W9-BXQ-486

evidence

Also by John Weisman ━━━━━━━━━━━━━━

Guerrilla Theater:
Scenarios for Revolution

John Weisman

evidence
a novel_____

The Viking Press·New York

Copyright © John Weisman, 1980

First published in 1980 by The Viking Press
625 Madison Avenue, New York, N.Y. 10022
Published simultaneously in Canada by
Penguin Books Canada Limited

LIBRARY OF CONGRESS CATALOGING IN PUBLICATION DATA

Weisman, John.
Evidence.

I. Title.
PZ4.W427EV   1980   [PS3573.E399]   813'.5'4   79-20562
ISBN 0-670-30041-1

Printed in the United States of America
Set in CRT Optima

*For Sally Bedell*_____

evidence

*chapter 1*_____

I have always been somewhat
preoccupied with the keeping of records. Of course, in my
present line of work, narcotics reporting, accurate files are
vitally necessary. This is because there are people, I am told,
who would like to see me disappear for good. Now that may
seem slightly paranoid. It is not. After more than three years
of covering the dope scene here in Detroit I have made enemies. People with whom one must take precautions.

For example, I have had the wooden door to my apartment replaced with a steel door and frame, which, when
combined with two burglarproof locks, a heavy steel dead
bolt, and a 360-degree peephole of two-way bulletproof
glass, makes my tenth-floor aerie virtually assaultproof. I
have replaced the sixty-watt light bulb in the hallway with a
three-hundred-watt lamp for added brightness. And, in a
cupboard close to the door, there is a loaded Remington
model 870 twelve-gauge pump-action shotgun with four
shells of double-ought shot in the magazine, and one in the
chamber.

Of course, they're subtle, my enemies are. They are not the
sort of people who call you up in the middle of the night,

threaten to cut off your balls and make you eat them. They know my phones are unlisted (although they probably have the numbers), and it would be out of character for them to stage a frontal assault on my apartment.

Still, you can never be absolutely sure, which is why I have the steel door, the shotgun, and some other protection available. My enemies have been known to hire some nasty hypes from the West Side to hit you in your home and make it look like a robbery (it's midnight, and there's a knock on the door; if you make the mistake and open it even a crack, you're dead. And not nicely or neatly either. Really dirty— the kind of scene that makes the La Bianca murders seem tame by comparison). Indeed, my enemies know a lot of people who enjoy messing up white folks just for fun. Carve them. Stab them. Draw graffiti on their chests with straight razors. Apply cheap cigars to the genitals. Stick fingers in the electric toaster. I have seen that sort of thing happen before. Believe me, Detroit hypes are real bad news.

My former partner and I were talking about what bad news Detroit hypes are only last week. Seven days ago I shared a byline in Detroit and Nancy Susan Roberts was alive in Los Angeles. Today I write alone and Nancy is dead. I got the word yesterday. It came from a former source of mine, a sergeant in the Los Angeles Police Department. In the form of a gray legal-sized envelope containing a coroner's memo, a comprehensive homicide investigation report, three diagrams, and a series of photographs, all of which establish beyond any reasonable doubt that Nancy Susan Roberts, with whom I lived for six years, was shot to death by a person or persons unknown while standing on a street corner in West Venice, California, roughly sixty hours ago.

Nancy is dead. I am totally alone now. Except for my files, that is. My files; my memories; my nightmares; my stories. But then Nancy always said I'd end up like this. She was prescient about me.

Actually, she didn't always say I'd end up alone. That prediction came only toward the end of our relationship. In the beginning she—like I—was optimistic. I remember calling her late one night a decade ago. So late it disrupted her dor-

mitory in Northampton, Mass. I called her from the Ace Motel, just outside Indianapolis, where I was staying. I was on my way to a job at the Los Angeles *Times*. I called Nancy and woke her up to tell her that I was in love with her. She said that she loved me, too. I asked her that night to live with me in Los Angeles after she graduated from college and she said that she would. We made each other all sorts of promises that night. It was probably a very maudlin conversation. But I didn't think so at the time. I was ten years younger then, and in love.

If I had been as sophisticated then as I am now I would have recorded the call. I record almost everything these days. It is a form of protection. Ten years ago, however, I recorded nothing. Journalism school never taught us about recording. No one gave courses in the use and misuse of the Nagra body recorder. The professors never bothered to teach us how to tap phones or instructed us in the intricacies of wireless radio transmitters. Instead, we ran around with notebooks and covered press conferences for credit. We wrote capsule news summaries from wire stories. We learned all about feature leads and studied the rules of inverted pyramid structure. We read Ernest Hemingway's articles for the Toronto *Daily Star* and pored over bound copies of *Yank* magazine. We were inculcated as idealists. No one told us what it would be like in the real world.

So I had no tape recorder at the Ace Motel, no telephone pickup. Only my M.S. from Columbia's Journalism School, a job offer from the Los Angeles *Times*, and a dozen reporter's notebooks—a graduation present from Nancy.

My former partner, Juliet Walker, and I worked together for the past eight months—until last night. I never told her about Nancy Susan Roberts, although she probably suspected that I had been in love with somebody once. What Juliet and I had in common was not our pasts. We shared the present: Detroit's corruption, its narcotics traffic and its organized crime. We also shared a joint byline and my double bed. In every other way we were opposites.

I am a city kid, brought up in New York. The product of private schools, a liberal arts education, and Columbia's

3

School of Journalism. I am light-complexioned, clean-shaven, and slight of build. I do not stand out in a crowd, a great asset for a reporter.

Juliet is a five-foot-ten-inch brunette. A healthy WASP. A Navy brat with wide hips and a weak chin who became a reporter after a failed marriage to an ensign who wanted four kids and a military wife.

But Juliet never had that kind of stamina. She did, however, turn into a gifted organized-crime reporter. We decided to team up eight months ago after I had had a very traumatic day on the job and she was kind enough to invite me up to her apartment for a drink.

For more than a year prior to that we had sat at facing desks in the city room. But usually I work at home, and hence we seldom spoke. Then, on that very traumatic day eight months ago, Juliet and I started talking about Henry Fielding, John Gay, and some other eighteenth-century writers, an unlikely subject for city room discussions.

One thing led to another, and Juliet invited me to her apartment for a glass of wine. She said I was looking pale. We had the wine. And a dinner of hamburgers and frozen vegetables. Then, after some brandy and a couple of joints, I found myself rolling on the imitation Persian rug in front of her glowing fireplace trying my damnedest to remove Juliet's clothes while her two German shepherd attack dogs prodded us somewhat impudently with their cold, wet snouts.

I remember looking at Juliet's ample, aroused breasts and thinking, I am here because two telephones were not answered today and I do not want to be alone tonight. I did not tell her that, of course. I didn't tell her much of anything. Except that I was very horny and that her nipples tasted great and that her dogs had very cold noses.

I pulled Juliet out of her clothes that night much faster than she got me out of mine. But then she seldom wore a bra, while I had to wrestle out of the cup supporter in which I customarily wear my Nagra body recorder. I think I first thought about working with Juliet when she showed no surprise at the Nagra. She didn't even ask me to turn it off. She just smiled and looked at the apparatus and hung it on the

back of a chrome and leather rocking chair. Then she settled down on the rug next to me, next to our pile of combined clothing, with her head facing my groin.

Neither one of us had had what you'd call a meaningful relationship in some time. We lay there and looked at each other's crotches, explaining our mutual horniness and why sleeping together would be the very worst thing we could do, how it would spoil a budding across-the-desk-in-the-city-room friendship.

But while we talked, we touched. I could feel her body shake as I ran my fingers up and down her legs and brushed the soft dark triangle of hair where they met. My own self quivered, too, as she stroked the outside of my thighs and slipped a hand between my legs to worry the hair behind my balls. Somehow her legs parted, too, and I moved my hand up between them. Where they came together she was very wet. I felt inside and then took back my probing fingers and licked them. Juliet rolled over onto her back and spread her legs, her hands moving my head to where I could lick and kiss. My damp-fingered hand lay at my side. I could feel the two dogs nuzzling up to it, sniffing.

It seemed that we lay stoned like that for an hour, touching, caressing, tasting. When I checked the tape at home, later that evening, it timed out at sixteen minutes.

"I haven't taken a pill in three months," said Juliet's voice on the tape.

"We can do this. We can lie here and do it like this."

"Just this, then, tonight."

"Nothing else. Only this."

I came first. I could feel myself growing in her mouth. Her fingers were kneading my scrotum, massaging the lower part of my cock. Her tongue drove me crazy, pushing me, coaxing me, enticing me to explode. When it came, there was no stopping it. We rolled over, my legs wrapped around her back, my tongue buried as deep inside her as I could get. My hands spread her buttocks and played with the soft skin inside. She held me in her mouth while I found her tender clit and worked it with my tongue and nose and teeth and fingers. I stroked it in counterpoint to her breathing. Her thighs

5

started to move rhythmically above me, her knees pressing against my torso like a bareback rider's. She came with grunts and groans and tiny cries, while the soft brown hair between her legs rubbed wet against my forehead.

Then we lay head to head and kissed a lot and decided that since our beats were compatible, perhaps we should work as a team.

We never talked about Henry Fielding again.

As a matter of fact, we didn't talk about much except our work. And we never talked at all when we made love.

In the city room we'd sit at our facing desks, coming in two cars at different times and leaving separately, never speaking except for small talk. At my apartment it was different. We'd spread our notes out on the parquet floor, notes written on small index cards, some with police mug shots attached. Juliet had been covering organized crime for four years. My own specialty is the heroin trade. Between us we had 561 three-by-five-inch index cards, which, when we weren't using them, were locked into the safe that is lag-bolted to the floor of my bedroom closet.

So you might say that during the past eight months there has been no past for me. Only the present and the work on which Juliet and I collaborated. Which made it a dangerous time emotionally. I have always been a solitary worker. Sharing things is painful for me. Nancy used to tell me that, and she was right. But in these three years after leaving Los Angeles and Nancy, I have come to prefer the loneliness gained by shunning company.

Yet in some ways working with Juliet was exhilarating. I grew to trust her, rely on her. But relying on another person means that you live in the present. Yet you cannot forget the past. If you do, it will come crashing down on you when you least want it to.

For eight months, I forgot about the past and Nancy Susan Roberts. Until yesterday, when the gray envelope arrived from Los Angeles.

Then my past caught up with me at the worst possible time—three hours before Juliet was to interview a source named Johnny Psycho.

Part of our job consists of doing source interviews (I was always nervous when Juliet met with a source. With dope dealers you know where you stand. They are crazy mother-fuckers, all of them, and they'd just as soon off you as look at you. Dope dealers have few subtleties. Never have I met one who has read Machiavelli. But the majority of Juliet's sources were Greek and Italian. Southern Italian. Mean Greek), and last night Juliet was scheduled to interview a mean Greek we knew as Johnny Psycho.

So far as the state unemployment office knows, Johnny Psycho is an unemployed spot welder who, every week, drives his Cadillac Fleetwood Brougham to the unemployment office and collects a check for $105. What they don't know is that from the state unemployment office, Johnny Psycho drives his thin, manicured, Right-Guarded, suede-clad body over to Georgie Rugg's bar on North Road, where he sits patiently in the corner for hours at a time, listening to the jukebox play Frank Sinatra and Mel Tormé. Perhaps twice a week or so Georgie Rugg slips Johnny Psycho a small piece of paper with a name and an address on it. Johnny Psycho picks up the slip of paper, stuffs it into his pocket, and walks out of the bar. Then he drives to the address he has been given and asks to speak to the party in question.

He mentions that he represents Georgie Rugg and that the party owes Georgie Rugg some money. He suggests that the party make an immediate payment—in cash. If the party says no, Johnny Psycho walks out to his Cadillac Fleetwood Brougham and takes a Louisville Slugger baseball bat out of the trunk. He returns and intimates that a Louisville Slugger is harder than shins, knees, or fingers. After such an inducement, the money is usually paid.

Sometimes, however, it isn't, and Johnny Psycho is called up to do a little mischief with his Louisville Slugger. For this, Johnny Psycho collects fifteen percent of the total debt owed to Georgie Rugg. Now, as you can imagine, Johnny Psycho is not very talkative—especially to the press. Notoriety is frowned on in the loan-sharking profession. So although Juliet had kept a file on Johnny Psycho for almost three months, she never found a way to talk to him. Then

7

one day she discovered one of Johnny Psycho's deepest secrets, something she knew that would squeeze him into
talking.

She discovered that Johnny Psycho, aside from collecting
money from both the state unemployment office and Georgie Rugg, was also earning a monthly stipend from the federal government. Johnny Psycho, it turned out, was a paid
snitch for the FBI. When Juliet contacted Johnny Psycho and
hinted about what she knew, he became more than willing
to meet with her.

We set up the interview in a bar on Outer Drive, a place
called the Falcon Club. It was clean. No one would attract
any attention there. I didn't want Juliet going alone, of
course. So we planned for me to get to the bar half an hour
before her meeting with Johnny Psycho. I would be armed. I
would watch the interview. Then she would ask Johnny Psycho to leave. After he was gone, we would split out the back
door. We'd come back for her car later—taking time to make
sure that Johnny Psycho hadn't done anything nasty, like at-
tach some dynamite to the ignition wires. To give us some
extra protection, I wired Juliet with a small Motorola transmitter. The battery pack was taped to her inner thigh with
the transmitter in her bra and the antenna running down her
back. I wore a portable five-watt receiver on my belt, with an
earpiece just like the ones the Secret Service uses. In an
ankle holster I carried a S&W .38 Airweight pistol with a
walnut grip and blue finish that I had bought on the street
for $150.

I got to the Falcon Club right on schedule. Having been
there before (in situations like this there is no being too
careful), I knew that there were bars across the windows in
both the men's and women's rest rooms, that the back door
was secured with only a dead bolt during business hours,
that the unlit alley led to the unlit parking lot. I also knew
that the customers tended to dress in Qiana nylon print
shirts and double knit slacks. So when I walked into the Falcon Club last night, I was not wearing a coat and tie. I had on
a Qiana nylon print floral shirt and a pair of gray herring-

bone double knit slacks. I also wore a green cardigan sweater with an alligator on the left breast. I wasn't wearing the sweater to be fashionable, but to conceal the Motorola receiver that was clipped to the belt of my trousers. The clear plastic wire and earpiece were not visible in the bar light, although they would have been obvious at midday, outdoors.

Things first started to go wrong when Johnny Psycho showed up ten minutes early. He walked through the door and spent a minute or two looking around. He wrinkled his nose; then he walked back outside.

Juliet showed up. I leaned my hand against the earpiece.

"Right on time."

"I don't like you standing so close to my car. Can we go inside?"

"I don't like the way it looks inside. We'll talk in your car. Drive around and talk."

"No way. Neutral ground was the arrangement."

"Okay. You don't trust me. But not the bar. Too many people. See the Burger Chef across the street? What about there?"

I didn't like that at all. The Burger Chef was empty. It was all glassed in. I couldn't walk outside to watch. All I could do was listen.

It was going to go sour. I could feel it deep in the pit of my stomach. We had wanted to flip Johnny Psycho, make him into our snitch, too. That way we could learn what the feds were up to as well as glean some information about Georgie Rugg's operation, which, according to our file cards, would take us one step closer to the large drug-smuggling operation controlled by Rugg's very organized partners.

But all of a sudden Juliet and Johnny Psycho were walking across the eight lanes of Outer Drive toward a Burger Chef that I had not checked out. I slid off my barstool and left the Falcon through the back door. I never even looked back at my change lying on the bar. I ran across the alley, to the parking lot, hand clasped to my ear, trying to make out Juliet's voice above the traffic noises and static. They were talking about mutual trust. I slid the key into the VW's igni-

tion but didn't turn it over. Reaching down to my left ankle, I undid the strap on the holster and brought the Airweight up, shoving it under my left thigh.

"Listen, Juliet, it's not that I don't trust you, you know, but I gotta pat you down."

"Sure, Johnny. You want to make sure that I'm not carrying anything in my bag."

"It's not just your bag, honey. It's bad luck for me if you're carrying a wire or anything."

Jesus Christ. I knew we had blown it then and there. If Juliet got into trouble, all she had to do was say, "Pudding," the attack word for her dogs, and I'd come and get her out. But she didn't say, "Pudding." She didn't say anything except: "You can pat me down if I can pat you down."

There was a lot of rustling following that. Then the Motorola transmitter died. I turned the ignition of the VW over and, without putting the lights on, eased out of the parking lot onto Outer Drive. Half a block away I flicked on the lights. Then I made a U-turn and cruised slowly past the Burger Chef. The place was empty. I went another half block and U-turned again. I still couldn't see anything, so I made the circuit one more time, sliding to the curb about five hundred feet from the Burger Chef lot and sitting, engine idling, lights off. Then I saw Juliet and Johnny Psycho come out from behind the Burger Chef, running hand in hand, laughing. Daring the traffic on Outer Drive, they crossed to the Falcon Club's unlit parking lot, where they climbed into Johnny Psycho's Cadillac Fleetwood Brougham and sped off.

I was frantic. Had Juliet been laughing, or was her smile a smile of pain? What had happened to the Motorola? There were no answers, so I concentrated on the Fleetwood Brougham's taillights, making sure that they never got more than two blocks from me, running red lights to keep up if I had to.

Johnny Psycho was not taking any precautions at all. He never slowed down, never cut into alleys, or zigzagged the way people do when they know they have a tail on them. He drove straight to Indian Village, where he parked the car in front of Juliet's house, and the pair of them disappeared in-

side. I drove past once, watching for lights on the second-floor front, where Juliet's living room was. None came on. So I went around the block twice, then doubled back and found a parking space in front of a hydrant where I could see the entrance to her house as well as the back-room windows. The bedroom windows. I turned off the engine and sat, waiting.

I sat there for three hours. After the first hour I pulled the gray LAPD envelope out of my briefcase and held it clutched to my chest. For a long while afterward I cried. I had not cried when a copyboy handed it to me or when I opened it and saw the contents. But sitting there, staring at Juliet's bedroom windows, waiting, I cried. I knew what was happening on the second floor. I knew what had happened in Los Angeles. Why either of them had happened I didn't know, so I cried.

By the time Johnny Psycho came out of Juliet's apartment I knew unshakably that Juliet did not matter. Not to me. Johnny Psycho's print shirt was undone to his waist. He carried his suede leisure jacket over one shoulder. As he climbed into his Cadillac Fleetwood Brougham, I took the .38 Airweight from under my left thigh and slid it back into the ankle holster on my left leg. Johnny Psycho drove off without looking up at Juliet's apartment. I had never left without looking back at the curtained windows of her living room, where the two German shepherds would stain the cool glass with their noses.

I was tempted to follow Johnny Psycho, but there was Juliet.

I blew my nose and rang the bell.

She came to the door obviously stoned, soft dark hair a mess. She was dressed in a red cotton kimono tied low around the hips. The shepherds sniffed at my hands as I came in, then stalked off in their stiff-haunched way, leaving us to talk. Only I couldn't think of anything to say, so I went to Juliet's antique liquor cabinet in the living room and poured myself a straight vodka—about three ounces. Then another one. Then I sat on the floor of her long hallway, my back to the avocado-green wall, and stared up at her.

She sat down next to me, hugging her knees. "It just happened," she said. "I was wired; he was wired. We thought it was funny."

I didn't say anything.

"I think he likes me. I think I like him."

I pulled at the cup supporter where my Nagra nestled uncomfortably. The tape had run out hours before.

"He's exciting."

I got myself to my feet and went back to the bar. I poured myself another three ounces of vodka.

"Can't we talk? Robert, say something."

I walked past her down the lime-green hallway, then paced back into the living room, across the imitation Persian rug and up to the mantel, where I plucked a generous thick joint out of a red-and-gold papier-mâché box. I lit it and inhaled deeply. Then I walked back up the hallway and sat down next to Juliet. I offered her the joint. She shook her head.

"I was adored once," I said. "Do you know who said that?"

Juliet shook her head.

"Sir Andrew Aguecheek in *Twelfth Night.*" I took a deep drag on the joint. I could hear, very distinctly, a dripping faucet in Juliet's kitchen.

Juliet sat hugging her knees. "Oh," she said. The two German shepherds came out of Juliet's bedroom and lay on the floor by us, waiting for our conversation. Idly I blew marijuana smoke at them and ruffled them behind the ears. We sat without saying anything.

"This is impossible." I pulled myself to my feet and went into the den. I found *Sticky Fingers* and put it on Juliet's turntable. I turned up the amplifier very loud.

Juliet followed me into the den. She turned down the volume. "Robert—"

"You know, I *was* adored," I said. "I was held. I was needed." I turned the music back up and started ponying to "Brown Sugar." The Nagra in my jock chafed my thighs. I said, "Do you think when Shakespeare wrote, 'If music be the food of love,' he was anticipating the Rolling Stones?" I

kept my feet moving in syncopation with Charlie Watts's back beat. I said, "I was adored. I was loved. I have documents. I can prove it." The room started to move slightly to my left. I compensated for the tilt and kept dancing.

Juliet turned the music down again.

"Leave it up," I shouted. "Leave the fucking thing alone." I was crying again. When the tears had started, I didn't know.

The room began spinning, and I fell backward, landing on a velvet couch.

"Hey, did you take downers or something?" said Juliet. "Did you take anything before you came here?"

I shook my head. One of the dogs came into the den. It started licking my face. Its breath made me gag.

"We all have to be needed sometime," I said. My eyes were shut tight against the spinning room. I started to feel the nausea then, rising in my throat. The dog kept at my face, licking it insistently. Alpo breath forced its way up my nostrils. Eyes shut, I rolled off the couch and by instinct lurched toward the bathroom. I made it on my hands and knees, relieved by the coolness of the tile floor. Crawled to the bowl and was sick. Reached for toilet paper to wipe my mouth. Couldn't find it. Rubbed away the drool with the sleeve of my alligator sweater.

Juliet must have come into the bathroom behind me. She turned on the light. I was blinded. I rolled over onto my back and pressed an arm over my eyes.

She grabbed me by my sweater and pulled me to my feet. My knees sagged. "Shit," she said. She threw one of my arms over her shoulder and hoisted me onto her hip, dragged me into the spare bedroom and dumped me onto a studio couch.

"Shit," she said.

I tried to say something. But my mouth filled up again with bile, and I rolled over onto the floor and was sick on Juliet's rug. I lay like a rag, sobbing. I tried to tell her about the gray envelope sitting under the front seat of my car, but I couldn't make my tongue work. I couldn't make my lips move.

Except to be sick again. So I retched, while Juliet watched.

I don't know how long she watched. I do know that she hoisted me back up onto the studio couch because that's where I found myself six-thirty this morning. The two dogs lay on the soiled rug head to head. I rubbed at my eyes, rolled off the couch. The apartment was dark. I walked into the living room. Juliet had left my shoes on the coffee table. Next to them was the .38 Airweight in its ankle holster. I picked it up and took it out to check the cylinder. All five bullets were still in place. I sat on the imitation Persian rug and slipped into my loafers. Then I stood up and, with one foot on the coffee table, strapped the holster to my left leg. The Motorola transceiver was still clipped securely to my belt, although the earpiece was gone. I had another at home.

When I slipped out of Juliet's apartment earlier this morning, I didn't check her bedroom. I didn't want to know whether or not she was there. I didn't care. I was beyond caring.

There was a cold mist in the street. I shivered as I looked up at Juliet's living-room windows. The dogs were there, muzzles pressed against the glass. We stared at each other for some minutes, the dogs and I. Then they grinned their big, foolish German shepherd grins and turned away, allowing the curtains to fall back into place.

chapter 2_____

I stood under the shower for a long, long time after I got home. It was symbolic, really: a ritual cleansing; a washing away of the present; a solitary immersion; a rebirth. I do my best thinking in the shower, free associating as the water cascades down on me. I have not always liked showers. As a small boy I was afraid of them. My parents had a house in Atlantic Beach on Long Island, one block away from the ocean. We would leave New York in early June, just after my school closed for the summer, and stay through Labor Day weekend. I have always remembered the house as huge. But last year, when I was in New York on business, I drove out to Atlantic Beach on an impulse and saw how my memory had deceived me.

It was in reality a small red-brick house with a green-shingle roof. I had not been there in twenty years or more, but when I drove from New York, my homing instinct was precise. A modest house; very unpretentious. The old shower was still there, too. A stall shower behind a wooden screen in the alley next to the side door, put there by my father so we could wash the sand from our bodies before going inside. I hated that shower. The nozzle had never been screwed on

correctly, and the water, which was never warm enough, would spurt into my eyes and sting my face. My father would have to catch me and take me into the shower with him because I would not go by myself. He would hold me aloft and turn me under the spray as I kicked and screamed.

I was four, or five, or six, and I cried.

These days I love my showers. I close my eyes and let the water rush over my body. I stand there for hours, thinking or not thinking. Daydreaming. Plotting. Writing my stories in my head. Sorting out my life. Reviewing my files. Nancy never understood showers. To her they were something utilitarian: To shower was to lather up, rinse off, and towel dry. Not to me. Standing on the mat, water running down the transparent plastic shower curtain, the bathroom door bolted, chained, and dead-locked, my shotgun resting easily across the toilet seat, I am completely safe, utterly at ease.

This morning I stood under the hot, soothing water, making plans. It was going to be much easier to close my file on Nancy than it had been to close another file eight months ago. Jack's file. Jack Fowler's file. Nancy was an open-and-shut case. Jack had been different. Jack had to be written about. Facts had had to be compiled; stories checked and sorted; confidences breached and rules broken. Such things know no bounds, few limits. This is why I will not compile material about Nancy; all I want to do is close out her file. I will not write about her. I will not break *that* rule again. Once was enough.

I have loved two people in my life. Nancy Susan Roberts and Jack Fowler. Both were killed brutally within the past year. Both were murdered because they did not play by the rules. Rules are important. Precautions are important. If you don't take precautions, if you stop paying attention to the signs, the signals around you, things can get dangerous. In my job, I never stop watching, looking, sizing things up. I never stop taking precautions. Those are the rules I play by. They keep me safe—from myself and from others.

Until recently, that is.

Nancy is dead. Jack is dead. I am alone. But they did not die because they had me in common. They died because

they broke, they disobeyed, the rules. I am not responsible for their deaths.

Nancy, says the LAPD report, died on the street in West Venice, California, of a massive hemorrhage. A single .22-caliber slug entered her left arm at a point six and a quarter inches below the point of her left shoulder, passed through the arm, and exited to enter the chest cavity two inches below the left armpit. The single round then punctured the left lung at a position of the third rib, deflecting off the fourth rib at the spinal column, finally coming to rest below the ninth rib at the left posterior of the chest, seven inches from the spine. The slug, a long, weighed twenty-eight grains. It had rifling marks: eight lands and grooves and a lubaloy-type coating.

There were no powder burns on Nancy's clothing or body, meaning that she had been shot from more than eighteen inches away. Witnesses saw a tan Econoline van, driven by two unknown Latin males, moving away from the scene.

I can see the LAPD report through my transparent shower curtain. It is sitting on the sink. It is open to a diagram tracing the path of the slug that killed Nancy. The diagram is neither male nor female. Just an androgynous human form, bald-headed, standing or lying vertically, arms away from the body, palms up. It bears no relation to the Nancy I once knew. It is not Nancy. My telephone call from the Ace Motel is Nancy. Nancy's freshly washed auburn hair is Nancy. The smell of Nancy's perfume is Nancy. The ache of separation from Nancy when I came here to Detroit is Nancy. The diagram is not Nancy. Just the way other, similar diagrams had not been Jack Fowler.

Jack Fowler, killed eight months ago. Stabbed to death in his apartment across the street from my own house by assailants to whom he opened the door when he shouldn't have. Jack Fowler: colleague; friend; corpse; ghost. I have closed the file on Jack Fowler, but still he haunts me. The dreams come less often now, but they recur. Jack alive and Jack dead. Pictures of Jack in the newspapers; pictures not publishable; stories about Jack, written by me.

I am not responsible for Nancy's death, or Jack's. I am

merely a witness to them. They were not my fault. They were not killed because of me but in spite of me. Damn her, she should have known. They both should have known, and God knows I tried to tell them.

I wrote about Jack Fowler. That was my mistake. I will not write about Nancy. Damn her, she should have known. Walking alone on the streets of West Venice, California, at one in the morning is an open invitation to mayhem. It is a clear violation of the rules. If Nancy had not broken the rules, her file would still be open. There would still be hope.

Hope for what? For reconciliation? For us? For me? For . . . something.

Eight months ago, when the cops came to talk to me about Jack Fowler, I told them that he was the first of my friends who had ever been murdered. The taller of the two detectives, whose name was Mercaldi, told me that perhaps I didn't have the right kinds of friends. More Negroes, he suggested. We laughed at that, the tall detective named Mercaldi, the shorter black one named Johnson, and I. Sometimes it is better to laugh than to cry. Policemen know this. It is one of the rules they live by. Like carrying a .25-caliber automatic as a backup weapon. It is just done. Reflexively. But then, why shouldn't they laugh? The greater part of their professional lives consists of seeing people at the worst of times. Very much like reporters. Oh, yes—we're quite similar. And they, like we, develop a protective veneer of cynicism. Nothing gets to them. Nothing gets to us. We are the professional survivors, the note takers, the onlookers, the chroniclers. Facts disappear into our notebooks, which in turn disappear into desks or file cabinets. Better to crack a joke than shed a tear. Listen to the victims, then go out to the car, the squad room, the city desk, the bar and laugh about it. Cops drink a lot. So do reporters. (I remember driving a young woman visitor from New York around Detroit once. I took her on a cruise through the neighborhoods I love to explore. Ghetto avenues of boarded-up FHA houses, with side-street-cool dudes standing on corners, stray dogs

feeding themselves from garbage cans, fires burning in va-
cant lots. We passed a couple in their fifties. He had a length
of two-by-four and was beating her silly with it, beating her
down onto the steps of a tenement, while she screamed at
him and tried to protect her bloodied head with a shopping
bag full of God-knows-what. The visitor cried in protest
when I refused to stop and break up the scene. She called
me uncaring. Unfeeling. Not compassionate. She did not
understand that when you drive through a wildlife preserve,
you leave the animals alone. If you participate, you break the
rules. You get bitten.)

Being a professional observer hasn't always been easy. I
used to have a hard time watching autopsies when I first
worked the police beat here. The cadaver would be lying
there on the table. With his scalpel the coroner would make
a long T-shaped incision. The top of the T would start above
the clavicles and center on the sternum. Then another,
longer one, which would run down the front of the corpse to
the pubic symphysis. The chest would be flayed open, and
rib cutters used to rend the cartilage and rip open the clavi-
cle joints. The whole process never took more than a minute
and a half, except in the case of shotgun wounds to the
chest, which made things messier than usual. I was not
bothered by the dissection, really. It was not a human being
on that steel table so much as a piece of meat. Indeed, the
sight of the medical examiner working on the body was similar to that of the butchers who section beef from whole steer
carcasses in the slaughterhouses across town. What used to
bother me most were the eyes. Most of the time the eyes of
the dead thing on the table were open, watching me watch
as the pathologist cut, sawed, severed, sliced, snipped, and
slashed his way through viscera and organs. At the first autopsy I ever went to—a kind of ritual indoctrination for police beat reporters—I was quite sick. Those eyes were what
did it to me. Unchanging, unmoving, they bored into my
own eyes as the doctor began his examination, the civil service high priest looking for omens in his human sacrifice.

I went to Jack Fowler's autopsy eight months ago. I went
as a last visit because the night he had been killed I was

supposed to have been with him, and had I been with him he would not have been killed. But I turned down his invitation for dinner and went out, instead, to finish work on a project I considered important. The following morning I skipped breakfast and went to the morgue. I did not cry at that autopsy, nor was I sick. I simply watched as the body, white and tallowy from lack of blood, was systematically torn apart by the city's chief medical examiner and his findings spoken into a microphone that in turn took the voice, transmogrified it into electrical impulses, and transferred them onto a tape machine running in an adjacent room. When the medical examiner's office finished transcribing the coroner's report, I obtained a copy of the eleven eight-and-one-half-by-fourteen-inch pages and brought them back to my apartment. I opened one of the three locked file cabinets that stand in my dining room in place of a table and chairs and made up a new file, labeling the manila folder "JACK FOWLER" in large block letters. Within days the file grew until it filled almost a drawer and a half.

Jack Fowler and I were more than neighbors, more than colleagues. We shared secrets. We were best friends. The kind of best friend you have in high school, the one you share your deepest feelings with. I trusted Jack with thoughts and emotions I had told no one else—even Nancy. He did the same with me, or so I believed. He was my best friend, and I was his. We were, we felt, responsible for each other. It was the only time in my life I have not hidden my emotions from other people.

Still, we lived distinctly separate lives. My apartment, for example, is sparsely furnished. My couch is secondhand. My bookcases are college-modern: bricks and boards. The only two extravagances are a ten-by-fourteen-foot hand-loomed antique Persian rug of silk and wool, bought at auction some years ago, and a custom-built wine cellar that holds two hundred bottles of better-than-average Bordeaux, Burgundy, and champagne at a constant fifty-six degrees.

Jack, on the other hand, furnished his apartment elaborately. He was well set up—his family owned a chain of groceries in the South, and he had been given the best of

everything, including a Princeton education, a graduate degree from Oxford, and a trust fund that provided him with $3,500 a month, tax-free, over and above what he earned at the paper. So he spent money on art and furniture. Real Chagalls, Vasarely temperas, Klees, and Kandinskys. A perfect preserved poster of Toulouse–Lautrec's. All hung in a brown and white setting both very modern and very tasteful. It was, I always thought, a real home—a womb to come back to every night.

Of course, Jack and I had our similarities, too. We both were studious file keepers, although our techniques differed. Jack's files were, as he was, southern romantic: dozens of leather-bound books filled with lined writing paper, on which he recorded, in a firm hand and with a $100 fountain pen, his daily journal. Just in case he became famous, he used to tell me. He loved to read sections of his journal. He would pull a volume from one of the custom-built bookcases in his study and read about Oxford, about drinking a 1934 port after long dinners with his favorite don. Or tantalize me with accounts eight years old of the wine auctions at Christie's, in London.

There were other files, too: transcriptions of our conversations, recorded while we sat in his apartment or mine, smoking good grass, drinking my wine or Jack's champagne. We talked a lot, Jack and I. About ourselves, our lives, our stories. Both of us had come a long way, professionally. We had reputations at the paper. We were different from most reporters. Neither of us, for example, had to deal with the city editor very often. Our story assignments came from the managing editor or from Mike, the executive editor. We also generated a lot of our own material. And neither of us spent much time in the city room. Jack kept a cubicle in the courthouse. I was allowed to do most of my work at home. As Mike once told me, "I don't give a damn where you work just so long as we're first with the story and your stuff is here before deadline."

Sometimes Jack and I would play our conversations back. We'd sit at my house or his, laughing, half-stoned, at our taped voices. God, the things we talked about: sex; life; writ-

21

ing. The dialogue always seemed to come back to writing, to newspapering. I guess that's because newspapering is all either of us really had.

We were most unalike, however, in our approach to the craft. Jack believed in making changes. He was convinced that what he wrote actually made a difference in people's lives. I used to think that; I don't anymore. For me it's the story. Gathering the facts. Laying them out. Watching the pieces come together. That's the exciting part. That's the part that can be controlled; that makes me come alive.

I haven't always been that way. In the beginning, in Los Angeles, I thought the way Jack did. I went after stories not for their own sake but because I thought writing them would help people make changes in their own lives. I used to take people's problems, their miseries, seriously. I would bring them home with me in note form and talk to Nancy about them. We would spend time analyzing, becoming emotionally involved in what I was writing. Then, after a year and a half or so, I stopped talking about my work at home. It was just easier not to. My work was depressing. In almost a decade of reporting I have never written a story with a happy ending.

In the beginning, in Los Angeles, I felt all-powerful. I didn't mind the fact that my articles never ended on an up-beat. Sooner or later, I thought, they would. And of course, there was Nancy. She was working for CBS, developing prime-time comedy shows. She loved her work. She kept files on comedy ideas just the way I kept them on juvenile crime and urban decay. But somehow the more my files grew, the less I wanted to hear about TV pilots. Everything I wrote about ended unhappily. Nancy's stories always ended after twenty-two minutes with a big laugh. I began to think that she worked in a totally unreal environment. I guess she thought the same about me. I could not comprehend how she was able to talk about Mary Tyler Moore's situation-comedy character as if it were a real person. For her part, she could not understand what she called my unhealthy fascination with violence and misery. I began to think of her colleagues as venal. She considered mine bloodthirsty leeches.

22

I remember taking Nancy with me one night to Hollen-beck, in East Los Angeles, to watch as I put together a story on juvenile crime in the Mexican ghetto. Her vision of crime had been shaped by movies and television. In her world the kids in trouble always went straight in the last reel or the final segment. But that's not the way it is. So she watched, revolted, as two fifteen-year-old armed robbers were man-handled by a pair of burly detectives. The kids were hand-cuffed and kept in a closet-sized holding room. They were pushed and bullied and shoved around. Nancy said, "They're only children. Why are they treated like that?"

I said, "What about their victims? What about the old Chi-nese grocer they stabbed?"

To Nancy it didn't matter. To her, the cops were the vil-lains; the system was the villain. But I knew better.

We went out for a beer with the detectives who had made the arrest, went to a bar called Jack's, across the street from Hollenbeck Division. It is a policeman's bar, filled with off-duty cops, detectives, narcs, playing pool and drinking to ease the memories of what they've seen during the watch. A buffer zone, a no-man's-land between their jobs and their lives. Nancy sat silent, sullen. She did not allow herself to be drawn into the conversation. Later she told me she found it impossible to talk to men who roughed up children for a living.

And afterward, when the story ran, she asked if it would make any difference. I was in my ambivalent period then. I told her what I considered the truth five years ago. I told her that I didn't know.

Now, of course, I do know. Now I'm not naïve anymore. Or ambivalent. Instead, I am a professional observer, a gath-erer of facts, a reporter. I make no judgments. I simply re-port; I tell what has gone on. I do it alone. And I get the story before anybody else does.

Of course, there are always doubts. That is why I try not to think about what I do, not analyze my profession or myself. Doubts prevent the story from being written. But still, some-times, I am not sure. How important is any single story any-how? I have covered the narcotics trade for most of my three

23

years on this paper. Because of my articles, thirty-three police officers are currently facing indictments for taking payoff money from dope dealers. Two dozen of the worst shooting galleries on the West Side have been shut down. The Westvale, a rock-and-roll hall, has lost its license to operate. There is presently a federal task force investigating the connections Juliet and I drew in a series of articles about the Italo-Greek crime families here and their relationship to the so-called Black Mafia. Last April the Press Club gave me a plaque and a check for $100 as an award for writing the best news feature of the year. It was a profile on an eight-year-old heroin dealer who sold more than $150,000 worth of junk before they caught him. Because of his age, of course, he went unprosecuted. The father, who had put the kid on the streets in the first place, also got off scot-free.

And what have been the actual results of my reportage? The federal task force files reports to Washington, D.C., but nothing is done. The thirty-three corrupt police officers have been replaced by thirty-three other, more corrupt police officers. The two dozen shooting galleries have recently reopened in new West Side locations, where, instead of paying protection to the Eighth Narcotics Division, they pay off the narcs of the Tenth Division—who demand more money.

We can no more change things than the cops can. Yet we, like they, hit the streets every day. Looking for something to write about. Something awry. A new victim, a different story, a fresh snitch. Something with a twist. Like Parnell R. Brown, Jr., the operator of a shooting gallery on Fenkell Avenue who killed an unwanted customer by dropping a thirty-pound watermelon on the poor dude's head from the third-floor window of his rat-infested junkie's pad. That made page one because it was a slow news day. Seldom do we save a life, force a change. We simply watch as "they" do damage to each other. We keep the score, tote the victims in the obituary column. We stand ready with the shrouds; no need to buy a winding sheet. We wrap 'em in newsprint and bury 'em in the three-ball final.

The night Jack Fowler was stabbed to death, blood running out of the twenty-five wounds in his upper torso, I was

dressed in my best rock-and-roll clothes, watching the action at the Westvale, a pop music emporium on East Harper Street. Jack and I had gone there together once, but that night I was working alone, watching as dealers lined the former movie house's mezzanine and hawked their wares to the youngsters who came from the safe white suburbs into the city to hear music and score dope.

By the time I got to my apartment after writing the story in the back seat of my VW police cars were already parked three deep across the street and Jack had been dead for two hours. Had I not chosen to visit the Westvale I would have been at Jack's for dinner. Had I been at Jack's he would not have opened the door. I would not have opened the door. But who knew? Who could have told at eight in the evening that he would be dead seven hours later?

*chapter 3*_____

There was a memorial service for Jack, held in the meeting hall of the Newspaper Guild building downtown. I did not go. Neither did I accompany the body on the private plane Jack's parents chartered to fly him home to Savannah, although I had been invited to be a pallbearer and eulogizer at the funeral. Jack's mother, whom I had not met before, accused me of being unfeeling. She said that I was doing Jack's memory a disservice by not coming, not speaking. But I knew better. There is nothing to do at a funeral but grieve. Or laugh. And partaking in the eulogies would do me no good, would do Jack no good. I already had Jack's definitive eulogy. It was folded neatly inside the manila folder with "JACK FOWLER" in block capital letters.

This eulogy described in clinical detail exactly how Jack Fowler—a male Caucasian stated to be thirty years of age and appearing to be as stated, whose complexion was medium, whose body had a length of 70¼ inches and a weight of 171 pounds and bore no visible scars or identifying marks, whose hair and irides were brown, whose spinal fluid was clear, whose musculoskeletal, gastrointestinal, hepatobiliary, and hemolyphatic systems were all anatomic, whose kidneys

weighed 148 grams, spleen 326 grams, and testes 26.5 grams, whose cerebellum, cerebrum, pons, medulla, and midbrain were all anatomic—had died because a nine-inch kitchen knife had, in the course of causing multiple stab-type wounds to the chest, severed the major arteries to his lungs, resulting in expiration caused by massive exsanguination and shock.

Spare, lean prose transcribed from the taped monologue of the city's chief medical examiner as he stood, scalpel in hand, in the tan tiled autopsy room of the morgue on St. Antoine Street, a room with four steel tables and fluorescent lighting.

Although you couldn't tell from the transcript, it was rushed prose, hurriedly spoken because three other bodies lay on the clean tables. A ninety-year-old man whose head had been caved in by a ripping-claw hammer, an infant dead of SID, and the middle-aged victim of a juvenile street gang's senseless violence all awaited silently, uncomplainingly, the pathologist's scalpel. And outside the tan tiled basement room five more corpses, the night's total, lay on wheeled carriages, waiting to be measured, weighed, and then dissected before they, like Jack Fowler, would be rolled upstairs to the first floor, to the white-walled corridor that contains 186 crypts all kept at a constant thirty-eight degrees. The work would keep the medical examiner and his three assistants busy most of the day.

No, I did not go to the memorial service. I did not climb on a plane and go to the funeral or the grave site. Jack, I knew, would ride sealed in a brass or steel box, which would be lowered hydraulically into a bunkerlike concrete shell. Jack's funeral would be conducted by rote, by machine. And the living would stand watching as the casket dropped out of sight, after which they would leave. There would be nothing to be learned visiting the grave site.

That is why instead of going to Savannah, I used my police-issued press pass and bullied, wheedled, and cajoled my way into Jack's apartment across the street from my own. I knew things no one knew—except Jack. The crime-scene lab crew had finished dusting for fingerprints. Photographs had

been taken. One of them even appeared in the newspaper: a graphic study of the bedroom where Jack had lain dying while the killers tore the apartment apart, looking for booty to carry off.

Now I am used to these sorts of things. The heroin trade leaves little room for astonishment. When one dealer decides to rid himself of a competitor, usually a mess of some kind is made. I am accustomed to seeing brains, looking like strawberry yogurt, splattered over tangerine velveteen sofas. I do not cringe at the sight of a spade slit from ear to ear, all flashy, gaping smile where a straight razor has cut evenly across windpipe and carotid artery. An OD'd hooker sitting on the toilet, a syringe protruding obscenely from her vulva, has brought as much crude humor from my lips as from the cops who have to remove the instrument, pack her in a rubber bag, and tote her away. So my reaction to the carnage at Jack's apartment I later ascribed to my familiarity with it in better days.

Simply, the place had been raped. The bedspread that lay on his king-sized bed had been shredded and tossed aside. The mattress, too, was torn apart. Its ticking clung like cotton bolls to the walls, mirror, and thick café-au-lait wool carpet. Drawers from the dresser and bedside table were overturned, miscellaneous contents strewn about. In the living room the couch had been attacked, the jacquard material violated with some weapon. A Picasso on the wall was slashed—rent by a jagged Z for Zorro. Two Chagalls had been punched out of their frames; they lay in the shards of the thick smoked-glass coffee table through which a heavy planter had been dropped. In the den, Jack's desk had been ravaged, its oiled finish marred with scratches. Someone had written "FUCK" across it. Not a single book remained in the heavy cases. The journals, lovingly handwritten, bound in antique calfskin, had been ripped apart. The record of Jack's life lay confettilike at my feet. I picked up a fragment, a rough rectangle with two lines written in Jack's sure script. "Oxford, April 197 " ran the first line. On the second I could make out the words "elighted you." Nothing else. I stuck the shard of heavy paper in my pocket. Walked into the kitchen,

where a fat black detective was prowling through the utensils. My Nagra captured the conversation.

"Get much?"

"Jewelry. Watches. Camera. The portable TV."

"Anything else?"

"We're having a muthafucker of a time going through what's here. What you think they got?"

"I don't know—I knew where things were when the place was together, you know. Now—"

"They really did a job, huh? Masterful. Not one decent latent. Smears. But them scrotes were crazy, you know."

"Huh?"

"Look at the art. Dumb sumbitches messed around with the art. Coulda cut it out from the frames, rolled it up, and walked off. 'Stead of that, they go an' fucked it over. Shit. I'da took the art."

"Hypes?"

"Maybe. Shit, though, after those pieces he wrote about the courts last year it coulda been judges. Looka this, will you? That's a fucking copper pan. Solid copper. My wife went out, priced one—seventy-five bucks. Just to fry eggs."

"Take it. Who'd notice?"

"Nah. It's too big. Maybe there's something smaller."

I knew they hadn't found Jack's hiding place yet. So I walked back into the bedroom, onto the rug, where the thickened bloodstains looked like hardening pools of Hershey's syrup. Bent over and put my index finger on one of the bloodstains. There was still moisture. I brought my finger up to my nose and smelled. Nothing. Rubbed thumb and forefinger together. Jack's blood. Rich blood, dead blood; already oxidized. Wiped my stained thumb and index finger on the rug. A small crescent of blood remained under the nails. It could be washed out later. Went to the corner, where the rug ran flush up to the wall below the pedestal of Jack's Mediterranean pecan dresser. Moved the dresser with my shoulder and reached behind it. Lifted the rug where Jack had installed four blind grommets, installed them to ensure that the rug would never buckle or bulge, so no wrinkle would ever betray the fact that he had painstakingly

29

chiseled out a square-foot by three-quarter-inch-deep section of the parquet floor. I lifted the corner of the rug and slid aside the thin steel plate that covered Jack's secret cache. Fingers exploring, I felt inside. The tapes were there. Jack's tapes. Research on the story that had probably killed him. I retrieved them all and slipped them into the inside pocket of my sports jacket. I replaced the steel cover, rubbing the metal on both sides with my handkerchief so as not to leave any telltale fingerprints. Carefully regrommeted the rug in place. And then, using my shoulder, I pushed Jack's dresser back into the corner. I knew that when the police took up the rug, they would find the hollowed-out space. But they would have no way of knowing whether or not anything had been stored there on the night Jack was killed or, indeed, even what the space had been used for.

There was no need for them to know. That part of Jack's life was his secret. And mine. I stood at the bedroom door and looked back into the room. I wondered what would happen to the furniture, to the paintings, now ruined. I wondered what Jack's family was thinking. It didn't matter. I closed the bedroom door and walked back toward the living room, toward the kitchen, where the policeman was still sifting through the pots and pans.

On my way out I flashed a smile and a wave at the black detective, whose raincoat bulged slightly at the pockets. We both had souvenirs to take home.

chapter 4_____

We start with such high ideals, all of us. I remember how pure I felt when I got my M.S. from Columbia. I knew, a decade ago, that I could cure the world's ills. I was young and in love with Nancy and believed in us both. I did not know about aloneness or fear or terror. I did not sit in my apartment at two in the morning watching an old movie and crying at the TV screen as I do now. I did not have any files to go through. There were people to talk to in those days, friends to see, dreams to dream.

I have come a long way since then.

I have, but *they* haven't. I see it at the paper now. The young reporters arrive each summer with their master's from Columbia or Northwestern. So eager to write; so eager to right the wrongs they see around them. Anxious for a Big Story. Wanting to cut a swath about them. We old-timers look them over carefully as they are introduced, like veteran NFL backs sizing up the rookies who come to take their jobs away. Once in a while we worry, but not often. We know too many tricks. We play too dirty. Ethics is a lovely word, but it never won anybody a Pulitzer.

Yet looking over the new arrivals does have its small plea-

sures. What with the number of women holding degrees in journalism, women reporters are getting better-looking on the whole. And Mike, our executive editor, who oversees the final hiring, prides himself on being able to select the creamies of the crop. We are, after all, the seventh largest daily in America. That gives us some latitude in the hiring process. It also gives us some clout in the sack.

The incident that brought Jack Fowler and me together began one night eight months after I arrived in Detroit at the London Chop House, a downtown restaurant we both used to frequent, but separately. There are a number of so-called newspaper bars in Detroit, but I did not hang out in them. Listening to shoptalk can become depressing. Instead, I opted for the dark wood and leather banquettes of the Chop House, where I would sit alone at the bar watching high-priced ladies and their expense-account dates bolt their food before retiring to king-sized beds at one of the neighboring hotels.

I was sitting at the bar, working on a dozen oysters and sipping at a tidy Moselle, when Jack Fowler walked in with a twenty-two-year-old knockout on his arm. I had nodded to Jack in the city room. But we had never really spoken. Jack was a loner. Much the way I did, he kept to himself. He had a reputation as a lady-killer, and I had seen him before in one or another of the Chop House's back booths engaged in earnest conversation with a series of nubile young lovelies. He had been at the paper for two years. His stories were good. Painstaking exposés that took weeks and months of research. But most of the city room crowd thought Jack was stuck up. He had an independent income. He had a Ph.D. in English from Oxford. His clothes were custom-made; his shoes were shined and never worn down at the heel.

I was surprised when Jack and his date came over to my barstool. Her name was Nina Thatcher, I was told, and the executive editor had asked Jack to take her out to dinner. She was being interviewed for a slot in the features section.

Normally the executive editor would have wined and dined the succulent Ms. Thatcher, after which he would

have escorted her back to her hotel and done his damnedest to get into her Pucci panties. But this was Wednesday, and Wednesday evenings were reserved by our beloved leader for his mistress, a farm-fresh blonde from the outer regions of South Dakota who worked in the classified ads department and astride whose ample hips the executive editor would unfailingly spend the hours of five-thirty until eight, Wednesdays, forty-nine weeks a year.

So Jack had been asked to fill in. And after I had been introduced, he asked if I would like to join them for dinner—it was on the paper's expense account, after all. Besides, I, like Nina Thatcher, was a product of Columbia's J-school. So I had my oysters sent from the bar to one of the black leather banquettes and exchanged my tidy Moselle for an extravagant Pauillac. We sat over soft-shell crabs, rack of lamb, and steak tartare, talking about the pros and cons of working for the paper. Before the entrées arrived, we had already started on a second bottle of wine. Before we ordered dessert, we had finished a third. And we ended the meal with the excellent Framboise for which the Chop House is known, served in crystal shot glasses set deep in shaved ice.

The conversation ranged from the satyrism of our executive editor, whose reputation, it seemed, had preceded him all the way to New York, to Jack's stint as a court reporter, to the intricacies of narcotics reporting, which I had just begun in earnest. And we talked about life-styles in this city, most of whose white, middle-class population left at rush hour for the security of suburbs.

"How's the grass?" Nina Thatcher asked.

"It all depends what you want to pay," Jack Fowler said. "Good street reefer goes for about fifty the ounce. Colombian or Hawaiian sells for more. If you're lucky, or know people—like Robert, here—you can score some fancy Thai sticks for a hundred an ounce."

"One twenty," I said. "But it's definitely one-hit stuff."

"Like this?" asked Nina Thatcher, who took a small leather purse out of her handbag and unzipped it. "Or should I bring half a pound when I move from New York?"

I looked at her stash. All buds and flowers. No seeds, no stems. Not even many pieces of crushed leaf. Jack looked, too, and whistled.

"You guys have been out in the sticks too long," said Nina Thatcher.

"Hey," said Jack, "that's quality stuff. But I've got some at home that's even better. Not so many buds, but it's laced with hash oil."

"Horse puckey," said Nina Thatcher. "Horse shit."

"Wanna bet?" asked Jack. "We'll let Robert judge." He called for the check. "Back at my place. Then we'll drop you at the hotel—if you can still walk."

"You're on," said Nina Thatcher.

Jack drove a Buick in those days. A long, low Riviera in basic black with a single thin racing stripe in red along the side. We snuggled into the front seat and just for fun hit seventy on Jefferson Boulevard. Nina asked Jack if he always drove like that.

"Only when it's a matter of life and grass," Jack said, laughing, turning the FM radio up so that the interior of the car reverberated with the Supremes.

I had never seen the inside of Jack Fowler's apartment before. It was, to say the least, a masterpiece. Thick white shag rug in the living room; the two sofas done in a jacquard brown and white fabric. Plants everywhere. He had a two-bedroom apartment on the twenty-eighth floor of a new high rise directly across the street from my pre–World War I paradise, and his terrace overlooked the river. On a clear day he could see almost all the way to Toronto.

But it was the artwork that surprised me most. And Nina Thatcher, too. We walked through the linen-walled living room the way one would visit a museum. Two Klees over the sofa; two Chagall oils on the far wall. In the master bedroom five Vasarely temperas; in the dining room three Rouault oils. The second bedroom had been made into a paneled office, redolent with leather and dark wood fixtures. The only color was provided by a Josef Albers oil, about eighteen inches square.

"I like to get high and watch the colors change," Jack said.

"I thought reporters were poor," said Nina Thatcher. "You're really a pimp, right?"

Jack laughed. "I'm a rich kid," he said. "You're looking at my trust fund."

We settled into the deep sofa in the living room. Nina Thatcher kicked off her shoes, took the stash out of her purse, and produced some rolling paper. "All right, Fowler," she said. "Cut the impressive shit, and let's get down to business."

Jack removed his jacket. Whoever his tailor was had done an excellent job of concealing the fact that Jack Fowler worked out with barbells. His pectorals were full; his triceps, thick and ripply. "Business," he said. "Okay—first we prime the senses."

A small silver pillbox was brought out, and Jack dumped its contents—crystalline white powder—onto the smoked-glass surface of the four-foot-square coffee table. From his office he brought a French straight razor and with precise movements began to cut the powder into three separate piles. These he divided in twain, so that we soon looked down on six separate lines of good-quality cocaine, each about three inches long.

Jack proffered a short silver straw to Nina Thatcher. "Madam?" he said.

Nina Thatcher went to her knees in front of the glass-topped table. One line of coke, then another disappeared up her delicate nostrils. Then it was my turn; then Jack's. He went away for a moment, returned almost immediately with a trio of Irish linen handkerchiefs, which he handed out with a flourish and a Restoration bow. "I've been to Oxford," he said, slipping into a nasal English accent. "So very, very pleased that you could visit." He laughed. "Now that we've keened our senses, let's get on to the tasting." He produced three joints, each rolled in American Flag paper.

"Yours first," Jack Fowler said to Nina Thatcher.

Nina Thatcher took a *Gourmet* magazine from Jack's coffee table and, sitting on his couch with the magazine in her lap, proceeded to roll one large joint. She sat cross-legged. She was wearing a white dress that was belted and buttoned

down the front. The buttons stopped six inches above her knees, and with Jack's high-grade cocaine coursing through my head, I felt suddenly like stroking the firm thighs that had become visible.

I took Nina Thatcher's joint and looked it over carefully: a tobacco connoisseur evaluating a cheroot. "Evenly rolled," I said. "No outward sign of airholes. Probably clean-burning." I passed the thing under my nose. I looked up at Nina Thatcher. The top three buttons on her dress were open; I could see one strap and the top of a light-colored bra. Her breasts, I noticed, weren't very large. "Probably"—I sniffed again—"licked by someone who recently tasted wine. A 'sixty-one Pauillac. Château Lynch-Bages. North side of the hill." We all laughed. I passed the joint under my nose again, holding it there while I raised my eyes to sneak another look at Nina Thatcher. She had a little bump on her nose. It was just enough to give her nose character. I sniffed at the joint again. "Definitely Colombian," I said, "a hybrid red-gold with a hint of Oaxacan Sinsemilla. It's not pure, but a mixture."

"How did he know?" asked Nina Thatcher.

"When the paper trusts a reporter with five grand to buy dope," said Jack Fowler, "the paper wants a reporter with a dealer's nose. Robert has the making of a first-class dealer."

I took Jack Fowler's table lighter and applied its flame to the tip of the joint, let it catch fire, then blew it out. I waved the smoke in front of my face but didn't inhale yet. The aroma was sweet and slightly smoky. "Lacks the tempering that comes from being rolled on dark thighs," I said. "But then, de dark meat is always sweeter."

"Always?" Nina Thatcher asked.

"Always," I said. I noticed for the first time that Nina Thatcher wore a sensible Rolex watch on a gold bracelet. Not one of those tiny secretary's things, it was a watch that told you the time. She had nice wrists, too.

Then I placed Nina Thatcher's joint in a crystal ashtray the size of a pie plate and turned my attention to Jack's American Flag reefers. "Oh, say, can you see?" I said. Selecting the one in the middle, I rolled it between my thumb and forefin-

ger. "Professional," I announced. "Thick and tightly packed. Like Luckies. I could strip this and the boo would remain cylindrical." Jack nodded. I sniffed at it. "Mesopotamian Milkweed," I said. "Grown on slopes near the Chaldees of Ur. Laced with Siamese syrup." Again I lit up and sniffed cautiously at the gray smoke. It had an acrid kick. "Dangerously potent."

"So what's the verdict? Nina's or mine?" Jack's knuckles rapped on the smoked-glass coffee table.

"For smoking pleasure, Nina's," I said. "A long, luxurious, feline high. But for getting hard-ass stoned, ripped within an inch of your mind, you got it down cold, Jack."

We all laughed. And we lit up Nina's joint again, and Jack's, passing them among us with great pomp and ceremony. Jack turned on his quadraphonic sound system, and Sam and Dave came flooding into the room. Jack kicked off his shoes and lay back on the larger of his two couches, his hands in back of his head. "That beautiful Memphis sound," he said. "Jungle music. I love it."

I excused myself. "The wine's getting to me," I said and I lurched toward Jack's bathroom, where the combination of grass, wine, and coke caused me to waver unsteadily in front of the john. I made a mess and wiped up the spill with some toilet paper, flushed, washed my hands, and was turning out the lights to go back to the living room when Nina Thatcher appeared and slid by me in the narrow bathroom doorway.

"My turn," she said.

I don't know how it happened or why, but all of a sudden she slipped into my arms, and her tongue was in my mouth, and her breasts, pushing against the front of her silk dress, were touching my chest. I couldn't stop myself. My hands were all over her—feeling her arms, shoulders, back, thighs, ass, tits. I had an erection and pressed it into her groin. I massaged her stomach, reached my hands under the dress, and slipped one down the front of her panythose. Then out of the corner of my eye I saw Jack Fowler come down the hallway. He saw us—saw what we were doing and made an abrupt about-face. My face reddened. This was Jack's place, after all. If Nina Thatcher was anyone's for the night, she was

Jack's. I pushed away. "See you inside," I said, and let Nina Thatcher proceed into the bathroom. I guess we had stood there for three or four minutes, but I don't know for sure. I didn't start wearing my Nagra until later—in those days I could get a hard-on and women would feel it; now I'm protected, and so are they, by a machine—so I never timed that little sequence. When I got back to the living room, Jack had turned the lights down low, and Sam and Dave had been replaced by Marvin Gaye.

"Be cool," he said. That's all he said. Then he disappeared into his hallway. I sat quietly in the dark for some time. Then Jack reappeared, with his arm around Nina's shoulder.

"Listen," he said, "would you like to slip into something more comfortable? I think I have just the perfect little item—" And off he went again, almost scampering, toward his bedroom. He came back with a huge Detroit Lions jersey. "This belonged to Alex Karras. I bought it at the last PBS auction." He draped it in front of Nina Thatcher. The garment came below her knees, dwarfing her. "A perfect fit."

Nina Thatcher took the jersey and headed toward Jack's bedroom. "It's not fair to wear anything underneath," he called after her. Jack looked at me. "Calvados?" he asked.

It was probably the Calvados that did it. I don't recall details afterward, except for specific moments. Like Nina Thatcher reappearing in the silly oversized jersey and settling herself between Jack and me on the sofa. Then kissing him. Then kissing me. Then somehow we were rolling, all of us, on the floor, and Jack and I didn't have any clothes on, and neither did Nina Thatcher. Breasts to bite and soft, fuzzy pubic hair in my face. My cock in her mouth and Jack going down on her. Fucking Nina Thatcher while she went down on Jack. Jack in her ass and me up her snatch, I could feel his cock tight against mine separated by a thin wall of flesh. The shower in Jack's bathroom coming down hot and cold while we soaped and rinsed and licked and touched. Drying each other off and flicking at buttocks, cocks, balls, breasts with wet, thick terry cloth. And then bed. Sweet, big king-sized bed. Under the covers hugging each other like life-sized teddy bears, feeling, kissing, stroking, moaning.

I do remember the morning. Nina Thatcher between Jack and me, her dark hair spread out on Jack's blue pillowcase, a hand on my cock massaging it into early-morning life; a hand on Jack's, too. We rolled over and snuggled up to her like babes, suckling each on a small breast. She scratched our backs. "My boys," Nina Thatcher said. "My men."

We had her again, both of us did. But in the light. I watched Jack, critically, as he entered her. His cock was uncircumcised; the head grew. I could see the foreskin pull back as he disappeared slowly into Nina Thatcher. I watched as she massaged his balls, pumping them almost, as he rocked her back and forth, her legs point past his shoulders, the hair in her crotch like dark mattress ticking, wet with sweat and come and her own juices. My turn. She was warm inside and very wet from Jack, and she welcomed me. Jack watched as she took my cock in her fingers and rubbed it up against her clit, suddenly turning and taking just the head of it in her mouth, then rolling over so that I could enter her from behind.

We had fresh grapefruit juice for breakfast. Jack squeezed it while Nina and I took a shower. Then, while he rinsed himself off, Nina poached some eggs, and I fried a full pound of bacon. We ate and kissed and ate some more, feeding each other strawberry jam on whole wheat toast. Jack and I went to the bathroom and relieved ourselves, pissing streams into the pot in tandem while Nina Thatcher watched and applauded our aim. We brushed our teeth with the same toothbrush. All for one and one for all.

Jack drove like a madman, and we stopped by the Pontchartrain long enough for Nina Thatcher to get her blue Ventura carry-on bag and check out. Then we drove the twenty-five miles to the airport at a more leisurely pace. We had her at the terminal with ten minutes to spare but decided to race each other to the gate anyhow. Nina Thatcher kissed Jack Fowler good-bye. Then she kissed me good-bye. "I think I'm going to like it here," she said as she started down the boarding ramp. "A lot."

We watched the plane back off from the gate, our noses pressed against the glass like a couple of kids. "Have you got

anything to do today," Jack Fowler said as we walked back to
where he had left his Riviera double-parked in a space reserved for police cars.

Nothing really, I told him.

"Good. Neither do I. Let's go back to my place and talk."

We walked out of the terminal, our arms around each
other's shoulders, feeling like a couple of teenagers; to slay
the dragons of poverty, filth, crime, and corruption that fill
this city. Young knights, riding on charging white paragraphs, their shields emblazoned with the escutcheon of the
First Amendment. Nancy once described me that way. She
said it three years after I called to tell her I loved her from the
Ace Motel.

But that was seven years ago. I was still a greenhorn. I believed that there was something gained—some good to be
done—by writing stories, by exposing wrongs. I thought that
the notes I took, the people I interviewed, the misery I saw
were only means to an end, the end being change. I was so
serious in those days, so much older then.

Sometimes, when I'm in the shower, I remember what it
was like waking up in the tiny trinity apartment Nancy and I
shared in the Silver Lake district of Los Angeles. I would roll
over and admire the fine, gentle line of her back as she lay
sleeping next to me. She had a beautiful back. A back in a
million, I used to tell her (Nancy's response was always the
same. "How would you know from a million," she would
say. "You're a one-back man").

I used to kiss her awake a decade ago. Kiss her awake and
then watch as she went to brush her teeth. I'd follow her
sleepily into our minuscule kitchen and look as she stood
barefoot in front of our three-burner stove in one of my old
button-down shirts and fry up the most incredibly good jelly
omelets ever to be consumed. I would do my share, too,
pouring exactly the right amount of real cream into mugs of
rich, black, steaming coffee. And I would light our morning
cigarette, which we invariably shared.

But that was all before. Before I came here. Before Jack
was killed. Before Juliet slept with Johnny Psycho. Before I

received the damnable gray envelope. Before I was totally alone.

I could afford to be serious in those days. I could afford to care. Life was simple and good. Pleasures were easily come by and easily returned. I was so much older then: ambitious; optimistic; committed to making waves.

I'm younger than that now. I know better.

*chapter 5*_____

I never wanted to write Jack's story. I have said that to myself many times in the eight months since he was killed. It is true. Of all the rules I live by—and there are many—two of the most important are never to hold back on a story and never to write about a friend. I know they are important: I have broken both of them, and I have been hurt each time.

Nancy once compiled a list of my rules. She typed them on thick bond paper and bound them in a leather folder. I received them for my twenty-fifth birthday. A big, intricately wrapped package, inside of which was this folder, inscribed "Robert's Rules of Order." Nancy thought it was quite a joke. But then she never understood about rules. She thought it was possible to go to work, come home, and live a normal life, whatever that is, and not become changed by what you see on the streets. Of course, Nancy never worked on the street. She had a small but pleasant office at CBS. She read scripts written by writers who had never seen the street. I remember telling her once that her image of society was incredibly naïve. People in television scripts never have real problems. Their cars always start; they always find parking

places. Their houses are filled with good furniture. Their clothes match. When they get sick, they are cured by doctors who never seem to send bills, doctors who still make house calls.

Nancy accepted these things. I never did. It was impossible for me to accept them because I saw life at its worst on a daily basis. The doctors I came in contact with worked in emergency rooms. The people I covered were either victims or victimizers. It became harder and harder for me to accept Nancy's vision of society.

Take sources, for example. Often we would go out to dinner with one of my sources. Nancy never understood the reality of having sources. She couldn't comprehend why I would spend so much of my time coddling my sources, why I would literally drop whatever I was doing if a source called and asked to meet with me.

She did not understand that without sources there are no stories. Hence one's sources become one's most important resources. You play confessor for them. You deal with their problems. You stroke their egos. You massage their consciences. You develop their trust. It is very important to do so.

Yet sources are not friends. You try to get them to the point where they tell you their innermost secrets, but you never divulge any of your own. This sort of thing took me awhile to master, but I did it. At first I was vaguely guilty about manipulating sources. But not for long. I learned to repress the guilt, to overcome it. I discovered that much reporting is role playing. You become the person your source wants you to become.

It sounds cold, I know. And calculating. Even unscrupulous. The problem is that it is necessary. So I would tell Nancy that some of the people with whom we would have dinner were not my friends, but sources, and therefore, we should talk as little as possible about ourselves. She found this hard to do. She argued that business lunches were just fine but that dinner should be something special, that it should be reserved for friends.

Still, sources are not friends, even after you get to know

them. Even the word is a lie. Source. It looks great on the page. But among reporters, in the sanctity of the city room or over a drink, sources become what they really are: snitches; finks; stoolies.

As a narcotics reporter you learn never to bring a source home because then he knows where and how you live. He knows how many locks you have on your door and where you keep your weapons, if you have any. Snitches, we know, aren't snitches because they are sterling people. They always want something. Sometimes it is publicity. Sometimes they want to air a grudge. In government, sources leak information to push one side of a question, or to force their opponents to act prematurely, or to kill a certain project simply by disclosing its existence.

In my own field, sources talk to me because it helps their business. Say I have a snitch working for Dealer A. He gives me reliable information about Dealer B. I write a story. Dealer B gets busted, and Dealer A takes over his business. But my snitch is probably telling his boss everything he knows about me. My habits, the way I look and talk—anything he knows. Because Dealer A is no dummy. He understands that sooner or later I will find a source who works for Dealer C, who hates Dealer A and would like to take his business over.

Hence I will meet my snitches. I will buy them lunch or dinner or drink with them in bars. But I will not become their friend. I will not talk about myself, except in the most general of ways. I will not give up my secrets.

Nancy never understood the impeccable logic of this. "They are people," she would tell me. "All relationships are built on mutual trust," she would say. I could never convince her that in my case, trust was simply the source's faith that I would never divulge his name. That the other kind of trust—the sort that makes for long-standing personal relationships—simply could not exist.

Just before I left Los Angeles for Detroit three years ago, Nancy said I was emotionally dead. She said that in the six years we had lived together she had watched my emotions petrify into stone. She called me cold, calculating, and ma-

nipulative. Maybe she was right. Probably she was. Yet I couldn't see any other way to live my life. As my stories got better, my personal life got worse. It couldn't be helped.

Nancy said, "If you don't let me back into your life, then I will find someone who will. Someone to share things with. Someone who's not afraid to let his emotions show."

I took it as an idle threat. Nancy was good at making idle threats. But it was not an idle threat, and when I came to Detroit, I came alone.

But I still loved her. In Los Angeles and even in Detroit she was a constant factor in my life. The idea of Nancy was a constant factor, I should say. I could work the streets and return to my empty apartment because, somewhere out there, Nancy existed. And if I wanted to, I could go back to her. I kept telling myself that. I have told myself that for three years.

Until yesterday, when going back became impossible.

———

I never wanted to write Jack's story. That is God's own truth.

I took the tapes from his ravaged apartment to protect him from other, more unscrupulous newsmen and the police. The cops hate our newspaper. They would have leaked Jack's tapes to the competition. But I had them, and they were perfectly safe with me.

Or so I thought until I got a call from our executive editor. I was taking the morning off, sorting through two cases of new wines when the phone rang. It was my private line, which is connected to the paper's switchboard. I use it to receive calls from sources. That way my unlisted home number stays out of people's hands. As usual, I flipped on the recording switch after two rings. It was a short call.

"Robert, it's Mike."

"Hi, boss, what's up?"

"Jack's place is a mess. Have you been up there?"

"I went over to take a look. They kicked the hell out of it. How in God's name did the security people let anybody in without calling up first?"

"We're not sure. I had a team interview some tenants. No-

body's talking for attribution, of course—they're all scared shitless. One guy said that security in the building has been screwed up for months. Told us that nobody's being checked at the desk, that the night clerk spends all his time reading or sleeping in the manager's office."

"What about the security guards?" I asked.

"We discovered that they go down into the garage at about ten," Mike said, "and they play a regular poker game almost every night. It's a great scam—one guy makes all the rounds, punches the clocks, while the others screw off."

"And the doorman?"

"He's supposed to work until midnight. Generally he leaves at about ten-thirty."

My transcription indicates that there was about a six-second pause on the tape at this point. Then Mike said, "Robert—"

I said, "Mike?"

"Look," said Mike's voice, "this isn't easy. I know you and Jack are—were—friends. I know you used to hang out together. I want you to work on the story. Do the personal side. The background. Write about Jack Fowler the man, who he was, what he meant to us, to the city."

"That's impossible," I said. "No way."

"You've got the insight for it," Mike said. "You knew the guy. You were neighbors. You could write this out of your head with all the background you've got. Come on, Robert, it's an easy piece."

I said, "I don't write about my friends. There are a dozen people you could put on the case."

"I've already got a dozen people working. But nobody knew him like you did. You could do a hell of a job on the background stuff."

"Which is exactly why I'm going to stay the hell off. Jesus Christ, Mike—"

"Robert, just shut up and listen to me for a second, okay? First of all, we've got a dead reporter. A rich dead reporter. Second, he's your buddy-buddy. Third, our competition is busting ass on the story. It makes us look bad."

True, all true, I thought. But there was so much more, so

much Mike did not know about. I sat silent for a few seconds. "Let me think about it," I said. "Call me back in an hour." I didn't wait for a response but cut off the line.

Yes, I had background. For two months before he was killed Jack Fowler had been working on a story about young male prostitutes. Chickens they're called on the street. And he had gotten on to the story through me.

Jack and I were close. He was the only person at the paper with whom I had ever discussed Nancy. In return, he told me about Madeleine, a lady at Oxford, who, as Jack put it, "spoiled me for any other woman." But we shared more than secrets about our personal lives. We backed each other up on the job as well. Every reporter needs a sounding board, someone to go to and say, "Look, here's what I've got—do you think it'll stand up?" Jack and I were each other's sounding boards. And occasionally, we'd let the other observe a story in progress on a firsthand basis.

One night, two months before he was killed, I took Jack with me to the Westvale, the rock-and-roll emporium on East Harper. I went to the Westvale over a three-month period, buying an assortment of uppers, downers, mumblers, laughers, cryers, cocaine, heroin, PCP, THC—the whole alphabet soup of central nervous system depressants and mood elevators. The paper had given me $6,000, and I spent it all easily. It was a simple story to write. The gist was that every weekend hundreds of kids from all over the Detroit area come to hear the music and buy narcotics, and the management of the Westvale (with the tacit cooperation of the Detroit Police Department) lets everything go on in the open.

I wanted to shut the place down. Indeed, I did shut it down, with a story written the very night Jack was killed. But two months before that night Jack had decided he wanted to visit the Westvale with me.

At first I was against it. Basically Jack was no street reporter. He was gifted at covering the court system. He was a digger. He never minded spending days and weeks searching through the files at the City-County Building. He used to say he actually enjoyed working his way through umpteen

rolls of microfilm. But on the street he was vulnerable. On the street his English clothes, $200 tinted eyeglasses, and Gucci boots made him a mark. Especially on East Harper, in the center of a ghetto that stretched five miles in every direction.

But Jack insisted, so I took him with me, "just for kicks," as he put it.

He really dressed up for the occasion. A velvet hacking jacket, silk shirt open to the waist, tight French jeans, fancy cowboy boots. I was in my normal work clothes: bump-toed shoes with inch-thick soles and three-inch stacked heels, jacquard-knit double knit trousers in forest green, and a patterned shirt, over which I wore a fringie vest.

We spent five hours at the Westvale. Jack watched as I worked my way down the gauntlet of dealers, sampling their wares, buying what I thought was the best and the worst dope available. He said later that he had been fascinated. But he was even more fascinated by the kids who hung out at the Westvale. Mostly they came from Detroit's wealthier suburbs—Grosse Pointe, Southfield, Birmingham, Oak Park. The Westvale was an ideal place to visit because the action was fast and the dope easily obtained.

But there were other kids, too. Eleven-, twelve-, and thirteen-year-olds from Detroit's West Side. Black kids who pulled tens and twenties out of dirty jean pockets to score Dilaudid and Leritine from Harvey, a male nurse out of Detroit General who supplemented his income on the weekends by selling narcotics, or Quaalude and pink tabs of THC from Lester, a high school vice-principal who wanted to retire on more than a city pension.

"Where do they get their money," Jack had wanted to know, "the ghetto kids?"

"From robbery, purse snatching, mugging," I told him. "Or by selling themselves."

"Oh," Jack Fowler had said. And we hadn't talked about it until later, at his apartment, when he asked how I thought kids of eleven or twelve went about selling themselves. I started to answer, but Jack said, "Wait a minute." And he went into his office, got his tape recorder, slipped a fresh

cassette into it, and turned it on. "Speak," he commanded.

"Say you are a poor kid from the West Side," I said. "How do you get cash for dope? You can steal it, which means that you might get caught—not that the cops would do anything to you, but you could get caught. Or there's a simpler way. You hit the Six Mile Road area, where the gay community lives. You stand outside a porno bookstore, or a bar, or a gay movie theater, and you wait. Sooner or later somebody comes along, and you ask him if he wants to play with you—five bucks for five minutes. If the answer is yes, you either take him into an alley and let him jerk you off or go into the balcony of the movie house, where he can blow you, or play with you, or something like that.

"Or if you're really serious about things, you can hit on one of the charge-it-by-the-hour hotels and let the trick really go down on you for half an hour or so, but that usually costs more—like fifteen or twenty."

"Oh," Jack Fowler had said.

"It's called chicken hawking," I said.

"I know," Jack Fowler said. "It's big in New York right now."

"Really," I said. "I guess like all good things, it gets around."

"But the kids aren't all gay," Jack said. It was a statement.

"From what I know I don't think so," I said. "Look, you take a twelve-year-old. He lives somewhere on Rangoon Street or in the Northwest ghetto. He wants to score some dope. Maybe he doesn't belong to a gang. Maybe he does. But using his body is much less a risk than if he went out and rented a gun or stole one or bought one and stuck up a store in his neighborhood. Besides, the rip-off possibilities are better. A lot of the guys who dig kids are bisexual from what I can tell. They have homes and wives and kids. So once a month, say, they go out and give some kid a blow job. And let's say that the kid keeps a straight razor in his jeans, as well as his prick. And let's say that after the blow job, or during it maybe, he decides to rip off the trick's wallet. Nobody's gonna go screaming to the cops, is he? Who's gonna say he was ripped off while committing sodomy on a minor? It's

like the hookers downtown. They'll French you for a dime, but they'll rip you off afterward, you know? Right in your own car."

Jack was silent. There is silence on the tape at this point. Then he said, "How come we haven't done anything about it?"

"I don't know," my voice said.

There is another silence here. A longer silence. "It could be my kind of story," Jack said.

I tried to talk him out of it. But the more I argued, the more convinced Jack became that he should tackle it. We talked for hours, but he didn't listen to me. I knew he was wrong, though. Jack was not a street person. I knew him better than anybody, and I knew that outside the courts, the document rooms, the legal libraries, he was a naïf, an innocent. He had none of the smarts necessary to survive on his own. He was not callous or sneaky; he was not cold or calculating; he was not sufficiently cynical. He was a bad liar. I could tell when he was lying, every time.

I told him all that and more. I explained about my rules to him, about survival. But he wouldn't listen. He said that it didn't matter, that he could take care of himself. "I'm not a child, Robert," Jack said. "I have my reasons," he said.

When I asked what they were, he had told me that he was sick and tired of covering the courts. "This piece will get me out of the courts for good," he said.

He swore me to secrecy, too. He'd work the story on his own time, he said, then hand it in and ask for more investigative pieces.

"But you're already doing investigative pieces," I said.

"Street pieces then," Jack said. "I know, Robert—all articles are investigative. That's what they tell us. And I guess it's true. We should always take the time to make the extra phone call, check the umpteenth source. But for once in my life I want to be out on the street."

Jack said, "It'll make my bones."

The story did more than that. It killed him. I felt I was the one who had literally set him up. I had broken one of my primary rules for survival. It was as if I had taken Jack to a wild-

life preserve and, instead of making sure that he stayed safely inside the Land Rover, I had allowed him to jump out to pet the hyenas.

And they had eaten him alive.

So having once broken my own rules, I broke them again. I called the executive editor back and told him about Jack's two-month secret investigation. Then I told him that I'd work on Jack's story. It would be one way to protect Jack, to make sure the hyenas stayed safely in the background.

"You'll be doing Jack's memory a service," Mike told me. How could either of us know that just the opposite was true?

*chapter 6*_____

          I did not like myself very much
after I hung up the phone. There is a certain peculiar, ineffa-
ble, empty gut feeling reporters get when they start a project
they know will end badly. I had that feeling. Moreover, I did
not enjoy the fact that I had Jack's tapes and notes locked in
my closet safe. They gave me an unfair advantage, I thought,
insights into Jack's life that were dangerous to him. Jack and
I had shared secrets that one does not tell an analyst. This is
the reason that we should not pursue stories about our
friends, our loved ones. Our friends trust us; our loved ones
trust us. Jack had loved me. I knew that. He had trusted me. I
knew that, too. And I had trusted him. With the trust came
the sharing of secrets—his and mine. But secrets, as all reporters know, are the cornerstone of any good story.
   Some of my secrets died with Jack, although by dying he
betrayed others. Most of the rest died sixty hours ago, when
Nancy was killed. So I am pretty safe, I think. Eight months
ago, eight months ago, I thought I had all of Jack's secrets
locked in my closet safe. But they were not safe any longer.
Nor were they to be secrets very much longer. In the seconds
after Mike's phone call they had become evidence.

They documented a facet of Jack's life that no one in Detroit but I knew. They were notes, tapes, and conversations proving that Jack was bisexual. Under normal circumstances this fact would not be startling or damaging. A person's lifestyle is his or her own business. Except in Jack Fowler's case. Jack had been working on a story about homosexuals. And in doing that, he had broken another of my rules: He was writing about people with whom he had a conflict of interest. Thus he became a part of his own story.

Jack told me about his life-style early in our friendship—perhaps three months after we had shared our night with Nina Thatcher. We had been sitting in my apartment, tasting a bottle of Pichon-Longueville-Baron '59, ruminating about who else at the paper Ms. Thatcher might be cohabiting with. Despite occasional waves and smiles in the city room, we'd never repeated our happy ménage, and neither Jack nor I saw Nina Thatcher socially.

Jack had insisted on turning on my tape recorder. To capture, as he put it, the eclectic brilliance of our repartee. We ruminated for a while about Nina Thatcher's sex life, inventing all sorts of lovely fantasies.

Then Jack changed the subject. "How often do you get laid?" he asked. He sipped at his wine.

I thought about lying and decided against it. "Not very often," I said. "There's work, you know, and tapes to transcribe. Besides, I work odd hours."

"I know," said Jack. "All the fashionable excuses."

"What do you mean?" I asked.

"You damn well know what I mean," said Jack. "You just don't want to get laid, do you?"

He was right. "You're right," I said. "It's just that—oh, hell—you know—I just don't think I can handle relationships very well right now."

"Nancy," Jack Fowler said. "You've been here almost a year, and you're still living inside a relationship that ended in Los Angeles. It's Nancy, right? You think you're still emotionally involved with Nancy."

I nodded. "Also," I said, "I'm not very stable now. I have enough problems with the work. A relationship would—"

"Complicate things," Jack's voice said. "But the core of it is Nancy. There's always a Nancy. A Nancy whom you want and can't have. A Nancy whom you can fantasize a relationship with. It's Nancy, right?"

"Yes," I said.

There is a pause on the tape. Then Jack said, "I was in love like that once. I was in love with a woman who spoiled me for other women. I mean she really messed me up, Robert. Screwed my mind up good." There is another pause on the tape: the sound of Jack shifting his legs. Then he said, "Her name was Madeleine."

Jack had met her in the sixth month of his residence at Christ College, Oxford. She was twenty-five; he was twenty-seven. She was a medievalist working toward her doctorate. He was an English scholar trying to perfect his skill at baccarrat and his Oxford drawl. It was all, Jack said, like living in a dreamworld. His rooms were furnished in what he chose to call Early Christopher Wren. Jack's vintage ports were all crusted and three decades old. He had put Aubussons on the floors and Gobelins on the walls. He had affected a habit for Cuban cigars and fifty-year-old brandies. He had made a point of going to dinner parties where evening clothes were the rule, not the exception.

And at one of them, at the home of an American diplomat, he had met Madeleine.

"She was perfect," said Jack's voice. "Classic English. Hair halfway between butterscotch and chestnut brown. The kind of complexion that looks best after a two-hour walk on the moors. She could ride and shoot; her family was well-off. She was tall and lithe and beautiful. We would have had beautiful, lithe, tall children. She was everything I had ever dreamed about. Oh, yes, Robert, something I shouldn't leave out. She was a virgin. Can you believe it? At twenty-five."

"What you are talking about," I said, "is an old-fashioned girl. An old, old-fashioned girl."

"As usual, you have grasped the kernel of the situation," Jack said, slipping into his Oxford drawl. He sipped at his wine and dropped the English accent. "We courted in the old-fashioned style. None of that rolling around the back

seats of cars or groping each other in dormitory bedrooms. She really wanted to be courted. Flowers, notes, long talks about metaphysical subjects. Walks in the rain. Do you know it was a month before I ever held her hand? She was like no one I had ever known."

"What was your first kiss like?" I asked.

"Incredible. Absolutely unbelievable. I had this old red Austin two thousand at the time. We drove into London for the weekend to see the Vic. We'd been seeing each other for about six weeks at that point. So we saw *Measure for Measure*, then had dinner at Mirabelle and finished the evening at the White Elephant. It was one of those perfect days. We did a lot of hand holding.

"I had gotten us rooms at Claridge's. They were on separate floors because Madeleine thought it better form." Jack took a long swallow of wine. He can be heard gulping it on the tape.

"And?"

"And I take her to her room. She puts the key in the lock. Then she opens the door. I remember thinking that she was going to invite me inside. But all of a sudden she gives me a quick little peck that landed halfway between my cheek and the left corner of my mouth, and slam—she's gone. And I hear the bolt turn on the inside of the door.

"I think I stood outside her door for half an hour. I went through all kinds of changes. I remember thinking that Claridge's is costing me a hundred quid, that dinner, tickets, and the Elephant was another hundred and a half. And I am standing in the hall like some idiot, having been pecked on the cheek. I felt like a character in a Trollope novel."

"It might have been a good idea to have a little Trollope waiting by your bedside that night," I said.

"Don't be patronizing," Jack said. "I was in love, man. We're not talking about anything rational. Give me some more of that *vin extraordinaire*. I mean, we are dealing here with lunacy: crazy, insane lunacy.

"I had taken one look at this lady and told myself that she was going to be mine. Like, I was going to win her hand. Can you get behind that phrase, Robert? Win her hand. Consider

the implications of that. I was playing the game on her turf, by her rules. They were new rules, but I believed that I could play by them and win. It's out of Henry James, isn't it?"

I played straight man. "What happened?"

"We spent six months courting," Jack said. "We were together most of the time. Everybody thought we were sleeping together, but Madeleine said she couldn't give herself—that's exactly how she said it—give herself to me yet. I was climbing the bloody walls. Here I was, an Oxford scholar, rooms at Christ College. The world's most beautiful lady on my arm day after day. And at midnight I'd be back in my rooms standing on my Aubusson with my shorts around my ankles jerking off into a piece of Kleenex.

"And I was happy doing it, I thought."

There is a short pause on the tape at this point. Jack can be heard sucking in his breath. "Then my brother, Teddy, killed himself coming home from a tea dance. Teddy was six years younger than I, but we were close. You know the kind of thing, Robert: a big house, lots of people to run it, and two kids left more or less to themselves. We didn't have a lot of friends, and my parents are horrendously active in social affairs. Anyway, Teddy got drunk and ran his car into a light pole. I had to fly home to be with my parents. I couldn't book a flight the day they called with the news, so Madeleine and I went to dinner. I planned to drive to London the next morning.

"She was perfectly lovely at dinner. Sympathetic as hell. I guess I was pretty unsettled. I knew I needed more than sympathy. I don't know—it was an empty feeling in my gut. An animal need to be held. I didn't want to spend eight hours on a plane and have to face my father. I didn't want to be alone. That's what it was, you know, a feeling of dreadful aloneness.

"We walked back to Madeleine's rooms. She said I looked white and offered me a brandy. She poured one, too. We sat in facing armchairs. It was so damn civilized. God, I remember the pattern of those chairs. Tiny yellow roses on light blue silk. There was a butler's table between us. She sat there with her legs crossed at the ankles and stared at me.

"I really wanted to be held, Robert. I wanted primeval body wamrth. Something to take the pain of death away. I sat there and drank brandy and thought about Teddy, about being alone, with no one to talk to, no one to share my secrets with. Madeleine sat there with her ankles crossed and looked at me. I don't know whether she was empathizing or whether she was incapable of dealing with me—I still don't know." There is a full thirty-second silence on the tape at this point. There is the sound of wine being poured into a glass.

"You know I've never told this to anyone," Jack's voice said. "No one knows."

I was silent.

"I raped her.

"Maybe I went crazy, I don't know. I wanted . . . something. Madeleine, sex, body warmth, to make some sort of physical statement about being alive. I saw her sitting there with her legs crossed at the ankles, and I came apart at the seams. I ripped her dress. I turned over the chairs. I broke the brandy snifters. It wasn't rape, you know. At least I didn't think of it as rape at the time. It was something else. A way to share my grief. A need to be inside somebody. Not to be alone.

"I left for Savannah the next morning. I was away for a month. When I got back, Madeleine wouldn't see me. She wouldn't even talk to me. It was like being excommunicated. I was a nonperson.

"I couldn't work or study or anything. Sometimes I'd go and sit outside her rooms like a dog. My whole world was collapsing. And of course, it was compounded by something only she and I knew—that I'd raped her. I knew that I had violated her whole value system. At times I wanted to castrate myself, you know. Cut off the offending member.

"Three weeks after I came back from Savannah Madeleine announced her engagement to some fucking marquis. I locked myself in my rooms and cried for two days.

"On the third day the senior don of Christ rapped at my door. He invited me upstairs to his room for dinner. He said that he was concerned about me, that I hadn't been myself,

that he wanted to help. He was a lean little man named Williams Pierce. A historian and classicist. He would have groups of us up for port and cigars.

"He fed me sole meunière and overcooked flageolets and we drank a bottle of warm Bâtard-Montrachet. Two bottles, actually. He said that he understood that Madeleine was engaged, and I'd have to pull myself out of it, and could he be of any help? He didn't know anything, of course.

"I had a stiff brandy after dinner. I took it down fast. He poured me another, and I chugged that one, too.

"Then I got very sick. I lost the dinner and the wine and the brandy. I was hysterical, I think. I know I was drunk. But he held my head over the toilet, and he actually carried me to his bedroom. He put me down on his bed and wiped my face with a cool cloth.

"And then he said, 'Can I hold you, dear boy?' I was still crying, but I must have nodded yes because all of a sudden he was getting out of his clothes and lying next to me in this narrow bed of his. I remember that he was wearing green briefs, and somehow I thought to myself how strange that a historian would wear green briefs.

"He held me and kissed the back of my neck and rubbed my chest, and for some reason I rolled over and kissed him full on the mouth. God, my breath must have been disgusting.

"And then, oh God, Robert, I remember thinking that he was Madeleine, and I kissed him harder, and I stroked him, and I wanted him. And I got hard, you know, and he wriggled out of his green briefs and rolled over, and I fucked him. I was thinking about Madeleine, but I fucked him. God, I was thinking about Madeleine but I came in his ass and then he rolled over again and I went to sleep in his arms.

"The worst part of it was that I hadn't slept so soundly in months."

There is another pause on the tape at this point. Then Jack sighed.

"We were very discreet," he said. "More discreet than Madeleine and I had been. But he taught me things, Robert. And much to my disgust, and my amazement, I liked what

he taught me. I'd never been so close to anybody in my life. Women are lovely creatures, you know. But I discovered there is a closeness between men that cannot be duplicated."

"Are you—" I asked.

"Yes," said Jack. "But quietly. I cover the courts. If my character were questioned, my stories would become invalid. I'm no fag, Robert. I don't want to be the interior decorator reporter. I don't want to write about hairdressers. It's just that once in a while I have to be close to a man, to feel a man's strength."

"No one knows? No one at the paper knows?"

"Except for you, now."

"Me and the tape recorder," I said.

"I went to a shrink for a while," Jack said. "I think she knew I was hiding something from her. I don't even know why I told you, Robert. You never suspected, did you? I don't think anyone suspects."

"No, you're right. I don't think anyone suspects anything," I said. "But why can't you just be you—whatever that means? If you're bisexual, then be bisexual. If you're homosexual, or whatever—"

"I prefer not to pronounce it that way," Jack said. "Not homo like 'home.' It has a cheap sound to it, like calling me a faggot or a pansy. It should rhyme with 'om.'"

"Home, hom—it doesn't make a difference," I said. "You wouldn't be an outcast these days."

"Wanna bet?" asked Jack. He blew his nose. "We don't do such things in my family. The merest hint would kill my parents. And I swear to you, Robert, it would kill my career.

"Look at me. What do I have? A trust fund and a lot of art and a family of supermarket owners just waiting for me to come to my senses, go home to Savannah, and run the business. There's nothing my mother would like better. After Teddy died, there was no one else to pass the business to. But I don't want the business. Reporting is my life; it's what I do. It makes me happy. It makes me forget about everything else.

"I can't control much about my life, Robert. My life is all

screwed up. I think Freud would pay a million bucks for a look at my subconscious. I have no way of controlling how I live or whom I love or desire or anything like that. But I can control the stories I work on. They're the single consistent factor of my fucked-up existence, and I will not give them up."

"You're right," I told Jack.

I told him he was right because I had made much the same speech to Nancy some years before. "I cannot control us," I had told her. "I cannot take responsibility for anything but my work. I can control the stories I do." And I had told her that nothing equals that feeling of control: not love or companionship or sex or anything.

I told Jack what Nancy had said to me. "You are going to be a lonely young man, you and your stories," she had said.

"Are we going to be lonely young men?" Jack's voice asked. He sounded like a little boy just then.

"I don't know," I said. "I hope not." I was lying. I knew the answer. It was not a pleasant answer. I couldn't bring myself to tell him. I think he knew.

"In the meanwhile," Jack's voice said, "we can rely on each other. I guess we have to rely on each other. You've got my life in your hands, Robert."

"I know," I said. "I know." When I replayed the tape later, the tone of my voice was very uneven. I had not wanted that sort of responsibility.

But I had taken it. I had held Jack's life in my hands for more than two years. Then he had been killed, and I had been assigned to write about it.

No, I did not like myself very much after I hung up the phone from Mike's call. I was very lonely then. I wanted to call Mike back and get myself taken off the story. I wanted to call Nancy in Los Angeles and tell her I didn't want to be a lonely young man anymore. I wanted not to break any more of my rules.

None of these things was possible, of course. My life was out of my hands. Only the story remained: a story to be written, controlled. Nancy had given me my choice years ago. A relationship or a story. I had picked the latter. Now I

was stuck with it. Jack's life, too, was out of my hands. What remained of him were the facts. Who. What. When. Where. Why. How.

Eight months ago, lying in his grave, Jack Fowler had become source material. I hated myself.

But not enough. Not enough to let the story go.

chapter 7_____

Two days after Jack was killed, the day Mike called and I accepted the assignment to write about Jack, I had a terrific need to be with somebody, to talk to somebody. I wanted very much to call Nancy in Los Angeles and talk things over. That was impossible, of course. I hadn't called Nancy since I'd come to Detroit, although I had thought about it. But Jack's tapes had to be transcribed. His notes had to be scrutinized. His research had to be checked, analyzed, sorted out. Besides, even if I had called Nancy, it wouldn't have helped. Neither of us would have revealed secrets. Neither would have shared our lives. It would have been a very civilized conversation. I would have asked how her job with CBS was going; she would have asked me what stories I was working on. She would have inquired whether I was eating properly. Then I would have told her about Jack and my assignment, and she would have wanted to know the reason I was doing the story in the first place. She would have accused me of trying to expiate my guilt over having to write the story by laying some of it off on her. Then, she would have said, I'd be able to be the callous, unfeeling person I like to be. Once I'd confessed my guilt,

she'd say, I could go right ahead and betray Jack by digging into his secrets.

I was able to play the conversation in my head because Nancy had said the same sort of thing before. When I was offered this job in Detroit, I asked Nancy to come with me. She refused. She had watched me change, she said, from a person who enjoyed people into a person who saw only the bad in others. I was suffering, she had said, from a reporter's version of "John Wayne Syndrome." Life was a game to me, she said, and she didn't like the way I was playing it.

So on the day I left Los Angeles for Detroit she was not around to send me off with a kiss. She stayed with friends while I packed my things into my car. What she did do was write me a letter. I still have it in my files. I know it almost by heart.

"For the past six months, Robert," it said, "I have been living alone. We share a house and a bed. We talk about sports, or movies, or the weather, but we do not talk about us. You have (and very successfully, too) depersonalized our relationship. You may touch me, but you have forgotten how to *touch* me. I cried twice last week at night, and you slept right through. You clutched at your pillow instead of me (and I am made for clutching, believe me. I have it all over pillows—even the best goose-down ones).

"Last week—our last week together—you came home drunk (and very late, and you never called to tell me that you would be either). When I asked you why, you said it was part of the job, and it didn't matter anyhow. I took that graciously, if I do say so. I oozed charm, reheated our dinner, and waited for you to talk to me over the wine. A bottle of Corton, if you remember. But even an exquisite Burgundy couldn't open you up. You gobbled your food in silence; you refused to tell me what was on your mind, what was bothering you.

"Then you went into the bedroom and switched on the TV set and left me to the dishes and myself. I cried then. Softly, so you would not hear me (but, I thought to myself, not so softly that you wouldn't hear me if you wanted to).

"And when I came to bed, having brushed my teeth and

63

perfumed my body and put on my most seductive mini-nightie to see if I could coax some tenderness from you, you were already asleep, clutching your pillow like a long-lost lover. And I cried again, louder, but you never woke up. It was not the first time this has happened, Robert, but I swore to myself that it would be the last.

"I work, too, Robert. I hold a full-time, high-paying job. There are stresses and pressures on me, too. But somehow, when I come home, I like to think that your presence and your love can help relieve those stresses and pressures. When I come home, I want to laugh, to share, to be held—and to hold you. But you have stopped needing, I think. You are intent on shutting yourself off from me. Are you so terri-fied of life that you cannot open your arms and hold me? Is the street so bad that you feel you must become impervious to emotion to survive?

"I will not go to Detroit with you, Robert. I cannot. I will not cry myself to sleep anymore. I will not share a silent din-ner table with you, or anyone, ever again. I will not be taken for granted."

There was more to the letter. As I reread it eight months ago, I realized that I could not call Nancy. She would not have understood. Yet I needed to talk to someone. I remem-ber thinking at the time that the person who would have understood my problem best was Jack Fowler. Jack would have been supportive. But Jack was unavailable, of course.

What I did was dial the features department and ask for Nina Thatcher. Although neither Jack nor I had dated her once she arrived at the paper, I felt, somehow, that she would understand what I was going through. And in truth, she was the only person I could think of to call.

Could she come over? I asked. I explained that what I had to discuss couldn't be done on the phone.

"It's about Jack, isn't it?" she asked.

"I'll tell you when you get here," I said. She rang off abruptly; I wondered why. She also must have driven like hell because she was knocking on my door fifteen minutes later. It had taken me almost that long to set up my wireless

transmitters and mike the living room, kitchen, and bedroom. Sometimes WTs are valuable. Mine is called a Kel system. It is built into a Royalite attaché case. Inside the case is a radio receiver wired to a four-hour-capacity tape recorder. The transmitters themselves are battery-powered and have mikes about the size of chewing-gum packets. They have two watts of power and a range of roughly three hundred yards through steel and concrete. And because of their size, you can wear them and pass safely through most metal detectors, something that is impossible to do with a Nagra body recorder, which is the size of a package of international-size cigarettes and which also contains a lot of metal.

She knocked on my steel door. "Robert?"

"I'm coming," I said. I peered through the mirrored peephole and saw that Nina was alone. I threw off the dead bolt, unlatched the Fox police bar, and opened the door. As she passed me, walking into the living room, I closed the cupboard door where my shotgun lay.

"I'm sorry about Jack," said Nina Thatcher. She looked around. "God, this place is a mess—don't you ever clean it up?"

"I've been working," I said. "It's always messy when I work. You know, I have this habit of throwing things around, and—"

"Robert," said Nina Thatcher, "why did you call? You sounded desperate on the phone, almost hysterical." She folded her raincoat inside out, punched through the armholes, and laid it across my single armchair.

"I'm in trouble," I said. "Mike wants me to write about Jack."

"Holy shit," said Nina Thatcher. She sat on one of my overstuffed pillows and stretched booted legs out straight. "Are you going to do it?"

"I said I would," I said.

"Holy shit," said Nina Thatcher again. "You know we've got three people on the story already. Have you seen the paper today?"

I must have shaken my head because the tape indicates no response here.

"Straight stories," Nina Thatcher said. She leaned back, resting on her arms. Her face turned up toward the ceiling. "An obit that starts above the fold on page one, two sidebars on what the cops are doing, and a box signed by the publisher offering a five-thousand-dollar reward for information leading to the conviction of Jack's killers. The obit jumps to page five, and we've got two pics: a file shot of Jack in a column and a half and a four column of the bedroom after the body was removed. Do you have something to drink?"

"What would you like?" I asked.

"Some wine," said Nina Thatcher. She flicked something from the lapel of a black velvet blazer.

"Come into the kitchen and take your pick," I said. I offered my hand and pulled Nina Thatcher to her feet. "Who wrote them?"

"Jim Schmidt did the obit," she said. "It was a heady piece of work. The progress piece on the cops was done by Howard Mahler at Thirteen hundred Beaubien and that bitch who covers organized crime."

"Juliet Walker," I said.

"Walker," Nina Thatcher confirmed. "Jesus, Robert, look at that cabinet. How the hell did you get it in here?"

"I brought it up in pieces," I said. "Put it together myself. Wiring and all. It does the job."

"I guess it does," said Nina Thatcher. "How many bottles does it hold?"

"About two hundred," I said. "Any preference?"

"I don't know," said Nina Thatcher. "What do you have?"

"Montrose 'sixty-four and 'sixty-seven, Magdelaine 'sixty-two, 'sixty-four, and 'sixty-six, Pichon-Baron 'fifty-nine and 'sixty-two are pretty good if you want Bordeaux," I said. "In Burgundies, I've got some 'sixty-six Corton, a couple of lovely 'sixty-nine Clos de Bèze, and an outstanding 'seventy-one Corton."

"I don't think I'm up to Bordeaux," said Nina Thatcher. "Could we try the 'seventy-one Corton?"

"Lovely," I said. "The perfect wine to discuss journalism by."

"Didn't anybody ever tell you not to end sentences with prepositions?" said Nina Thatcher. She watched as I uncorked the bottle, found a pair of deep-bowled glasses, and poured the wine.

I sipped at the Corton. "Nice," I said. "It'll get better when it's had some air."

Nina Thatcher took glass in hand and wandered back into the living room. She didn't sit down, however, but walked over to the window facing east, where she stared at the seven-stacked power plant in the distance. She sipped at her wine. I stood in the doorway, looking at her back.

"Why did you call?" she asked. She didn't turn around. "You haven't said ten words to me in the last year and a half."

"I had to talk to somebody," I said.

"It's crazy," Nina Thatcher said. "We had that one wild night, you know, you and Jack and I. It was a crazy night. I'd never done anything like that before, and I certainly haven't since, and when I came here full time, you treated me like a nonperson. You and Jack. The two of you, like Heckle and Jeckle or Frick and Frack. Always together. Always hanging out. Always sharing some private joke or something.

"I felt like shit, Robert. For a year and a half I've felt like shit because you never even called. Jack never even called.

"Now he's dead, and you've got to write about him, and now you call." She turned away from the window. There was a tear rolling down her cheek.

"You are a little shit, Robert," she said. "An absolute little shit. And I guess I am a shit, too, because here I am standing in your apartment, which you have never asked me to visit before, drinking your wine, which you have never invited me to drink before, all because you call me when I am in the middle of a story and you sound desperate. And like a real asshole, I jump in my car and come over here.

"Has it ever occurred to you that I never asked you where you live or what your apartment number is? I knew, didn't I,

Robert?" There were tears rolling down both cheeks. Nina Thatcher drained the glass of wine and held out the glass toward me. Her face was puffy.

I went over to the window and refilled her glass. I tried to talk but couldn't think of anything to say.

"I'm right, aren't I," she said. "Now that Mike has you scared shitless over writing about your best friend you decide to call me. You are really incredible, Robert. Get me a Kleenex, will you? My liner is running, and I'm not going to soil the sleeve of this blouse on it."

I started to put the bottle down.

"Never mind," said Nina Thatcher. "I'll get it myself." She walked toward the bathroom.

"Kleenex is in the bedroom," I said. "The table next to the clock radio."

She changed direction and turned into the bedroom. I picked up the bottle again and sipped at my wine. After thirty seconds, when she didn't reappear, I walked into the bedroom. Nina Thatcher had put her wineglass on the night table and was daubing at her eyes with a gold tissue. She looked small and vulnerable, her dark hair bound with a scarf, the blazer and sleeveless V-neck vest and plaid blouse offset by a severe A-line skirt and dark leather boots.

"I'll be all right," said Nina Thatcher. "Just leave me alone for a few minutes, please."

I went back into the living room and sat on my couch. I reached down and picked up the file marked "JACK FOWLER" that contained the coroner's report. I looked at my shoes. I read the wine label. I stared at the ceiling and noticed a cobweb above the radiator.

Nina Thatcher reappeared. Her eyes were dry.

"You know," she said, "I used to think, for a while, that you and Jack were queer for each other. I thought that for about six months. Then I realized that you weren't queer; you were just a couple of infants playing kindergarten games with the rest of us. Sharing your secrets privately. Snickering behind our backs. Behind my back.

"What the hell did you say about our night together, you and Jack? Did you think that our little ménage was some-

thing normal for me? Christ, Robert, what did you think? What did you think I thought?

"You never asked, did you?

"The funny thing is, I'm not an easy lay. And I don't think I would have repeated our little evening with you and Jack ever again. It just happened, you know.

"But you never even asked how I was. Neither of you." Nina Thatcher took a deep breath. "What are you thinking, Robert?"

I didn't say anything. I stared at the cobweb above the radiator. The tape is blank at this point.

"What are you thinking, Robert? Huh? Tell me. Say something."

I couldn't look at her. "I'm sorry," I said.

"You are incredible," Nina Thatcher said. "You are the selfishest human being I have ever met. You're sorry. Okay, Robert, you're sorry. I accept that. But what the hell have you been thinking for the past year and a half, almost two years? You and your dear, departed pal Jack Fowler?"

"Nothing," I lied.

"Horse puckey." She threw her balled-up wad of Kleenex at me. "Horse shit. You and your buddy have probably been laughing at me and joking about me and comparing notes on my twat since that night. Jerking off together while you do it.

"I really used to think that you were queer, you and Jack. You couldn't screw each other, so you screwed me." Nina Thatcher walked over to the couch and stood above me.

"To hell with you, Robert." She threw her wine in my face, then turned and pitched the empty glass against the wall.

"Fuck you," she screamed. She stood astride me, her knees pinning my legs to the couch, her hands flailing at my wet face. I threw my arms up and grappled with her, grabbing at her wrists, struggling to my feet. I got her in a bear hug, my arms circling her shoulders, hands clasped together in the small of her back. Her face was red and puffy; her eye liner stained my blue shirt. She hit and kicked and sobbed while I held her immobile.

And then I kissed her. I got her head back by pulling on

her hair, and I forced my tongue into her mouth, and I kissed her. What was more amazing, she kissed me back.

Still struggling, I picked Nina Thatcher up and carried her into the bedroom. I pulled at her blazer, vest, boots, skirt, pantyhose, until she was naked except for blouse and bra. I shed my trousers and undershorts, shoes and one sock, and then I covered her with my body and kissed her again and again.

"You prick," Nina Thatcher said. "You shit. You inhuman son of a bitch." But she was wet inside and warm, and I slipped into her, and she locked her legs around my back, and I reached up under her blouse and undid the catch of her bra and slipped my hands up front to cradle her breasts, all the while kissing her and moving inside her.

"This isn't for love," said Nina Thatcher. "I hate you, Robert," she said, but she brought her hands under my shirt and clawed at my back. She unlocked her legs and brought her knees onto her own chest. I could feel my balls slapping into her crotch as I thrust inside her.

We didn't last very long, either of us. She reached a hand down between my legs and felt my cock as it moved in and out, and I came almost immediately. I held her around her back, her knees pressed against her chest, moaning as I exploded. I felt her back; it was wet with perspiration. My chest was wet, too, through my shirt. I stretched my legs out, carefully, so as not to slip out of her, reached toward the foot of the bed, and pulled a comforter over us.

We lay huddled together for quite some time, neither one of us talking. Finally I slipped out of her. I rolled over onto my side and cradled Nina Thatcher to my chest, arms around her tightly. I kissed the top of her head. Her scarf had come off and lay next to us.

After a while Nina Thatcher sat up. She ran her hand over the front of her blouse. "I guess I don't have to worry about soiling it anymore."

I pulled her down next to me. She turned away, offering her back. I snuggled close to it, my knees bent slightly behind her own. I held her around her waist. I kissed the back of her neck.

"Now what?" Nina Thatcher asked.

"I am a shit," I said.

"I already know that," she said. "So now what? Now I have come over here and told you what I think of you, and you have responded by tearing my clothes off and jumping on top of me, and I have been even a greater fool than I ever thought by letting you do it, and now we are lying here, and I don't think I like you very much at all, now what?"

"I am a shit," I said.

"Don't repeat yourself by stating the obvious," Nina Thatcher said.

"I am in trouble," I said.

"You've been in trouble for years," said Nina Thatcher. "Somehow I get the feeling that you have the emotional life of a rock. Come on, Robert, out with it. For once in your life, trust somebody. I don't like you very much, but I think you think I can be trusted. So out with it."

In replaying the tape later, I was amazed at how freely I spoke with Nina Thatcher. I told her about Jack, and Madeleine, and Jack's bisexuality. And about the story Jack had been working on when he was killed.

"He was the perfect setup," she said. "Closet homosexual, big reputation here, working a story he should never have touched. Ripe for blackmail."

I nodded.

"You really must feel like a shit," she said. "A real asshole." She sat up and hugged herself. "And now what? Now you've told me your secret and we've been to bed together. So do you send me on my way and not talk to me for the next year and a half?"

I shook my head. "I think I'd like to be friends," I said. "Could we pretty please be friends?" I rolled over and put my head on Nina Thatcher's lap.

She stroked my shoulder. "Yes, Robert, you shit," she said. "I will not sleep with you again. But we can be friends."

*chapter 8*_____

Some hours after Nina Thatcher left I pulled one of the cassettes I had taken from Jack's apartment out of my safe and slid it into my transcriber. It was the earliest of the chicken-hawk tapes, made five weeks before Jack had been killed.

Many of the older reporters on the paper have an abiding dislike for tape recorders. They do not relish the thought of being tied to an electronic box, preferring instead to make notes on a sheet of yellow newsprint, a legal pad, or a reporter's notebook. But they are wrong. Notebooks cannot capture the whole truth of a story, only the impressions and facts told to you. Not even all the facts either, just those you manage to scratch at the time, hoping all the while that the scrawls you're making on the page will be decipherable in an hour's or a day's or a week's time.

Notebooks leave a wide margin for error. And when you are in the business of collecting evidence, there should be no margin for error; none at all. Notebooks allow you only partial recall. But tape recorders are the true notebooks of the eighties. They provide a complete sound track. They leave nothing to the imagination.

Still, the old-timers argue with you. Batteries go dead, they say. Worse, they say, people have become wary about giving out information if you walk into their homes or offices and set your little machine down. People seize up, they say, when they realize that what they are telling you is being captured indelibly, that once it's on tape, it cannot be called back or forgotten. In this the old-timers are right. It is bad business to plunk down a tape machine and ask for secrets.

This is one reason I use my Nagra body recorder so much. I give the appearance of carrying no equipment at all, and my interviewees think I am harmless. Sometimes I take a notebook with me, but leave it closed and in plain sight. I tell my subject that I am interested purely in background. It is a very disarming technique. People talk to me very freely. And I record it all.

So I cleaned up my apartment, wiped the wine Nina Thatcher had thrown at me from the floor, then set a pair of earphones into the transcriber's jack and rolled a piece of paper into the IBM. Transcribing has always been something of a joy to me. The merging of mechanics and craft, the ability to listen accurately and transfer what comes over the earphones onto a piece of paper with the least possible repetition or effort. Nancy used to accuse me of getting off on transcribing. Jack Fowler did, too. "Aural sex," he'd say. And we'd laugh. "Do your snitches give good ear?" he'd ask, and we'd laugh. We would always laugh.

I wasn't laughing when I transcribed the first of Jack's tapes. I tried as I typed to disassociate Jack's voice from his whole being. It wasn't easy. When I heard his voice, I could see him in my mind. I guessed how he had been dressed, where in that once-beautiful living room of his he had been standing, sitting, moving around. It was like playing a movie inside my head while my ears, brain, and hands transferred the sounds to words. Took them from the tape to be examined, scrutinized.

"I'm coming," said Jack's voice. The two-tone chime near his doorway rang again. "Coming." You could hear his shoes on the eight-foot patch of bare floor that separated the entrance foyer from the living room proper.

73

"Hi," said Jack's voice. It was calm, inviting, and, I thought, anticipatory.

More feet on the parquet. Three pairs? Four pairs? I ran the tape back. Jack's own shoes were unmistakable. He wore steel taps and lifted his feet carefully on the bare floor. His walk sounded like *nip, nip, nip.* There was another distinct sound. A draggy *thunk-eee* that made me think of someone wearing a pair of stacked boots who habitually walked on his heels. They sounded worn down. There was the unmistakable squeak of sneakers. The next I could not make out because the sound conflicted with the worn-heel sound. I ran the tape again and again. There was a fourth pair of feet in the room. But without leather soles or rubber soles. Neolite? Work boots with Neolite soles? I let the tape run on. Three, four steps, and the foot sounds disappeared into the thickness of Jack's white shag carpet.

"Sit down. Make yourself comfortable. You want something to drink? Scotch? Something cold?" He was moving around. I wondered where he had stashed the tape recorder. He obviously wasn't wearing it. From the sound, it might have been under the couch or inside the huge planter that held a six-foot dieffenbachia. Jack's voice was pitched half an octave higher than usual. He was excited.

"Scotch would be nice," said a voice. I ran it again. "Scotch would be nice." Flat, Detroit accent. Nasal. "Scotch would be nice. With a little Coke." I tried to visualize a body to go with the voice. It was impossible.

"Just Coke for the boys. That okay with you, fellas?"

Two younger voices, one on top of the other: "Uh-huh." "Sure."

Jack moved across the living room toward the kitchen. The man's voice said, "Real nice place." He wasn't talking to Jack. "High-class," he said. "Whaddya think, fellas," he said.

One of the younger voices said, "Uh-huh." It was indistinct. It sounded as if he had taken a mouthful of the dry-roasted cashews Jack kept on his coffee table.

The man's voice again. "Hey, take your feet off the table."

Jack had come back with the drinks. "Scotch and Coke—

it's okay, he can put his feet up if he wants. Let me go get the others."

The sound of a hand slapping material. "I told you to get 'em off the table."

"He told me I could. He said it was okay. He told me." A young, petulant voice. Even with a mouth full of cashews it was unmistakably young. Ten, eleven, maybe twelve.

"You never listen, do you?" Jack had come back into the room. Two thunks as two crystal old-fashioned glasses came down on the glass coffee table. "See how they treat me?" The man's voice. "I tell you—kids. . . ."

Obviously he was looking at Jack. There was a pause. Maybe five seconds. Then: "Hey, don't be nervous pal, we just came over to visit, you know. Let you meet a couple of the boys. No pressure or nothing. Just time to get acquainted, you know."

"Scotty. . . ." Jack's voice was hesitant. I put an asterisk in the margin opposite the name.

"Hey, Jackie boy." Scotty's flat voice was reassuring. But there was a subtle change. It had assumed the dominant role in the conversation. "Relax. We're here to give you a good time. Give you whatever you want. You want to talk, we'll talk. You want to play, we'll play. Listen, why don't you get yourself a drink and sit down? You haven't met the boys."

"I don't want anything," said Jack's voice.

"Jackie boy," said Scotty. "Jackie boy, Jackie boy. Ease up. Come on. Get yourself something. It'll relax you. You were drinking wine in the bar the other night. Get yourself some wine."

Jack's voice broke slightly. "I've never done this before," he said. "It's different from the bars."

I ran the section again. It was hard to tell whether Jack was role-playing or not. He had told me he didn't frequent gay bars. He was much too discreet for that. His habit, when he got what he self-mockingly called "the curse," was to take off for New York for a long weekend. "I couldn't handle it here," he had once said. "There's a chance I'd be discovered. In New York I'm anonymous. Besides, I don't need much,

75

Robert. I think it's more an intellectual thing than physical. Closeness, touching, tasting. The fucking aspect of it doesn't really turn me on. I'd rather do that with women."

That's what Jack had told me. On this story, however, bars were mandatory. So he was role-playing; he had told me he'd hit the bars to get a line on some pimps. I rewound the tape and played it one more time. "I've never done this before. It's different from the bars."

"Bars got no class," said Scotty's voice. "Besides, Jackie boy, bars are dangerous. You never know who you're gonna meet in bars. Some people will rip you off, you know? For example, Jackie boy, like, what do you do?"

"I don't think that's any of your business," said Jack's voice.

"Nah, nah, nah," said Scotty. "I didn't mean anything by it. Just, say, that you're a doctor or something, you know. Or you work at Ford or Uniroyal—you got a nice place here, you make decent bread—and some queen thinks she can put the squeeze on you, right, boys? So that can happen in a bar much faster than it can right in the comfort of your own home, right, Jackie boy? Forget the bars. Bars are a bad scene. Take it from me." Scotty—I thought it was Scotty— took a pull at his drink.

"Listen to me, will you?" Scotty said. "I'm going on about bars, and you haven't even met the boys. This is Eric—he's the quiet one. And this guy, who gives me smart talk all the time, is Neil."

"Hey, Neil. Hi, Eric," said Jack. "You doin' all right?"

"Yeah," said a young voice. It was the petulant voice—the one with his feet on the table. The other must have nodded.

There was an awkward silence. It must have been horrible for Jack right then. But perhaps not. Perhaps Jack had wanted to create tension, to give the impression of being a nervous, first-time chicken hawk. Perhaps he was playing the role he knew best: a young, rich guy with a problem. And Jack knew the tricks: If you don't talk, you force the other guy to. You wait him out. I rolled the tape back and listened.

"Hey, Neil. Hi, Eric. You doin' all right?"

"Yeah," came the petulant voice's response. I ticked off

the seconds. One, two, three, four, five, six, seven, eight, nine, ten, eleven, twelve. Then Scotty's voice began. Just as if he'd picked up a cue. "So, Jackie boy," he said. "So we're here. What can we do for you?"

Jack must have thought about it because there was a three-second pause. "I need a good time," he said.

Jack and I had talked about entrapment. Keep things as general as you can, I had warned him. Always let them do the soliciting, I had said. I ran the section of tape once more. He had paid attention to me. He was following the rules. "It's been a long time since I had a good time," Jack's voice said.

"That's why we're here, Jackie boy," said Scotty. "A good time. But I gotta tell you something—I hate to be crass, you know, but this ain't no bar scene. Nothing comes for free. You get that, Jackie boy? Nothing comes for free, I said." Scotty laughed.

Jack was silent. Then I heard the sound of his steel heel taps on the wood floor, and I knew that he had walked into the kitchen. Perhaps to get himself some more wine. Perhaps to give Scotty the chance to be specific, to have to call out the specifics and capture them on the tape.

"We got several options," said Scotty. "You look like a nice guy—you don't go for any of that leather stuff, do you?" He didn't wait for Jack to answer. "Nah, you don't look the type. So you're a nice guy, and I tell you what I'm gonna do. Maybe you'd like Neil here to stay with you for a few days. Keep you company, you know. Help out with the housework. Make the bed—" Scotty stifled a giggle. I reran the tape to make sure. "Make the bed—you know what I mean. Now Neil likes housework, don't you, Neil?" Again Scotty didn't wait for a reply.

"All you got to remember is to be nice to him. Like a big brother. If you're nice to him, he'll do anything that you want, right, Neil?"

No answer. Scotty continued: "Or here's a second option. I know you gotta be a busy person, Jackie boy. You gotta be busy to keep a crib like this, right? So maybe you don't have time for somebody to be around here twenty-four hours a

day. So maybe Neil here, or Eric, one of them stays with you tonight, just to see if you're compatible—if you get along. Then you put 'em in a cab in the morning."

Jack's heels tapped across the parquet floor. "What kind of, ahh—"

"Fee?" said Scotty. "You mean what kind of allowance do we give the boys? Well, see, Jackie boy, they're kinda young to handle their own financial affairs, and they've been staying with me for about two months now, right, kids? What you do is, you and I we sit down and work out kind of a scholarship fund for the boys. And then you pay me, and I hold it in trust for them.

"For example, you want Neil here to stay a few days? Then you contribute fifty bucks a day to his scholarship fund. You want Eric to stay over? You donate twenty to his fund. Maybe you gotta lot of upkeep, Jackie boy, and you need two houseboys. Then we work out a nice deal: you get 'em both for three fifty a week. Or one for three hundred. See, if they're not with me, I don't have to feed 'em. And you got no idea how much kids eat these days."

Another pause. "Jackie boy, I tell you, these kids'll eat anything. *Mmmmmmm.*" Scotty sounded as if he were running his tongue across his lips. I ran the tape back. "*Mmmmmmm.*"

Then another silence. Good. Jack was waiting him out. Letting Scotty make all the moves. And Scotty would become more confident; he would spell everything out.

"You're so quiet, Jackie boy," said Scotty. "What you thinking about? The money? Don't sweat the money, Jackie boy. We can always work something out."

"It's not the money," Jack's voice said. A certain hardness had crept into it. He had cast the hook out, and now he was going to set it. Set it hard. I touched the rewind pedal of the transcriber. "It's not the money," Jack was saying. "It's the goods. Face it, Scotty, I don't know what I'm getting into. You know, I like the way Neil and Eric look, but that's 'cause they're nice kids, and we're all sitting here friendly, you know."

"Jackie boy, Jackie boy, Jackie boy." Scotty's voice was

calming, avuncular. "Of course. You gotta forgive me. I'm so dense these days, you know." Scotty's voice shifted on the tape. He must have stood up. Walked across the thick white shag rug to where the boys were. "Up," Scotty's voice said. It had an edge to it. It wasn't a request but a command. "Up. Pare down," he said.

Pause. Sounds. Clothes rustling, zippers unzipping. The dull thunk of shoes being dropped on the rug.

"Lovely, aren't they, Jackie boy?" Scotty said. "Eric, come over there. Turn around so Mr. Fowler can see you all over. Look at that back, will you? Check out the tuckas. So cute you wanna pinch it to death, isn't it?"

Jack's voice said nothing.

"Neil, go over to Mr. Fowler. Lovely kid, isn't he? Go on, Jackie boy, feel how soft his skin is. Like butter. No hair any-place, right, Neil?"

Jack said nothing.

"Turn around, Neil," said Scotty's voice. "That's it. Look at the little dingus on that one, will ya? God, I tell you, Jackie boy, they really turn me on. I can hardly keep my hands off them.

"Come here, Neil. Lemme show you something. You know how old he is? Twelve. Twelve. He could pass for ten, though, 'cause he's small. And not a hair on him. Come here, Neil. That's a good kid. You know, Jackie boy, these kids'll do anything for me, 'cause I treat 'em right. Right, boys? Come here, Neil. That's it. Stand—yeah. Like that. No, no—spread your legs little bit . . . right. Now, Jackie, watch what happens when I—see, just touch him, see? Take those lovely, hairless—God, it's good. He likes that, don't you, Neil? See how he likes that, Jackie boy? Good boy, Neil. See, Jackie boy? See. God, I tell you, it feels so good. Now watch. See how it's standing up? You could take it in your hand now, Jackie boy. You could play with it."

Jack said nothing.

"Incredible, isn't it?" Scotty said. "They're so easy. Just touch 'em and they get hard. You know the bar scene, Jackie boy. You drink too much; you go into a stall in the john; you find somebody. Maybe he can't get hard; maybe you touch

him and he's dirty. Maybe a lot of things, right? That's it, Neil, just stand there." Scotty's voice came in gasps. He took a breath before each sentence.

"Not this way, Jackie boy. Look at how clean that little dingus is. You could eat off it. No hair, no nothing. And watch, Jackie boy—hand me one of those little napkins off the table. See? Just a little more English, see? And just a little harder, and—don't move, Neilly, don't move—see? Look, will you? A couple of shots is all it took. That's it, Neil, into the napkin, kiddo. Good boy, good boy." Scotty was breathing hard now. Neil didn't make a sound.

"You got another napkin, Jackie boy? Lemme wipe my hands here. Yeah. Good boy, Neil. You did just fine. You want another Coke?" A pause. "No? Okay. You sit there on the rug. You go sit by him, Eric."

"What are the marks on Neil's backside?" Jack's voice was hollow. He sounded as if he had been gulping air, too. "Scabs? Burns?"

"Oh, them," Scotty's voice said. "Sometimes, Jackie boy, you gotta discipline kids, you know. Like Neil, here, he's an independent sort. You'll see that. Two months ago I found him at the bus terminal, you know. Isn't that right, Neil? Kid was running away from home. He didn't have a dime, Jackie boy. Not the price of a phone call. And you know what? I took him in. I fed him, and we went to Sears and bought new clothes, didn't we, Neil? And he has his own room—of course, he shares it now with Eric—and he gets to watch all the TV he wants, right, Neil?

"But he's independent. And one day he decides he's gonna run away from his uncle Scotty, you know.

"I tell you, Jackie boy, you can never let the kids get the upper hand, you know? I mean they'll run all over you. So Neil and I had this little talk. A kinda show and tell, right, Neil? Yeah, a kinda show and tell." Scotty's voice laughed. "I showed him a cigar, and he told me he wasn't gonna run away ever again. Right, Neil? Isn't that what you told your uncle Scotty? You promised you'd be a good boy. So I touched him light, Jackie boy. Those things'll disappear in a week. Not a trace, right, Neil?"

"And Eric? What about Eric? He ever try to run away?" asked Jack.

"Eric? Naw," said Scotty. "Eric's a sensitive kid, you know. He took one look at that cigar, and he wasn't gonna cause any trouble, were you, Eric?"

A small voice said, "No."

"Okay, fellas," said Scotty. "You take your clothes and find the bathroom. Get dressed so Mr. Fowler and I can talk a little grown-up talk, okay? That's good boys. See, Jackie boy? Jeez, they're obedient. I wish all kids was as good as them, you know.

"Listen, you got any more scotch?"

"Sure," said Jack.

"With Coke, remember?"

"I remember," Jack said.

"Look, Jackie boy," said Scotty, "you got a nice place here, and I'd like to do right by you. So which one you want? They're both good kids, right. You saw that Neil—he's something else, right? I could get a hundred a night for him on the streets, you know. But I'm not a greedy man, Jackie boy. And I want to do good by the kids, right. Not overwork them or anything. You know how it is with kids. You kinda get to feel responsible for them and everything. So I don't want 'em out on the streets where they could meet the wrong kind of people, dig? You know, Jackie boy. The street is something else, right? Thanks, Jackie boy. You got real nice glasses, you know that? What are they, crystal?"

"Yeah," said Jack Fowler's voice. "They're crystal." He was pacing. You could hear it on the tape as the voice moved around the living room. "I, uh, don't think I'm ready to buy anything yet, Scotty," Jack said. "I mean, I appreciate your coming up and everything, but I—"

"Jackie boy," said Scotty, "I understand. Here we are, three strangers, coming into your home, right? You're a little nervous, right? I can dig it. I tell you what, though. I can't walk away empty-handed. I mean, you took up my time and everything, and I had to drive over, and it'll cost me a fin to get my car out of the garage. Why don't you slip me fifty? Let's call it a deposit, okay? If you want one of the boys, I'll

take the first fifty off for you. That way we're both happy."

"Sure," said Jack's voice. "That sounds fair."

I ran the section again. What was Jack saying? His tone of voice was strange, hollow. That half-an-octave-higher-than-normal tone of voice. Did he want to keep one of the kids with him? Was he afraid? Or was he just setting the hook deeper? I ran the section once again, then let it play on.

"Sure, that sounds fair." A pause. "I don't want to sound pushy, Scotty, but suppose I wanted to check you out. You see I've got nice things here, and—"

"You are a righteous smart cookie, Jackie boy," said Scotty. "Hey, I come with the best credentials, you know. Ask anybody on Six Mile. Check me out at the Golden Dove or the Pit, you know? Everybody knows Scotty. Ask my boys. They'll tell you. I keep 'em clean, Jackie boy. Some guys, you know, they fuck around with their kids. They shoot 'em up with dope; they keep 'em on downers. It's like screwing a corpse, you know. Shit, man, I'm like a father to these two. They'll tell you. Shit, Jackie boy, I'm not into ripping people off. A lot of good that would do my business.

"Naw. A nice relationship with good people who'll do right by my kids, that's what I like. All on the up and up. Hey, fellas, you all dressed? That was quick. Okay, we gotta get a move on. Let Mr. Fowler take care of some business, you know. He's gonna give Uncle Scotty a call, and maybe you'll come back and visit soon.

"Right, Jackie boy?"

"Sure," said Jack's voice. "Come back soon. Real soon. Okay, let me see you to the door."

"That's all right." Scotty's voice seemed to be in motion. "We can let ourselves out." More motion on the tape. Foot sounds on the bare floor. The lock being turned back. "So long, Jackie boy. We'll be in touch." The door being closed. Then silence. The hissing of the condenser mike with nothing to record.

It ran on for fully a minute, and Jack hadn't come to shut it off. What was happening? I ran the cassette back to the point where the door closed and turned up the volume. "So

long, Jackie boy. We'll be in touch." The door closed. Click. Then hissing. Silence.

I turned the volume up full and adjusted the transcriber's tone control. There was something there. Faint sounds. I ran the tape again. Something was there. It was very hard to pick up, but it was there, unmistakably.

It was the sound of Jack being sick.

*chapter 9*_____

Jack had made six cassettes in his apartment. I transcribed them all. He wasn't sick again; he hardened himself to what he heard and saw. He had seen black pimps and white ones, chickens who were runaways and ghetto kids who needed the protection of a grown-up. Jack played the right role. He coaxed the pimps to talk, flirted with the kids, and always, always managed to extricate himself before any hard deal was struck.

But the children got to Jack. They really never stopped affecting him. That was one of his flaws: He felt too much. I had tried to warn him, but it was impossible.

"It's the look in their eyes," Jack had said ten days before he was killed. We were sitting in his living room, my Nagra on the table taking the words down. It was one of the few nights in a six-week period that we had been able to get together, as Jack was spending most of his time in gay bars, discos, and clubs and I was scoring dope from dealers who used the Westvale as their base of operations.

"They all have that pleading, vulnerable look," Jack had said. "They're all searching for approval."

"What do you mean?" I asked.

"Maybe you were right," Jack said. "Maybe some of the kids are doing this purely quid pro quo for the money. But most of them have really fucked-up home lives, and they're looking for some sort of father figure. They've been rejected, and they want the approval and love of an older man. That's why they stay with the pimps for so long, even when they're tortured or burned or doped up. Somewhere in their screwed-up minds, they think that what they're getting is approval, a family life, a father's discipline."

"That's perverted as hell," I said. "That's incredible."

"It may be perverted," Jack said, "but it's not incredible. When I really face myself, Robert, really look at myself, I'm doing the same thing. Shit, once a month, once in six weeks, I take off for New York, check into the Regency, change into engineer's boots, jeans, and a plaid flannel shirt, carry a leather jacket over my shoulder, and hit Christopher Street. Now what the hell am I looking for? Company? I've got that here. You're company. You're somebody to talk to.

"So it's something else. A person to be close to. A male person to be close to, to hug me like my brother used to. Except that in New York the male person takes my dick out of my jeans and sucks on it for a while, and then he hugs me. Okay, that's where I am, you know, and I feel guilty as hell about it. But it provides me with something I can't get any other way.

"I enjoy screwing women," Jack said. "But I can't relate to them, you know. You see a foxy lady, and you want to lay her. But that's it. There's a closeness with a man that can't be duplicated."

"What is it?" I asked.

"I can't really put it into words," Jack Fowler said. "I remember, though, after I screwed that Oxford don the first time, I was closer to him than I had ever been to anyone in my life. I mean, I really felt wanted, adored, you know.

"Now it's all so casual. Hit the clubs, trick once or twice, maybe end up at somebody's apartment or take somebody back to the hotel—we're close. We share the guilt; we talk afterward. We have something we never had as kids at home.

"I need that, Robert. I need it once in a while. Just like I need to be a reporter. Now you can call it perverted. I think I am perverted, I guess. But I don't think it's so incredible.

"Just like the kids. Sure I empathize with them. They're looking for closeness because they don't have it where they live, wherever that is. It's not all for money, Robert. Not always.

"Look at yourself, Robert. Do you really like who you are right now?"

"Not really," I said. "But it's all I know, all I want to know, at this point in my life. After Nancy—"

"You're evading the point," Jack Fowler said. "You turned Nancy off on purpose. You did it on purpose. You used the work for an excuse, just as I use it."

"It's easier, isn't it," I said.

"Sure it is," Jack Fowler said. "It's much easier than facing yourself. But the question is, Robert: Do you like yourself?"

"Not much," I said. "Not much these days."

"Then you're making progress," Jack Fowler said. "Six months ago you would have lied to me. You would have told me you were just fine."

"I'm getting soft," I said. "In my old age."

"No," Jack said, "you're just beginning to open up a crack."

"Do you think so?"

"Yeah, I do, Robert. Frightening, isn't it?"

"I don't know," I said.

"Sure you do. Come on, Robert, own up."

"Okay, you're right," I said. "In those last few months with Nancy I used to hide from her. I stayed away on purpose. It was just—oh, you know, Jack, it wasn't easy. I didn't want to go home to her. I didn't want to share what I was doing. She was so good at her job, and she still had room for an emotional life. I guess I felt inadequate, so I just shut off. I clicked myself off. I hated myself for doing it, but I did it anyhow."

"Why?" Jack asked. "How come?"

"I don't know. I really don't know. I guess if I knew, Nancy

would be here and you and I wouldn't be sitting like this." There is a pause on the tape at this point.

Then Jack Fowler said, "Shit. Oh, come on, Robert, shut off the damn machine and let's go out for some pizza and beer."

It was the last time we shared a meal. Pizza and beer and small talk about little boys who sought approval from father figures by letting strange men fondle them and suck their cocks. Pizza and beer and small talk about how it feels to watch such things and not be able to do anything to help, to observe and be paid for it. Pizza and beer and the shared knowledge that each of us would go home to an empty house where we would transcribe the day's conversations, annotate the events, and file them all away.

Others might go home to wives or lovers. We had our stories. They justified our existence. They were our families. Love your story, and it will love you back. If that is the case, why do I cry when I'm alone?

I didn't used to cry. Not with Nancy. Being with Nancy allayed incipient hysteria. But she never understood some things. Like the need to know. I remember walking down a street with her one night. It was late, and she had picked me up at the office. We were on our way to a midnight dinner at one of her colleagues' homes, and we were walking to a parking lot. It was early fall in Los Angeles. The Santa Ana winds were blowing. It was a hot night. An ambulance was pulling to the curb near Spring and Second, and I dragged Nancy by the hand to see what was going on. A black man in a white shirt yellow with age and old-fashioned high-rise trousers held up by suspenders lay bleeding in the gutter. I wanted a closer look, but Nancy pulled at my arm. "Let's go," she said.

"I want to see," I told her. I shook free of her hand.

"Why?" She stood her ground at the edge of the crowd.

I started to elbow my way through. I stopped. "To see the kind of wound," I said. "Stabbing, shooting, blunt instrument—"

"Why?" said Nancy. "What does it matter?"

"It matters," I said.

"But why? It doesn't concern you. Can't you just leave it alone?"

"No," I said.

"That's crazy," she said. "I'm beginning to think you get off on this sort of thing."

I denied it, of course. But she was right. Nancy backed away and stood in a storefront doorway while I pushed through the crowd and knelt by the man. He was bleeding badly. Blood stained the black asphalt. An onlooker dropped a lit cigarette into a red puddle to extinguish it. It hissed and fizzled out.

I saw what I had to. I rejoined Nancy half a minute later. "Happy?" she asked.

"Yes," I said. "It was a stabbing."

"Why are you happy? Why?"

I offered her my hand, which she took. "Because now I know," I said. "Let's go."

———

The police paid me a second visit shortly after the first of my stories about Jack appeared in the paper. It was not a routine call. But then, it hadn't been a routine story. While half a dozen of our own reporters and a similar team from the competition were covering Jack's murder from a straight robbery-killing angle, I had used Jack's tapes and notes to construct a scenario in which Jack had probably been killed by sources who were fearful of being exposed. I wrote carefully, keeping Jack's sexual orientation out of the piece.

"New material," I wrote, "shows that Fowler was researching a series of stories about the homosexual underworld in Detroit. And his investigation, although incomplete, nevertheless indicates that young boys, called 'chickens,' are for sale by the hundreds in this city. Further research shows that many of the pimps involved are members of a loosely formed organization. It is probable that Fowler's work on this story led to his execution by still-unknown parties."

I had time to prepare for the visit because Mike called

from the city room to warn me that the cops had stopped by to ask me some questions. So I pulled my files off the floor and stuffed them into my closet safe. The police, Mike had said, were not carrying search warrants. Even so, there was no sense in giving them probable cause to go through my apartment because they saw something that might be construed as evidence.

When I unlocked the door after checking credentials through the peephole, I was greeted by three men. Two had the look of cops: oversized double knit sports coats; flared trousers, baggy at the knees; and scuffed boots. The third man was younger and dressed with real style: Burberry raincoat, herringbone tweed sports coat, and matching vest over a pair of pleated gray flannel trousers and shined black Gucci loafers. He carried an oversized lawyer's briefcase in one hand and a tape recorder in the other. I knew him well. He was Jerry Daley, an assistant DA who had organized and headed a special strike force of supposedly incorruptible undercover cops to prosecute the narcotics trade.

Daley was known as the Animal by the men who worked for him and by more unprintable adjectives by the dealers he brought to trial. He was politically ambitious, and because of his eastern background, boyish good looks, hazel eyes, pretty southern wife named Lucy and her family's money— not to mention a high conviction rate—it was altogether possible that at the age of thirty-six he could become the city's next district attorney.

Still, Daley had a few flaws. His strike force was not incorruptible, for example. I had proved that when I once observed one of his sergeants taking an envelope of $50 bills from a dealer outside a bar near Fenkell and Livernois. Jerry Daley had an Irish temper, which often made for colorful quotes, but for morning-after statements that he had been quoted out of context. He also held grudges, not wise for those who aspire to elective office. But hold them he did. And because of my story about his bribe-taking sergeant, one of Jerry Daley's biggest grudges was against my newspaper. He loved to leak tidbits to the competition.

So I was not really surprised to see him standing there in

his Burberry, an Irish fishing cap at a rakish angle on his head. I invited everyone inside, took Daley's coat and hat, nodded as he introduced his companions, and indicated that we might all sit down.

"I'm going to tape this, Robert," said Daley. "Do you mind?"

"Not at all," I said. "I thought I'd tape it, too." I took a cassette machine from the top of a file cabinet and set it on the rug next to Daley's. Simultaneously we pushed the record buttons.

"This recording is being made with the interrogant's permission," Daley said, pulling an unfiltered cigarette out of a leather case and tamping it on his signet ring. "It is being conducted by Jerome Daley, assistant district attorney, city of Detroit, county of Wayne, and assisted by Detroit Police Sergeant Michael Palmer and Detective Third Grade Thomas J. Ritchie, Jr. For the record, interrogant Robert Mandel is simultaneously making his own recording of the interview." Daley pulled a gold Dunhill lighter from his vest pocket and applied its gas flame to the end of his cigarette.

"Robert," he began, "a story appeared under your byline this morning that makes some serious allegations about a murder investigation currently being handled by my office. I'd like to ask you some questions about your story and about your friendship with the victim, Jack Fowler."

I said nothing.

"You did write the story?" Daley said.

"It was under my byline," I answered.

"And you were a friend of the deceased?"

"I think I've answered that question before," I said. "Yes."

"How long did you know the deceased?"

"As long as I've been at the paper," I said. "Just under three years."

Daley leaned forward and unlatched his oversized briefcase. He pulled out a green paperboard folder, from which he extracted a clip of my story. "How did you come by the information in this story?" he asked.

I said nothing.

"How did you come by it?" Daley tapped the clipping

with a manicured finger. His cigarette dangled from his lips.

"I'll get you an ashtray," I said. I walked into the kitchen and pulled a saucer out of the cupboard. When I returned to the living room, Daley was exhaling smoke from his nostrils and grinding a piece of gray ash into my carpet. He looked up at me.

"It's good for the rug," he said.

"Maybe your rugs. Not mine."

"You haven't answered my question," Daley said.

"You know I can't tell you that," I said.

Daley pointed at the tape machines.

"All right, Jerry. For the record, I am standing on my First Amendment rights. I will not disclose my sources, to you or to anyone. Is that plain enough?"

"Don't get holier-than-thou," Daley said. "Jesus."

"Aw, look, Robert," said the older of the two detectives, "can't you see we need your help on this?" He was going to play the nice guy. He shifted toward me, gray eyes crinkly and friendly. "We don't want you to burn your sources. You know that. But we need some leads. We know that you were up in Fowler's apartment the day after he was killed. You also know that we don't have a thing to go on. The night he was killed there was nobody at the desk and the security men were down in the basement playing cards."

"They were in the garage," I said. "Don't you guys ever get just the facts, ma'am?"

"Jeez, that's right," said the detective. "The garage. But that's what I mean, Robert—we need your help. We got no prints, no nothing. Don't you want Fowler's killers caught? Jeezus, the guy was your friend."

Daley cut him off with a look.

"Okay, Robert," he said. "Let's say we know that you took something out of Jack Fowler's apartment while you were up there. How's that for the facts?"

I looked at him. "What makes you think I took anything?"

"Because you're a sneaky little bastard, Robert," Daley said. "We found a hollowed-out section of floor under Fowler's dresser. Very fancily done, you know. Blind grommets in the rug, flush metal plate—very tidy. A nice little

hiding place, too. Good for all sorts of things. Like dope, maybe—oh, you could keep half a pound of cocaine there at least. Or maybe notebooks, or cassettes, or films. I tell you, Robert, it was a swell hiding place. Just the kind of hiding place a sneaky reporter would use. You know how sneaky reporters are, don't you, Robert?"

"No," I said. "Why don't you tell me? I'd love to get this on tape."

"My pleasure," said Daley. Another piece of ash fell onto my rug. He ground it in delicately. "Sorry," Jerry Daley said.

"Now I know why they call you pigs," I said. "Do that again and you can all leave."

"You really are on edge today, Robert," Daley said. "I wonder if that means you've got something to hide? What was I saying? Oh, yes, I was telling you how absolutely devious reporters are, and I mentioned that we had found Jack Fowler's little stash—hey, Robert, do you have one, too?" He tapped at my rug with a black loafer. "You seem to me like the kind of guy who keeps a stash. Oh, and yes, Robert, we know that you were up at Jack's place. And now you sit down and write a story that no one else has written."

Daley slammed an open palm into the green folder. "Just how stupid do you think we are, Robert?" He didn't wait for an answer. "Jack Fowler had his research in that little cubbyhole. You got up there, and you took it. Now in my book that is called stealing evidence."

"I'm glad that you all came to visit," I said. "But if you can't prove what you're saying, I think you're about to leave." I stood up. "Bye."

"I'm not ready to leave yet," said Daley. He hadn't moved toward his tape recorder. "There's another aspect of this killing we want to discuss with you."

I sat down again. "What's that?" I asked.

"Did you know that Jack Fowler was gay?"

"What does that have to do with anything?"

"You know, Robert, you surprise me," Daley said. He reached down between his legs and shut off his tape machine. "How about turning yours off, too?"

"Sure, Jerry." It didn't matter. My wireless equipment

would still be running. Besides, if Daley was as sharp as I knew him to be, he had wired one of his cops and had a Kel sitting in the car I guessed was parked at the bus stop in front of my apartment house. It was an incredible charade.

"Let's put this off the record, okay?" Daley took another cigarette out of the leather case, bounced it once against his signet ring, stuck it in the center of his mouth, applied the flame, took a deep draw, then settled back onto my couch. He crossed his legs, making sure that the crease in his gray flannels would be preserved. Daley did this in court, too. He was known as a theatrical prosecutor who wooed juries with his appearance as well as his facts.

"Cozy?" I stood up and paced in front of Daley. "Okay, Jerry," I said. "I've had the Columbo act, and now you're settling into your 'just a friendly chat' character. Why not just cut the shit and tell me what's happening?"

"Like I said," said Daley, "you surprise me, Robert. Now I've done some checking on Fowler. This isn't some spade on Wyoming who's been killed. Your paper is upset, the family back in Georgia is upset, and now I'm upset because I'm stuck with the case."

"It's not a dope prosecution, Jerry. How come you got it?"

"I shouldn't have said I'm stuck with it, Robert. I asked for this one."

"You'd love to catch us dirty, wouldn't you?"

"As a matter of fact, I would. I was thinking, for example, how nice it would be to turn this apartment of yours upside down and come up with a twentieth of a gram of cocaine, you know. Or one little, innocent marijuana seed. I'd like nothing better, Robert, because I think you really screwed me.

"But that's not why I took it on. You tell me, Robert—when's the next city election?"

"The primary's in, what—sixteen months?"

"Seventeen," said Daley. "Now tell me how much chance I'd have without your paper's support."

"Oh, somewhere between zero and none," I said. It was true. Daley needed the black vote to win, and our competition was not geared to Detroit's sixty-five percent black pop-

ulation but to the white middle class who fled the city nightly.

"So—"

I threw up my hands. "Go no further, Animal," I said. "I see it all. You want to get your hands on Jack Fowler's killers, throw them into jail, reap the gratitude of our editorial-page editor, and—grudges thrown away like so much Kleenex—win the primary next year."

"You're a sneaky little bastard, Robert, but you're smart," Jerry Daley said. "If this were an interview, I'd tell you no comment. But it's not an interview. It's a private, off-the-record conversation."

"Now that we've settled your political future," I said, "what does Jack Fowler's being gay or not being gay have to do with it?"

"Oh, he was gay all right," Jerry Daley said. "Not a full-time queer, you understand. Bisexual. Kinky. But you already know that."

"I do?" I asked.

"Yes, you do," Jerry Daley said.

"Who told you?"

"Jack Fowler." Daley smiled. He crushed his cigarette carefully in the saucer I had provided. "Jack Fowler told me.

"I'm not a stupid man," said Jerry Daley. "Arrogant, maybe. Egocentric, perhaps." He leaned forward. "But I'm not stupid, Robert. So when we found Fowler's little stash yesterday, I had half a dozen of my guys go through every shred of paper we found in Jack's apartment. You know all those lovely journals he kept? Kept them in longhand."

I nodded.

"Well, guess what he wrote in them, Robert. We don't have everything, yet. But the partial entries we were able to reconstruct give us all sorts of interesting information. We have Jack's sources on the court investigation that won him that award last year—I don't think they'll stay employed too much longer, even with civil service.

"And we've got some juicy descriptions of what Jack used to do in New York. I tell you the man was kinky—kinky.

"But you know that, don't you? Sure you do, Robert, be-

cause Jack says"—he dug into the oversized briefcase and brought out another green folder from which he extracted a sheet—"it's from an early September entry two years ago: 'Robert came up for some Pichon-Baron 'fifty-nine. Deep and lovely, though not so big as I would have liked. But an elegant wine. Perhaps should have opened the Pichon-Lalande 'fifty-nine instead. Talked about Madeleine; night I came out with Williams Pierce at Christ. I trust Robert, I think. Am not attracted to him physically, but we share our aloneness well, and I like his taste in wines. A growing friendship that will last, I think.' " Daley passed the sheet of paper to me. Ripped fragments of Jack's journal had been pieced together like a jigsaw puzzle. There were bits missing, but the entry was clear and unmistakable.

He had evidence. In Jack's own precise southern handwriting. I handed the page back to Daley.

"Okay," I said. "Now what?"

"Robert, I'll be honest with you," Daley said. "Six months ago, a year ago, this might have been leaked to your competition. But now I think it'll stay quiet. I noticed your story didn't mention the fact that Jack was gay. So you're trying to keep it quiet, too."

Daley indicated the two policemen. "They work for me, Robert, not that idiot in homicide. And I think we can say that what's been said here won't leak out."

"Lovely," I said. "Okay, the lid is on."

"Which brings us back to my original question," Daley said. He took out another cigarette and went through the tamping and lighting procedure again. "We know that you took stuff out of Fowler's apartment. Material that Jack hadn't put into his journals yet.

"So I've got a couple of choices. I can ask you for it, and you could slip me the information without anybody knowing. Or you can withhold it, in which case I am going to make your life miserable over the course of this investigation.

"Hard or easy, Robert?"

At that point I knew that Daley had one of his cops wired. Handing out evidence to the cops would blow my credibility

95

with every source in town. If I agreed—something I would never do—he'd be able to squeeze me every time he needed something. I would become one of his snitches.

"Hard," I said.

Daley stood up. "I'm sorry about that, Robert," he said. He reached down and slipped the two green files back into his briefcase.

"For the record, I'd like you to know that I'm going to be all over your case from now on. Up and down and all around. How would you like to appear before a grand jury, Robert?"

"You'll have to talk to the paper's lawyers," I said. I walked to the hall closet and got Daley's coat and hat. "If you like," I said, "I'll make sure that you get early copies of the paper by messenger."

"Robert, you're all heart," Daley said. Cigarette between his lips, he slid into his coat, perched the fishing cap on his head, and picked up his case and recorder. The cigarette ash fell onto my rug. Daley rubbed it with his toe.

"Sorry," he said, smiling.

"Get the hell out of here," I said. I opened my front door. Daley rapped on it as he walked by.

"Steel," he said. "You worried about B and E, Robert?"

"Sometimes," I said.

"Steel never stopped a search warrant," Daley said as he closed the door behind him. I could hear him laugh in the hallway.

*chapter 10*_____

Jerry Daley was a fool, I thought. He had telegraphed his moves; he had mentioned a search warrant; he had given me warning. Of course, Jerry Daley was no fool. By talking about a search warrant, he had virtually made sure that I would move the Jack Fowler files out of my apartment. The courts have not been kind, of late, toward reporters trying to shield their sources. I knew this. So did Jerry Daley. So I sat and thought for a while. Then I walked down the service stairs into the basement laundry room and called Nina Thatcher at the paper. By this time Daley probably had tapped into my home phone line; one cannot be too careful. It is a rule.

Nina Thatcher picked up after one ring. She said, "Hello."

"Recognize the voice?"

"Of course I do," she said.

"Good," I said. "Let's not use any names."

"Okay."

"Remember where you and Jack and I met the first time?" I asked.

"But of course," said Nina Thatcher. "How could a girl forget?"

"Okay. Daley the Animal and a couple of his friends have been visiting, and I'm worried about search warrants. Meet me there in forty minutes." I hung up the receiver and sprinted back up eleven flights of stairs. Then I took Jack's files and spread them out between my mattress and box spring. Just in case Daley decided to break in while I was out. I pulled a dozen old clip files from the corner of my closet, stuck them into a liquor carton, sealed the top with masking tape, and after double-locking my apartment door, carried the box down the service stairs to the garage. If Daley were as cunning as his reputation indicated, he would have someone watching the elevator to see who got on at the tenth floor.

Inside the garage I checked my VW for bugs before unlocking the door. Scanned the underside with a flashlight; ran my fingers carefully under the wheel wells, the bumpers, the exhaust system. Pried off the hubcaps and checked the wheels. The car was clean. I unlocked the door and looked inside. Under the cocomats, dashboard, behind the radio. Beneath the seats and rear storage area. Nothing. The Bug was bugless.

Opened the garage door with my card key and edged the car onto Hibbard Street, northbound and one way. As I shifted from second to third, I saw an olive-green Plymouth pull away from the curb perhaps a hundred feet behind me. That would be car number one. According to the Detroit police manual on physical surveillance, there would be two other cars involved, running on parallel northbound streets to the east and west of me.

Surveillance by car is complex. Movies and TV shows usually show one vehicle trailing another. In real life it's different. You don't want to break traffic laws if at all possible, and unlike *The French Connection* or *Bullitt*, you can't go careening around corners, caroming off parked cars. In one form of the classic three-car tail, the first vehicle stays behind the object of surveillance until he turns left or right. Then car two or three picks up the tail, while the first car assumes the parallel course. This method is effective on city streets. It is not, however, effective on freeways.

So, maintaining a steady twenty-five, I drove down Hibbard to Gratiot, turned right, and headed toward the Ford freeway.

Even making the turn onto Gratiot, which is six lanes plus parking, would give my pursuers trouble. Gratiot runs diagonally to intersecting streets; that means it is impossible to parallel tail. All three cars would have to follow me directly, taking turns staying directly behind me. One, perhaps, would pass, pull over, and play catch up.

I cruised along Gratiot slowly, in the right lane. Pulled over alongside a package store, walked inside, and bought a pack of cigarettes, which I opened after I got back into my VW. I also took the time to turn on the police radio scanner that sits in the Bug's glove compartment. My tail, I discovered, was operating on a channel known as Tach 3. They were calling themselves Deacon-Adam One, Two, and Three. I was being called Adam Henry, which is radio talk for asshole.

I pulled back into traffic. "Adam Henry moving east again. Deacon Adam Two taking the point K," said a voice.

"Four, Deacon Adam Two," said another voice. "We have an eyeball K."

I eased into the middle lane, then the left-turn lane, and swung off Gratiot in second gear, accelerating the Bug as much as I could.

"Deacon One, take the turn," said a voice. "Deacon Two, go north and parallel."

I slid the car hard left into an alley before the olive Plymouth appeared in my rearview mirror, found a garage alcove in the alley, and pulled into it. The olive Plymouth's tires screeched to a halt a hundred feet away. I could hear it.

"Deacon One to Deacon Leader," said the voice, "pick him up. He's running south now."

I heard the Plymouth reverse itself and K-turn in the one-way street. I pulled out of the garage alcove and slipped into the southbound street, so that they could see me head back toward Gratiot, toward the Ford freeway.

"We've got an eyeball, Deacon Leader" came the voice. "Adam Henry back on Gratiot, heading east."

Now they knew that I knew that they were following me, and we could play our game successfully. So I obeyed the traffic laws, making all sorts of turns and figure eights as I drove along Gratiot, to keep them on their toes. Finally, I slid onto the Ford and headed back to the center of the city, where, still tailed, I wove my way to the front door of the London Chop House. Nina Thatcher was standing outside.

"You're late," she said.

"I am the proud owner of a tail," I said.

"No shit," said Nina Thatcher. "How come you're leading them to me?"

"Because you are my decoy," I said. "We're going to your place and drop off my files."

"What files?" asked Nina Thatcher.

"The ones back there," I said. Nina Thatcher swiveled in her seat and looked at the carton on the back floor.

"Are you crazy, Robert?" she asked.

"They are dummy files, dummy," I said. "But even so, you are about to get your apartment searched. I hope you don't have anything incriminating around."

"I have five ounces of the best grass you've ever smoked," said Nina Thatcher, "as well as what the cops refer to as marijuana paraphernalia. You want to get me busted?"

"I will pay you back for the grass," I said. "You're going to have to flush it. We can stash the bongs or whatever in your garbage can."

"Do you realize how long it took me to find decent grass in this city," Nina Thatcher said. "Robert, you are going to do more than pay for my smoke. You are going to replace it."

"Anything you say," I said. "But where do you live?"

Nina Thatcher lived, she said, in Palmer Park, on the West Side. We took the long way, moving slowly up Woodward, listening to the police scanner as we made plans. As soon as we got to Nina's, she would start grinding her dope into the garbage disposal; I would call the paper and tell Mike that we were about to be busted. Then I would slip out the back way, and Nina would take the fall, as they say, by herself. Meanwhile, I would run back to my place and stash the Fowler files in a safe place before Jerry Daley, who would be

very mad, came screaming back to my place with a search warrant. I also wanted Mike to get the paper's lawyers over to my place and up to Nina Thatcher's apartment, just to prevent Daley's people from wholesale destruction of our property.

Ostentatiously I carried the liquor carton from my car through the front door of Nina Thatcher's apartment house, a four-story affair built before the Second World War. She had, I discovered, done a nice job of fixing it up, custom-painting two of her living-room walls in a rich dark-green enamel and hanging a half dozen more than decent museum posters. But there was no time to be admiring. Nina went to her stash and, after giving me a very dirty look, began running cold water in the sink.

"This is incredible," she said as she turned on the disposal and emptied the first of five Baggies of rich-looking dope into the drain. "This is a month's salary," she said.

"I'm sorry," I said, punching Mike's private number on Nina Thatcher's kitchen phone. "I'll make it up to you."

Mike assured me that a lawyer would be waiting for me at my home and promised another was on his way to Nina's. Yet a third, he said, would try to get a restraining order. "We'll pull the First Amendment gag," Mike said. "We'll try to slow the sons of bitches down," he told me. I thanked him and watched as Nina emptied the last of her delicious boo into the sink.

"I'm sorry," I said.

"Horse pucky," said Nina Thatcher. "I have just made the ultimate sacrifice for you," she said. "Now I'm going to check all the ashtrays for roaches, which I will flush down the toilet. Then I am going to put my two bongs, three pipes, and the Cheech and Chong roach clips I love so much into the dishwasher, so that all the residue can be washed off. Then I am going to sit here and sulk, Robert, because of what you have made me do."

"I am going home," I said, "and hide the files and wait for the Animal."

But Jerry Daley was no fool. Jerry Daley didn't want my files; he didn't give a goddamn about my files. He just

wanted to bother me. Put me on notice. Stick a tail on me for the hell of it. Keep me busy. Which is exactly what he did. By the time I got home from Nina Thatcher's the green Plymouth was gone. Besides, the Animal had better ways of getting information. Through systematic leaking of secrets, for example. He leaked the fragment of Jack's journal with my name in it to the opposition. It came out in the final edition. DEAD REPORTER TIED TO GAY SCENE is how the headline read.

It ran in a box just under the masthead. The story, which read as if it had been dictated by Daley himself, alleged that Jack had had connections in the homosexual community, connections that had prevented him from being able to write the true account of the city's chicken-hawking trade. There were inferences that Jack might have become involved with some of the children he was writing about. Then the story jumped to page five, where the journal fragment was shown in its entirety. That's where my name appeared. "The 'Robert' in Fowler's journal entry," the story said, "refers to Robert Mandel, the op's crack dope reporter. According to police sources, Mandel and Fowler were very close friends, although the true extent of their activities together is not known. It is possible, however, that Mandel and Fowler had some of the same connections to Detroit's homosexual community. Mandel was unavailable for comment."

It was a cheap shot; I was never called for comment, which I wouldn't have given in the first place. But Daley had done his job. He had kept me busy while the competition put the story together. It was an effective but sleazy thing to do. And it got my ass chewed out good.

I got called on the carpet. Not the carpet, exactly, the linoleum tile floor of the executive editor's office. Mike was there, his feet on his glass-topped desk. So was Tom Collier, the managing editor, and Larry Chesler, the city editor. They were not happy.

They were most unhappy, in fact. Mike put it succinctly. "You really fucked up," he said. "I get three lawyers at two hundred bucks an hour, and you fuck up. And you end up on the front page of the competition."

"Page five," I said.

"This is really funny," Mike said. "There are fifteen cases pending—crooked cops, cops on the take—all based on your stories. One of them is Daley's guy. Now Daley gets you by the shorts and jacks you around, jacks the paper around. Our reputation is at stake here, Robert. Your reputation is at stake."

"I know, I know," I said.

"I don't want you holding back," Mike said.

"You've got to write what you know," Tom Collier said. Larry Chesler nodded. I looked at him. A yes-man. No balls. He had no right even to be at the meeting.

"I know, I know," I said.

"So what you want to do?" Mike asked.

"I'll write what I know," I said.

"Were you and Jack involved," Mike said. He didn't ask; he said it.

"No," I said. "We were friends. Close friends."

Tom Collier looked up. "Asshole buddies," he said with a smile.

I launched myself at him, grabbed the lapels of his jacket and twisted him down onto the floor, lashed out at his face, grabbed his tie just below the knot, and tried to smash his head into the side of Mike's desk. They were all over me, pulled me off Tom Collier. They were yelling at me. I wanted to kill Tom Collier at that moment.

Finally, they got us separated. Mike held me back. Mike's big arms pinned me to the wall. I looked through the glass doors of his office and saw twenty pairs of eyes staring at us from the city room.

I pointed at Tom Collier. "I'll kill him," I said. There were tears in my eyes. "Get him out of here, or I swear I'll kill him." I pushed against Mike's forearms. Mike added the weight of his shoulders, and I stayed pinned to the wall. He gestured with his head.

"Tom, why don't you take a break for a minute, huh?"

With Collier gone, he relaxed the pressure against my chest.

"He said something stupid," Mike said. "Forget it."

"Forget it," said Larry Chesler. "It was a stupid thing to say."

I pulled a handkerchief out of my pocket and blew my nose. I paced up and down in front of Mike's desk. Larry Chesler began to straighten the chairs that I had knocked over. "I'm sorry," I said to Mike.

"You should be," he said. He looked at me for a few seconds. "It's okay, Robert," he said. "It's okay. I know you're upset."

I walked in tightening circles until I couldn't walk anymore. Then I sat in one of the steel chairs facing Mike's desk. "What next?" I asked.

"Take the rest of the day off," Mike said. "Tomorrow I want you out on the street. You messed up, Robert," he said. "You screwed things up pretty good. So you're going to have to unfuck yourself and unfuck the paper. We don't want to have to print any skin-backs about Jack or about you.

"Now get the hell out of here and get some rest."

chapter 11_____

The call came late. After two. I had been asleep less than two hours. The phone rang four times, I think, before I was able to struggle out of a deep sleep. In the dark I flipped the switch that turned on the phone tap and cassette recorder simultaneously. Then I picked up the receiver. I wasn't awake.

"Is this Robert Mandel?" a voice asked. "Hello? Is this Robert Mandel?" It was a scared voice, a young voice, I wished it were a louder voice. I wished I had not had five shots of vodka to help me sleep. I couldn't get myself awake.

"This is Bob Mandel," I said. "Who's calling?"

"I called the paper. They put me through to you," the voice said.

"Yes," I said. "Yes?"

"The paper put me through to you," the voice said. "This is Robert Mandel? You're not listed in the phone book."

"Yes," I said. "No," I said. "Who is this?"

"It doesn't matter," the voice said. "I have to talk to you. I have to talk to you, you know. It's very important."

"Yes," I said. I was struggling to clear my head. I was fuzzy. "What about?"

"About Jack," said the voice. "I have to talk to you about Jack."

I sat upright, tried to kick the quilt away. It was wrapped around my legs. I had fallen asleep on top of the bedclothes. I panicked when I couldn't extricate my feet.

"Wait a second, please," I said. "Don't hang up." I rolled over and turned on the bedside lamp. Kicked the quilt onto the floor. Piled my pillows against the headboard so I could sit up. I rubbed my face. My hands were sticky from sleep. I had been sweating heavily. I couldn't remember if I had been dreaming or not. It didn't matter. The word "Jack" had got me up, made me fully awake. I looked for the receiver and couldn't find it. I traced it by following the wire from the wall.

"Hello," I said. "Sorry," I said. "Do you have any idea what time it is?"

"I have to talk to you about Jack," the voice said. "You're Robert Mandel. I read about you in the paper. I called your paper, you know, and they put me through to you."

"Yes," I said. "But why did you call?"

"You loved Jack and he loved you, didn't you," the voice said.

"He was my friend."

"He was my friend, too," the voice said.

"Yes?" Even struggling out of sleep I knew I had to keep him talking.

"He loved me, too. I loved him, too," the voice said. "And now he's dead, and I don't know what to do."

"Yes," I said.

"It's crazy," the voice said. "He's dead. He's dead."

"Yes," I said. "And . . ."

"We have to talk about Jack," the voice said. "Did he give you money?"

"What?"

"Did he give you money? He gave me money."

"Who is this," I said. "Can I come and meet you? Can we talk?"

"I just had to talk to somebody," the voice said. "You loved Jack. I read it in the paper. You'll know what to do."

The voice approached hysteria, I thought. Such a young voice to be so hysterical.

"Yes," I said. "Can I meet you someplace now? We'll talk."

"I can't," said the voice. "Not now. Can't, now. To-morrow."

"Tomorrow," I said. "Okay," I said. "Yes. Whenever you want."

"Promise? Do you promise?" the voice said.

"Yes," I said. "Ten o'clock. Tell me where and I'll be there."

"No," said the voice. "I can't. Later. After school."

"Okay," I said. "Anything you say. Where?"

"You know the Stage Deli on Nine Mile Road?"

"Yes."

"Three-thirty. I'll meet you there."

"Three-thirty," I repeated. "How will I find you?"

"I'll find you," the voice said. It had dropped to a whisper. "Please be there. I have to talk to somebody. Oh, God, I have to. It said in the paper that, you know, you loved Jack."

"What's your name?" I said. "What's your name?"

The line went dead.

I sat there for a while, propped against the headboard, and realized that I would not get back to sleep. So I walked into the kitchen and made a pot of cocoa. There were some old marshmallows sitting in the cupboard, and I dropped three of them, hard as pumice, into the mug. They took forever to dissolve. I sat in the living room and sipped at the cocoa, Jack's thick file on my lap.

I wanted to sleep; I needed to sleep. So I went back into the kitchen, took the sweet basil jar from the spice shelf and a package of cigarette paper from the towel rack, and rolled myself a joint. I lighted it, took the bag of stale marshmallows with me, and went back into the living room to pore over the file again.

The marshmallows made me queasy, and I lay down on my rug, using Jack's file as a pillow. I closed my eyes. A kid calls at two-thirty in the morning and wants to talk about Jack and I have no idea who he is. I ate another marshmallow, then went back into the kitchen and found a box of gin-

ger snaps, which I brought and set next to me on the rug. Marshmallows to the right, ginger snaps to the left. Two-handed munchies.

I stood up again and walked to the hi-fi and found the Beach Boys' *Holland* album. I put it on the turntable, turned out the lights, took a pair of stereo earphones, and slipped them on. Lay down again. Jack's file my pillow. Listened to the waves of sound. Sang along. Cried for a while. Had he lied to me? Had Jack lied to me? And what were the lies he had lied to me if he had lied? I lied. I lied to Jack. I lied to Nancy; I lied to Nancy when I told her it didn't matter that she wouldn't come to Detroit with me when I got my job here. I lied a lot. I lied in print when I wrote what I had written about Jack. Or what I hadn't written. Don't we all spend a lot of time lying to each other, I thought. Whose voice was that? Mike Love's, I thought. No, on the phone, I thought, the voice on the phone, who told me he had loved Jack and Jack had loved him. Somebody's lying, I thought, and what money was he talking about anyway? I put another marshmallow in my mouth and followed it quickly with a ginger snap. I could taste neither. The waves of sound moved from left to right through my head and I wiped my eyes with the sleeve of my shirt because I couldn't reach into my trousers for my handkerchief, and wiped my nose, too. What money? Everybody lies, and the center of my head throbbed electric bass guitar and Moog synthesizer and I knew I would be asleep before the third track finished playing.

⎯⎯⎯⎯⎯

I knew him as he walked in the door. He was out of place in a delicatessen. At three-thirty in the afternoon, the Stage is half-empty. The lunchtime shopping crowd has gone on to Hudson's for the afternoon's buying. The kids who arrive from the Oak Park schools arrive in groups. He was alone. Gangly, blond, nervous, dressed in a leather windbreaker, corduroy jeans, and sneakers. He was carrying a textbook with a University of Michigan cover, although he couldn't have been more than seventeen. He ran a hand through his longish, curly hair and looked around, slightly wild-eyed.

You could see him tick off the possible choices. No, I was not the middle-aged man working his way through a dish of flanken, or the bald construction worker with a beer and a Danish, or the teenager with a toasted English muffin and a cup of coffee in front of him. That left me, the thirtyish person sipping on a Cel-Ray tonic in the back banquette. A waitress asked if he wanted a table, and he shrugged her off, gesturing toward me. His lips moved: "I'm meeting somebody." He walked toward the rear of the dining room, unzipping his windbreaker as he came.

"You're Mr. Mandel," he said.

I nodded.

"Look," he said, "I don't want to get involved, you know." He looked at the reporter's notebook that lay on the Formica tabletop. "Please don't write anything down," he said. He was still standing.

"Sorry," I said. "I was just going over some old interviews." I slipped the notebook into the back pocket of my trousers. It didn't matter. I was wearing a Panasonic minicorder in a shoulder holster. There was a microphone that looked like a pen in the breast pocket of my sports coat, and a remote control on-off switch ran down the inside of my jacket into my left trouser pocket. I reached down and switched it on, removing a handkerchief as I did so. I coughed discreetly into it and put it back.

"I couldn't talk last night," he said, slipping onto a steel and plastic chair opposite me. "I was calling from home, and I thought I heard my parents wake up."

"Uh-huh," I said. "Look, um—what's your name?"

"I don't think I should tell you," he said. "I don't want people to know who I am," he said. "Can't we keep this sort of anonymous?"

"You've got to trust me," I said. "You called me because you loved Jack and something about his death bothered you, and you wanted to talk. But that's kind of hard if I have to call you Mr. X all the time. I'm Bob. So what do I call you?"

"Mark," he said. "Okay, my name is Mark, all right?"

"Fine, Mark," I said. "It's good to meet you. I'm glad you came. Why don't you tell me first why you called, and

maybe I can help you out, or we could just talk about Jack?"

He scrunched his chair closer to the table. "Um, could I have a Coke or something?" he asked.

"Sure you could," I said. I tried for a waitress's attention and was finally able to order a Coke and a refill for my Cel-Ray.

"What is that?" Mark asked.

"It's made from celery," I said. "It's a New York drink."

"Heavy," Mark said. "I don't think I could ever get into it, you know," he said.

"It's an acquired taste," I said. "Like caviar."

He sipped at his Coke. "My mother doesn't know," he said.

"What?" I asked. "What doesn't your mother know?"

"About Jack," he said. "About me, you know, that Jack was my, you know, my lover. Like he was yours."

I was not about to contradict him. "Oh," I said.

"We met about a year ago," he said. "I never stayed around the house much, you know. I don't get along with my parents. Like my mother's always bugging me, getting on my case real bad, you know, and my father—he's not my real father—he doesn't give a damn anyway, so I was better off by myself, you know."

I nodded. "How did you meet Jack?"

"There's this guy," Mark said. "An older guy, maybe twenty-five, twenty-six, you know, and I used to go over to his place a couple times a week. Listen to music, you know, get a little high, do a little PCP. So I was over at his house, you know, and Jack was there."

"What's this guy's name?" I asked.

"It's not important. It doesn't matter, you know," said Mark. "Why are you asking all these questions?"

"Hey, kid," I said. "That's what we're here for. If I'm going to help you, you've gotta talk to me, okay?"

"Like it's not important," Mark said. "Names aren't important."

"What's his name?" I asked.

"I gotta go," said Mark. He started to stand.

"Okay, okay," I said. "Names aren't important."

Mark sat down again. He sipped at his Coke. He thought for a while. "His name's Larry," he said.

"Oh," I said. "See, that wasn't hard. Now, what does Larry do?"

"Oh, nothing, I guess," Mark said. "Deals a little, you know. Pills and stuff. He's a very hand-to-mouth kind of guy."

"Did you ever see Jack and Larry together again?" I asked.

"Um, I don't know," Mark said. "Not often, you know," he said. "See—that's all I was going to tell you, you know, that I met Jack at Larry's house and we didn't know he was a reporter or anything. We got high, see, and then Jack told Larry that he'd take me home. To my house."

"I see," I said.

"I really called you from Larry's last night," Mark said. "I was staying with Larry for a few days," he said. "The day that Jack was killed," he said. "I've been doing a lot of PCP," he said. "I loved Jack," he said. "I did, Mr. Mandel."

Mark looked at me. "He believed in me," he said.

"Sure he did," I said.

"So like he took me home that first night, you know, and he leaves me off down the block from where I live. I asked him to, you know, but before he lets me off, he looks at me, you know, and he says, 'You're not happy, are you?' Weird, huh? I wonder how he could tell. So I tell him that the scene at home is a drag, and I'm always at Larry's, you know, and getting high. And he tells me, 'There's more to life than that, kiddo.' And then he gives me his home phone number and says that if I'd like to be somebody, to give him a call, you know. Then I get out of the car, but before I get out, he shakes my hand, you know. He shakes my hand, and says, 'Look, call me. I'll take care of you,' you know. He told me, 'You look like a nice kiddo.' That was heavy, you know."

I nodded. "So?"

"Okay," said Mark. "So I called him, you know, and he brought me up to his place, which was really out of sight and had all these paintings, and we got high, and he asked me all about myself and how I grew up and why I got high all the time. And he asked me how much of an allowance I got, and

111

when I told him five bucks a week, he said how would I like a job part time working for him, you know. And we're talking and smoking, you know, and I thought how much I'd like to have a brother like him, you know, an older brother. But anyway, you know, we were getting high, and he was drinking this wine, you know, and he got a little drunk and asked if I'd mind staying because he was too wrecked to drive me home or anything, and I could stay in the guest room if I wanted and he'd take me home in the morning.

"But I didn't want to stay in the guest room really. I wanted to be with him, you know. I mean I wanted to be close to him. He was different, see? Kind, you know. So I helped him to bed, and we got our clothes off, you know, and then a fantastic thing happened. Like we didn't do anything; we just held each other. He let me put my head on his chest, and he held me, and I rubbed his shoulders, and we went to sleep like that. Did it happen with you like that, too? Did you feel that way with him?"

I thought about Nina Thatcher, and I smiled. "It was a little different," I said.

"We made love in the morning," Mark said. "We took a shower together, and then we made love, and it was the best, you know."

"Mornings are nice," I said.

"See, I can tell you this because it said in the paper you loved Jack, too," Mark said. "You understand."

"I understand," I said. I was only beginning to understand. I said, "But why are you so upset? Why did you call?"

"Don't you see?" Mark said. "Now I don't have anybody. And the paper talked about those journals, and the cops are gonna come and question me, you know, and my mother is going to find out, and she'll probably kill me. And besides, there's the money."

"What money?" I asked.

"I told you on the phone," Mark whined. "Jack's money. He gave me five thousand dollars last month. I told him that my grades had gone up, you know, like I don't get high at school anymore, just like he asked me not to. And I showed him my report card, and I got a B minus and two Bs and

three A minuses, and he was so happy he said he'd start a scholarship fund so I could go to college—not a junior college but a real college. And he gave me a check for five thousand dollars, and I cashed it and started a bank account, and I've only spent a little of it on clothes and stuff; but my name is on the check, you know, and they'll think that I killed him, you know, and I didn't. I swear, Mr. Mandel. But they're gonna think that I did, you know."

"How often did you see Jack?" I asked.

"Not too," he said. "The first couple of months we spent one, two nights a week together. Then it got down to once a week, once every two weeks, you know. But I would always call him, and we'd talk on the phone, and he'd ask me about school and stuff. Last year he took me to New York for a weekend. Thanksgiving weekend. We went to see the Macy Day parade, with all those big balloons, you know. It was incredible, just absolutely fantastic. He showed me all around New York, and we stayed at the Regency Hotel in a suite with three televisions, and we had lots of room service—I could order anything I wanted, you know—and we went to see *Chorus Line* which was fantastic, and he took me to dinner at this incredible French restaurant called Le Petite Ferme—"

"La," I said. "La Petite Ferme. *Ferme* is feminine."

"Oh, yeah," Mark said. "Jack was always correcting my French, too. That was my B minus. I'm not too hot in languages, you know."

"I see," I said. I sipped at my Cel-Ray. "Order us another round," I said. "And some food if you want it." I pointed at the empty soda bottle. "This stuff runs right through me." I edged out of the banquette. "I gotta hit the head. I'll be back in a second."

"Sure, Mr. Mandel," he said. "I'm kinda hungry, you know?"

I nodded and headed toward the john. Once inside I took a seat in an empty stall, pulled my pants down, and my shorts, so I'd look occupied, and flipped the minicassette over. I had three more in my pocket; four hours of tape in all if it became necessary. I sat there for a minute. Jack had lied

to me. "When I get the curse, I go to New York," he said. I had it on tape.

I thought of Nina Thatcher. "Horse puckey, horse shit," I said out loud. I pulled my trousers up, adjusted the minirecorder, put the remote on-off switch back in my pocket, flushed the commode, and then went to wash my hands. You never can tell who's listening outside the door. And a flush is proof of use, just like wet hands.

He hadn't moved. He was sitting, back to the door, hunched over a bologna sandwich. "Hi," I said, "I'm back."

He nodded. "What you think I should do?" he asked, his mouth full of sandwich. He had ordered it on white bread. I wondered if that had been Jack's influence. Jack was not an ethnic food eater.

"Okay, Mark," I said. "I'm going to be straight with you. Sooner or later the cops are going to find Jack's check, and they're going to come calling. Which will probably happen within the next two days. Then just think about what'll happen. Jack was working on a story about gay kids. You are a gay kid. You took money from Jack—don't say anything, we may know better, but that's what they're going to think. And you're going to be dumped right into the middle of this mess."

"But I haven't slept—I didn't sleep—with Jack for more than two months," Mark said. A tear formed under the center of his right eye, welled up, and began to roll down his cheek. "I swear, Mr. Mandel," he said. "Jack said that he didn't want to sleep with me anymore. He said that all he wanted was to be my friend."

"I believe you, Mark," I said. "I believe you." I reached across the table and patted his hand. There was mayonnaise under two of his fingernails. I wondered why kids always manage to eat messily. He saw me looking at the greasy crescents and moved his hand to his mouth, sucked on the fingertips. "The problem is," I said, "maybe the cops won't believe you. Like you say, Mark, they're going to find that check with your name on it. Think of what your mother will say when she finds out that you've been sleeping with an older man."

"Oh, God," he said. Now there were tears in both eyes. He crumpled up the paper napkin sitting beside his plate and wiped his eyes with it. "My mother doesn't *know*," he said. "Oh, God. Please help me, Mr. Mandel."

"I'll try," I said. "But I have to know why you called me. I mean, why you called me as opposed to, say, telling Larry or somebody else."

"Because it said in the paper you loved Jack," he said. "I knew Jack was involved with other people, you know, but I didn't know who. And it said in the paper you were a reporter, and I thought you'd know what to do. I couldn't tell Larry anyway."

"Why?" I asked.

"I just couldn't," he said. "I can't tell you, you know; it's private."

"Okay," I said. "It's private." I could find out why later. First, however, I had to put Mark on ice. The cops would find him sooner or later. Jerry Daley would go through Jack's records piece by piece. He would get to Mark. On the other hand, if I could keep the kid out of sight for two or three days, we'd get a big jump on the story.

"I'll tell you what, Mark," I said. "I think you're being honest with me. And if Jack loved you, then I have to protect you."

"What do you think I should do?" Mark asked.

"I'm going to get you a place to stay for a couple of days," I said. "You'll be with me and a friend of mine. We'll talk. I'll try to get you off the hook. You can call your folks when you get settled."

The kid wiped at the tears that were still running down his cheeks. "Thanks, Mr. Mandel," he said. "I knew you were the right person to call."

I smiled reassuringly and patted his hand again. "You did good, Mark," I said. "Come on, let's get out of here." I put some money on the table. I knew that once we stashed Mark whatever-his-last-name-was we could squeeze him. If Jerry Daley wanted to leak goodies to the opposition, fine. Let him. He'd have to read us to get the story from now on.

I had my arm around Mark's shoulders as we walked out

to my VW. I looked at the kid in the sunlight. A child. Just a child. Damn Jack anyway, I thought. Damn Jack for lying to me.

I thought about Jack's smiling face, his tinted glasses. Jack's London-cut clothes. Jack's T. Hodgkinson, Ltd., shirts. Jack's Gucci boots; his secrets.

I walked Mark toward the blue Bug. Had Jack been alive, had he been with us, I would have hit him.

*chapter 12*_____

Mike was not happy. Mike did not like the idea that I brought Mark up to his office. "I don't want to know what you do," Mike said. We had left Mark sitting in the glass-walled office and walked down the hall into a small conference room to talk things over. "It makes things difficult for me," he said. "If you want to hide somebody who might know something about a crime, Robert, that's your business. But I don't want to know about it. There are too many pressures on me. I can't think about one story, you know that."

"Mike," I said, "listen. Here is a kid who says that Jack slept with him. Here is a kid who says Jack gave him five grand. Then he mentions the name of some other guy, a faggot who runs dope, whom Jack knew. If we give the kid up, Daley's gonna be all over us with the fag reporter label. Smear us through the competition, you know; you can see the stories, right? 'Paper Harbors Homosexual in Midst. Pederast Covers Sex Scene.' Great, right?

"Okay, Mike—you were right. I screwed things up. Jack was my friend, and I tried to protect him in print. That was wrong. He lied to you; he lied to me. Maybe he lied to a lot

of people. The thing is, now we've got to do the story first."

"I don't want to know," Mike said. "All I want is ten books by deadline tomorrow and ten books every day after that until this thing is cleared up. I want your sources checked. I want facts."

"You are an amoral son of a bitch," I said. "Just give you the stories and you're happy. Do I have stolen files? Don't tell you, you say, because that would be conspiracy to something or other. Hide a witness, okay, but don't tell you about it. That's great, Mike. Why? Because then you can go in front of a grand jury and say you don't know anything; you're clean. And it's my ass they'll be after. Shit.

"What the hell do you want me to do? Put the kid in my apartment? Daley's probably gonna get a warrant for it. Or for Nina Thatcher's place. I don't want to use a hotel. Jesus Christ, I need some help."

"What are you thinking?" Mike asked.

"The corporate apartment," I said. "It's big and comfortable, and it has an unlisted phone."

"Oh, that's great," Mike said. "Get the corporation involved. That's all I need."

"They don't have to know," I said. "Is anybody expected in for the next three or four days?"

"Not that I know," Mike said. "But I'd have to sign the keys out. There'd be a record."

I looked at Mike. The bastard really knew how to lie. "Bullshit," I said.

"What do you mean, bullshit? Corporate keeps the keys. I don't."

"Wednesdays, five-thirty to eight," I said.

Mike's eyes betrayed him. Psychologists say that the eyes always betray you. They tell you that there are things called micromomentary expressions, flashes that, instead of the fifth-of-a-second blink, begin at about a twentieth of a second, sometimes flashing as fast as a fortieth of a second. Blinks, twitches, contractions. It's the subconscious, they say, releasing a lie and the conscious mind yanking it off the face. I watched Mike's face. Twitch, blink, twitch, blink. Eyes roll-

ing back and forth. If I had blinked myself, I would have missed it.

"You have a key," I said. "If you give me your key, you won't have to go to corporate."

Mike was silent.

"Oh, come on," I said. "Own up, Mike." I wanted him to say something. I wanted him to tell me something so that the pen-shaped mike in the breast pocket of my jacket would capture it.

Mike was not to be pinned down. "Go out for a couple of minutes," he said. "Then come back and check your pigeon-hole for messages." Mike was not an executive editor for nothing.

"Think of it as your contribution to journalism this year," I said. "You can say that you missed getting laid in the line of duty."

"I don't know what you're talking about," Mike said. "Just take a break for ten minutes, okay? And take the kid with you."

So I took a break. I called Nina Thatcher up in features and asked her to meet Mark and me at the luncheonette in our lobby.

"What is it now, Robert?" Nina Thatcher asked. She stirred a quarter of a packet of Sweet 'n Low into a mug of black coffee. She looked over at Mark, who met her eyes with his and then concentrated on a large paper cup of Coke.

I didn't say anything for the moment. Nina Thatcher pulled a fresh package of Benson and Hedges menthol cigarettes from her brown leather handbag and put them on the white Formica surface on the booth's table. "Who's your friend?" she asked.

"How would you like to room with me for a few days," I said.

"How would you like to get stuffed," said Nina Thatcher. "Excuse me, kid."

"It's okay," said Mark.

"This is Mark," I said.

"Hi, Mark," said Nina Thatcher. She burrowed through her

purse until she found a disposable plastic lighter, which she set on top of the cigarettes. She sipped at her coffee, unwrapped the cigarettes, took one, and put it in her mouth.

As she applied the flame, I said, "Mark, here, was a friend of Jack Fowler's."

"Oh," said Nina Thatcher. She held the lighter to the cigarette.

"Mark, here, was a very close friend of Jack Fowler's," I said.

Nina Thatcher dropped the lighter back into her purse. "Oh," she said again. She took another look at Mark, taking her tinted glasses off to do so. Nina Thatcher smiled at the kid as she peered at him. "Oh, I see," she said.

"Mark was such a close friend of Jack's that I thought it might be better all around if we looked after him for a few days," I said.

"Aha," said Nina Thatcher. She put her glasses on top of her head.

"Mark," I said, "this is Nina Thatcher. She knew Jack, too."

The kid nodded. He did not catch the look that passed between Nina Thatcher and me.

I reached across the table and took one of Nina Thatcher's cigarettes. "I thought that you might like to—"

"Baby-sit with you," said Nina Thatcher. "Excuse me, Mark, I didn't mean it personally."

"Sure," said Mark. "Can I have a cigarette?" he asked.

"Help yourself," said Nina Thatcher. She relocated her lighter and put it on the table. "Here," she said. She pushed the cigarettes at Mark.

I toyed with my unlit cigarette.

"I can't have him at my place," Nina Thatcher said. "There's no room."

"I've got a place," I said. "Three bedrooms, nicely furnished, quiet."

"Oh," said Nina Thatcher.

"We can talk there," I said. "Right, Mark?"

He nodded.

"See," I said, "the p-o-l-i-c-e are going to be looking for

Mark here, and he tells me he's not quite ready to face them yet. Are you, kid?"

Mark shook his head. "Mr. Mandel said he'd protect me," he said. "I don't know what to do, you know."

Nina Thatcher nodded. "I know," she said. "I think I know," she said. "What should I tell Jerry?" she asked. Jerry was the features editor. Jerry was also a loudmouth.

"Tell Jerry you're taking your comp time," I said. I looked around the small luncheonette room. A couple of copyboys were having coffee two tables away. Down at the takeout counter Mike's secretary was exchanging a dollar bill for three doughnuts and a tea to go. Mike obviously wanted to spend five minutes alone.

"Take Mark with you," I said. "I've got an errand to run," I said. "Meet me out back by the loading dock in an hour."

"What'll I do for an hour?" Nina Thatcher asked.

"Walk over to Hudson's and buy Mark a change of clothes," I said. I took $50 from my wallet. I slid out of the booth. "And I want some change," I said.

———

There was a lot to do. The apartment had to be wired. I got the key from my mailbox and drove out West Lafayette Avenue to the high rise in which the corporation kept a three-bedroom pied-à-terre for visiting executives. I own two Kel units. One of them is at home; the other sits in the trunk of my Bug. The bugged Bug, Jack used to say. He was fascinated by Kels and also by the three narcotics test kits I carry. One for opiates, another for cocaine, a third for amphetamines. Actually, my Bug is outfitted like an office on wheels. There is the Kel, a dozen cassettes, the police scanner, a portable typewriter, a ream of copy paper, the test kits, a high-intensity lamp that can be run off the cigarette lighter and a file of maps, along with two changes of clothes, a pair of rubber boots, and an army-surplus poncho. If I stocked food, I could live out of my car for a week should I have to. The only thing I do not carry in the trunk is a weapon.

It was a well-stocked apartment. Our corporation execu-

tives like to live well. As a company we project a spare, even lean image. The papers—sixteen of them in all—are profitable. The wire service makes a modest profit these days, too. But the corporation is not flashy. Our executives drive Fords or Chevys, not Lincolns or Buicks. Expense accounts are scrutinized for the stockholders' benefit. Privately, though, the brass lives good. Especially when they're on the road. The apartment was on the top floor of a nineteen-floor glass-and-stone building. It overlooked the Detroit River and downtown. There was nothing special about the furniture, except that it was good quality. But the place had been outfitted beautifully. Three console TVs; an ample bar stocked with Chivas, Russian vodka, and Beefeater gin. Cut crystal glasses; Spode china; sterling silver flatware. The art was unimaginative but all authentic: Agam, Kandinsky, Rauschenberg. For a southern corporation, I thought, the art was very New York. But then the place had probably been put together by a decorator.

I stashed the Kel transmitter in a planter and ran the antenna wire up the back of a seven-foot dieffenbachia. The recording unit went into the master bedroom suite. I checked the kitchen. There were staples, but we would need milk, eggs, bread, butter, and soda. Those could be picked up on the way over, and I'd need some sleeping pills. I was pleased to see that the place had two entrances. A main door leading into the apartment and a service entrance that led to fire stairs. Both doors were steel and had inside dead bolts. It would do, I thought. I turned the thermostat up and went to get Nina Thatcher and Mark whatever-his-name-was.

We'd be all nice and cozy, I thought, and the kid would have the opportunity to talk his brains out.

———

There is a problem with tape. That problem is that there is a lot of it. A two-hour conversation may contain ten or fifteen seconds of real information, but each word has to be transcribed nonetheless. It is a long process, especially when you're on a deadline. Nancy used to watch me transcribe in the early days of my career. I would sit in the living room of

our rented house. A lovely house, really, four rooms in a row. You'd walk into the kitchen, pass through into the dining room, where we had a picnic table and two benches set up against the windows, which looked out into a tall hedge of bushes. Then back into the living room—long and narrow—and finally the bedroom. There were no doors. When we had a houseguest, whom we would put on the studio couch in the living room, Nancy and I would have to be very quiet in bed. My best friend in J-school, who works for *Time* now, once came to visit. Nancy and I lay awake listening to him snore. At one point I walked into the living room to find him sitting bolt upright on the couch.

'We've got to stop eating," he told me.

"Eating what?" I asked.

"People," he said. "If we don't stop eating people, they're going to eat us one of these days." He was talking in his sleep.

"Of course they are," I said. I went back into the bedroom, and Nancy and I giggled.

"He's having a reporter's nightmare," I said. "Devoured by his readers."

"Is it a real fear?" she asked.

"Absolutely," I said. Then I snuggled close against her and ran my hand up the front of her nightie. I fondled a breast, two breasts. I made the nipples stand up.

"We'll wake him," she said.

"I don't care," I said. "You have small, delicious, perfect breasts," I said. "I want to eat them."

We were so close in those days. We did share. I know it. We were a duo, a pair, a couple, a unit. It was us against the world. We had our private jokes, our personal giggles. Nancy taught me how to play chess. I taught her backgammon. We did things together. We laughed a lot. We held hands in restaurants and necked during the screenings that Nancy was sometimes required to attend in the evenings.

I worked at home whenever I got the chance. Nancy used to watch me transcribe on weekends. Sitting in the living room. I worked at a portable typewriter table, my electric machine, transcribing unit, and foot pedals all jammed to-

gether. I used to sit on a rickety bentwood chair. Nancy was very unfair. She would try to distract me. Often she would succeed. It is hard not to be distracted by a woman wearing one of your old button-down shirts and nothing else when she parades in front of you, flashing perfect breasts, nice legs, and a tanned, firm tummy.

After a while I stopped transcribing my interviews at home. I was accelerating at the paper, getting better stories, bigger stories. I was working on a tighter schedule, and distractions became harder to take. I was gaining a reputation; it was important to me. So I saw less of the tanned, firm tummy and perfect breasts. I told myself at the time that it could not be helped.

I thought about Nancy the first night that Nina Thatcher, Mark, and I shared our corporate hideaway. I thought about Nancy because after the three of us had talked for more than three hours, I slipped into the kitchen and put two Dalmanes in Mark's cocoa. The kid got very, very sleepy. So we put him to bed. Then we replayed the tapes, taking notes as we went along. The transcribing would come later, when there was time. I was glad to see that Nina had asked Mark to call his house. He had told his mother that he was staying with a friend for a day or so. Her voice was not anxious. It was something he had done before.

I thought about Nancy because Nina Thatcher asked if she could borrow one of my shirts. She shed her tweed jacket, boots, and skirt, tied her hair into twin pigtails, and emerged from her bedroom looking like a little girl, my blue button-down like a minidress stopping three inches above her knees. She had taken off her bra, too, I saw. And when she curled into a low stuffed velvet chair, I saw a flash of panties.

"Keep your mind on your work," Nina Thatcher said.

"I'm not thinking about that," I said. "You remind me of somebody, that's all."

"Sure I do," said Nina Thatcher.

"No, it's true," I said. "I have a friend who used to borrow my shirts," I said. "She lives in Los Angeles."

Nina Thatcher sat cross-legged in the armchair. She pulled

my shirt over her knees as best she could. "This is no time to tell me your life story," she said.

"I hadn't planned to," I said. "It's just—"

"Robert," said Nina Thatcher, "I really don't want to hear. I am your partner in crime. I am your friend. But I don't want to hear about your past, okay? All I want to hear is the tape."

"Of course," I said. "Sure," I said, and went to get it.

We had problems with the tape. The conversation had been halting at first. Mark did not trust Nina. I had the feeling that he didn't like anyone female who might remind him of his mother. But Nina was good. She didn't press the kid. She kept the conversation general. She told him about her own background, about her own childhood and parents. She ignored my warning looks and opened up to Mark. I could never deal with a source like that. But Nina did, and it worked.

The conversation was convoluted. Sometimes it even became hysterical. But the kid cracked. He talked, willingly, openly, freely to us. And afterward Nina and I sat with two legal pads, scribbling as the sounds played back over my cassette deck. Often we reran sections. Sometimes we sat, listening for ten to fifteen minutes at a time as the conversation ran on inanely. But there were nuggets. Good nuggets. Stuff that stories are built of.

"... my mother," Mark's voice said. "My mother's going to kill me when all this comes out."

"No, she won't," Nina Thatcher said. "Believe me, Mark. It'll be all right."

"Do you really think so?" he asked.

"I do. And if you need me, I'll be there," she said.

Mark sniffled. "Thank you, Miss Thatcher," he said.

"What about your father?" Nina Thatcher asked.

"My stepfather," Mark's voice said. "He doesn't give a damn, you know. I mean, after my real father died, my mom took over the business. When she married my stepfather, he went to work for her. They always spend time together. I guess I was on my own a lot."

"You spent a lot of time on the streets?" I asked.

"Sure," he said. "When I was twelve, I had, um, relations with a man for the first time. Excuse me, Miss Thatcher."

"It's all right," she said. "I know this is hard for you. But you can trust us. Just be as open as you can be. Robert and I are here to help."

Mark said, "I dug it, you know. I mean, I had always felt kind of different. I didn't know what it was. Just different, you know. I used to hate the showers after gym class. I'd always been small for my age, and the other guys were flicking towels at me and stuff. They used to hold my head under the shower. It was real bogue. The pits."

I said, "Tell me about Larry, Mark."

Nina Thatcher cut in. "What about the first time, Mark?" she asked.

Mark looked at her. "It was in a movie," he said. "A guy came up to me in a movie theater, and he put his hand on my leg. I kind of liked it. It was exciting, you know. Then he moved his hand up, you know. And I got an erection. I never thought that a guy could give you an erection. Anyway, he did. He just sat there and touched me. It wasn't bad—I mean, I didn't feel bad about it or anything. I was even kind of relieved because all the other kids were talking about hard-ons, and I was small, you know, and I guessed I was shy, or backwards, or something."

He looked at Nina Thatcher. "That isn't bad, is it?"

"No," she said. "No, Mark."

"I guess after that I just knew that I was different," Mark said. "I never said anything to anybody. I knew my mom would kill me. She's always talking about how she's living for when she has grandchildren, you know. So I never say anything. Sometimes I really wish that I could just shout it out at her, you know. 'Hey, I'm queer, and you're not gonna have any grandchildren.' But I can't do that, I just can't. I guess that's why I spend a lot of time outside the house, you know, like at Larry's place."

Nina looked at me. A slight nod. "Tell me about Larry," I said.

"Larry's great," Mark said. "I met him two years ago. He was selling pills at school, you know, and he looked at me."

"Looked at you?" Nina Thatcher interrupted.

"The eyes," said Mark. "Gay people look at each other. It's a look. You look, and you know. It's something you just know."

"What does the look mean?" asked Nina Thatcher.

"I guess it comes down to sex," Mark said. "Like, are you available? Will you sleep with me?"

"Oh," Nina Thatcher said.

"This is hard," Mark said. "I used to talk to Jack about this stuff. It's like real different to put into words. It's all feelings, you know."

"Try," I said. "Try."

Nina Thatcher said, "Just talk, Mark. It'll feel better. I promise you. There's nothing I haven't heard before. Really, you're not going to shock me."

"Promise?" Mark looked at Nina Thatcher.

"I promise," said Nina Thatcher. "If you catch me blushing, you can stop."

"So Larry had the eyes, you know. And we talked. And he invited me over to his place, you know, and then we, um, went to bed together."

"That day?" I asked.

"No, about a week later," Mark said.

"Anyhow," Mark continued, "Larry let me use his house. And sometimes he'd take me to clubs. Private clubs, you know. And I didn't like being at home, so Larry let me stay with him. He has a beautiful house. Incredible, you know. But Larry was weird, too.

My voice: "How come?"

Mark said, "He was into rough stuff, you know."

Nina Thatcher asked, "Rough stuff?"

"He liked violence," said Mark. "Sometimes he'd hit me. Not hard or anything. But he's hit me. Once by mistake he chipped a tooth." Mark pointed to an incisor. A small corner of it was missing. "I thought Jack would kill him for that."

"How did Jack meet Larry?" I asked.

"I don't know," Mark said. "Yes, I do. Jack told me. It was in a club."

"I see," I said.

"Jack was incredible," Mark said. "He understood me. He really loved me, you know. He'd say like 'You want to be held, don't you?' And I did want to be held, you know. He knew that. Making love with him was something special. It really was. He was so gentle, you know."

"Were you gentle with him?" I asked.

"He didn't like that," Mark said. "I mean, he liked to be inside me. But he never let me be, you know, in him." The kid looked at Nina Thatcher. She hadn't blinked. She sat there, still. But when Mark looked away, she swallowed hard.

"What did Larry do for Jack?" Nina Thatcher asked.

"Mostly sold him dope, I think," said Mark. "They didn't go to bed a lot, I don't think. Not after Jack met me anyway. But Jack was funny about Larry. He used to tell me that Larry had some exciting friends—you know, the rough guys. I already knew that, though."

"How did you know that?" I asked.

"It was just after I met Jack," Mark said. "I owed Larry about fifty bucks. I mean, he let me stay at his place and everything, but he never gave me any dope free, you know. He used to tell me that business was business. Anyway, I owed Larry this money, and he said I could pay it off by sleeping with one of his friends—a guy he owed a favor to."

"What did you think?" Nina Thatcher said. "How did you feel about that, Mark?"

"I don't know," Mark said. "You know, like I wasn't an innocent kid, you know. I mean, I've done it for money before."

"You have?" Nina Thatcher lit a cigarette.

"It's called tricking," Mark said. "Yeah—I've tricked. But not a lot, you know. I mean, it wasn't a constant thing, you know."

We nodded.

"So I said okay because I figured it was an easy way to pay Larry off, you know. So we drive over to Highland Park, you know, and go to the Hotel Orleans. And there's this guy. Murray Fast, Larry calls him. Murray Fast. The thing I remember is how his ears stuck out from his head. And he had all

this frizzy hair, like very thin, you know, and he had this little mustache, too.

"But mainly he smelled. Like his room hadn't been cleaned up in ten years, you know. And it smelled real bad, and Larry knocked on the door and said go in, and I went in, and it was a real downer, you know. And Murray Fast is lying there, and he says to me to turn the lock on the door, and his pants are open, you know, and he's rubbing his thing and looking at me. And he says, 'Come here,' and he's running his tongue all over his mustache, you know, and saying that I look like a nice piece of ass. So then he gets up from the bed. He's all dressed, see, in this weird velvet suit with lapels out to here, you know, and he has to shave his eyebrows, you know, because they looked all funny and narrow. He looks like the kind of guy who, when they don't shave, they have one big eyebrow all across their foreheads, you know, and his thing is sticking out of his pants, you know. The room smells real bad, too, and I say maybe I better go because I can trick at a bar or something and pay Larry the fifty. But then he gets between me and the door, and he locks it himself.

"Then he takes off his clothes. I didn't want to, Mr. Mandel. You know, I really wanted to get out of there. But he's like locked the door, and when I don't do anything, he drops his pants, and he's standing there in his shirt and his jacket, and his little skinny legs with no hair, and I see he's dirty around the ankles.

"He says, 'I'm going to be gentle with you,' you know. Well, I know he's not gonna hurt me because his thing's too small, you know. But jeez, you know, he tried to make me suck it, you know. I got so sick I threw up. I was crying and everything, and asking him please to let me go, and he says he wants to show me his whips, and when he walks into his closet, you know. I push the door shut and slam a chair in front of it, and I run out of the room—I didn't even have all my clothes or anything, but I got the hell out of there and hitched to Jack's place, and Jack gave me the money for Larry and took a shower with me and let me spend the night."

"What did Jack say?" I asked.

"Nothing," Mark said. "He didn't say anything. I told him what happened, and he dried my eyes and kissed me, but he didn't really say anything."

"Do you know why?" Nina Thatcher's voice asked. It sounded hollow.

"Not right then," Mark said.

"But later Larry told me that Jack knew Murray Fast."

"Oh," I said.

"Larry told me that Jack and Larry and Murray Fast once tricked together," Mark said. "Larry laughed about it, you know. He said that Jack liked weirdness. I couldn't understand that because Jack was, you know, so kind to me."

"Who were some of Larry's other friends?" I asked.

"I don't know," said Mark's voice. "Miss Thatcher, could I please have some more cocoa?"

"Sure," said Nina Thatcher's voice. "And what about some cookies?"

"Yeah," said Mark. "Cookies, too."

"Do you remember some of Larry's other friends?" I said again.

"Sure. There was a guy named Al who used to come by. And another named Tony, and Phil and Bosco, you know. They all score dope from Larry, regular."

"Did Jack know any of them?" I asked.

"Thanks for the cocoa, Miss Thatcher," Mark said. "Sure," he said.

There was a pause here in the tape. Then Mark yawned. "Listen," he said. "I'm really tired, you know."

"It's been a long day," Nina Thatcher said.

"Can I go to bed? I'm really tired, you know."

Nina Thatcher's voice was positively motherly. "Come on, Mark," she said. "I'll tuck you in. Go brush your teeth."

There was another silence on the tape. Then Nina Thatcher's voice: *"Caramba!"*

"Wait a couple of minutes," my voice said. "Put him to bed first. And don't forget to bring his wallet out here."

"I am going to change into something comfortable after he's out for the night," said Nina Thatcher. "Do you have a shirt I can borrow?"

"Sure," I said. "How do you feel about blue button-down?"

"Exquisite," Nina Thatcher said. "Just so long as it isn't starched."

"*Jamais,*" said my voice. "Is he asleep? I'm going to switch the machine off."

chapter 13_____

A lot of role playing goes on in my trade. Some reporters, for example, "Columbo" when they do interviews. They ask silly questions, appear disorganized, and are endlessly repetitive in their inquiries. Often the subjects get so exasperated that they divulge all sorts of goodies. Others—Juliet Walker is an example—sometimes come on like naïfs. I can remember watching one evening as Juliet met with a certain bagman from the trucking industry. She actually looked at him with her big brown eyes and with absolute innocence said, "Skimming? What's skimming?" And he told her precisely what skimming is and how, specifically, he had collected more than $300,000 in skimmed money from the purchasing department of the Ford Motor Company.

Then there's outright impersonation. A friend of mine in Washington often calls people from his press cubicle at the White House and tells them, "This is so-and-so calling from the White House." He is technically correct. Another of my colleagues keeps a white doctor's coat and stethoscope in his car. When he has to interview someone in a hospital, he puts them on so that people will think he belongs. He never

says he's a doctor, of course; he merely looks like one. When I had to get into a local TV station, I simply picked up a coil of electrical cable and carried it past the security guard.

In narcotics reporting there are all sorts of characters to impersonate. I have pimp clothes, addict's clothes, and bum's clothes. My street look was developed after weeks of cruising the neighborhoods in which I was going to work. One of my rules is always to look as if you belong. It keeps you healthy.

Our competition has a narcotics reporter. He does his job in a three-piece suit. He doesn't do very well. Last year he attempted to write a series on the abuse of methadone. The simp actually walked up to some addict outside a methadone clinic and asked if he could score some methadone. The junkie looked him over and said, sure, meet me in an alley in five minutes. When my distinguished competitor showed up, he was confronted by three spades with knives, who took his money, his press card, his three-piece suit, his shoes, and his socks. They did not, needless to say, give him any methadone.

Undaunted, he went back to the paper and wrote an article about what it is like to be ripped off by three junkies. When I read it, I went home and changed clothes. Then I visited the methadone clinic he had written about, scored fifty bucks' worth of the stuff, and had it messengered over to him with my compliments. He hasn't spoken to me since. It is no loss.

I knew after Nina Thatcher and I ran the tape we had made with Mark that I would have to pay a call on some of the people the kid had talked about. The question was which of them to see and what cover to use. Obviously the key was Larry. But Mark had been adamant about not giving us Larry's last name or address. On the other hand, he had said that Murray Fast lived at the Hotel Orleans in Highland Park. It was as good a place to start as any. I decided to play a little head game with Murray. So I left Nina Thatcher with Mark and drove home to my place, where I took the .38 Air-weight from my closet safe and slipped it into a shoulder holster. Then from my dresser I plucked a Detroit police

shield and put it on my belt. It is a real detective's shield, given to me by a cop who owed me a big favor. He reported it as lost and was issued a replacement. I have never said that I am a cop when I use it. Nor do I have a counterfeit police identity card. In many situations, when people are nervous, a quick flash of gun and shield are sufficient to create the right impression, if you adopt an aggressive personality.

So, feeling like Kojak, I drove to Highland Park and found the Hotel Orleans. I parked the Bug around the corner—there is no use coming on like a cop if you climb out of a Volkswagen—and sauntered inside. The lobby was deserted. It was near midnight. I rang the service bell and waited. Finally the office door behind the desk opened, and a sleepy middle-aged man came out.

"I have something for Murray Fast," I said.

"Three-twelve," the man said, and disappeared back into his office. There would be no call upstairs. There was also no elevator. It was a walk-up hotel, one of those places the city likes to stash welfare cases. There was mildew and peeling wallpaper, and I went up three flights of stairs with decaying risers to find Murray's room. I unzipped my windbreaker so the Airweight would be obvious when Murray looked at me. The detective's shield was on my belt, at my hip. The only thing not showing was my Nagra body recorder, safe in its jockstrap.

I hit Murray's door with my fist five times. "Hey," I said. I said it loud. "Hey, Murray." There was no response.

I hit the door again. "Open up, you shithead," I yelled. Two other doors cracked; two sets of eyes looked at me. I turned toward them, flashing shield and pistol. "Get the hell back inside," I said. "This is business," I said.

The doors closed. I pounded for Murray again. "Open up, you asshole," I called. When you play a cop, aggressiveness, I have found, is the key. Let the subject call you Mr. Mandel, for example. You call him nothing but Murray or whatever his first name is. It creates an inferior-superior relationship from the beginning.

The lock on Murray's door turned over, and it cracked open. "Who is it?" a voice inside asked.

I didn't answer. I hit the door with the flat of my hand and barged inside. I closed the door in back of me and stood against it. I made sure he saw the shield and the pistol and then closed the windbreaker halfway. I did not want him remembering a badge number.

Murray stood there in a pair of filthy boxer shorts and gray T-shirt. The room was fetid and messy. He looked at me wide-eyed and started to say something. I pointed a finger at him and said, "Not a word, scumbag." I peered around the room. "What a shithole!" I said.

There was movement in the iron-framed double bed. "Whoever's in the bed get your ass out of there," I said.

A nappy black head appeared. The head of a child with the face of an old man. Its eyes were wide with fright. "Get your ass out of the fucking bed," I said. Murray started to move. "You freeze," I said. "You put your hands behind your head, and don't even think about breathing."

I was role-playing then. But as I looked at Murray, sorry, disheveled Murray and his ten-year-old paramour, it wasn't hard to play the role at all. I was a cop who hated faggots. I looked Murray up and down. I thought about what Mark had said. That Jack had tricked with Murray and Larry. I thought about Jack's well-groomed body, Jack's lovely apartment, Jack's expensive paintings. The secrets I had shared with Jack. At that moment I did not find it hard to hate faggots. Not hard at all.

"Get your pickaninny ass out of the bed," I said.

The kid climbed out. He stood naked, scared, confused.

"Where are your clothes?" I said. The kid pointed to a pile on the floor. He couldn't have been more than ten or eleven. He didn't say a word. It was cold in the room, and his black body had a grayish cast to it. "Get your clothes on, and get the fuck out of here," I said.

Murray started to move. I walked over to him and pushed him onto the bed. I am neither big nor powerful, but because I was in command of the situation, I could do damn well what I pleased. Besides, Murray was a small man. An aging queen of perhaps fifty with spindly, hairless legs, patchy hair dyed an awful brown, and a sunken chest. His

135

mustache, which ran the length of his upper lip, was thin in spots. His lips were broken and cracked. He had hair growing out of his ears. "Put your hands on your chest," I said. He did. There was dirt under the fingernails, grime worked into the knuckle creases.

The kid edged toward the door. I moved with him and cuffed the back of his head as he left. "If I ever see you again, I'll blow your fucking face off," I said. "Now get the hell out of here," I said. I locked the door and leaned against it.

I looked at Murray, who resembled a corpse with his hands folded across his chest. "Oh, we are in trouble," I said. "We are in big trouble, Murray."

Murray stared at the ceiling. "Who are you?" he asked. "Who the hell are you?"

"Who the hell do you think I am," I said. "I am Snow White, and you are one of the Seven Dwarfs. You are Scumbag the Dwarf."

"Come on," said Murray.

"Oh, Murray," I said. "Think about it. I pay a nice social call, and I find you in bed with a ten-year-old. That's endangering the morals of a minor, Murray. That is not pandering or soliciting; that is a violation of PM three-fifty-A; that is a felony, Murray." I didn't know what the hell I was talking about. On the other hand, neither, probably, did Murray.

"We got sodomy here, Murray," I said. "You are a dirty person."

"What do you want?" Murray asked. "What the hell do you want?" A whining quality slipped into his voice. On the streets Murray would be more the victim than the victimizer. There was an obvious weakness to the man. It could be played upon.

"Let's talk about, oh, Jack Fowler," I said.

Murray's eyes went wide.

"You recognize the name," I said. "Good. That's a start."

"Who told you guys?" Murray sat up. "I didn't have anything to do with it. I don't know nothing."

I moved across the room and stood over the bed.

"Bullshit," I said.

"Nothing," Murray said. "I swear."

"Oh, Murray," I said. "You are a pitiful asshole. A sorry scumbag if ever I saw a sorry scumbag. And you lie so badly, Murray." Now it was my turn to lie. "Larry says you know everything."

"He's lying," said Murray. "I don't know nothing. All I did was trick with him—Fowler—a couple of times. We had a ménage, him and Larry and me. Larry said Jack wanted someone to piss on—I like that sometimes. It was no big thing. I just tricked with him and let him piss on me."

"You killed him," I said. "You learned about Fowler and his stories, and you killed him," I said. "Yes, you did, Murray. I know you did." I pulled the Airweight out of the holster. If it had been loaded, I probably could have pulled the trigger. I cocked it and pushed the muzzle just under Murray's ear. I was sweating; I could feel it under my arms. I was mad as hell.

"No," Murray said. He looked up at me, pleading. His eyes brimmed with tears. He smelled awful. His teeth were yellow-gray; the upper left front had been badly chipped.

I uncocked the pistol. "Get me your wallet," I said. Murray scrambled out of the bed and went to his dresser. He took a thick billfold out of the top drawer. He handed it to me. "Get back on the bed," I said. "Lie down," I said.

"Can I cover up?" Murray said. "I'm cold."

"Fuck you, asshole," I said. "You stay on top."

I started to go through the wallet. There was not much money. But there were other things. Receipts, food stamps, and a small imitation leather address book. I turned my back and slipped the book into my trouser pocket.

"Tell me about Jack Fowler," I said. I threw Murray's wallet under the bed. I leaned against the door. "Tell me," I said.

"I met him through Larry," Murray said. "Larry said he had this friend who liked a little rough stuff now and then," Murray said. "Larry told me he could arrange something and I'd make some money. I met Jack at Larry's, and the three of us did a little rough-and-tumble, you know, that's it."

"There's more," I said.

"No, really," Murray said. "Larry and Jack tied me up, and Larry did some bondage stuff, nothing real heavy, and then

Jack came in and saw me tied to the bed, and then he got undressed, and Larry oiled him up, and Jack rolled around on me, and I sucked his cock, and then he pissed in my mouth, and then he fucked Larry on top of me while I was tied down. Really, that's all."

"How many times did that happen?"

"Two. Three. Three times."

"How much did you make?"

"Fifty bucks," Murray said. "And Jack bought me a dozen amyls one time from Larry."

"And what did you know about Fowler?"

"Nothing, I swear," Murray said. "Nothing. Larry told me that he was a rich guy looking for kicks, is all. I didn't know he was a reporter until the stories came out, I swear. I never even knew where he lived, you know.

"Hey, man, come on, give me a break, you know. I'm being straight with you."

I looked at Murray. "You're being what, asshole?" I said. "You couldn't be straight with your dick. I've got a good mind to take you downtown and beat the shit out of you—except you'd probably like it, scumbag."

"No," said Murray. "I can't take another bust, you know. Hey, I'm on probation now."

"And I catch you with a kid, huh, Murray?"

"Look, what do you want? You know, there's two pimps upstairs. They got eight-year-olds. Hey, they're on the fifth floor. Five-oh-eight and five-oh-three. They're tricking like crazy. What about it, huh? You take 'em. Just leave me alone, okay?"

I didn't want the pimps upstairs. What I wanted I already had in my pocket. Murray's address book. If he had noticed me palm it, he hadn't said anything. I walked over to the bed where Murray lay. He was shivering, his bony knees quivering like a nervous dog's. "Okay, scumbag," I said. "I'm gonna let you off the hook this time." I took his ears and held them like mug handles. I pulled his face close to mine. He had blackheads all over his nose; his Adam's apple bobbled nervously. That face sucking Jack's— It was unbelievable.

"I am going to keep an eye on you, Murray," I said. "I am going to watch you very, very closely from now on. And the next time I catch you with an underage piece of ass I am going to plug your sphincter with hot lead and put a hatpin through your cock. In other words, Murray, I am going to take you out of the the pederast business." I shoved Murray's head backward. The top of his skull grazed the bed's iron frame.

"Ow," he protested.

I put a finger to my lips. "I thought you liked being hurt," I said. I moved toward the door. "See you around, scumbag."

————

I was still shaking as I climbed into the Bug. I decided against going directly back to the corporate apartment. Mark was asleep and would stay that way for another eight hours. Nina Thatcher needed her rest. And I wanted to have some time alone. Well, not exactly alone. I drove to my apartment and rummaged through the files, looking through some of the tapes Jack and I had made. I pride myself on being able to read people. It is my stock-in-trade. I am hard to bluff at the poker table. But Jack had bluffed me. I had loved him, and he had lied.

There is a scene in *The French Connection* in which Gene Hackman, playing a hard-nosed cop, trails two suspects—French dope smugglers—through New York City. The pair end up at a classy restaurant called Copain, which is slang for pal. You can see them through the window, ordering a really sybaritic meal. Meanwhile, there's Hackman across the street in a doorway, shifting his weight from foot to foot in the same kind of standing-in-place dance cops have done for generations. He is cold, and he is hungry. And he watches the pair of high-living dealers with increasing hatred. And at that point in the movie you see in Hackman's eyes that he's going to get them. Not because they are smuggling heroin. Not because they are breaking the law. He'll get them because they are sitting in Copain, sitting on soft leather, drinking vintage wine and eating a $100 meal, while he is outside, his feet freezing, eating cold pizza and slurping a

soggy paper cup of dishwater-thin coffee. He hates them for what they have and he doesn't, and he'll get them for it.

Driving back from the Hotel Orleans, shivering not from the cold but Murray Fast, I hated Jack in much the same way. For having all the advantages and not using them. For betraying himself and me. For lying to us both. I hated Jack during that drive. Hated him like a six-year-old whose best friend won't play fair. And like a six-year-old, I swore revenge.

"It's complicated." Jack's voice came over my earphones. I had taken one of the tapes, a tape made a year before—made at about the time Jack had tricked with Murray Fast and Larry—and put it on my big cassette deck. The stereo speakers had been switched off, and Jack's voice, running through a one-hundred-watt amp, played inside my head.

"It's complicated," he was saying.

"What is?" my voice asked.

"My problem," said Jack's voice. My transcript noted that the tape had been made in my apartment on a Sunday night. Jack had just returned, he said, from a trip to New York.

"Nothing's simple," said my voice on the tape.

"I know," Jack had said.

"So?"

"It's just," Jack said, "it's just that I'm finding it harder and harder to deal with myself. To make the transitions. Straight to gay. Gay to straight."

"Aha," said my voice. "Classic identity crisis. A schizo. Quick, Doctor, the lithium."

"Don't make fun of me," Jack said. "Please, Robert."

"I'm sorry." I had been sorry, too. It was not, I remember thinking at the time, something to be dealt with lightly.

"What brought this on?" I asked. Playing back the tape that night, I remembered how we had been. We were lying head to head, sharing a four-foot-square pillow in the middle of my living room. From above, our bodies looked like six o'clock on a watch, the tape machine the hub from which we extended. Jack had a glass of wine balanced on his chest.

"I had a bad weekend," he said. "I met somebody," he said. "I like him," he said.

"Oh," I said. "What's he like?"

"This has never happened before," Jack's voice said. "Relationships are always so transient, you know. Three glorious days in New York. Nights in the clubs; cruising the bars. You really should come with me sometime, Robert. Especially the leather bars. Just for the experience. I think you'd dig it."

"I don't think I'm ready," I said.

"No, you'd really dig it," Jack said. "It's kinetic as hell."

"I get enough kineticism buying dope," I said. "That's all the catharsis I need right now."

"This weekend was different," Jack's voice said. "Really different." He paused for a while. The tape hissed, even though I had the Dolby switched on.

His voice picked up again. "I was in a club—the name doesn't matter—and I met a friend. Someone I saw last month. Do you have any dope? I'd really like a joint, you know."

"I'll see what's around," I had said. I could hear myself get up. My voice called from the kitchen. "Nothing special today. Street reefer okay?"

"Sure," Jack's voice called back, "if that's all you've got."

My voice got stronger. "Here."

"Thanks, Robert." Another pause, followed by a whistling intake of breath. "Not bad," Jack said, "for ordinary shit, except it's got something of a bite to it."

"Maybe I should use filters," I said.

"Aren't you smoking?"

"No," I said. "The wine's enough right now."

"I met this guy," Jack's voice said. He said it while he was holding his breath in. It came out with a whoosh. "And we went back to his place, you know, and he had a friend over visiting. Somebody younger, you know. Not a kid or anything, I'm not into that, you know, but just somebody younger than we are."

I ran the tape section again. He was doing it. Unmistakably. He had been talking to me in Mark's speech pattern. All those "you knows." Jack hadn't talked like that. Jack had al-

ways prided himself on his speech. The Savannah accent had been whittled away, then melded with the flat tones of Princeton and the nasal drawl of Oxford. Jack had always been precise with words. He did not, like so many others, "um" and "hum" and "er" and "uh." He spoke in sentences, most of the time, and thought in paragraphs. Why hadn't I seen it? He was talking like a sixteen-year-old.

I hadn't seen a thing. I hadn't been listening, back then. "And so," I had asked, "what happened?"

"The physical attraction was immediate, both ways," Jack's voice said. "And my friend, you know, wasn't in love with this guy or anything. It was just like a friendship, you know. So we sat around and had some wine and smoked a little dope and listened to some music, you know, and my friend's friend's head, you know, is on my shoulder all of a sudden, and he kisses me on the neck, really soft, you know, and runs his hand under my shirt. Robert, it was magic time. I mean, this guy has incredibly sensitive hands.

"So we get up to dance, you know, me and my friend's friend, and my friend puts on Georges Moustaki—the real slow stuff. And we're dancing close, you know. He's got his hands in the back pockets of my jeans, and I can feel him hard up against me, you know."

"What's that like?" I asked.

"Like dancing with somebody with a cucumber in his shorts," Jack said.

"Is that a pickle in your pocket or are you just glad to see me?" I said.

"Mae West," Jack said. "When the music stopped, we kept dancing. I couldn't take my hands off him. He was so soft, you know.

"We went on like that for a couple of hours, dancing and kissing and talking, you know. And my hand was touching him, and he was touching me, like we were holding hands on the dance floor rubbing each other, you know."

"I think this is making me uneasy," my voice said.

"I'm sorry," said Jack Fowler. "Do you feel threatened or something?"

"No," I said. "Uneasy. I've never heard you talk like this

before. It sounds like you were with some lady, you know."

"Different altogether," said Jack's voice. "Robert, a woman never made me feel like this."

"Why?"

"That's why it's so fucking complicated," his voice said. "I think I had a pretty normal childhood for a screwed-up kid. My father is successful, although he married into the business. But he runs it well, you know. My mother's kind of the forceful one, though. She likes to be important, you know. So she's always running charity affairs and pushing my father into new clubs, and between them they have a full life. Maybe it's not the happiest, but it's as full as hell. So my brother and I were always left on our own. We had somebody to look after us, of course. An English nanny. And I always thought of our lives as pretty normal. Except for the fact that my brother and I didn't have very many friends. Not more than two or three that my mother thought suitable, you know.

"Anyway, I remember when I was about thirteen and Teddy was seven. I'd just begun to masturbate—it was an adventure then—and I remember going into the bathroom to lock myself in and play a little one-on-one, and I opened the top of the john, and there was a used sanitary napkin. The water was pink from the blood. I'd never seen something like that before. I knew about menstruation and periods, of course. But I'd never seen a used Kotex, you know.

"So I jerked off into the bowl, and wiped up after myself, and flushed everything away.

"But you know, I never was able to look my nanny in the eye again. I knew something about her, you know. I had seen her blood, you know, and it was like she was less than human after that, you know."

There was a pause on the tape. Then Jack Fowler's voice said, "It's hard for me to deal with women. I like going to bed with women, Robert. But I always feel dirty afterward. Like they've stained me or something. It's always been that way."

Jack took a long drag on his reefer. "It felt so, so clean, with my friend's friend, you know." He let the smoke out of

his lungs slowly. "Yet here I am, a grown-up adult, you know, with a job and a career and a family, who expect me to get married and raise kids, you know. And part of me wants that badly, Robert. Really. But there's another part of me that doesn't want it at all. There is a piece of me that would like to move to New York and live on Christopher Street and find a lover and live happily ever after.

"Except," Jack's voice said. "Except that I could never do that. It would kill my mother. And besides, there's the job here. If I didn't have the courts to cover, I think I'd go crazy. When I'm sitting there, when I'm interviewing, then I know who the hell I am. Other times I'm not so sure, you know."

I switched the cassette deck off. I looked at the transcript I had been reading as the sound played into my head. It all became so clear. Jack hadn't gone to New York. Jack hadn't met some friend of a friend in New York. He had been at a club here, in Detroit, with Larry, and had gone back to Larry's place, where he had met Mark. And then he took Mark home with him. But he couldn't tell me that—not then, not ever. And I had trusted Jack enough to take him at his word. My trust had betrayed me. He'd been talking like a teenager, and I had never seen it.

*chapter 14*_____

I stood under the shower for more than an hour after I played back Jack's cassette. It gave me time to think about what I was going to have to write, and I had to write with a clear head. Often we have guilts, recriminations about the stories we write. Nagging guilts about what our words are going to do to the people we write about. Not during the writing process, but afterward: in the short space between the time the copy books go to the editor and the time they appear in print. That space of time is the worst, a lacuna in which nothing can be done, nothing happens. In that gap comes the worrying. Are the facts right? Are the sources accurately quoted? Is the thrust correct?

Once it is visible, in print, the gnawing doubts vanish. It is real. The story is in black and white. It cannot be withdrawn. But before, before it rolls off the press, before is a bad time. There have been nights I waited at the loading dock to grab a copy of the hot-from-the-press paper just to make sure that what I had written was real, was really in type. I've always been that way. Nancy used to tell me I was overreacting. I remember a series of mine in Los Angeles about Beverly Hills restaurants and their use of illegal immigrants.

It was, I thought, a real heartbreaker. Mexicans paid a few cents an hour by plush establishments because the owners knew their employees couldn't complain to anyone. I named names. I told horror stories. It was a good series. But in the interval between the time I handed in part one and the time it appeared—no more than eight hours—I never stopped pacing, calling my editor, worrying about how the story would look.

Nancy couldn't understand why I acted in what she called a childish way. "It's a good piece," she said. "It's so good that one of the networks will probably rip it off."

She didn't understand my feeling of helplessness, of doubt, of worry. The qualms that only other reporters would know about. The paranoid conviction that you have really screwed things up and have gotten the facts completely wrong, that you have not made that last phone call, and that you, and your paper, are going to be sued by someone who is actually justified. It is a horrible feeling and can be quashed only by your seeing the article in print. Once you see it, you know you're okay, that your sources are straight, that your facts are right. The story has its own life.

After my shower I replayed the tape I had made at Murray Fast's hotel room. I also played the tapes of Mark. Then I took Jack's files and spread them out on the floor of my living room. I rolled a sheet of paper into the typewriter and began to type. The writing process is something like a religious experience in that it cannot be defined. Once the facts are known, once the quotes have lodged themselves inside your head, once the parameters are blocked out, there remains only communion between writer and machine. How, exactly, stories get written I do not know. Perhaps it is a form of temporary madness. It is the only facet of my job in which there are no rules. Or nothing but rules. Who, what, where, when, how. . . .

So I wrote myself a memo, telling whom Jack had been associated with, what he had been doing, where he had been doing it, when he had been doing it, and how. Ten books—two thousand words. I built sentence upon sentence, paragraph onto paragraph—I do not know how—and

three hours later took my ten pages of copy, put them inside a manila folder, and drove back to the corporate apartment.

Nina Thatcher whistled as she read. My Nagra captured it.

"Jesus," she said. "Do you think they'll print it?"

"Yeah," I said. "They'll print it. It's true."

"How do you feel?"

"I don't know," I said. "We gotta tell the story."

"But this is a family newspaper," Nina Thatcher said. "I'm just kidding, Robert."

"No, you're not."

"How do you feel?" she asked.

"Not good."

"I mean about Jack?"

"That's what I said," I said. "Not good."

"But—"

"He lied," I said. "He lied to me. Do you know what that makes me feel like? I told him things. I didn't lie to him. I told him things, and he made tapes, and now Jerry Daley has the tapes, and he probably knows more about me than I do. The only good part of it is that I made more tapes than Jack did. I have a couple of dozen; Jack didn't tape more than five or six times."

"Robert." Nina Thatcher put the manuscript on her lap. "Robert, I've never asked you this, but did you tape the night you and Jack and I played our little game?"

"No," I said. "I wasn't into big-scale taping then."

"But you are now."

"Yes."

"Are you taping this?"

"Yes," I said.

"Why?" Nina Thatcher asked. Nancy would have asked the same question.

"Because," I said.

"That's no answer."

"Yes, it is," I said. "Records have to be kept."

"Why?"

"If I hadn't kept records of what Jack and I said, I wouldn't have the story you're clutching in your lovely hands," I said.

"That's not enough," Nina Thatcher said.

"It is for me."

"Are you wired?" Nina Thatcher asked. "How are you wired?"

"Nagra," I said. I stood up, undid my belt, started to unzip my fly.

"Hold it," Nina Thatcher said.

I turned my back. "Sorry." I reached into the cup supporter and pulled out the Nagra. "See?" I held it above my head. Then I replaced it and zipped up again.

"That's gotta be very uncomfortable," Nina Thatcher said.

"You get used to it."

"I think you need professional help," said Nina Thatcher.

"I think you should let me have my story back," I said. "How's Mark?"

"Still sleeping," Nina Thatcher said.

"It's just as well. Whatever happens, don't let him see the paper when it's delivered."

"You know," said Nina Thatcher, "I'm getting pretty tired of sitting here playing nursemaid to a kid."

"We need Mark for another day or so," I said.

"Then what?"

"Then we give him to Jerry Daley."

There was a cry from the bedroom. Nina Thatcher and I stood up and walked back to where Mark lay sleeping. He was bundled under the covers in a fetal position, clutching at a pillow as if it were a teddy bear. He looked very young and vulnerable. He was breathing hard, irregularly. He was not resting well. Nina Thatcher stroked his forehead.

"He's so pretty," she said.

"He likes guys," I said. Mark's arm moved around the pillow, and his thumb entered his mouth. He moaned. "He's probably dreaming about Jack."

Nina Thatcher hit me in the small of my back. "Bastard," she said. "Shit," she said. She pulled me by my shirt sleeve toward the living room.

We were halfway there when Mark called out again. "Oh, God," he said distinctly.

"He *is* dreaming about Jack, the little cocksucker," I said. I turned back toward the bedroom.

Mark was sitting up in bed. He was awake. "Help me," he said. "Oh, help me." There were tears in his eyes. I watched him in the half-light. Nina Thatcher came from behind and pushed me away. She went to Mark.

"It's all right," she said. "Mark, it's all right." She looked at me. "He's feverish," she said. "Get me a washcloth."

I got one. She wiped Mark's forehead. She held him and rocked him. "It's all right," she said over and over. She laid Mark's head on the pillow. "Just a nightmare," she said. "Nasty old nightmare. It's all gone." She looked at me.

"I'll stay with you for a while, Mark," she said. "I'll stay with you."

I walked into the living room and sat down. After ten minutes or so Nina Thatcher came out. She was holding the damp washcloth. "He's asleep," she said. "I don't know what it was. A bad nightmare maybe," she said. "Can't we send him home?"

"We all have them," I said. "With his life I'm surprised he can sleep at all."

"Mr. Big Heart," Nina Thatcher said. "Mr. Nice Guy." She threw the washcloth at my head. "Let's send him home."

"We can't," I said. "We need him. He gave me Murray Fast. Murray leads me to Larry. Maybe, just maybe, Larry will lead me to Scotty or some other pimp or to some of the kids. If we're lucky, we'll beat the Animal to the story. If the Animal gets hold of Mark, he'll squeeze him like a tube of toothpaste in a couple of hours. Then who'll have the story? Not us."

"I never did well in aggression at J-school," Nina Thatcher said. "Maybe that's why I like being in features so much. We don't bother people. We don't sell them out. We don't trade them in like poker cards."

"I'm sorry you don't like what I do."

"I didn't say that," Nina Thatcher said. "I said—"

"You don't like what I do. Okay, you don't. That's fair. Well, sometimes I don't like what I do either. But it's got to be done."

"Why?" Nina Thatcher dropped herself into a chair.

"Because," I said.

"That's no answer."

"It's the perfect answer," I said. "You do what you have to do to get the story. It's not how you feel that's important; it's the story. Hey, how do you think some public defenders feel when they've got to stand up in court for a scumbag who's just raped a six-year-old? Their feelings aren't important; the defense is."

"But that's a constitutional right," said Nina Thatcher. "A defense."

"So's the First Amendment," I said. "Look, I can't go into this now. I've got a story to finish. I've got a deadline."

"It doesn't make sense," said Nina Thatcher.

"I'll explain it to you later. Mike needs the piece now. Look, just trust me and keep the kid under wraps until I get back. We need one more session with him."

"Then we give him to the cops," Nina Thatcher said. "We ruin his life for him."

"The kid's life is already ruined," I said. "I've got to go."

"Finish this out," said Nina Thatcher. "You're running away from an argument."

God, she sounded like Nancy just then.

She picked up my story and shook it at me. "Here is an article about the man you call your best friend. In it you describe—in what I would call graphic detail—an assignation between him and the child who is sleeping in the next room. You know what an assignation is, Robert? It is a dirty meeting. I won't characterize the prose as lurid because it isn't. But it is, shall we say, picturesque. Factual, I guess, but picturesque.

"Now, instead of helping poor Jack's memory, you are destroying it. What is the logic in that? What is the good in it? What the hell does it all mean?"

"It means," I said, "that what I have written is what happened. Facts are facts. We don't choose the bad guys, or the villains, or the victims. They do that to themselves. We just tell about them. If Jack Fowler lied, then I have to tell people that he lied."

"Horse puckey," said Nina Thatcher. "Horse shit."

"It's true."

"It's a crock," Nina Thatcher said. "You are enjoying doing what you are doing because Jack lied to you. You're like a child, Robert. 'Play by my rules or I'll get you.' That's what you're saying."

"Look—"

"Oh, don't rationalize," said Nina Thatcher. "Jesus. Save it. I said that I would be your friend. Remember that? I said that I would help you. You may even be right in what you're doing. It's just that I don't have to like it."

"I have to go," I said. I held my hand out. I wanted my article back.

"Here," said Nina Thatcher. "Take it. Print it. Enjoy it."

"I will," I said. "I will," I lied.

"You know," I said, "I have this friend. Actually I have this former friend—"

"I can see why," Nina Thatcher said.

"This former friend who lives in Los Angeles," I said.

"Tell me, Robert," Nina Thatcher said, "did you write about this former friend, too?"

"No, I lived with this former friend. Now she lives by herself."

"So do you," said Nina Thatcher. "So what?"

"I told you before," I said. "You and she sometimes sound a lot alike."

"That's why neither one of us is living with you," said Nina Thatcher. "I told you before, Robert, I don't want to hear about your former friends, or your life, or your feelings, okay? I don't need to hear about your former friends. I have just read about one of them, and I'm not feeling very friendly toward you right now despite any promises I may have made in a weakened condition."

"Look," I said. "I'll be back soon. We can talk."

"Don't rush yourself," Nina Thatcher said. "Take your time." She placed my story on the coffee table and walked toward the kitchen. "I need a drink," she said. "Did you remember to buy us some Tab?"

*chapter 15*_____

Jerry Daley did not like my story. He did not like my story at all. He paid a visit to Mike just after our metro edition came out and hinted that in the light of the Stanford *Daily* case, he might just search the city room for evidence about Jack's murder. Mike called the corporate apartment. I remember thinking that my paranoia must have been contagious because Mike called from a pay phone at the Chop House.

"The Animal is mad," Mike said.

"Too bad," I said. "What's he going to do about it?"

"He's making noises about searching the city room," Mike said. "He knows we don't have anything; he just wants to inconvenience us."

"Nice guy," I said. "We still gonna back him when he runs for DA?"

"It all depends," Mike said. "I don't know. What does it matter anyway?"

"I was just making small talk," I said.

"What do you want to do?"

"I'm not sure," I said. "Thatcher and I have Mark here. She's feeding the kid some dinner now. Then we're going to

do another session with him. I hope we get more information out of him. Then we'll put him to sleep, and I'll pay a couple of people a visit. I'll write another story tonight based on what Mark has to say. And I've got Murray Fast's address book. I got that last night."

"I don't want to know," Mike said. "I don't want to know how you got any of your information or who gave it to you. The less I know, Robert, the better off we all are."

"Sure," I said. "Maybe I should send my stories in a plain brown wrapper."

"It's for your protection."

"Sure it is," I said. I wasn't about to start that old game with Mike.

"Do you have any ideas?"

"I'm not sure," I said. "There are any number of scenarios. First, that Jack was killed by one of the chicken pimps. But I don't really believe that. It's more likely that he was killed by some faggot he met in a bar or was fixed up with by a guy named Larry."

"Have you talked to Larry yet?"

"No," I said. "That's one of the calls I have to make tonight."

"I see," Mike said.

"I don't think so," I said. "Never mind what I just said," I said.

"Then what?"

"Then I hit a few of the gay bars," I said. "Local color for the story. It'll give us a nice lead—you know, 'Jack Fowler covered the courts by day and the cruise bars by night.'"

"That sounds great," Mike said. "Just great."

"Yeah."

"Robert." Mike paused.

"Yeah?"

"You're really into this story, aren't you?"

"I don't have any choice, do I, boss?"

"That's not what I meant," Mike said. "Are you all right?"

"I'm fine," I said. "I just want it all to be over."

"Okay," Mike said. I knew he couldn't understand. "How's Thatcher?"

"She's fine," I said. "She doesn't like the story," I said. "But she's been good for the kid, you know?"

"Uh-huh," Mike said.

"Look," I said, "I'm going to need some help later tonight."

"Anything I can do?"

"Yeah," I said. "I'm going to need a beard when I hit the clubs. Somebody to pair up with and dance with. From what I understand, Daley is working his way through the bars, and a single guy asking questions ain't gonna get any results. At least not the results I need."

"Can you think of anybody?"

"Halloran," I said. "Halloran would be perfect."

"Halloran?" Mike sounded positively shocked.

"Remember when I helped him out last year? He was working on that term-papers-for-a-fee story. He's perfect."

Johnny Halloran stood five feet two inches tall and weighed 173 pounds. At the age of twenty-six he still needed to shave only once a week. Johnny Halloran bore a distinct resemblance to a Rubens cherub, except for his bright red hair and his green Irish eyes and his freckles. He was always being asked to produce proof of age in bars. Whenever the paper needed high school pieces, Johnny Halloran would be put on the case. The first time he interviewed a vice-principal, the woman thought Halloran was a reporter for the school paper.

When Johnny wrote his term-papers-for-profit story, I worked as his backup. He walked into the office near Wayne State where they sold the damn things and passed himself off as a high school student whose New York cousin—me—was going to put some family money into a similar venture. Wide-eyed and innocent, he asked if the owners of the firm, College Research, Inc., would like to franchise their operation. The people in charge took one look at him and spilled their guts. He walked away with facts, figures, profit margins, lists of available writers—everything. They never knew what hit them.

But more recently Halloran's life had become a shambles. His wife, who was getting her Ph.D. in clinical psychology at

the University of Michigan, had left him for her thesis adviser. Halloran had moved out of their suburban apartment and into a downtown hotel. His stories started to suffer. And he had broken the rules. He let his personal life affect his work. You cannot do that. You cannot feel anything on the job except the job.

"Ask Johnny to shave his beard off, will you?" I asked Mike.

"You're demanding the ultimate sacrifice," Mike said. "I'll see what I can do." It had taken Johnny Halloran six months to grow his red beard. "Are you sure you want Halloran?" Mike said.

They never understood, the editors. They sense that we are children, that we have the emotions of children. So they play parent with us. They dangle cookies in front of us in the form of good assignments. And then when we screw up, or we have a personal problem, they take away the cookies. They never understand that losing those goodies will make us paranoid, will make us screw up even more because then there's absolutely nothing to care about. Johnny Halloran's personal life had collapsed. His stories suddenly weren't so good anymore. Did he get support from the so-called family? Of course not. What Johnny Halloran got was on Mike's shit list. So instead of purloined term papers, he covered supermarket openings in Monroe. Mike had had Larry Chesler, the city editor, assign him a three-part series on Detroit's biggest potholes. What a waste. They call newspapers familial. They tell us we're all one big family. Maybe we are. But don't ever be the black sheep. Don't ever appear weak to the patriarch who gives out the assignments. Don't let your personal family life interfere with your professional family life, with what your professional family thinks it needs.

"Are you sure you want Halloran?" Mike asked the question again. What the hell did it matter to him? He was sitting in the number one booth at the Chop House, his regular booth, drinking the fourth or fifth of his usual eight-martini afterwork quota. The tab would be charged to the paper. There were probably five or six sycophants from the city room along for the ride. There always were. Like pilot fish. I

155

remember thinking that neither Nina Thatcher nor Johnny Halloran had ever been members of Mike's afterwork martini society. Nor had I. Nor had Jack.

"Yes, Johnny Halloran," I said. "Ask him to meet me outside the loading dock at about midnight."

"Okay, will do," said Mike. Mike's voice was uncannily even. How he could do it after five martinis I never knew. I still don't know. "What about the kid?" Mike asked.

"We give him to Daley tomorrow," I said. "By then we'll have a step-up on the story, and it won't matter what the kid tells Daley. Besides, the kid's uptight. He's afraid for his life, you know, and we'll be able to say that we've spent a couple of days convincing him to cooperate with the authorities."

"Sounds good to me," Mike said. "Look, Robert, I've got to go. There's some business to take care of here."

"What's she wearing?" I asked.

"Too much," Mike said.

"Does she work for us?" I asked.

"What do you think?" Mike said. "This is the time of the year I review staff salaries."

"Give my regards to your wife," I said. I hung up the phone. I switched off the tape recorder, unplugged the phone jack, and pocketed the cassette. Then I walked from the master bedroom back into the living room, where Nina Thatcher sat with Mark.

"Well?" Nina Thatcher put down a copy of *People* magazine.

"Mike says hello."

"What else did Mike say?"

"Mike said that the Animal has been around," I said, as much for Mark's benefit as Nina Thatcher's.

"What does that mean?" Mark asked.

"It means, kid, that we got problems." Mark looked at Nina Thatcher for assurance, an empty-eyed look of desperation. She turned his focus back to me.

"Mark," I said, "we've got some more talking to do. What I think we have to determine is that you had no involvement at all in Jack's death."

"But I didn't. You know I didn't, Mr. Mandel," Mark said.

"I know," I said. "And Miss Thatcher knows, too. But we want to go over your story one more time, just to make absolutely sure. Then tomorrow, after you've had a good night's sleep, we think you should talk to the police—"

"No," Mark said. "I can't."

"Mark," I said, "sooner or later you're going to have to."

"But why?"

Nina Thatcher said, "Because you know about Jack, Mark. Because you were close to Jack."

"Besides," I said, "there's the question of money. You'll have to answer some questions about the money."

"Will I have to give it back?" Mark looked from Nina Thatcher to me.

"I don't think so," I said. "The money was a gift. You'll be able to keep it."

"I only spent a little of it," Mark said.

"I know," I said.

"Mark." Nina Thatcher sipped at a tall glass of Tab. "We want to hear your side of things one more time. Let's start at the beginning, okay?"

"Sure," said Mark. "Like I told you—I met Jack when Larry brought Jack home from the Spike one night. No, it wasn't the Spike; it was the Anchor. I was staying with Larry to get out of my house for a couple of days, you know, because it was like real bogue, you know. My mother was real down on me and everything, you know. Real jive and everything, you know. So I was staying with Larry. I'd planned to go home that night, though, to get a change of clothes, you know, and then Jack walked in with Larry. He wasn't like the usual kind of guy Larry'd bring home, you know."

"What do you mean?" Nina Thatcher asked. She had incredible patience. I walked into the master bedroom, where the Kel receiver was picking up the conversation from the wireless mike stashed in the living room. I flipped the cassette, giving Nina Thatcher another forty-five minutes of taping time, and stretched out on the bed. If I was lucky, I could get fifteen minutes of sleep before I had to shower,

157

change clothes, and go out. I hadn't slept in almost two days, and I was beginning to wish that I had some speed.

———

Johnny Halloran was early. I could see him pacing in front of the loading docks as I edged the Bug down the cobblestone alley at the rear of the paper, slaloming slowly to avoid the remnants of newsprint rolls that littered the pavement. Halloran looked like a walking figure eight. A small red-thatched circle—his head—set atop a larger circle—his torso. He was wearing a knee-length car coat that accented the rotundity. I reached across the Bug and popped the lock. Johnny Halloran slid in.

"Hey, Mandel," he said, "what's happening?"

"Hey, Halloran," I said, "you're about to become a faggot."

"I'm bitter about my wife," said Halloran, "but I'm not that bitter. Couldn't I just jerk off?"

"Later," I said. "Right now we're going to play some games at the gay clubs."

"The Fowler story," Halloran said. "Fantastic. I'm off Mike's shit list. Okay."

I reached across Halloran's chest and opened the glove compartment. There was a Panasonic minicorder and a shoulder holster inside. "Put it on under your sports coat," I said.

"What sports coat?" Johnny Halloran said. "Mike didn't say anything about a sports coat. He said to show up at midnight and take my beard off." Johnny Halloran rubbed at his chins. "I left the mustache on," he said. "is that okay?"

"Sure," I said. I didn't really care about Johnny Halloran's mustache. But I did care that he couldn't be wired. The Kel, which he could wear under his shirt, was at the corporate apartment. I wasn't about to give up my Nagra. I shook my head.

"What's wrong?" Johnny Halloran said. "I didn't screw up, did I?" When you are on Mike's shit list, you tend to become paranoid and infantile. You develop a persecution complex. It is not imagined.

"Nothing's wrong," I said. "Nothing." I slipped the Bug into gear. Everything was wrong.

"What's the score?" Johnny Halloran asked.

"Simple," I said. "Just like the term-paper scam. We are a couple of gay guys. We hit three, four clubs. We do some dancing and some talking. We listen."

"Who leads?" Johnny Halloran asked.

"What?"

"Who leads?" Johnny Halloran was insistent. "When we dance, who leads?"

"Oh," I said. "We'll trade off, okay?"

"Dynamite," said Johnny Halloran. He started to gyrate his body. "A little outrageous boogie," he said. "Just what I need."

I made an illegal left turn onto Woodward and started north toward Six Mile Road. "How's life?" I asked.

"Okay," Johnny Halloran said. "Well, not really," he said.

"Found a place yet?" I asked.

"Yeah," said Johnny Halloran. " A nice one-bedroom in Grosse Pointe."

We both were silent for some minutes. Life at the paper may be familial, but you don't generally intrude on your colleagues' lives. Not in person, at least. Everybody talks about everybody else, but seldom to his face. Only behind his back. It's the family way.

"You hear from Martha?" I asked. We were stopped at a light.

"Not really," Johnny Halloran said. "She forwards my mail to the paper. I guess she's happy."

"You still paying her tuition?"

"Just till the end of the year," Johnny Halloran said. "What the hell, you know."

"Uh-huh." I reached between my legs and shifted the Nagra, which was already on and working.

"Jock itch?" Johnny Halloran buckled his seat belt.

"Something like it." We drove on in silence for some blocks. "Look at these streets, will you?"

"Incredible, aren't they," said Johnny Halloran. "Newark without the charm," he said, gesturing with his head at a

group of half a dozen men warming themselves at a fire set in a trash can.

"Better," I said. "Cleveland without the money."

We drove silently.

"You know," Johnny Halloran said, "you know, there was a distinct moment—a precise instant—I knew that something was going wrong with Martha."

"Uh-huh," I said.

"Her diaphragm," Johnny Halloran said. "About a month before we split up she started taking her diaphragm to school."

"Oh," I said. "You know," I said, "it doesn't matter to me—"

"It's okay," said Johnny Halloran. "I understand. It's just weird, you know. I mean, I'm not a suspicious person. It's just that one day Martha left the medicine chest open when she went to school, and you know how you look at things for years and never pay any attention to them. So I started to close the medicine chest, and all of a sudden I saw that something was missing."

"Oh," I said.

"The diaphragm case. A blue plastic case. Looks like a compact. And the tube of jelly was gone, too."

"Maybe she was going to replace it," I said.

"That's what I thought, too," Johnny Halloran said.

"So like a good reporter, you checked up on her the next time she left the house, right?"

"But of course," said Johnny Halloran. "And the case was gone again."

"You didn't say anything?" I asked.

"No," said Johnny Halloran.

"I see," I said.

"I'm not all that fond of confrontations," Johnny Halloran said. "Then one day I checked the medicine cabinet—I was doing it on a daily basis then—and the case was right where it belonged. You know, I felt good about not talking to Martha because I figured, what the hell, she'd felt threatened or something or attracted to somebody for a couple of

160

weeks, and now it's over. I felt really good about Martha."

"What happened?" I asked.

"After about a week I decided just for fun to check inside the diaphragm case. You know, we'd been married for three years, and I'd never seen the thing. So after she left for school, I took a look inside. And the case was empty."

"Shit," I said.

"That's mildly what I felt like," Johnny Halloran said.

"Of course," I said, "we both know that you weren't looking inside the case just because you'd never seen a diaphragm before."

"I felt like such a criminal," Johnny Halloran said. "I mean, I was alone in the house. Martha had gone to school and everything, but I put the chain on the outside door and locked the bathroom up."

"How did you feel—aside from like shit?"

"Hateful," Johnny Halloran said. He ran a hand through his red hair. "I wanted to kill her, you know. That was my fantasy."

"But you didn't."

"You know," Johnny Halloran said, "I couldn't even confront her. Talk to her. I followed her to school one day. Drove all the way to Ann Arbor. Sat outside the classroom and staked it out. Followed her to a tutorial session with her professor. Then they climbed into his car and drove off. I followed them. I felt like a cop. To his house. They went to his house and went inside. I felt like going to the door and ringing the bell, and when he came to answer it, I'd say, 'I have a message for Martha Halloran,' and then I'd pop him one, you know. A thirty-eight with a silencer right between the eyes."

"You didn't, of course," I said.

"Well, first, I don't have a thirty-eight with a silencer," said Johnny Halloran. "Second, even if I did, I wouldn't know how to use it. Third, I'm not really a physical person."

"I know," I said. "That's one of your charms."

"Sure," said Johnny Halloran. "The fat kid doesn't like to mix it up."

"So you moved out."

"Sure," Johnny Halloran said. "I never said another word to Martha. I felt so—"

"Hurt," I said.

"A mild description but accurate," Johnny Halloran said. "Shit, Robert," he said. "Here I am running off at the mouth, and I don't know what the hell we're doing."

I turned the car onto Six Mile and looked for a place to park. "I told you," I said, "we're coming out of the closet."

"I knew that already," Johnny Halloran said. "But what are we looking for?"

"I don't know," I said. "First, we get, you should pardon the expression, the lay of the land. What goes on here? How does it all happen? Who does what to whom. Then, after the ambiance, we're interested in conversation. Are people talking about Jack? What are they saying? That kind of thing. Then we're looking for some specific people. A pimp named Scotty, and a dude called Murray, and someone named Larry, to name a few."

"No last names?" Johnny Halloran slid out of his seat belt.

"Not yet," I said. "Look, we go in and we play it by ear."

"How do we know which bars?"

"A snitch told me," I said. "We start at the Sand Box, then we hit the Spike, and after that the Golden Dove."

"Sounds good to me," said Johnny Halloran. He leaned over the gearshift. "Blow in my ear, and I'll follow you anywhere."

"Fuck you," I said. "And I think we should drink ginger ale."

"What else?" said Johnny Halloran, who did not drink anything stronger than ginger ale.

"Some Irishman you are," I said.

"I've got a potato jones," said Johnny Halloran. "It's enough."

"Ready?" I used the car key and locked my side of the Bug.

"Willing and able," said Johnny Halloran. "Hey, Mandel," he said, "thanks."

"Who else'd be willing to take a beard off just to become a

beard," I said. I put my arm through Johnny Halloran's, and we walked up to the Sand Box's solid steel door.

It was going to be hell on my Nagra. In fact, my Nagra was useless. Any recorder would have been useless. We walked in and paid $2 each and got our hands stamped by someone in a fishnet tank top and French jeans. I looked at my hand. There was a purple 69 above the knuckles. I showed it to Johnny Halloran, who laughed. "Free advertising," he shouted to me above the noise. We pulled ourselves out of our coats and checked them, then struggled toward the bar. The Sand Box was dark inside, except for the dance floor, where a huge mirror ball cast thousands of spears of light at dozens of dancing couples. As far as I could see, there was not a woman in the place.

I am pretty much at ease in any situation. My trade calls for me to be that way. But in the Sand Box I simply felt out of place. As I said to Johnny Halloran later, it was like being a black at a Klan meeting, as if a black man had put on a sheet and a hood and a pair of gloves and walked in on a bunch of Ku Kluxers to watch and to listen. I had not been threatened by Jack's sexuality. I guess I knew him too well—or thought I did. But at the Sand Box I felt unprotected and vulnerable. I was out of my element.

Johnny Halloran pointed to a couple on the dance floor. The mirror ball was bathed in red and blue lights, and the disco DJ was playing "Le Freak." I followed Johnny Halloran's arm and saw a tall, fiftyish, balding man dancing close to a young partner. They were oblivious to the music. They swayed like lovers. Their mouths never parted. Their hands ran up and down each other's back, sides. The young one took the old one's hand and put it between his legs. Johnny Halloran cupped his hand and put it to my ear. "I'm going to have a lot to talk about at confession this week," he said.

"You think *you* are," I said. "Think about them."

Halloran smiled and nodded vigorously.

We fought our way to an edge of the bar, where we could watch the dancing. I waved at the bartender until I got his

163

attention. I kept calling, "Nurse, nurse," until he came over.

"What'll it be?"

"Two ginger ales, please," I said.

He nodded and grabbed a couple of ice-filled glasses, sprayed them with soda from a spigot, and sloshed them toward us. "Five," he said.

"Five?"

"Everything's two fifty each," he said. "Whatever you drink is two fifty."

I dug into my jeans and handed him six singles. "Keep it." I offered a glass of ginger ale to Johnny Halloran, and we turned our backs to the bar so we could watch the action.

The music was still telling anyone who'd listen that Le Freak was chic.

"What do you want to do?" I said.

"Gee," said Johnny Halloran, "I don't know. What do you want to do, Marty?"

"I dunno, Ang," I said. "Maybe we should dance. Get in the swing of things, you know."

Johnny Halloran looked at me. Then he looked at the couples on the dance floor. Then he said, "Why the hell not?"

We elbow-speared our way down two steps and edged onto the floor, gyrating with the music, bumping shoulders and hips with others, sometimes stepping on toes, insteps, whole feet. The sound was incredibly sharper on the dance floor. As I moved with the beat, I looked up. Eight studio-quality speakers hung above the floor, angled down toward the moving, swaying, jumping crowd. Every time the phrase "Freak out!" was repeated the dancers echoed it. The lights started to change. The DJ brought a bunch of strobes into play, and Johnny Halloran's movements became stylized and jerky, as if I were flipping through one of those old Cracker Jack prize books where you flip the pages fast and watch a clown do somersaults. Johnny Halloran's eyes closed. He clapped chubby hands above his head and boogied, bumping his hips to the music. I thought what the hell and closed mine, too, moving inside the loud framework of incessant disco beat repetition.

"Freak out!" My knees buckled as someone slid into them. I moved away and kept going. What the hell was I doing here? I thought. A trio of men danced together like a curious human sandwich. The one in the middle kept sinking to his knees, moaning, "It's a meltdown; it's a meltdown." What the hell did Jack get from coming to places like these? I watched as two lithe twenty-year-olds with dancers' bodies did the Latin hustle, twirling each other with the grace of a pair of Fred Astaires.

Let it go, I thought, and clapped with the syncopation, mouthing the words. The couple Johnny Halloran had first pointed out to me were still locked in their lovers' embrace, oblivious to the meaty, beaty music.

"Freak out!" It was hard not to give myself up to the music completely. Maybe that's what Jack had come here to do. To let himself go. Not to think. The strobes went out, were replaced by reds, blues, greens, flashing in time with the dancing. It was getting hot on the floor, and the Nagra chafed my crotch. I opened the two top buttons on my shirt and kept moving, kept dancing. If I concentrated, I could shut out everything except the beat. Is that what Jack had come to do? Or had Jack been looking for other, more tactile pleasures? The human sandwich started jumping up and down. They moved closer, closer with each ba-bump until the three bodies touched and moved in unison, side to side, up and down.

"Freak out!" I clapped in time with the music. I could smell the dancers, sweating Aramis, Canoe, Patchouly, and Vetiver. I closed my eyes and gave myself to it, threw my body inside it, swung with it. There were no stories. There was no Jack. There was no Nancy even. Just the music, coming down so hard it made my head reverberate from the inside. No present, no past, no future. Just the dance.

The DJ cross-faded, and a poignant, wailing guitar led the way into Luther Ingram's "If Loving You Is Wrong, I Don't Want to Be Right." The crowd shifted pace, slowing down, moving together, holding each other, dancing close. I looked at Johnny Halloran.

"If you don't mind," I said, "I think we'll skip this one."

165

Johnny Halloran laughed. He wiped a patina of sweat from his forehead. "Shucks, Mandel," he said, "I was hoping you'd ask me to stay. Jesus, that was great."

I played the cynic. "It was okay," I said. It had been great. I hadn't danced in months.

We pushed our way back to the bar against a stream of couples heading for the dance floor. Our ginger ale glasses had been removed. I waved at the bartender again.

"Nurse, another round, please."

They were delivered. I looked at the glass. Five ounces of ginger ale and three ice cubes for two fifty.

"There's gotta be money in this," I said to Johnny Halloran. "Maybe we should open a bar."

"Good idea," Johnny Halloran said. He had sweated through his sports shirt, and dark circles had appeared under his arms. "God, I'm wet," he said.

A man to his right said, "That makes you all the more attractive, dearie."

Johnny Halloran turned. He looked the man up and down. A dark, tall man in a Lacoste shirt, tight jeans, white socks, and Nike training shoes. "Sorry," he said, "I'm into blonds." He put his arm through mine. "See?"

"Well, excuse me," said the man, "I was just trying to make conversation." He ran his hand along a close-cropped, manicured beard. "I'm sorry if I interrupted a tryst."

Johnny Halloran smiled demurely. "We've just only met, and we'd like to be alone," he said.

I watched as the tall man wandered into the crowd. On a railed balcony above the dance floor another man watched the action. "If you're into blonds," I said to Johnny Halloran, "why not talk to him?" I gestured.

He was moving with the music, in a world all his own. Dressed in motorcycle jacket, red plaid shirt, engineer's boots, and jeans so tight they looked sculptured. He was almost an albino he was so light-complexioned.

Johnny Halloran stared. "Jeezus," he said.

A voice from my left. "He's something, isn't he?"

I swiveled to see who was talking. A smallish man, beardless, with close-cropped butterscotch hair. Almost preppy in

his dress: well-worn chinos; blue button-down shirt; boating moccasins; dark-green web belt with a brass buckle.

"Yes," I said.

"I don't know who he is," the man said. "He comes here three, four nights a week. He never dances. He never talks. He just looks. Maybe he can't make up his mind."

"Can't make up his mind?"

"Whether to come out or not."

"Oh."

"It's hard, you know."

"I know," I said.

"I haven't seen you in here before," the man said. He held a glass of coffee in his hand. "I'm Joel."

"Hi, Joel," I said. "I'm Bob. This is my friend Johnny." The three of us shook hands.

Joel put his arm around the man to his right. "This is my friend Ralph," he said.

"Hi, Ralph," said Johnny Halloran. "How're you doing?"

"Maintaining," said Ralph. "I'm okay."

There was a silence.

"It's a nice place," I said.

"Thank you," said Joel.

"Is it yours?"

"Mine and the bank's," Joel said.

"Great," Johnny Halloran said.

"You should come back, now that you've made it the first time," Joel said.

"Do you know everybody who comes here?" I asked.

"Just about," Joel said. "It's a neighborhood bar, you know. Nothing fancy. Good music, some drinks, some conversation. Not a heavy cruise place."

"The music's great," said Johnny Halloran. "The music's marvelous."

"Thank you," said Joel.

"Say, Joel," I said, "I was wondering if you know any of my friends."

"Your friends?"

"Yeah," I said. I looked at Johnny Halloran. "Our friends. They come in here sometimes."

"Oh," said Joel. "Maybe I—" He was interrupted by the bartender, who tapped him on the shoulder, mimed a man on the telephone, and pointed toward the rear of the bar.

"Excuse me," said Joel. "I'll be back."

Johnny Halloran, Ralph, and I stood in silence for some time. I didn't know what to say.

Finally, I said, "Nice place."

Ralph nodded.

"Has it been open long?"

"About six months," said Ralph.

"It's really doing well," I said.

"People need to get out," Ralph said. "Have a good time."

"I guess," I said.

The beat on the dance floor picked up. Ralph looked at me. "Want to dance?"

"Not now, thanks. I'm still pretty winded."

He gestured to Johnny Halloran. "How about it?"

"Sure," said Johnny Halloran. "It's cool, Robert," he said.

I watched the two of them push their way toward the music. I wondered how gay men kept their hips so narrow and their asses so small. The dancers seemed to suck Ralph and Johnny Halloran into their midst, and I lost sight of them in the stew of bouncing, boogieing couples, trios, and quartets. I stood with my back to the bar, my elbow resting on the dark wood, my foot on the rail, watching, looking, observing. Was Scotty here? I wondered. Was Larry here? Had Jack come here? I thought about what would happen if there were a fire all of a sudden and I couldn't get out. Trapped in a gay bar. Who'd believe I was doing research? What would my family say? I wondered whether Jack had worried about those things. Of course he had. But he had gone to bars like this one anyhow.

I felt like such an outsider. Was it my own knowledge that I didn't belong? Perhaps. But I was used to playing roles. Why did playing the gay role disturb me so much?

A hand on my shoulder. It was Joel. "You were somewhere else," he said.

"I was just thinking about a friend," I said.

"I see," he said. Did he? I didn't think so.

"I hear you've been open about six months," I said.

"Just over."

"It's doing really well."

"I'm pleased with it," Joel said. "Where are you from?"

"I live on the East Side," I said.

Joel nodded. "Work in town?"

"Yes," I said.

"What do you do?"

"Not much," I said. "As little as I can." I smiled.

Joel shook his head. "Would you like a drink?" he asked. "I see Ralph and your friend have gone dancing."

"Great music," I said. "Absolutely great music. Sure, a ginger ale would be nice."

Joel signaled the bartender. He pointed to my glass. He sipped at his coffee. "I don't drink much when I'm working," he said.

"I can understand that," I said.

I saw Johnny Halloran's head bobbing through the crowd. "Here they come," I said.

"Boy," said Johnny Halloran, "that was something. That music is incredible, Robert, really incredible."

I watched as Ralph settled himself next to Joel. He wiped his neck with a red bandanna.

"I was wondering," I said to Joel, "if you knew any of our friends who come here."

"Do they live in the nabe?" Joel asked.

"Yes," I said. "A couple of them do."

"Like?"

"One guy named Larry," I said. "Another's named Scotty. And then there's my friend Jack—" I looked at Johnny Halloran. "Our friend Jack."

Joel looked at Ralph. He shook his head.

"What's wrong?" I asked.

"Would your friend Jack's last name happen to be Fowler?" he said.

"Yes," I said. "I guess so," I said. "Yes."

Ralph said to Johnny Halloran, "And you dance so well, too."

"What do you mean?" said Johnny Halloran.

169

Joel sighed. "You're either cops or reporters, right?"
Silence. Discovered. Unmasked.
I tried to bluff. "No, it's just that—"
Joel said, "Oh, come on." He looked at Ralph. "I wish that
they'd just leave us alone."
"Hey," I said. "We're not—it's all right—"
"I think you are," Joel said. "You know, you're the third
pair of guys in the past twenty-four hours come in here and
started asking questions. It would have been a lot less obvi-
ous if one person had come in. But I guess you all feel threat-
ened by what we've got here."
"Hey, come on," I said. "We're cool, you know."
"Sure you are," said Joel. "Why can't you just be upfront,
huh?"
"What do you mean?"
"Are you cops or reporters?"
I looked at Johnny Halloran. I faced Joel. "Reporters."
"Thank you," said Joel. He started to turn away. I stopped
him. I put a hand on his shoulder. He looked at it and said,
"Don't you think you'll become infected?"
"Hey, come on," I said. "Give us a break, will you?"
"Why should I?" Joel looked at me. "Bob, right?"
I nodded.
"Bob Mandel?"
"Yes."
"You wrote the piece about Fowler today. So tomorrow
you'll write another one, and you've come here to give it a
little local color. Jesus. You guys—" He shrugged my hand
away.
"So give me a break," I said. "Talk to us."
"About what?"
"Your side of things."
"Our side of what," said Joel. "Our side is the same as your
side."
"Oh, come on," I said. I was thinking of Jack and Mark, of
Jack and Murray Fast, of Jack and Larry whatever-his-name-
was.
"You're here to get fag background," Joel said. "Okay,
you've got it. Your pal here danced with a real live homosex-

ual. So why don't you both crawl back to the paper and write about it?"

"You're not giving me much choice," I said. "I mean, to write anything other than what you say."

"What do you mean?" Joel set down his glass of coffee.

"Okay," I said. "We're reporters. I'm working on the Fowler story. I admit it. But if you don't talk to me, then I have to go with what I've got. And what I've got right now is a bunch of guys dancing with guys and a nice, suggestive stamp on my hand." I waved the purple 69 under Joel's nose. "So give me a break, will you? Talk to me. Make me understand all this, and maybe I won't do the hatchet job you've just about committed me to writing."

Joel looked at me.

"Hey, come on," I said. "I'm after a story. I'll get it with or without your help, Joel. But I'd like to get my facts straight, okay?"

"Straight facts from a gay bar owner." Joel laughed. "Oh, shit, I guess there's nothing to lose."

He pointed toward the rear of the bar. "Come into the office," he said.

We talked for over an hour. I even took notes, on a borrowed legal pad Joel offered me. There was no use telling him that I was recording his words as well. Even afterward, however, I was confused. I thought about Mark, back at the corporate apartment. A kid looking for a father figure, a big brother figure, who thought he had found it in Jack. Then there was Larry, who arranged for people to meet people and dealt pills to school kids on the side. Then there was Murray Fast with his smelly underwear and his green teeth. There was Scotty, with his two little boys—chickens waiting to be plucked.

Finally, there was Jack. Jack, who had slept with Mark and Nina Thatcher and Murray and Larry and God knows who else, but who had slept with Madeleine only once.

Yes, Joel said, he had seen Jack in the Sand Box. Jack had flashed a lot of money. Everybody thought he was an auto company executive from Bloomfield Hills or Birmingham, catching a little action on the side. Just like a lot of the men

171

outside, Joel said. Nice, normal people, Joel said, who for one reason or another needed to escape from their families, or their straight world, and become part of a group with whom they were truly comfortable.

Gay, Joel said, was the same as straight, only different. Did I understand that? No, I said, I didn't. It was all so fuzzy. Good gays and bad gays; queens, transvestites, and macho men. Gay cops and teachers and judges; homosexual decorators and hairdressers; fag plumbers and steel haulers. Even queer reporters. Like Jack.

But there was so much more. Leather and satin. Doilies and steel-tipped whips. Trick books. Was Jack's picture in someone's home? Somewhere out there was there a Polaroid of Jack lying strapped to a bed, being whipped? Of Jack doing things I couldn't even picture?

Why had Jack lied to me? I would have understood. I know I would have understood. I told myself, sitting there, taking notes as Joel talked, that I would have understood. I would have allowed Jack to break the rules. Maybe. Maybe not. He died because he broke the rules. I knew that. Maybe he broke them on purpose. I didn't understand.

Johnny Halloran and I left the Sand Box at about two-thirty. I drove him out to his nice one-bedroom in Grosse Pointe and refused an offer of cold ginger ale. Then I drove to a phone booth on the corner of Jefferson and East Grand and called Nina Thatcher, waking her up. I told her we'd be delivering Mark to the cops late in the afternoon.

That way our competition would miss the story. Their final deadline comes at about two-thirty. After four they can't even drop news of the Third World War into the paper without printing an extra. Jack's story was good, but no Third World War. Our exclusive would be safe.

I drove back to my own apartment, where I dropped off the tape of the interview Johnny Halloran and I had done with Joel and Ralph. I threaded a new tape in the Nagra and replaced the batteries. It was about time to play the old cop game with Larry. That, at least, was a role I was comfortable playing.

chapter 16 _____

Reporters do not solve crimes. They merely chronicle the solving of them or write about crimes being committed. Those newspaper novels in which the journalist becomes a participant, the quick-fisted hub around which the story revolves, are romantic but unreal. We may precipitate action by what we write; we may even uncover crime or wrongdoing. But we seldom solve anything. Besides, the facts in our notebooks do not become materials used in arrest reports or district attorneys' memos. They serve only to help us get the story right when we write. On the other hand, reporters often fantasize about solving crimes. I certainly fantasized about getting a handle on Jack's murderers, confronting them, .38 drawn. Spread-eagling them on their car or against a wall, handcuffing them (where I'd get the cuffs was a problem I never solved, but in fantasies such details aren't important), and delivering them to Jerry Daley complete with signed confessions.

Those were the fantasies. The realities are always much simpler. Like driving up to Larry's house—his address was in Murray Fast's little black book—and discovering five police cars and an ambulance parked outside. I pulled down the

block and removed my .38, police shield, and shoulder holster, to stow them under the front seat of the Bug. Then I clipped my press pass to my shirt and pushed through the early-morning crowd of neighbors and onlookers. There didn't seem to be any other reporters around, so I made my way to the front door and confronted the cop blocking the path.

He was adamant about not letting me inside. Actually we got into quite a nasty little shouting match until I saw Jerry Daley over his shoulder. Daley was in shirt sleeves, and his Irish fishing cap was pushed back on his head. I called past the cop to him, and he looked up.

"If it isn't the newshound," Daley said, walking to the doorway.

"What's happening, Jerry?" I asked.

"I thought you could tell me," he said. "You seem to know everything about faggots these days."

"Faggots?"

"Faggots," said Jerry Daley. "Guys who like guys. Like your pal Jack."

"You're an incurable romantic," I said. "What's going on?"

"A lively, messy murder," Daley said.

"Can I take a look?" I asked.

"Can you see? Take a look?" Jerry Daley said. "Well, I don't know, Robert. Why should you?"

"Because of my natural curiosity," I said. "And my love of blood and guts."

"Of course," said Jerry Daley. "You're one of those people who likes to watch autopsies, aren't you? A charter member of the cadaver society, right?" He removed a cigarette from the corner of his mouth and flicked the ash through the open doorway.

"Come on in," he said. "You'll love this one."

The house was singularly unimpressive. A red-brick two-story affair built in the late thirties, probably for around five thousand. But thick walls, arched partitions, and real wood floors. Still, Larry had done nicely when it came to furnishings. I walked with Daley into the living room. It was full of antiques. Not the boxy Victorian stuff that's so cheap and

plentiful these days either. Larry had done the place in Empire. Real damask on the sofa, which was Egyptian. Good rococo gilt scrollwork around the edges of patterned-wood inlaid tables. Ornate porcelain lamps. The walls were covered by *trompe l'oeil* murals. A display case held two dozen pieces of exquisite heavy crystal. The rugs were Aubusson or good copies.

I whistled. "Not bad," I said.

"**Too** precious," Jerry Daley said. "Follow me upstairs." He led me up a narrow staircase to the second floor. I could see three doorways. Probably two bedrooms and a bath. The problem with these houses was they had only one bathroom. Daley walked into the front bedroom.

It, too, was impressive. Done in Napoleonic campaign style. A king-sized bed styled like an Egyptian chaise, in damask crimson and gold stripes. Matching fabric wall covering. The chairs also matched. They were campaign chairs, with leather straps and brass fittings. A trestle desk sat atop two sawhorses. Except the sawhorses were mahogany and the desktop, four inches thick, was inlaid in the center and edged with flush brass fittings.

There was a man slumped at the trestle desk. He looked as if he were resting, except that his eyes were open and a pool of blood like an inkblot emanated from one of them.

"Pretty piece of work, isn't it?" said Jerry Daley. "Come on, Robert, move on up and take a good, close look."

I walked up to the side of the desk and knelt to get a better view, balancing myself carefully so as not to touch the polished wood. A nice clean job.

"What do you think?" asked Jerry Daley.

"Like you said, it's a pretty piece of work," I said. "One bullet in the eye, probably very small caliber because it didn't come out the back of the head. Neat."

"Motives?" Jerry Daley lit a cigarette and pocketed his lighter.

"Oh, I don't know," I said.

"Sure you do," said Jerry Daley. "Come on, let's go downstairs and talk."

I followed Daley down the narrow staircase, through the

living room and small dining alcove, back into a country kitchen. Daley picked up two mugs from the counter and poured coffee into them from a Norelco drip pot.

"You do like to make yourself at home," I said.

"What the hell," said Jerry Daley. "You only live once." He motioned me over to the kitchen table. "That's Larry," Jerry Daley said.

"Oh," I said. "Larry who?"

"Larry Perkins," Jerry Daley said. "One of Jack's lovers."

"Aha," I said.

"The same Larry you were probably coming to interview."

"It sounds plausible," I said.

"Of course, it's plausible," Jerry Daley said. "Mark told you about Larry."

"Mark who," I said.

"Mark Brown," Jerry Daley said. "The sixteen-year-old Jack gave five grand to."

"He did?" I said.

"Of course he did," said Jerry Daley. "It was in your story. Except you didn't name any names."

"Of course," I said.

"Of course," Jerry Daley said. He walked over to the sink and ran water over his cigarette, then flipped it into a paper bag that sat next to the wastebasket.

"Somehow you got to Mark. Mark told you about Larry. Meanwhile, we went through Jack's journals and came up with Mark and Larry, too. Now it occurs to me that you've got Mark stashed somewhere. Larry, as we both know, is stashed upstairs."

"Killed—" I said.

"To shut him up," Jerry Daley said. "Now," Jerry Daley said, "our next task is to locate Mark Brown. I'll be honest with you, Robert: I could slap you with a subpoena right now and haul you into court, where you'd be found in contempt because you'd hide behind the First Amendment. On the other hand, that might get your paper upset. And we both know that while I like to needle you guys once in a while, there's an election coming up next year, and as your

city-county bureau chief wrote, I'm an ambitious person."

"But of course," I said.

"So I'll trade," said Jerry Daley. "You give me Mark Brown, and I'll go along with the fairy tale you're probably going to hand out about his being afraid to come to the cops. And in return, I'll give you a nice exclusive."

"On what?" I asked.

"On these," Jerry Daley said. He pulled an envelope out of his shirt pocket and tossed it across the table.

I opened the flap. There were two Polaroid pictures inside. I pulled them out.

"Oh, shit," I said. "Where did you get these?"

"From Jack's place," Jerry Daley said. "Unique, aren't they?"

I turned the prints face down. They had been taken with a self-timer. They showed Jack and Mark together. They were graphic. They were sickening.

"They're yours," said Jerry Daley.

"How come?" I couldn't take my eyes off Jack's face.

"They're copies," Jerry Daley said. He removed his fishing cap and set it on the kitchen table. He ran a hand through his thick hair. "I've got the originals sealed as evidence," he said. "Hey, Robert, don't look so unhappy. Think of the bright side. If Rupert Murdoch owned the competition, they'd probably already be in print."

"Who else has these?"

"I told you. This is your exclusive," Jerry Daley said. "I want the kid."

"He's yours," I said.

"Good," said Jerry Daley. "You're probably wired, you sneaky little bastard, so I'll say it again clearly: I agree to playing out the little charade we have decided upon. And that's for the record."

"Agreed."

"Good," said Jerry Daley. "Now, let's go back off the record. There are a couple of other things."

"Such as?"

"Well." He walked to one of Larry's chopping-block

counters and opened his brief case. "Take a look at this."

Jerry Daley handed me a ring-bound leather book. A photo album. "Larry's trick book," he said.

I flipped it open. There were pictures of Larry's liaisons carefully mounted under clear plastic. Larry, it seemed, liked everybody. There were black men, Hispanics, whites. Most were in their twenties. There were no pictures of Jack. Daley came around in back of me and riffled through the pages.

"Here's a beauty," he said. It was a three-picture sequence of Larry with a young black man whose cock had to be ten inches long. The first shot showed Larry on his knees holding the cock as if it were a hot dog. He was licking the top of it. The second shot had the black dude standing in back of Larry, with his cock between Larry's legs. It looked as if Larry had two cocks. "The old double-barrel shotgun number," Jerry Daley laughed. The third shot had Larry bent over and the dude halfway inside his ass.

There were other pictures. Jerry Daley pointed at one. "That's Zero," he said. Zero was a potbellied Neanderthal who had one big eyebrow and was pictured wearing only an ornate earring. The shot showed Larry sitting on his chest, dangling his balls in front of Zero's mouth. "Zero," said Jerry Daley, "is a KSO—a known sex offender. He likes little boys. Of course, he also likes little girls, and big boys, and big girls. He also probably likes dogs and chickens and sheep."

"A real egalitarian," I said.

"Bet your ass," said Jerry Daley. He looked at me and laughed. "That's funny," he said. "You're not laughing."

I went through the book. About halfway there was a page and half of pictures that interested the hell out of me. The first, taken in Larry's living room, showed Murray Fast and Mark. Both were naked. Murray was on his knees. He was kissing Mark's feet. The second and third were shots of Murray and Larry. I pointed a finger at Murray Fast's face. "Who's he?"

"I don't know yet," Jerry Daley said. "But will you look at the tiny pecker on him? I wonder what fun he was."

"Look at the ears," I said. Murray Fast's ears stood out from his head like jug handles.

"You have a perverted mind," said Jerry Daley. "Of course, you're probably right."

There was another interesting sequence that followed. Larry and Murray and Mark were joined by two other men. They looked like hustlers, with unkempt hair and stringy, muscular bodies. One was a dark, small man of about thirty. He stood naked in the picture except for a knit watchcap on his head. He had a thick mustache and a hairy body. He looked very uncomfortable posing in the nude. The other man was dressed only in a mesh T-shirt. Thin-lipped, with short blond hair and tiny ears, he looked like the prototypical Hitler youth. He was virtually hairless as far as I could tell. The pictures showed several ingenious combinations of oral-genital contacts. But the most fascinating part was that the two new men were more observers than participants. I poked the pictures with my index finger. "Who are these guys?" I asked Jerry Daley.

"No idea," Daley said. "I'm due downtown in about half an hour, and we're going to try to match faces with criminal records later. But as we both know, that's just about impossible."

"But it's fun," I said. "What about things like fingerprints?"

"We lifted some," said Jerry Daley. "But you never can tell."

"Hey, Daley," I said, "why is it that you're so nice to me all of a sudden?"

"I told you," Jerry Daley said. "I want the kid."

"Horseshit," I said. "Come on, talk to me. You already know we're going to give you Mark."

"But how are you going to give me Mark?"

"Any way you like."

"What about in public?" Jerry Daley said.

"You mean a press conference?"

"Why not?"

I thought about it for at least a full second, then said, "Why not? Right in the middle of our city room."

"I'll arrange the coverage," said Jerry Daley.

"Which is why you're being so lovely," I said. "I get the

feeling that you've been talking to your campaign manager."

"I don't have a campaign manager," said Jerry Daley.

"Not officially," I said. "But this friendliness just isn't like you. You really do need our endorsement, don't you?"

"I could get by without it," said Jerry Daley. "I've done okay so far."

"So far you haven't run for anything," I said. "Look, Jerry, I'm not going to quibble. Anything you want to give me, whether it's on the record or background, I'm going to take."

"That's good of you," Jerry Daley said.

"I thought so," I said. "Okay, how do we work this little charade?"

"First we set the time," Jerry Daley said.

"Five o'clock," I said. "Early enough for the local TV stations to make their six P.M., news, late enough so the competition has already gone to bed with their final edition."

"And I'll notify everybody," said Jerry Daley. "The announcement should come from me."

"Actually it should come from us," I said. "But I'm not going to argue. Besides, we both know that Mark isn't going to say anything. And I don't think it's going to hurt you when Mike stands next to you and tells the cameras what a great job you've been doing solving the brutal murder (is how the phrase usually goes) of one of our top reporters."

"Have you ever thought about a career in politics?" Jerry Daley said. "You've got the natural sense of timing for it."

I looked down at the Polaroids of Jack and Mark staring at me from the kitchen table.

"No," I said. "I like what I do too much."

————

"Where the hell have you been?" Nina Thatcher was livid.

"You're sounding like a wife," I said. "I've been out with the boys for a few boilermakers after a hard day's work on the assembly line," I said. I pulled the two Polaroid shots of Mark and Jack out of my jacket pocket and dropped them in front of her on the coffee table. "We were having such a delightful time we even managed to take a couple of snapshots to prove it."

Nina Thatcher picked the pictures up and looked at them. She put them back on the coffee table facedown. "Shit," she said.

"That about sums it up, yes," I said.

"What are you going to do?" she asked.

"I'm going to talk to you for a few minutes, and then I am going to start writing," I said. "What about the kid?"

"Well, since you left me here to play nursemaid, I played nursemaid," Nina Thatcher said. "We talked some, and watched a little television, and talked some more, and then Mark went to bed."

"And you?"

"I've been dozing on the couch, waiting for you," said Nina Thatcher. "Jesus, I *am* sounding like a wife."

"Mark say anything?"

"Nothing that would interest you," Nina Thatcher said. "He talked a lot about his family and how he knew at the age of ten or so that he was different from other boys. He's got deep guilts over his homosexuality and just this unbelievable love-hate thing with his mother."

"Welcome to abnormal psychology one-oh-one," I said. "Makes you think twice about having children, doesn't it?"

"My children wouldn't grow up like that," Nina Thatcher said.

"How do you know?"

"I wouldn't let them," Nina Thatcher said. "What else do you know?"

"Larry's dead."

"Larry who introduced Mark to Jack?"

"Yeah," I said. "That Larry. Larry Perkins."

"Oh," Nina Thatcher said. "Of course. Mark told me what Larry's last name was. He trusts me, you know."

"That's nice," I said. "Did he talk at all about Murray Fast or Larry or anybody else?"

"Mostly about Jack," Nina Thatcher said.

"Anything good? Anything I can put in the story?"

Nina Thatcher shook her head. "I really don't know about you," she said. "You are one in a million. The story. The story. Is that it for you? Is that all there is?"

"Just like the old song goes," I said.

"You must really hate Jack to be doing this to him."

I walked into the kitchen and took an open can of Tab from the refrigerator. I walked back into the living room with it. "Whose is this?" I asked.

"Mine," said Nina Thatcher. "Why?"

"Good," I said. I put the can to my lips and drained it. "From your lips is okay.

"Jack lied to me," I said. "Jack lied to all of us. I started on this thing because I thought, okay, it was a terrible shame, and Jack was working on a story he shouldn't have been working on. Now I find that he was lying. About everything. So maybe he was lying about his other stories, too." I walked back into the kitchen and dropped the Tab can into the wastebasket. "The story has to come out."

"Why?" Nina Thatcher stuck her lower lip out.

"You're sounding like my former friend again," I said. "It has to come out because it is a story. Because if we don't do it, somebody else will."

"Horse puckey," said Nina Thatcher. "You know what your problem is, Robert? You never examine the deeper motives. You've been out for the better part of two days chasing after your story. I've been sitting here with Mark talking. And I bet I have a deeper understanding of why Jack did what he did than you do."

"So you say," I said.

"Okay," said Nina Thatcher. "Why did Jack do what he did?"

"Well, I don't know," I said. "Madeleine, maybe. Or the thrill of living on the edge or some need to satisfy an animal craving. Or a combination of all those things."

"You're pigeonholing his emotions," Nina Thatcher said. "Damn you, Robert, Jack was a human being. Or can't you see that?"

"Of course I can," I said.

" 'Of course I can,' " Nina Thatcher said. "Horse shit. You have so few deep human relationships yourself that when you actually find one—Jack, in this case—you take him on without question. You accept everything he says. And if

there's a flaw anywhere, *anywhere*, then you think that he's betrayed you. Betrayed *you*—not himself. That's incredibly selfish, Robert."

"No, it's not."

"Yes, it is," said Nina Thatcher. "You're not leaving room for anyone's humanity. Face it, Robert. Have you sat down in the last few days and tried to think how Jack felt? About the pressures on him?"

"I knew about the pressures," I said. "Jack told me about the pressures."

"Not all of them," Nina Thatcher said. "Obviously not all of them, Robert."

"Okay, not all of them. But I knew about some of them. Some of them."

"Then why did Jack die?" Nina Thatcher asked.

"Because he was stupid," I said. "Because he broke the rules."

"Whose rules?" said Nina Thatcher. "Not his, certainly. Yours, Robert. He broke your rules, and I get the feeling that that made it okay for him to be killed. Jesus. You are incredible. Absolutely incredible."

"But that's what happened."

"That isn't what happened," said Nina Thatcher. "And if you'd really think about things, you'd know it." She slipped off the couch. "Is there any more Tab in the fridge?"

"I think so," I said. "All right," I said. "If you know so much, why was Jack killed?"

"I think he committed suicide," said Nina Thatcher's voice from the kitchen.

"Bullshit," I said.

"I knew you'd say that," Nina Thatcher said. "Of course, it's bullshit to you. Your logical, impeccable mind works in straight lines. Here's how you think: 'Jack is my friend. We share our secrets. I know he has this little sexual hang-up, but it doesn't matter because we are friends. Then he dies. But he doesn't have this harmless hang-up, it turns out, but a big, complex hang-up. Too complex for me to deal with. So he's not my friend anymore. He's a faggot. He has betrayed my trust and my friendship, and I will get him for it. He has

done me wrong, and I'll make sure every one of the paper's five hundred and sixty-eight thousand readers knows it.' That's the way you think.

"Are you blind, Robert? Think about it. Look at the family pressures Jack must have been under. Think about the guilt he carried with him. Jesus, how it must have piled up. Trying to live some kind of life without coming apart at the seams. It's not black and white for Christ's sake. And Jack's stories, Robert. Good stories. And okay, there was the other side. But you can't—it's—I mean, imagine how Jack felt in the bars here, and I know he told you he was in New York, but think of how he felt knowing, because he had to know, that someday somebody would find out just who he was and what he did for a living and blackmail the hell out of him."

Nina Thatcher walked over to a six-foot dieffenbachia and stroked one of the striped leaves.

"That puts real pressure on a person, Robert. Jack had to be pretty miserable down deep no matter how much good wine the two of you drank or caviar you ate or anything. And then he starts on the chicken-hawk story. He swears you to secrecy. But why the hell does he do *that* story? You know what I think, Robert? I think he did it because subconsciously he knew that it would kill him. I think in his gutty-wuts he knew that for him it was just as lethal as jumping out a window or blowing his brains out."

"I don't know," I said.

"That's your whole problem," Nina Thatcher said. "You don't know."

She paced in circles around the living room. "I'm finished sermonizing," Nina Thatcher said. "All right," Nina Thatcher said, "go write your story."

She held up her hand like a traffic cop. "Don't say anything, okay? Just go write your damn story. I'd like this whole nightmare to be over. Finished. I want to go back to my life, Robert. I want to get out of this apartment and go back to writing nice, comfortable features with happy endings. I have a normal life, Robert, if you can understand that. I'm seeing a man who appreciates me a lot. We go normal places on the weekends and see a lot of movies, and our sex life is

just fine, and the restaurants we eat at serve good food, and we talk a lot and share a lot. I don't know if you can understand that sort of thing, Robert. So go write your story because I want my life back. I'm happy with my life. I told you I will be your friend, and I am. I told you that I will help you, and I have. But I am finding it quite difficult to handle you on an up-close basis."

"I'm going," I said. "I have a deadline."

"Yes, you do," Nina Thatcher said. "You have a deadline. That's about all that you have, too. I'll have Mark ready midafternoon," she said. "You can give him to the Animal all wrapped up like a present." She crossed her arms and turned away. "Go off to your deadline," she said. "Get out of here. I'd like to be alone now."

Something in me did not want to leave. I had a tremendous sense of déjà vu. Almost three years before, Nancy had said the same thing to me. Nancy had been standing with her back to me in the Silver Lake apartment in Los Angeles and had said almost precisely the same thing. And I had gone then. I had left the trinity apartment while her back was turned. I had not kissed her good-bye. I had had a deadline and could not spare the time to talk. I looked at Nina Thatcher. Her shoulders were heaving slightly, but if she was crying, she made no sound.

"I'll see you later," I said to Nina Thatcher. Her back was still turned as I closed the door to the corporate apartment.

*chapter 17*_____

"How's the story going?" My voice on the tape had been clear. None of the usual cassette hiss because I had made the recording on my Dolby stereo deck, using two mikes, one for me, one for Jack, as we sat cross-legged on the floor of my living room sharing a magnum of Charles Heidsieck 1969, and two two-ounce jars of pressed Iranian caviar. We ate the caviar with spoons and drank the champagne from two Cartier crystal flute glasses that Jack had brought over from his place.

"Um, fine," said Jack Fowler's voice over a mouthful of food. The sound running through my stereo headset was superb. Studio-quality stuff. I followed the dialogue in the transcription I held in my lap like an opera libretto. It was like having Jack in the room again. "It's going to be great," Jack Fowler said. "Just great."

"Fantastic," I heard myself say. "We'll make you a star yet."

"Then we could work as a team," Jack said. "The Woodstein of Detroit. What do you think they'll call us, Fandel or Mowler?"

"It sounds like a wrestling tag team," I said. "What about Manler or Fowdel?"

"Too much like escaped Nazi war criminals," Jack Fowler said. "Maybe Mike will give us a column. We could call it the Jack and Robert Show."

"A guide to dope in the gay bars," I said. "Perfect."

"Six easy ways to shoot up," Jack Fowler said. "Recipes for the munchies."

"Some investigative column, huh?" I heard myself take a sip of champagne.

"What about a restaurant column? Lots of wine stuff. The most outrageous meals in the world," said Jack Fowler. "We could call it Hieronymus Gourmet."

"I think," said my voice, "that we'd better stick to street reporting."

"Maybe," said Jack Fowler. "Maybe." He took a spoonful of caviar.

"How are the streets?" I asked.

"Fine," Jack Fowler said. "Great," he said. He washed the caviar down with a mouthful of champagne. "It's so alive out there," he said. "Except. . . ."

"Yeah?"

"Except," Jack's voice said, "it's hard to deal with the situations sometimes."

"In what way?"

"It's so easy to go through records," said Jack Fowler. "Accounting reports, personnel sheets, or manpower figures. Like the stories about corrupt judges. It was all there for me on the public record. All I did was put the facts together—take one from Column A, another from Column B, and so on and so on. The bad guys were bad guys because they made mistakes that could be seen in dollars and cents, or they used bailiffs to paint their houses or took goods and services from people whose cases they heard. You write that kind of story, Robert, and all you have to do is enough research. It writes itself. All you're doing is laying out the facts for the reader."

"But?"

"But," Jack Fowler said, "this is different. I met a guy last week. A pimp named Scotty, okay?"

"Sure," I said.

"Okay, so I'm circulating in a gay bar called the Sand Box, and I meet this guy, and we start talking, and he propositions me. Solicits me, I should say. We have a couple of glasses of wine, and we strike a bargain. He invites me to his apartment to meet the boys, you know. But I'm not carrying a recorder or anything, so I put him off. I invite him up to my place the next night."

"You what?" My voice was incredulous.

"I invited him up to my place. I could wire my place. It was perfect."

"It's crazy," I said. "You should never invite them up to your place."

"Why?" asked Jack Fowler's voice.

"It's a rule," I said. "You never let them know where you live."

"Why?" asked Jack Fowler. "What's so bad about that? Shit, Robert, there's no place better to put someone at ease."

"And what happens if they guy decides to rip you off?" I asked. "What happens if he decides to come back and check you out? Suppose he walks up to the manager and asks about that nice guy Fowler who lives upstairs. 'Oh,' says the manager, 'you mean the newspaper reporter?' What happens to your cover then?"

"So you invite him late at night when the manager is off," Jack Fowler said.

"And you don't let him rip you off? How the hell can you stop him?" I asked.

"You stop him," Jack Fowler said. "We're getting off the subject, Robert."

"I'm sorry," I said. "But you can't do that."

"But I have," Jack Fowler's voice said. "So drop it, all right?"

"Okay," I said. "It's just breaking the rules, is all."

"I'm not talking about rules," Jack Fowler's voice was saying. "I have broken enough rules in my life, believe me. I don't need to be told I'm breaking yours, too."

"Okay, okay," my voice said. "Go on."

"What my problem is," Jack Fowler said, "is making the same kind of black-and-white decisions about the people in the story that I was able to make in the courts."

"In what way?" I asked.

"I told you," Jack Fowler said. "Records are hard fact. Lay them out, bam, bam, bam. But here, like Scotty—okay, Scotty is a real shithole. He's a pimp, and he makes his living selling little boys."

"So," I said, "what's the problem?"

"What about the boys?" Jack asked.

"What about them?"

"If I write this. When I write this, what happens to them?"

"What does it matter?" I said. "Probably you've done them some good. They'll go off the street. Maybe back to their parents. Maybe to an institution. But they won't be playing with strangers' dongs and giving the money to Scotty what's-his-name."

"That's not enough," Jack's voice said. "It's not enough."

"That's all there is," I said. I heard myself standing up. "Look," my voice said, "there are no results in what you're doing. There are no answers. You write something about judges' conflicts of interest, and maybe you're going to get results. Maybe there'll be an investigation. Maybe things will change. On the surface. For a while. Then you'll have to write the story again. Fine. Them's the rules. That's the way it works. But for Christ's sake, Jack, when I'm working on a dope story, I'm not trying to get results. Like this Westvale project. Maybe I'll close it down. I will close it down. But so what? In less than a week the action will move somewhere else. Maybe to the Cinderella, or the Riviera, or somewhere that hasn't even opened yet. All I can hope to do is to tell the readers, 'This is happening in your city. Know about it.' What happens to the people involved doesn't concern me."

"You're wrong," Jack Fowler's voice said.

"I'm not," I said. "Them's the rules, Jack."

"I told you they're your rules, not mine," Jack said. "What the hell good is writing what I'm writing if I can't help the kids?"

189

"Letting the readers know," I said. "This conversation is going nowhere," I said. "You refuse to take my word for something that's a rule. If I were working on a story about court reporters, I'd check with you for the lay of the land. You'd tell me what the rules were, and I'd play by them. That's what I'm doing for you. You're no street person. I am."

"How do you know?" Jack's voice asked.

"Because I know," I said. "Because you're not."

"Listen, old chap"—Jack's voice slipped into the nasal Oxonian drawl—"I can be whatever I want to be, and if that includes being a street person, then that's what I'll be." His voice changed. Now it became lispy, faggoty, pansified. "And if I have to sweet-talk a hustler, dearie, then that's exactly what I'll do. Listen, beautiful, it ain't no big thing."

"Great," I said. "You're great with accents. So what?"

"So nothing," Jack Fowler said. His voice was normal again. "But don't tell me what I am and what I'm not, Robert. I know what I am. And I know that what bothers me about this story is that there's no black and white. It's all written in shades of gray. Even the pimps, I guess."

"Bullshit," my voice said. "You sound like a bleeding liberal. Shades of gray. What horse manure."

I switched off the cassette deck and threw the transcript down. There was no use in listening anymore, in trying to pry significance out of month-old conversations. There was a story to write. It was out of my hands, out of Jack's hands. All that existed was the story: the pile of empty copy sets and my machine. I had three hours until my deadline.

———

The story was on Mike's desk by noon. It covered the ground pretty well, I thought. I used the background material Jerry Daley had given me, including a description of Larry Perkins's trick book, which I had trouble describing in words suitable to a family newspaper. But I managed. I showed Mike the two Polaroids of Jack and Mark, too.

"God, I'd love to use these," he said. "There's no way, of course." Then he had his secretary walk them down to the

photo department to be copied, instructing her to keep the originals in sight at all times and bring back all prints, including rejects. "Somebody," said Mike, "is leaking stuff out of this building to the competition. I don't think I want to take a chance with these." Then he read my story.

Mike buzzed Larry Chesler on the intercom. "We have Robert's second part here," he said. "Come on by."

Larry Chesler read my stuff in Mike's office. "Are you sure you want to print this?" he asked.

"Why the hell not?" Mike said. "It's the truth, isn't it, Robert?"

"It's the facts," I said. "There's a difference."

"It's brutal," Larry Chesler said. "Robert, you're crucifying Jack."

"I'm writing the facts," I said. "No more, no less."

Mike wanted it run. Mike wanted to get out to lunch, to his four martinis. Mike was impatient. He opened his desk drawer and pulled out one of the Polaroids, recently returned from the photo lab. "Here's a suitable illustration," he said to Larry Chesler.

"My God," said Larry Chesler. He put his glasses on top of his head. "You're not serious," he said.

"The story's sufficient," Mike said. "Run the story." He took the Polaroid back, slipped it into the drawer, and turned the lock. "Print it under the masthead in a box. Robert and I are going to lunch." Larry Chesler just stood there. "Good-bye," said Mike, "you have work to do."

We sat at Mike's regular booth at the Chop House. He drank; I watched. I was not very hungry. Some reporters are ravenous after finishing a story. I am not. I am drained and empty. To me it's like after sex. Actually the similarities between writing and sex are pretty close so far as I'm concerned. Everything from foreplay to postcoital sadness. Nancy used to accuse me of getting off on my stories. Maybe she was right. I was never any good at lovemaking after having written something. After research was something else. But writing just spends me physically. I couldn't get it up for very long. I have always wanted to be alone after writing an

article—a long, involved article. I have always needed the time: to calm myself down; to unfocus the energy; to become a human being again. Down time. And then, of course, it starts all over again. It's very sexual, I think. Writers who burn themselves out think of themselves as creatively impotent.

Mike was talking to me, but I was not listening. I was somewhere else. With Jack. With Nancy. With Nina Thatcher.

"How's Thatcher doing?"

I heard that. "Okay," I said. "She's holding up okay. She wants to get back to work."

"She is working," Mike said. "Has she been a help?"

"Tremendous," I said. "She's good with the kid. He trusts her. She really knew how to squeeze him. Got a lot of information."

"Good," said Mike. He drained his glass. Another was set in front of him without his asking. "And Halloran?"

"Halloran?"

"Was Halloran any help?"

"Sure," I said.

"I don't see how," Mike said. "The asshole."

"If you'd get off his back, he'd be fine," I said. "He's a good man."

Mike grunted and poked at the olive in the bottom of his glass.

"We're going to give the kid to the Animal," I said.

"Uh-huh," Mike said. He bit the olive in half.

"Five o'clock today in the city room."

"Fine," said Mike. He chewed the rest of the olive. He looked at me.

"Daley's calling the TV stations, right?"

"Right."

"And the wires, and the newsmagazines, and our friends down the street?"

"Yes," I said. "But it'll be too late for them to do anything."

"Great," Mike said.

"And Daley's going to want you to say something to the

cameras. You know, like how great he's been working on Jack's case."

Mike chased the olive with a swallow of martini. "I'll be happy to do it," he said. "I think," he said, "that this story is going to take off. *Time* and *Newsweek* called today. We'll probably make the press section next week. You're going to be famous, Robert. I'm going to make you a star."

"Thanks," I said.

"People are going to notice," Mike said. "This is going to do wonders for our reputation." Mike sipped at his drink.

"Why?"

"Because we're all over the story," Mike said. "It's not like we had to skin back, you know. Here's our own guy killed, and we've got the news out first. His secret life, his lovers— we're really going to build circulation on this one, Robert."

"Lovely," I said. I did not mean it. "Great," I said. I didn't mean that either.

"How long?" Mike said.

"What?" I hadn't been listening.

"When is Daley going to close this thing out?"

"I don't know," I said. "Soon," I said. I watched as Mike drained the second martini. He looked up. He did not like to have to wait between drinks. "Daley still doesn't have any ideas about who did what to whom," I said.

"How come?" Mike asked.

"Because he hasn't read my story," I said. "Daley doesn't know about Murray Fast, whose picture is in the trick book. And there's a connection between Murray and Larry and Mark and Jack. And two other guys. I don't know who they are. Hustlers, maybe."

Mike chewed a third olive. "Come on," he said, "eat something."

"I'm not hungry," I said. "Really."

"Even on my expense account?" Mike was smiling.

"Try me for dinner when this is all over," I said.

"You got it," Mike said. "The Jack Fowler Memorial Dinner." He drained the third glass. He didn't have to look up. Martini number four slid across the tablecloth.

"See," Mike said.

"See what?"

"Remember you were reluctant to take the story on," Mike said. "See what you would have missed."

"What?" I asked.

"An offer to buy you dinner," Mike said. He laughed. "Hey," he said, "do you think we could solve the case? You know more than Daley, Robert. Could we break it open?"

"What?" I said, I hadn't been listening. I had been thinking about the two Polaroids sitting locked in Mike's desk. I had been thinking about black-and-white stories versus gray stories. "We need background," I said to Mike.

"Do you think we could break the case open?" Mike said.

"We need background," I said. "Have we talked to any shrinks about Jack's mental state?"

"No," Mike said. "Come on, Robert, could we?"

"We should talk to somebody," I said. I was having second thoughts again. The the-story-hasn't-been-published-yet-and-maybe-I-haven't-checked-things-as-well-as-I-could-have blues. "No," I said. "We can't break the case open because I don't know enough," I said. "What about a shrink?" I asked.

"Why?" Mike held the fourth olive in front of his nose and stared at it. He crossed his eyes on purpose, then popped the olive into his mouth. "Why should we?"

"Added depth," I said. "Look, I'll go back to the apartment. Let Thatcher find a shrink and talk to him. We can make the first edition if she hurries. It'll make a good sidebar, I promise."

"Sure," said Mike. "Sure. Go ahead. I'll tell Chesler to carve a hole. Three books, though, okay? Three books."

I was sliding out of the booth before Mike finished talking. "Thanks," I said.

"For what?"

"For lunch," I said.

"I can't," Nina Thatcher said. "I won't," she said. "There's no time," she said.

"Come on," I said. "You were the one giving me all that

shit about not understanding the problem. Okay, so even things out. Here's a chance. It'll be a good sidebar. It'll give the story balance."

Nina Thatcher nodded toward the bathroom, where Mark was taking a shower. "What about him?"

"What about him?" I said. "I'll take care of getting him over to the paper. Come on, Thatcher. If you hurry, you can get out to Ann Arbor before two-thirty. You can talk to three people and phone the damn thing in in plenty of time. Come on. If you're so sure about all those pressures Jack was under, why not do something? And what about the suicide angle, huh? If you can find some basis for that, you've got yourself a great piece."

"Why me?" said Nina Thatcher.

"Because you put the idea in my head in the first place. It's only fair that you get part of the story. It's your part of the story."

"I don't believe you," Nina Thatcher said. "I think you're too chickenshit to find out that you're wrong, so you stick me on it." She sipped on a glass of Tab. She wasn't going anyplace.

"I think," said Nina Thatcher, "that you're incapable of dealing with this whole side of Jack, so you're sloughing it off on me. You never even thought of calling a psychiatrist to ask an opinion, did you? Just the facts. Now you're scared your story won't hold up because it's not fleshed out, so you get me to do your work for you."

"Think what you want," I said. "I don't care. I don't give a rat's ass. First you tell me about all these psychological pressures Jack was under; now, when you have a chance to prove it in print, you say no."

"You're worse than Mike," Nina Thatcher said. "Do you realize you probably have a great future as an executive editor someplace?"

"Hey," I said. "Let's just say that I may have been a little bit wrong, and you may have been a little bit right."

"I don't believe it," Nina Thatcher said. "You have just said that you could have been wrong."

"I'm only human."

"Don't overstate the case," said Nina Thatcher. But she walked over to the closet and got her Burberry out. "I'll do it," she said. "For Jack, not for you. Can I borrow your car?"

"It's double-parked downstairs," I said. "I'll call Mike."

Nina Thatcher tied the Burberry's belt around her waist. "I'll have something in by about four-thirty," she said. "Good enough?"

"Perfect," I said. Then there was a pause.

Finally Nina Thatcher said, "Well, okay." Then she said, "I'll see you. I have a deadline to make."

I said, "Drive safe."

"I will," Nina Thatcher said.

"I'll see you later." She was standing by the door. "Thatcher," I said, "good luck. And thanks."

"You're welcome," Nina Thatcher said. She reached for the door. Then she sort of skipped over to where I was standing and gave me a hug.

She ran for the door. "I'll make the deadline," she said.

*chapter 18*_____

By and large, reporters do not like being a part of the stories they cover. Reporters hate being interviewed. They do not like seeing their words in print, seeing themselves quoted for attribution. There is a reason for this. They know all too well what happens to interviews. A sentence here, a paragraph there, all cut apart and used, as politicians are fond of saying, out of context. Nancy came home one night years ago and found me in the middle of our living room, trying to make sense of an interview. It was a two-hour taped dialogue with a homicide cop, which I was putting together for the Sunday magazine. We had green wall-to-wall carpeting in the living room, and I was on my hands and knees with a pair of editor's shears and a giant Scotch tape dispenser, snipping lines from my transcript and pasting them on other sheets. She asked what I was doing.

I told her that interviews had to be structured. I explained that often you start talking about something, and then another subject comes up and you talk about that for a while, and then you return to the original topic. You just can't

publish things as they occur, I explained. There has to be a structure to an interview, I said. It has to follow a dramatic line. A rising action, climax, falling action, and denouement, I said. Nancy understood this. She spent the better part of her days reading and evaluating scripts for CBS. But, she asked, can you really tell me that you're applying Aristotelian rules to the construction of interviews? And is it fair to the subject?

That I couldn't answer. All I knew, I said to Nancy, was that you couldn't write an interview by taking the transcript and printing it as it was. Snippets and fragments had to be rearranged to make good sense. The reader had to be intrigued by what was being said.

We weren't fighting in those days, Nancy and I. Our conversations didn't deteriorate into arguments. So I stopped my work and gathered up my sheets of transcribed dialogue, and we sat on pillows on the green wall-to-wall carpet and discussed interviews and how they compared to television scripts. We listened to each other. Really listened. I remember that the conversation digressed, too. Nancy was under a lot of pressure in those days. CBS was number one in the ratings and wanted to stay that way. The network craved new series ideas, and that craving flowed down to Nancy's level.

She would come home tired and irritable, yet find the time to cook dinner. For my part I'd splurge on bottles of good wine—I was just beginning to build up my cellar in those days—and we would share our troubles over a bottle of Château Montrose '53 or a '59 Vosne-Romanée and then stretch out on the living-room floor, and I'd roll Nancy onto her stomach and massage her back, her legs, and her shoulders.

It was easy at first to let our troubles dissipate over dinner and wine. But as our lives grew apart professionally, it became harder and harder to do so. Each of us developed our own set of rules for survival, I guess. And they did not mix. Of course, Nancy's rules were less regimented than mine. She could never understand hard-and-fast rules. Hers were elastic, easily broken. For my part, I began to feel that with-

out definite limits I would eventually become the same as the victims I wrote about. Without rules I would be manipulated; I would just let things happen instead of making them happen.

Our files were different, too. Nancy clipped the newspaper for story ideas. They all were upbeat. She would scan for stories that might be transmogrified into series. One I remember was the story of a bum named Winston Pringle who lived under the First Street Bridge. He helped a couple of cops solve a robbery case. He was a colorful old guy, and Nancy thought a story based on his experiences might do very well. She dutifully filed the Pringle clip away. Six months later she threw it out when I showed her another story, a two-inch news story, detailing how Winston Pringle had beaten one of his fellow bums senseless with a length of two-by-four and had moved his residence from the First Street Bridge to the county jail.

Anyhow, the interview I was editing that night was a stream-of-consciousness kind of piece. A third-person narrative about a homicide cop who worked out of Hollenbeck Division. I used to get a lot of pieces in Los Angeles out of Hollenbeck Division. No one from the paper ever went down there, and the ground was fertile with stories. The cop's name was Dick, and he loved his job. We spent a week riding together in his olive-green Plymouth felony car. He used to love that car. He'd brag about what he called its four-seventy air conditioning. "You open four windows and go seventy miles an hour," he would say.

Dick taught me a lot about rules. He lived by rules. As Nancy looked at the transcripts of my conversations with him, she became fascinated by Dick's rules, too. Especially one of them. For years Dick had made a rule of keeping what he called his WBB file. He had a cop's sensitivity, finely tuned antennae for life's victims. And when he met one, that person's name was entered in the WBB folder. WBB, he said, stood for Will Be Back.

That's horrible, Nancy said to me as we sat on the pillows and looked at the transcript. That's really coldhearted, she said.

I told her, maybe so. But, I added, that's real. That's the way things operate. Those, I said, are the rules.

She couldn't understand that. Cataloguing potential victims was not something that Nancy could ever conceive doing.

Soon after the piece on Dick, the homicide cop, appeared, I started keeping my own WBB file. It served me very well. Life's potential victims and villains, neatly arranged alphabetically. There were always half a dozen good stories in that file.

I wonder now, had I met Jack Fowler under different circumstances would I have put his name in the WBB. Somehow I don't think so. Jack was too smooth, too good a liar. Until he died, he was not a candidate for my WBB. After he died, he never stopped coming back.

Take the press conference, for example. Nina Thatcher was in Ann Arbor, interviewing shrinks at the University of Michigan medical school. I was in the city room, which looked like the set of *All the President's Men,* with TV lights strung up and minicams on tripods and a dozen reporters milling in front of Mike's office.

I was inside the glass-enclosed space, with Mike and Larry Chesler and our ME, Tom Collier. And Mark. Jerry Daley was there, too, along with two of his investigators. We watched as the TV crews filmed us through the glass. We had plotting to do.

"I think Mike should make a statement," Jerry Daley said. "Something about the paper's convincing Mark to come forward. Then I can tell everybody that he has nothing to say until later. Then I can do a little fancy footwork answering questions, and we can all get out of here in time to see ourselves on the six o'clock news."

"Fine," said Mike. "But I'd like to wait for our attorney to get here. He's on his way."

"Okay by me," said Jerry Daley. He looked at Mark. "How you doing, kid?" he asked.

Mark nodded. "Fine," he said. "Okay." He looked at me with sad dog's eyes.

"It's all all right, Mark," I said. "It's okay. Everything's

gonna be cool." I looked at the kid. I closed my eyes, and I saw Jack. Jack the way I knew him. The real Jack. I opened my eyes. There was no real Jack. I looked at Mark again. Dressed in a tan pullover knit shirt with long sleeves and a pair of corduroy dungarees that Nina Thatcher had bought for him. I turned away and stared at the Pulitzer Prize on Mike's wall. I thought about the Polaroid pictures. It was very hard to look at Mark. There was absolutely no conversation in Mike's office. We could hear the noises outside. The TV crews. One reporter was doing a stand-up. He turned and pointed at us. I wanted to become invisible.

There was a commotion in the city room. Mike said, "The lawyer." But it wasn't the lawyer. Cameras swung around; lights flashed. A small woman with frizzy red hair was elbowing her way through the crowd of reporters and technicians. The cameras were on. People were thrusting microphones in her face, tape recorders were being held under her chin as she and a companion waded through the crowd toward Mike's office.

"Who the hell is she?" Mike stood up from his desk.

Mark knew who it was. "It's my mother," he said. "Oh shit oh shit you called my mother. You shits called my mother." He came at me with his fists. "I can't stand it, I can't stand it," he screamed. "You bastard, you called my mother."

I grappled with him. Jerry Daley's two cops picked him up and put him in an armchair. They held him down by his shoulders. Jerry Daley said, "I called your mother, Mark. You're a minor. I had to call your mother."

"Oh shit oh shit oh shit oh motherfucker piss piss piss shit." Mark was moaning. He was close to total hysteria. It was all happening so fast; much too fast. When I played the Nagra tape back later, there seemed to be no logical sequence to what went on. Only in transcription did it become orderly, one voice following another. On the tape, voice piled upon voice. It was hell to transcribe.

The woman burst into Mike's office. She saw Mark, held in place by the cops, and ran to him. "My baby," she cried. Then she hit him across the face. "What did you do?" she screamed. "My darling, I'm so sorry," she cried. Then she

shook him by the hair. "Do you know what I've gone through?" she said. She kissed him all over his face. Then she slapped him. "Louse," she said. "Little louse, you."

She turned to us. She didn't know whom to talk to. Mark buried his face in his hands and cried. "He didn't do anything," she said. "He's just a child," she said. "What have you done to him?" she asked. She looked, wild-eyed, for the man who had come with her. "Lawyer," she said. "My lawyer," she said. "He's innocent," she said. "My child is innocent," she said. "He won't say anything," she said. She looked at Mike, who was standing behind his desk. She must have realized that Mike had something to do with the paper. "I'll sue you," she said. "You kidnapped him. My child. My only child," she said. "A million dollars I'll sue you for. You made him part of this," she said.

Mike held up his hands. Mark's mother flung off the wool cape that she was wearing. It landed on Mike's carpet. Jerry Daley retrieved it and folded it over the back of a chair. "My child, my son," she said. "Oh, God." She dissolved in tears. The room was silent. It took Mrs. Brown only ten seconds to recover her breath. "I'll close you down," she screamed at Mike. "You kidnapped my child. I'll sue you bastards. You'll pay."

Jerry Daley took her by the shoulders and pushed her toward another of Mike's steel-framed armchairs. "It's all right," he said. "Please try to calm down," he said.

"Calm?" she screamed. She stood up again. "Calm? My boy is missing for days and I get a call from the district attorney and you say to be calm? He didn't do anything. He's a good boy. He goes to school. He has nice friends, and I should be calm? A murder case—the fruit who works for the paper—and I should be calm? I'll sue you bastards, all of you." She collapsed in the chair, out of breath.

I looked through the glass wall of Mike's office. The TV cameramen were having a field day. The camera eyes were panning back and forth on us. I looked at Mike. "Can we do something about that?" I said. I nodded outside.

"Curtains," Mike said. He walked to the corner of his office and pulled on a set of cords. A set of translucent curtains

walled us off from the lights. A chorus of boos went up outside.

Mark's mother was sobbing. The man she had come with walked over to her and put a hand on the back of the arm-chair, just above her shoulder.

"I'm Mrs. Brown's attorney," he said. "Sheldon Reiss. I'm looking after Mark's interests."

"They kidnapped him," Mrs. Brown said. Her mascara was running. There was a lot of it. Tire tracks, skid marks on her cheeks.

Jerry Daley looked around. "Let's all calm down," he said. "Please."

Mrs. Brown poked into a small purse that was strapped around her waist. She found a handkerchief inside and wiped at her face. She blew her nose and looked at the results before crumpling the handkerchief in clenched hands.

"Mr. Reiss," Jerry Daley said, "my name is Daley. I'm with the district attorney."

"I know," said Sheldon Reiss. "I know who you are."

"Good," said Jerry Daley.

Mike spoke up. "Perhaps we should all introduce ourselves," he said. "My name is Weston," he said. "I'm the executive editor." He pointed at Tom Collier, then at Larry Chesler. "Tom Collier," Mike said, "is the managing editor. Larry Chesler"—Larry nodded—"is the city editor." He looked around. He saw me standing in the corner, under the Pulitzer. "Robert Mandel," he said. "Robert is the reporter who's covering Jack Fowler's story," he said.

Sheldon Reiss nodded. "Mr. Weston," he said, "we appear to have a bit of a problem here. Mark has been missing for more than two days. Mrs. Brown has been very concerned, as you can well imagine." He removed his hand from the back of the armchair and walked to where Mark was sitting.

"This morning we got a call from Mr. Daley. Mr. Daley said that Mark was a material witness in the Fowler murder. He asked us to meet him here at five. Mrs. Brown called me, of course."

"Of course," said Jerry Daley.

"Now it appeared to Mrs. Brown that your paper"—Shel-

don Reiss indicated Mike—"had taken Mark and hidden him. It appeared to Mrs. Brown that you never let him call her and say where he was, or with whom, or that he was all right."

Mike looked at me, eyebrows raised. I shook my head. We had Mark's phone call on tape.

"Is that true, Mark?" Jerry Daley spoke up.

Mark was silent. He sat in the armchair, crying.

"Robert?" Jerry Daley looked at me.

"Mark called home," I said.

"Liar." Mrs. Brown stood up and pointed her finger at me. "He never—"

"I have a record of the call," I said. "There was a witness," I said.

Mrs. Brown sat down again.

Sheldon Reiss continued. "In any case," he said, "Mark was kept against his will."

"I don't think so," said Mike. "I think we have records to disprove that, too. Isn't that right, Robert?"

"Yes," I said. "We've got that, too."

"Mr. Reiss," said Jerry Daley, "before we start saying things that everyone here could be sorry about saying, I think you and I should go off into the corner and talk for a minute." He led Sheldon Reiss away. The room was silent, except for the two men murmuring to each other. Jerry Daley reached into the breast pocket of his jacket and brought out a glassine envelope. He showed the contents to Sheldon Reiss, whose eyes widened. I edged toward Mike.

"The Polaroids," I whispered.

It didn't take very long after that. Sheldon Reiss walked back toward Mrs. Brown. "I think," he said, "that you and Mark should cooperate with Mr. Daley," he said. "Harriet, I believe it's in Mark's best interests to cooperate. Mr. Daley assures me that Mark is not in any trouble. There are just some questions that have to be asked."

"What does he know? He's a child," said Harriet Brown.

"That's what we have to find out," said Jerry Daley. He looked at Harriet Brown and half smiled. He walked over to where she was sitting and knelt in front of her. "Mrs.

Brown," he said. He balanced himself with two hands on the arms of her chair. Jerry Daley became avuncular and homey. "There's nothing serious. But your son was acquainted with Jack Fowler, and we're talking to everyone who was acquainted with Jack Fowler. That's all."

"But he was a fruit," said Harriet Brown. She pointed at Mike. "Your stories. He was a fruit. He ran around with little boys. I read the stories. He had a little boyfriend. He—" Her eyes went wide "Oh, God," she screamed. "No, not Mark," she wailed. "It's impossible," she cried. She bolted from the chair and ran to her son, who had pulled himself into a fetal position in his chair. She beat him around the head. "You, you, you, you," she said. "Tell me, tell me, tell me, tell me," she screamed, slapping Mark's head with each word. Daley's cops pulled her away. They half carried, half dragged her back to her chair. "No, no, no, no, no, no," she sobbed.

Jerry Daley looked at Mike. "Is there a back way out of here?" he asked.

Mike shook his head. "I'm afraid not," he said.

"Can we clear the city room?" he asked.

Mike peered through the curtains. "I don't think so," he said.

"I'll call for more people," Jerry Daley said.

"No way," said Mike. "That's all we need. A roomful of photographers and reporters. No way, Jerry."

"You're right," said Jerry Daley. "Okay—here's what happens. I go out and say something. Then Robert, you and Mike take Mark, and Mr. Reiss, Sheldon, gets Mrs. Brown—one of my guys will help you—and the rest of us run interference."

"I don't think we can ethically do that," said Mike. "I don't want those cameras out there getting pictures of us looking like cops running through a bunch of reporters, including my reporters."

Jerry Daley sat on the edge of Mike's desk. "Ideas?" he asked.

No one said a word. Mark and his mother were sobbing. Sheldon Reiss ran a hand through his hair. Then he shot his French cuffs and cleared his throat. We looked at him.

"Nothing," he said.

Jerry Daley snorted. "Off the record," he said, looking at me, "if I were running for anything, this would be a hell of a way to start."

"Aren't you glad you're not?" said Mike.

"What?"

"Running," said Mike. "For anything." He emitted a sound halfway between a giggle and a hiccup. "I'd like a martini now," said Mike.

There was a banging on Mike's door. "Go away," he shouted. "We're busy."

The door opened. Nina Thatcher stuck her head inside. "I'm back," she said. "I phoned it in," she said. "You wouldn't believe the traffic," she said. She looked at Mark.

"Hi, Mark," she said.

Mark climbed out of his chair and ran to her. He was a head taller than Nina Thatcher, but he managed to throw his arms around her like a small child. "Oh, Miss Thatcher," he said. Then he burst into tears again.

"It's all right," Nina Thatcher said. She looked at Mike. She looked at me. She looked at Tom Collier and Larry Chesler and Jerry Daley and Sheldon Reiss and Harriet Brown. "Isn't it?

"It's not," she said. She edged Mark back toward his chair. He did not remove his arms, and Nina Thatcher had a hard time moving. "Take it easy, Mark," she said. "We're all here to help you, I think."

"She knows," Mark said to Nina Thatcher. He pointed to his mother. "She knows."

Nina Thatcher settled Mark in the chair. Then she knelt in front of him. "She had to, sometime," she said. "We talked about that, didn't we, Mark? We talked about that."

Mark rubbed his nose with the back of a hand. He nodded.

"Well?" said Nina Thatcher.

"But not like this," said Mark. He dissolved into tears again.

Nina Thatcher stroked the top of his head. "It's okay," she said. "It's going to be okay."

206

She looked at Mike. She looked at me. "What the hell is going on?" she said.

Mike threw up his hands. "I don't know," he said. "This was supposed to be a press conference," he said. "Mark was going to cooperate with Jerry Daley, and Jerry was going to thank the paper for getting Mark to cooperate. Sounds simple."

"So," said Nina Thatcher. She looked at Harriet Brown. "You must be Mark's mother," she said. "Mark has told me so much about you." Nina Thatcher looked me straight in the eye. "Mark is a fine young man," she said. Harriet Brown nodded. She looked up at Nina Thatcher.

"Yes," said Mark's mother.

Things seemed to pick up after that. Jerry Daley went out front and mollified the news crews, who made their six o'clock live remote feeds. He was able to talk them out of trying to shoot pictures of Mark and his mother leaving Mike's office, although I was never sure whether they left because of Daley's persuasion or because they had plenty of good footage before Mike closed his curtains. By six-thirty we were able to get the Browns and Sheldon Reiss out of Mike's office and down the freight elevator into an unmarked car parked by the loading dock. Nina Thatcher and I walked out with Jerry Daley and the Browns. Mark had his arms around his mother as they walked.

Outside the car Jerry Daley said, "Well."

"Well," I said. "What next?"

"We're still checking out the information in Larry's trick book," Jerry Daley said.

"Look," I said. "Maybe I have something for you. But I want to work a deal."

"Tell me, and I'll see," said Jerry Daley.

"Tomorrow morning," I said. "Can you meet me for breakfast?"

"Where?" said Jerry Daley.

"Pontchartrain Hotel at eight," I said. "I'd talk now, Jerry, but I haven't slept in a couple of days, and I still have a story to write."

"Sure, kid," Jerry Daley said. "We'll talk tomorrow. See

you." He climbed into the back seat of his unmarked car, squeeezing alongside Mrs. Brown. Jerry Daley's fishing cap was mashed in the rear window, and as they drove off, he pulled it from his head.

I watched them go. "How about a drink?" I asked Nina Thatcher.

"I deserve one," she said. "Let me make a phone call first," she said.

"Make it from the restaurant," I said.

———

"How was Ann Arbor?" Nina Thatcher and I were sitting at the Chop House in one of their rearmost banquettes.

"Busy," she said. "Robert," she said, "can I have a blackberry brandy straight up?"

"Sure," I said. "Why?"

"My mother used to tell me it settles the stomach."

"Does it?"

"We'll see."

"Why does your stomach need settling?" I waved for a waiter. I couldn't get anyone's attention. I have decided that the world is separated into two classes of people: those who can summon waiters and those who can't. I fall into the second category.

"I know this looks silly," I said. I was practicing semaphore with my napkin. Finally, a waiter took notice and I ordered.

"Oh, I don't know," said Nina Thatcher. "Three days with Mark—almost three days—and not eating and arguing with you."

"Who was arguing?"

"Listen to yourself," said Nina Thatcher.

"You know," I said, "It's funny."

"What is?"

"It all started here," I said. "At the Chop. Now we're back," I said.

"Without Jack," Nina Thatcher said. The waiter placed a snifter in front of her and a scotch and soda in front of me.

"Tell me," said Nina Thatcher. "What do you think about Jack now?"

"I don't know," I said. "I don't know. Really."

"Really," she said. "Why?"

"It's hard," I said. "Look, we were friends. We talked. We shared things. He lied to me. What am I supposed to feel?"

"Compassion maybe," said Nina Thatcher. She sipped at her drink. "Excuse me for a second, Robert, I still have to make a call."

"Do it later."

"No," said Nina Thatcher. "I have to call now." She slid out from behind the table and walked toward the phone booths by the maître d's rostrum. I sat and toyed with my drink until she returned.

"I can't stay long," she said. "I'm being picked up in a few minutes."

"Your friend?"

"My friend."

We sat silently for some moments.

"What's next?" Nina Thatcher asked.

"I'm going to tell Jerry Daley about Murray Fast," I said. "On the condition that he takes me with him when he goes to see Murray."

"Why?"

"I think there's something there," I said. "Larry's trick book. There are pictures."

"I know," Nina Thatcher said. "You told me."

"What about your suicide theory?" I asked. "I never saw your story."

"It holds up," Nina Thatcher said. "The shrinks said that it could have been an unconscious form of suicide. Almost an easy way out for Jack."

"I still can't believe that," I said.

"There are things that you don't know," said Nina Thatcher. "Believe it or not, Robert, there are things you don't know."

"Funny," I said. "Very funny." I played with my glass. "What are you going to do?" I asked Nina Thatcher.

"I told you," she said. "I'm going back to my life. First I'm going home and changing my clothes and taking a long, long shower. Then I'm planning to get a good night's rest."

"With your friend?"

"Probably," she said. "I don't think it's any business of yours."

"Just an idle comment," I said. "It's the reporter in me."

"Are you recording this?" Nina Thatcher said.

"You keep asking me that question."

"Are you?"

"Yes."

"Christ," said Nina Thatcher. She sipped at her drink. "I see now."

"See what?"

"Your friend in Los Angeles," Nina Thatcher said. "The one you keep trying to tell me about."

"You see what?"

"I can see why you're not together anymore."

"It wasn't taping. That's not why we broke up."

"But why do you tape?" Nina Thatcher asked. "Why is it necessary?"

"I have to keep records."

"Horse puckey," said Nina Thatcher.

"No, it's true—"

"Horse shit," said Nina Thatcher. "What are you afraid of, Robert? What are you so afraid of?"

"Nothing," I lied.

"You still won't talk, will you?" Nina Thatcher said. "What am I going to do? Hold it against you in a court of law? Blackmail you maybe?"

"You never know," I said. We sat in some silence for some seconds. Thirty-eight seconds to be precise. Thirty-eight seconds is a long silence when you're sitting at a table.

"You look lovely," I said.

"Jesus," Nina Thatcher said. "You really are an emotional cripple."

We sat silently for another twenty-nine seconds. I know, I timed it later. Then Nina Thatcher said, "You know, Robert, you did talk to me once. Was that so bad?"

"When you came up to my place the first time."

"When I came up to your place," Nina Thatcher said, "you really talked. You dealt with your emotions, your feelings.

210

You were vulnerable, and you made me feel your vulnerability. That's why I said I'd help you, Robert. Not because of Jack or because it's a good story—although God knows it is a good story and it's gotten to me. I told you I'd be your friend because you needed a friend. You weren't afraid to show that need. You weren't afraid to talk to me. For those few minutes you became very human, Robert, and that touched me. It really touched me."

"I don't talk very much about myself," I said. "It's just that people tell me things, not the other way around.

"Why?"

"Because," I said. "Because that's the way it is. Because I'm a reporter. Because I don't like to talk."

"What about you as a human being?"

"That's secondary," I said. "Of course, I'm a human being."

"Well, why don't you feel like one?" Nina Thatcher said. "Why don't you let your emotions out?"

"It's hard," I said. "It's hard—"

"Of course it is." Nina Thatcher licked at a drop of blackberry brandy sliding down the outside of her snifter. "Of course, it's hard. But you have to have a life, Robert. You can't live your whole existence just with your stories."

"Why not?" I said.

"It's not healthy. There has to be something more."

"There's not," I said. "The stories are what matter. I know that. Jack—even Jack knew that."

Nina Thatcher drained her snifter. "I don't believe you," she said. "I think you are full of shit." She puffed up her cheeks like a chipmunk. "Out to here," she said, bracketing her cheeks with her hands. She looked at her sensible watch and started sliding into her Burberry. "I have to go."

"Don't," I said.

"I have to," Nina Thatcher said.

She pulled her coat around her and buttoned it. "I do my job," she said. "I write what I'm assigned to write. But there's more to my life than my stories. I like being good at what I do. But I also like relationships. I like being held and holding someone. That's very important to me. I've got some rules,

too, you know—we all do, I guess. But mine are flexible. Yours aren't. And that's the pity, Robert. The real pity of it all."

I stared at my glass.

"So when somebody breaks your rules, you just cut him off. No more talking. No more needing. No more holding, right?"

I said nothing.

"Like you've done with Jack. You can tell me all you want that it's the story you're interested in. Horse shit. Jack broke your rules. Everybody you write about has broken your rules. So you punish them for it." She moved the table. "I have to go," she said.

"Don't," I said. I really wanted to talk, to explain.

"I have to," Nina Thatcher said. "Look, Robert, buried somewhere inside you is a person. A living human being person. At least I think there is. When you cried on my lap that day, you let him out for a while. I think you'd better let him out some more because otherwise, you're going to be a very lonely man. You and your stories and your recordings are going to be very lonely together."

She tied the raincoat's belt around her waist.

"I've always—" I said. I was gulping for air. I didn't want to be left alone.

"I don't have time to hear," said Nina Thatcher. "I really have to get out of here."

"Don't go." My eyes started to glisten. "I need—"

"You only need when you want to need," Nina Thatcher said. "Robert, that may sound cruel. I don't intend it that way. It's just the way you are." She slipped between the tables and walked past me. I didn't turn to watch her walk out. I counted to fifty, slowly. I dabbed at my face with my napkin. I caught a waiter's attention and ordered three shots of straight scotch. I was crying when my drinks came.

Psychologists, I am told, recognize uncontrollable crying as a sign of depression. I guess I was uncontrollably depressed.

*chapter 19*_____

Home that night was not easy.
I remember that. Dark apartment dead drunk. I had trouble
finding my keys and did not trust myself to pump a double-
ought shell into the chamber of the shotgun. Jerry Daley at
eight meant up at six. I took five aspirin and lay on the Oriental rug in the living room staring at the ceiling with my
eyes closed, head spinning. Oh, my aching head, shit, I remember it hurt. Call somebody, is what I kept thinking.
Nancy, not Nancy. Jack. Impossible. Nina Thatcher, not Nina
Thatcher. The tapes are what I settled on. The aloneness was
killing me nobody to talk to I did not want to be a star (yes, I
did). Crawl to the amp and find a cassette and listen to my
life play out; then I'm not alone anymore, right? With Jack I
was not alone, but Jack left, deserted, quit, bugged out, the
son of a bitch; damn him for being Jack; I could call him
drunk, and he would come over even though he was Jack.
Would he have come over if Mark were with him? He would
have had no choice; yes, he would: "I've got this little fox,
Robert, see, and it's, you know, difficult right now." He
wouldn't have come. Which is why the tapes. The tapes
never leave, desert, quit, bug out. Constant tapes. Friendly

tapes. Why record? Nina Thatcher asked. Could not tell her because they don't leave you. Tapes don't go meet a friend and leave me crying at a table. Tapes are there when you need them. I hear myself, and I know I am okay. I am okay, is how I thought, crawling on the rug toward the machine.

Blue light. Power on. Pillow and headphones somewhere, somewhere. Oh, I was drunk, was I ever. Little blue light never seemed so bright. Only light in the room, I could read by it (that's silly; ruin my eyes). Hit the Dolby switch, no reason to have hiss in my ears, not at this stage in my life. I deserve better than hiss in my ears. Push the buttons with my hands feeling as if I'm wearing mittens, I remember that. Hands felt like mittens. Amazing what whiskey does to your system. I remember wondering how I drove home. I did not remember driving home or parking the car or locking it. Did I chamber a shell in the Remington?

Sound at last.

". . . If you could write anything," Jack Fowler's voice was saying, "what would you write?"

"A story," my voice answered. "A story with a happy ending."

"Happy? Robert, hand me that delightful marijuana cigarette you are keeping all to yourself. How happy, Robert?"

"Happy-happy," said my voice. "Upbeat. Uplifting. Inspirational. Makes you cry when you read it. Smile and cry. Tears of joy."

"Happy stories," Jack Fowler's voice said. "Why, you closet sentimentalist."

My tone of voice was definitely defensive. "So what?" I said. "Everybody needs a happy ending once in a while."

"Not us," said Jack Fowler, his voice suddenly loud, as if he had leaned toward the microphone. "Not us. We don't get those kinds of stories, Robert. We just don't have any feel for them. When's the last time you wrote something with a happy ending?"

"Never," I said. "Never. I never have."

"Shit," said Jack's voice.

"Shit," came my reply. "That's it. Shit. I mean, I'd really like to do that, you know? Like—come on, hand it here—to

really—come on, Jack, hit me—to make everything come out all right in the last graph. Like in the movies or on television."

"Jesus," said Jack Fowler.

"Don't giggle at me like that," my voice said. "This is serious."

"Oh, we're serious?"

"Serious. Serious-serious. Happy endings are serious business."

"Come off it."

"They are," I said. "Nancy used to tell me that they hired literally dozens of writers for television series to come up with happy endings."

"You're bullshitting me," said Jack Fowler.

"No," I said. "It's true. They had all these writers, and they'd all come up with happy endings for comedy shows. See, they'd brainstorm, and five or six of them would work together, and they'd come up with something so that the show could end in twenty-two minutes, and all the problems would be resolved, and the last line would be a big laugh."

"Why don't you do that?" Jack Fowler's voice asked. "Write big laughs into your tag graphs?"

"Tie my stories up nice and neat," I said. "Make it all come out okay in the end."

"Right," said Jack.

"Because it doesn't," I said. "Because that's the whole point," I said. "We write what we see no matter what the ending is. We gotta do that. I'm only mad because I've never written about anything happy."

"But that's your fault, Robert," Jack said.

"Probably," I said. "It doesn't matter," I said.

"But it must; otherwise, you wouldn't have brought it up."

"I didn't bring it up," I said. "You brought it up."

"Bullshit. Hand me that thing again."

"Bullshit, bullshit. Okay, okay. Here."

"Bullshit," said Jack. "I didn't bring it up. Anyway, you'll get your happy ending one of these days."

"I doubt it."

"Believe me," he said. "But until you do, you'll get what we all get. You'll get your byline."

"And the gratitude of our five hundred sixty-eight thousand one hundred and twenty-nine readers."

"Twenty-eight," Jack Fowler's voice said.

"Why?"

"I just canceled my subscription." He laughed.

A pause on the cassette. Thank God for Dolby. No hiss. Just room tone. Roooooom tooone.

Then: "I am a person," I said. "I need gratitude."

"Oh, you must really be wrecked," Jack Fowler said. "You need what I need. Your byline to be defined by, as many times as possible, thank you. A little conversation with me now and then, and some good dope, and a bottle of wine to help you sleep at night. Can you sleep without the wine, Robert?"

"I used to," I said, "with Nancy."

"We all used to," Jack Fowler said. "We all used to be able to sleep with our Nancys."

"What?" I was confused.

"With our Nancys," he said. "It was so much easier with our Nancys. But we didn't learn that until it was too late, did we, Robert?"

"You're not making any sense," I said.

"I'm making exquisite, perfect, on-the-target sense," Jack Fowler's voice said. "You and your happy endings. Don't you know we're doomed?"

"Doomed?"

"Precisely," said Jack Fowler. "To not write happy endings. We could be hired for TV situation tragedies. We'd make a million."

"Jack," I said, "you're not making any sense."

"I'm making exquisite sense," Jack Fowler's voice said. It had an edge to it then. "Oh, Robert," it said, "we're alone. Madeleine's married, and Nancy's thrown you out, and what the hell do we do for body warmth on a regular basis?"

"Not much."

"And so?"

"We work," I said.

"We work," Jack's voice said. "God, how they must love us downtown. Because, God, do we ever produce for them. Someone to work on Thanksgiving, Christmas, New Year's Day? Call us. Call Fowler; call Mandel. Always available. God, I hate holidays."

A pause. I must have been thinking about it. "The city room," I said. "I remember last Christmas Day in the city room. I didn't even know you then. I came in at about eight to work on something. You came in at about eight-thirty. Remember? I didn't even know you then. We sat at our separate desks and typed. I remember thinking, Why the hell is he here? Doesn't he have something better to do? Actually I resented you. You broke up the lovely mood of self-pity I was reveling in."

"I know," said Jack Fowler's voice. "My first Christmas here. I was straight from Oxford, right? I did Christmas at the jail. Ate Christmas dinner at the jail with the prisoners. It was a maudlin little article, really, but effective. And it was better than being alone. It was a story. That was the thing. The story's the thing. You, I—we lose ourselves in the story. But I disagree, Robert, about happy endings. I don't like happy endings. Upbeat means we have to find ourselves at the end of it all. On the other hand, you and I don't particularly like what we see when we look at ourselves in the mirror. We need our Nancys to fantasize about, and we need our stories so depressing that afterward even we feel a bit better—without feeling good, of course."

"No," I said. "Not true."

"Bullshit," said Jack Fowler. A massive intake of reefer on the tape. "Here."

"Thanks," my voice said. "What you're saying doesn't leave us much."

"Of course," Jack Fowler said. "Of course it doesn't. But— maybe I'm wrong—isn't that the way we've set it up for ourselves? Hey, Robert, think about what you do. You descend when you write about dope. It's not higher stuff. It's what we snobs like to think of as Villonesque underbelly. Bullshit. It's an escape from normal values, a fantasy just the way Nancy is a fantasy. What you write is what you are."

"It doesn't hold true for you," I said.

"Why not?" Jack Fowler said. "I spend my time going through records, files. It's an escape from those other pressures. I don't have to think about myself when I work. When I'm tracing blind corporations, there's no Madeleine, there are no trips to New York, no interludes on Christopher Street; only the story. Hey, Robert, I know it's true." Jack giggled. "Besides, I can prove it. I read *The Outsider* and never forgot it." He giggled again.

"What?" My voice. "Now you're really not making sense."

"Oh, but I am," said Jack Fowler. "Alone again, naturally," he said. He laughed. "Oh, Robert," he said, "we're a mess."

———

"Don't you look the picture of health." Jerry Daley cut through an over-easy egg with his fork and then caught a piece of bacon with the tines. "You're late."

"I'm surprised that I got here at all," I said.

"Heavy night?"

"Yeah."

"Nice piece," Jerry Daley said.

"What?"

"The chick," Jerry Daley said. "Nina what's-her-name."

"Thatcher."

"Nice piece of ass," Jerry Daley said. "Did you have fun?"

"I always have fun," I said. "Let me get some coffee," I said. I settled into a chair facing Jerry Daley. I was wearing my shoulder-holster minicassette recorder with the fountain-pen mike.

Jerry Daley took out his cigarettes. "Could you wait awhile to do that?" I asked.

"Sure," Jerry Daley said. "You look awful, you know."

"I know, I know."

We sat silently as a busboy poured a cup of coffee in front of me, spilling some into the saucer. I waited as he mopped up the mess.

Jerry Daley said, "Nice piece."

"You said that already."

"She must be fun."

218

"I'll never tell," I said.

"Oh, but you have," Jerry Daley said. "You and Jack were quite talkative, you know."

I said, "Jack's tapes."

Jerry Daley smiled. "I have my sources, Robert. I don't have to tell you who or what they are."

"Shit," I said.

"Oh, don't worry," said Jerry Daley. "I promise you they won't get out. Unless, of course, there's a leak in my office. No one can help those things."

"Is there a leak in your office?" I asked Jerry Daley.

"Not yet," he said. "Not yet." He took another bit of egg and bacon and chased it with a mouthful of toast. "Have you spoken to Nancy lately?" he asked.

"Jerry, I know you have the tapes Jack and I made in his apartment," I said. "You don't have to carry on anymore, okay?"

"I know," Jerry Daley said. "Let's just say I'm interested in your personal life, Robert."

"Shove it," I said.

"You're not being very friendly," Jerry Daley said. "Let's not forget that you invited me to breakfast. I'm planning to stick you with the check."

"Just leave the tapes out of it, okay," I said. "Okay?"

"Don't worry about anything," Jerry Daley said. "It'll all be taken care of."

"That sounds very ominous."

"I didn't mean it to be," Jerry Daley said. "Come on, Robert, I've got a long day. Why the invitation?"

"I'd like to know how far along you are."

"We're doing all right," Jerry Daley said. "There are some leads."

"How close are you?"

"I told you, we're doing all right."

"If we can work things out, maybe I can give you another one."

"How do you mean, work things out?" Jerry Daley asked.

"When it all falls together, I'd like to go along for the ride," I said.

"Robert, you know that's impossible."

"No, it's not," I said. "Remember that shooting-gallery bust I did last year? I went right in with the detectives. Wore a bulletproof vest and everything. I didn't screw up anything for you guys."

"This is different," Jerry Daley said. "This is not shoot-em-up. This is all procedure, Robert. I don't want to lose this case on any technicality. There are going to be lots of lawyers arguing about their defendants' rights. All I need is a reporter. Shit, talk about your unfavorable pretrial publicity. I'd get my head handed to me."

"Come on, Jerry," I said. "If you really wanted to, you could work something out. Sooner or later I'd write about it anyway. This way what you want off the record I'll leave off the record. It's a perfect fly-on-the-wall piece. It'll do you some good, too. You know—crime-fighting assistant DA and all that crap."

"I don't like to think of it as crap," Jerry Daley said. "Okay, Robert," he said, "I'll think about it." He sipped at his coffee. "Now, what about your juicy lead?"

"The guy with the jug ears and the little cock," I said. "I know who he is."

"The one in the trick book?" Jerry Daley said. "The one in Larry's book?"

"Yes."

"You mean Murray Fast," Jerry Daley said.

"Yes," I said.

"What am I, some kind of idiot?" Jerry Daley pushed his plate toward the center of the table. "Mark spilled his guts to us last night while you were out pronging Nina what's-her-face." He smiled. "She really sounds like fun," he said.

"Cut it out."

"Ah, Robert," Jerry Daley said, "you blew it. You're out of your element. You have a lot of inside information and very little else. You know, this isn't like staking out some shooting gallery and watching for a cop to walk inside."

"So what do I have?"

"Right now, nothing that I don't have," Jerry Daley said.

"In fact, you've probably got less than I have." He waved to the busboy and pointed to his coffee cup. It was refilled. He stirred half a packet of Sweet 'n Low into it. He took a cigarette from his leather case and put it in his mouth.

"Come on, Jerry," I said. "Talk to me."

"Okay," Jerry Daley said. "I'll tell you what I think. Off the record. Completely off the record."

"Okay," I said. "Off the record."

"Jack Fowler was killed by three guys. Larry was one of them. The other two are rip-off artists. It was a simple case of robbery that got out of hand. Then the rip-off artists killed Larry because he's probably the one who stabbed Jack. Then they took off. That's what I think."

"Amazingly simple," I said.

"Most crime is amazingly simple," Jerry Daley said. "You guys always look for some kind of conspiracy. You're always writing about psychological motivation, about role modeling. Shit, Robert, most perps do what they do because it's all they know. They're stupid. They hate, they want, and they do things to other people because that's what they know how to do. Robbers rob. Muggers mug. Rapists rape. That's what they do best. It's their job. All that talk about sociopathic patterns, the messed-up childhoods, the resentment of the father-authority figure, I think it's a crock. The perp is a perp, Robert. They do what they know best."

"I think there's more," I said. "Did you see our stories? Did you read Nina Thatcher's sidebar?"

"Sure," said Jerry Daley, "but that doesn't change anything for me. What I have is a dead person who resembles a pincushion. You can write about suicide impulse all you want. It's hard for somebody to stab himself in the front twenty-five times. I'm not saying that Jack Fowler didn't have guilts or recriminations. But right now that's immaterial so far as I'm concerned. What I have is a dead body, and I've got to find out who made it dead."

"And Mark told you," I said.

"About Murray Fast. He told us about tricking with strangers. And about his life with Jack. And Larry. Not much

about Larry, though. He seems to have a block when it comes to talking about Larry. I think Larry was rough with him."

"Where is Mark?" I asked.

"At home," Jerry Daley said. "Listen, Robert, leave him alone."

"Okay," I said. "I will," I lied. I lied because I was thinking about Mark, about something Mark had told me, about the call he had made to me from Larry's house. About an inconsistency in Mark's story. And about Mark's dreams. Sleeping fitful sleep, disturbed sleep. I had thought it was just a nightmare. Just a nightmare. A nightmare.

". . . fuck things up," Jerry Daley was saying. "Don't mess, Robert. Stay away, and I promise you your story."

"Sure, Jerry," I said. "Sure," I lied. God, how we all lie. Jack, Jerry Daley, Mike, Mark, me. Especially me.

"So that's it," I said. "That's all you've got right now."

"Yup," Jerry Daley said. He handed me the check, which the waiter had put on his side of the table. "Thanks for the breakfast," Jerry Daley said.

"You're welcome," I said. "Anytime," I said. "Keep me posted."

"Oh, I will, Robert, I will."

chapter 20_____

"Come on, open up." I was pounding with a closed fist on the door of Nina Thatcher's apartment. "Come on, dammit." There was silence inside. After half a minute I heard stirring. I had my ear pressed against the door. She peered through the peephole, and I heard two locks being turned. The door opened six inches, and Nina Thatcher looked at me malevolently. Her hair was tied in a single pigtail; she was wearing a granny-styled flannel nightgown.

"Go away."

I put my foot in the six-inch crack between door and frame. "We have to go to work."

"Go to hell, Robert." She tried to close the door. My foot was in the way. "Come on, Robert," she said. "Get out of here."

I pressed on the door, pushing it inward against Nina Thatcher's weight. "Hey, Robert, come on," Nina Thatcher said. "Have you gone crazy?"

"Yes," I said. "Loony. Bonkers. Come on—we have work to do."

She had her full weight against the door. I pushed her

backward. I got inside. I closed the door against my back.

"You're crazy," Nina Thatcher said.

"Listen to me."

"Listen to *me*," Nina Thatcher said. "You can't come busting in here, do you hear? Come on, Robert, get the hell out. Call me at the office."

A male voice from the innards of the apartment: "Nina, what's wrong?"

"Nothing," Nina Thatcher called back. "Come on, Robert," she said. "Quit."

"I need you," I said. "I need you right now. We have to go see Mark," I said.

"You're crazy," Nina Thatcher said. "Certifiable."

"Mark was there," I said. "Mark had to be there," I said. I took Nina Thatcher's shoulders and shook them. "He was there, I know it," I said. "Get dressed." I spun Nina Thatcher around and walked her toward her bedroom. She did not want to go.

She tried to turn. I had her shoulders firmly, and she could not. "Stop it, Robert."

"Get dressed, for Christ's sake," I said.

"Mark had to be where?" Nina Thatcher said. "You're not making any sense, Robert." She fought my grip and turned. She stood her ground.

A man in a bathrobe came into the hall. "What's going on?" he said. "Nina," he said, "what's wrong?" He saw me. He cinched his robe tighter. "Who's that?"

"Go back to bed," I said. "We've got to talk."

"This is incredible," Nina Thatcher said. "Robert, have you lost your mind?"

I looked at the man. Late thirties, tall, clean-shaven, full head of dark hair. "Please," I said. "I have to talk to Nina in private."

"Who the hell—" The man took another step toward Nina. I held up my hand.

"I don't have time. Come on, Thatcher, get dressed."

"Peter," said Nina Thatcher, "you'll have to pardon Robert. Robert is a colleague of mine. He's crazy."

"I'm not crazy," I said. "Go back to bed, Peter."

I took Nina Thatcher by the arm and walked her into her kitchen. We were followed. I turned on the man. "I don't want to be rude," I said. "You're probably a decent guy. I hope you are. But I'm going to deck you if you don't get the hell out of here and go back to bed."

The man clenched his fists. Nina Thatcher looked at him and me. Then she said, "It's okay, Peter. I'll talk to Robert, and he'll leave, and we'll forget it."

I looked for the kitchen light switch and flicked it on. Nina Thatcher blinked and rubbed her eyes like an awakened child. "What is it?" she said. "Robert—I swear—"

"We have to see Mark," I said. I moved to the kitchen door and poked my head toward the hallway. Peter had gone back to bed. "Mark was there."

"Mark was where?"

"At Jack's," I said. "He was at Jack's the night it happened."

"Impossible," said Nina Thatcher. "Horse shit."

"No," I said. "Possible. Probable. True."

"How?"

"It's been right there all along," I said. "I've been a shmuck."

"I grant that you're a shmuck," said Nina Thatcher.

"Mark said," I said, "that he called me from Larry's the night he called me about Jack."

"So?"

"Mark said," I said, "that he had been staying with Larry for a few days."

"So?"

"Jerry Daley says that Larry was probably killed by the people who killed Jack," I said, "to keep him quiet."

"You're not telling me anything I don't know," said Nina Thatcher.

"If Mark was staying at Larry's, he probably saw the people who killed Jack," I said.

Nina Thatcher scratched her head. "So?"

"The nightmares," I said. "The nightmares. Mark has nightmares."

"Big deal," said Nina Thatcher. "We all have nightmares."

"I think his are about Jack."

"Why?" Nina Thatcher asked.

"What does Mark do?" I said.

"I don't understand," Nina Thatcher said.

"What does he do?"

"I don't know," Nina Thatcher said. "I guess he does his schoolwork."

"No," I said. "What does he *do*—what dope does he do?"

"I don't know," said Nina Thatcher.

"It's on the tape," I said. "He does PCP. He does PCP."

"So."

"So it screws up your mind," I said. "So maybe Mark wasn't at Larry's that night. Maybe he's lying to us, and he was at Jack's place. Fucked up. And maybe he sees Larry and Larry's pals come in."

"Impossible," said Nina Thatcher. "They would have killed him, too. Wouldn't they?"

"Maybe not," I said.

"I think you're full of shit," said Nina Thatcher.

"Maybe," I said. "But I don't think so." I shook Nina Thatcher by the shoulders. "I don't think so. Come on," I said. "Get dressed."

"Why, Robert?" said Nina Thatcher. "No."

"We have to go talk to Mark."

"Oh, come on," Nina Thatcher said. "He's been through enough."

"He's lying, I know it," I said.

"Then you go see him," Nina Thatcher said. "You go talk to him."

"I can't," I said. "Not alone."

"Why?" asked Nina Thatcher.

"Because," I said, "Mark won't be as responsive to me as he would to you. And I've got to get him out of the house. I've got to get him back to the corporate apartment for about eight hours."

"Why?" asked Nina Thatcher.

I dug into my pocket. I came up with a vial of Quaaludes, a bottle of sodium pentothal, and a sterile syringe in a blue and white wrapper. "This is why," I said.

"Jesus Christ, you are crazy," Nina Thatcher said. "You've lost your mind," she said. "This is insane," she said. "Where the hell did you get those?"

"I have my sources," I said. "Not everyone hates me," I said. "Some people owe me favors."

"I'm not one of them," said Nina Thatcher. "Talk about ethics. Talk about breaking the law. Christ, Robert—"

"Don't you see?" I said. "Don't you see? We've got to loosen Mark up. Got to get him to talk. Make him tell what he saw. I know he was at Jack's. I know it."

"Robert," said Nina Thatcher, "I am going to count to ten, and if you're not out of here by then, I'm calling Mike. And I'm calling the cops to tell them that you've got a hypodermic needle on your person and you're not a diabetic. And that you've got a bunch of Quaaludes on you and you don't have a prescription."

"Shit," I said. "Shit." I pounded on Nina Thatcher's countertop. I put everything back in my pocket. "Okay," I said. "No drugs. No drugs, I promise. But you've got to help me get to Mark. If I don't use the drugs, will you help me?"

"I don't know," Nina Thatcher said. "Robert. . . ."

"What?"

"Nothing," Nina Thatcher said. "You're just crazy, is all."

"Let me be crazy," I said. "Just help me."

"Why should I?" Nina Thatcher said.

"Because."

"You're always saying that," Nina Thatcher said. "It's not good enough, Robert."

"Because we can get to the bottom of the story," I said. "Look, if I'm wrong, then we know something. If I'm right, then we know what happened to Jack and how it happened and maybe why it happened. Okay," I said, "what are we after? We're after the story of what happened to Jack. That's what's important. The story is important. Jack is important."

"And what about Mark?" Nina Thatcher asked. "Is Mark important?"

"Mark's important, too," I said. "I told you, no drugs."

"And if you're wrong?" Nina Thatcher said.

227

"If I'm wrong, I'll go away," I said. "I won't bother you again. I'll leave you and Peter to perpetual bliss."

Nina Thatcher sighed. It was a big sigh. "I think you're full of it," she said. "And I think you're wrong," she said. "But I'll go along. I'll be your shill. But that's the end, Robert. After this, all bets are off. No more friends, okay? I don't think I can afford to be your friend. It's damaging, you know."

———

Nina Thatcher dropped me off at the corporate apartment. It would be better, we decided, for her to see Mark alone. It would also give me time to rewire the place. I set the Kel unit in the master bedroom and put the transmitter back in the planter. The wire antenna was taped to the dieffenbachia's stalk. I set another recorder in the bedroom where Mark had slept and ran a remote line and foot control under the bed. I could sit on the edge of the bed and still turn the machine on and off.

I took the elevator down to the building's convenience store, where I bought two six-packs of Tab and one six-pack of Coke. The Tab I put in the refrigerator. The Coke I kept on the counter. I used a can opener to pry the bottle caps off, very carefully. I set them on the countertop in a row. Then I took the Quaaludes from my pocket. I pulverized them on the countertop with the bottom of a drinking glass; eighteen of the 150-mg white tabs, three at a time.

I was not happy about lying to Nina Thatcher. I had not wanted to lie to her. But it was necessary. How many times had I taken someone I needed information from out to a bar, where I had fed him or her whiskey, wine, or martinis until the source was loosened up sufficiently to tell me what I needed to know? Fifty times? A hundred times? How many times had I traded heroin to a junkie in return for information? Lots of times. The Quaalude was no less ethical. Not in Mark's case.

I removed about a teaspoon of Coke from each bottle and then gently dropped the Quaalude powder in, watching it fizz. I worked very slowly, letting the powder dissolve before I added more. Would I kill for a story? Nancy asked me that

six, seven, eight years ago. I think she meant it figuratively. I was a greenhorn then, and I answered no. Now I know better. I would give it serious consideration if the story were good enough.

I was sweating by the time I finished spiking the six-pack of Coke. I recapped the bottles. I looked through the kitchen drawers for a pair of pliers. There were none. There was, however, an old-fashioned nutcracker, the kind restaurants give you to mangle lobster claws. I used it to reseal the caps. I tried shaking one of the bottles. There was no leak, no fizzing, no powder to be seen. I put the Coke in the fridge.

Would I kill for a story? What if Mark OD'd? It was a risk I knew, standing in the kitchen, I'd have to take. Ethics are what you talk to your colleagues about over a beer, I thought to myself. I am in the information business, I thought to myself. Sometimes that information has to be bought, squeezed, or coerced. Cops do it. So do reporters.

There are many reporters who do not feel this way; I know that. Reporters who say please and thank you a lot and still get good stories. Reporters who do not call their subjects nine, ten, eleven times an hour and still get interviews. Reporters who think that sitting outside someone's office door for eleven hours is a waste of time. I do not. I am willing to hole up in a car outside someone's house for a day and a half, peeing into an empty orange-juice bottle when necessary, waiting for a subject to make a move. If my snitches need money, I will give it to them, from my own pocket. This is not checkbook journalism; it is the way you get results on the street.

I wiped every trace of Quaalude residue from the countertop with a wet paper towel. Would I kill for a story? It is a hard question. It was a hard question when Nancy asked it in Los Angeles so many years ago. It was no less hard when I asked it of myself standing there in the kitchen of the corporate apartment.

Probably, if the story were good enough.

Which was not a pleasant thought. It is no fun to pay sources. It is no fun to badger secretaries, confidential assistants, or corporate factotums until they are almost in tears. It

doesn't make me feel very good to dangle a flat of heroin in front of a junkie's eyes, titillate him with what he needs most until he gives me the information I need most. But it must be done. Just as the taping must be done. The taping and snooping and spying and all those things we hate about the cops, FBI, and CIA. Of course, we like to think that we have a higher moral purpose than the cops, the FBI, or the CIA. And sometimes we do, I guess; not that this excuses us.

I hid the syringe and the sodium pentothal in a dresser drawer. My palms were sweaty. Sooner or later Nina Thatcher would find out what I had done to the soda. She would be upset. Upset. That was an understatement. But it would be too late by then. I hoped that she could be mollified. But I doubted it. Nina Thatcher was a lot like Nancy. She had ideals. She was no pragmatist. She was not one of us. Us. What a presumptuous thing to think. Us. Juliet Walker is one of us. Even Jack, in his way. Us. How pretentious. Except we do think of ourselves as different, as special. We exist for our work. We live for our stories. No story, no life.

I heard the doorbell. I remember thinking, Saved by the bell. I remember thinking, Or ruined by it.

I turned on the Kel before walking to the door.

Mark was nervous. Mark did not want to be anywhere near me. I could see it when I looked at him. He said to Nina Thatcher without turning, "You didn't say he was going to be here."

Nina Thatcher looked at the floor. She couldn't meet my eyes. "I know," she said. "I'm sorry," she said. "It's important."

"I want to go home," Mark said. "I said I'd talk to you," he said. He looked at me, through me. "I don't want to talk to him," he said. They walked inside. Nina Thatcher closed the door. I stayed behind and double-locked it.

Nina Thatcher threw her Burberry across the back of a stuffed armchair. "I understand how you feel," she said.

"No, you don't," Mark said to Nina Thatcher. He looked at me. "You sold me out," he said. "I don't have to talk to you,"

he said. "My mother said I don't have to talk to anybody," he said. "I want to go home."

"You can go home," I said. "Believe me, Mark, you can go home. We'll take you home right away. Just sit down for a second, please."

The kid ran a hand through his light, curly hair. He walked into the living room and sat down in a chair. He did not unzip his windbreaker. His hands clutched the arms of the chair like a dental patient awaiting the drill. His knees were pressed tight together.

I walked behind him. Wait him out, I thought. Give it time. I said nothing. Nina Thatcher sat down on the sofa, her hands in her lap. She looked away from Mark, from me. She was not going to make things easy either. After some seconds Mark slipped his hands into the pockets of his windbreaker. Then they came out again and went back onto the arms of the chair. No one said anything.

I reached into the breast pocket of my sports coat and extracted the two Polaroid pictures Jerry Daley had given me at Larry's house. The pictures of Mark and Jack. I dropped them onto Mark's lap, face down. He flinched as they hit. The kid let them lie there.

"Turn them over," I said.

Mark sat without moving.

"Turn them over," I said. "Take a good look."

Mark flipped one of the snapshots. He handled it by the edge. He looked. He choked. He jumped for the door. The pictures went to the floor. "I want to go home," he cried. He was almost to the door by the time I grabbed him from the rear in a bear hug and dragged him away from the knob. I wrestled Mark back into the living room and threw him on the couch.

"Louse," he said. "You bastard," he said. He began crying.

I stood over him. I didn't want him running for the door again. He was sixteen and the same size as I am. Stronger, too, if he had thought about it. You cannot let them think about such things. It is a rule.

"I gather you remember the picture," I said.

Mark was silent.

"Yes or no?"

"I have to go to the bathroom," Mark said, sniffling.

I pointed the way. "Go ahead."

He picked himself off the couch and shambled toward the hallway. Nina Thatcher and I sat in silence, not looking at each other. We could hear water running in the bathroom. We could hear the toilet flush. When Mark reappeared, he was wiping his mouth with the sleeve of his windbreaker. Then he wiped his hands on the back pockets of his jeans.

"I want to go home," he said.

"We'll take you home," I said. "We will. In a while."

Mark looked at me. "I'll sue the shit off you," he said. "I'll get you."

I dropped to my knees in front of the sofa. "You do that, you little cocksucker," I said. "You go ahead and sue me. I'd love you to try it because if you do, I'll put your picture on the front page." I reached under the coffee table and got hold of the Polaroids. I waved one of them under his nose. "I'll put this right on the goddamn front page," I said. "I'll let all your friends see what you do best," I said. "I'll give your mamma a real thrill," I said. "You sue, and this goes five columns wide on every newsstand in town."

Mark stared at the picture.

"But I don't want to do that," I said. "And you don't really want me to, do you?"

I waited. No answer. If the kid only knew. I couldn't do it. Nina Thatcher knew I couldn't. But the kid was a kid. The kid didn't know about bluffing, about empty threats.

"I don't want to put this picture in the newspaper," I said. "But I will if you sue me. Or if you don't talk to me. I'm gonna do it, Mark. It'll probably kill your mamma, kiddo."

If looks could kill, Nina Thatcher would have had me lying dead right then. Mark looked up. "What is it?" he said. He had tears in his eyes. "What is it?"

I softened my tone. "Let's talk about Jack and Larry," I said. "Let's talk about them," I said.

"No," Mark said. "There's nothing to say, you know."

"Okay," I said. I was pushing too hard. Ease up.

232

"Let's talk about drugs," I said.

"What drugs?" Mark asked.

"Any drugs," I said. "Like what drugs you're into."

"I'm not into drugs," Mark said.

"Mark, we both know that's not true." I said it gently. I did not accuse. "You told Miss Thatcher and me about Larry's place and Larry's stash. You did some PCP at Larry's, didn't you?"

"Yeah," said Mark, "but, you know, like not a lot."

"Okay, not a lot," I said. "I believe you." I didn't believe him. "But you did some."

"Yeah."

"But what else?" I said. "Hey, Mark, come on. I'm not taking notes, talk to me. Nobody just does PCP."

"No," said Mark. "It fucks you up too much. But I like it."

"Sure you do," I said. "But what else, huh?" Talk for the tape, I thought.

"I do downers sometimes," said Mark. "Ludes and Sopors, you know. They cool me out, you know."

"You do a lot of ludes?" I asked.

"No," said Mark. "Not a lot. Just sometimes when I'm really bummed out, you know."

"I know," I said. "There's a lot to be bummed out about," I said, "isn't there?"

"Sometimes, you know," Mark said. Nina Thatcher had been standing. Now she sat down in the armchair where Mark had been.

"You told Miss Thatcher that," I said. "You said there was a lot to be bummed out about."

"There is," said Mark. "You know, school and my mother. You know."

"And what about Jack?" I said. "Did Jack bum you out?"

"No," Mark said. "Jack never bummed me out. Jack was like a good force on me, you know."

"I know," I said. "I know, Mark." I sat on the edge of the couch. Mark scrunched himself over.

"And Larry," I said. "What about Larry?"

The kid looked up at me. "I don't know about Larry," Mark said.

"Come on, Mark," I said. "You know all about Larry. You called me from Larry's that first night. You were staying with Larry, remember? You said you were staying with Larry."

"Did I?" Mark said. "Maybe I was mistaken," Mark said. "I think I was at home," Mark said.

"No," I said. "I think you were at Larry's," I said. "And you were high, too," I said. "You were high when you called me."

"Was I?" said Mark. "I don't remember."

"Yes, you do," I said. "You were stoned, Mark. You were stoned. Hey, come on—I know when somebody's stoned. But it wasn't PCP, Mark. What was it, kiddo, ludes?"

"I don't remember," Mark said. "I just bummed out, you know. I mean I was really bummed out over Jack, you know."

"I know," I said. "I was bummed out, too," I said. "I was bummed out, too."

"I just wanted to get high," Mark said. "I didn't want to think about Jack," Mark said.

"I can dig it," I said. "But, Mark, how long had you been at Larry's?"

"A couple of days, I guess," Mark said. "Just after Jack was killed, you know."

"Yeah," I said. "A couple of days."

"I don't remember," Mark said. "I was doing a lot of stuff, see."

"Stuff?" I asked.

"I was bummed out," Mark said. "Larry had this PCP," Mark said. "Or maybe it was THC—I don't remember, you know. I did a lot of stuff. Just to cool me out, you know."

"Sure," I said.

Mark sat up. Both feet on the couch.

"Mark," I said, "where were you when Jack was killed?"

"I told you," he said. "I was at home," he said.

"No, you weren't," I said. "You told me that you were at Larry's."

"That was after," Mark said.

"Now you say it was after," I said. "The other day you said you were at Larry's.

"I lied," Mark said.

"I don't think so," I said. "What did you tell Jerry Daley, Mark?"

"What I told you," Mark said. "That I was at home."

"Bullshit," I said. "I know what you told Jerry Daley," I said. "You told Jerry Daley you were out tricking," I said.

"Did I?" Mark said.

"Yes," I said. "So now we have three stories, kiddo. First, you were at home. Second, you were at Larry's. Third, you were out tricking."

"So," Mark said. He was hugging his knees now. His body language said, "I am hiding something."

"I think there's a fourth story," I said.

Mark didn't say anything. Mark sat there and hugged his knees. Hugged them tight.

"You know what I think the fourth story is?" I said.

Mark sat quietly. He buried his chin behind his knees. Fetal position. Snug into a ball. Hiding. From what? I looked at Nina Thatcher. She had noticed, too.

"I think the fourth story is that you were at Jack's," I said.

Mark sat without saying a word. He lifted his head enough to shake it. He shook it. "No," he said. "I wasn't at Jack's. I wasn't there, not there." His head went back behind his knees. No one said anything.

"I was out hustling," he said to Nina Thatcher. "I was. You believe me, don't you, Miss Thatcher?"

Nina Thatcher didn't say anything.

"I was," Mark said. "I wasn't there. I wasn't."

"Hey, Mark," I said, "maybe you'd like something to drink?"

"Sure," he said. "You got any Coke?" he said. "A Coke."

"Okay," I said. I stood up.

Nina Thatcher said, "I'll get it. I'd like something, too."

"No," I said. "I'll get it." I stood up.

Nina Thatcher was already moving toward the kitchen. "Sit down, Robert," she said, "I'll get it."

Nina Thatcher disappeared into the kitchen. I sat and watched Mark, who had closed his eyes and was resting his forehead on his knees. No one said anything.

Except Nina Thatcher, who said quite distinctly, "Oh, shit." Then she said, "Goddamn it." Then she came back into the living room. She was holding a bottle of Coke in one hand and a glass of ice in the other. "Could I see you please, Robert?" she said. "In the kitchen please," she said. She was not being polite.

I stood up. I followed Nina Thatcher into the kitchen.

When I got there, she said, "You prick." Then she said, "You unconscionable bastard."

I said, "What is it?"

"Guess," Nina Thatcher said. She held the bottle of Coke for me to see. An eighth of an inch of white powdered crystal was visible at the bottom of the bottle.

"It's the real thing," I said.

"No drugs," Nina Thatcher said. "You promised no drugs," Nina Thatcher said. "You are a liar," she said. "A fucking hypocritical liar," she said. She poured the Coke down the sink. "I hate you," Nina Thatcher said. "I hate you for what you're capable of doing. I hate you for what you're capable of making me do. Almost making me do. I hate what you stand for, Robert.

"I'm taking Mark home," she said. "Right now," she said. "I don't give a rat's ass where he was when Jack was killed," she said. "I don't care if it blows your story, Robert. I really don't give a goddamn.

"That's it," Nina Thatcher said. She was opening the rest of the Cokes one by one and pouring them down the drain. "Eye-tee. Spells 'it.' No more. Good-bye. Farewell. Splitsville. *Arrivederci. Ciao.*"

"Come on," I said. "Come on."

"Fuck you," said Nina Thatcher. She tossed the last empty Coke bottle into the garbage can. "You are despicable."

"I need to know," I said. "I need to know where Mark was," I said. "Give me another half an hour," I said. "I'll do it without the drugs."

"If we're not out of here in three minutes," said Nina Thatcher, "I'm calling Mike. I'll bring you up on charges, Robert. Screw the kid—I'll sue you myself. You don't have pictures you can threaten me with, do you?"

"No," I said. "Come on," I said. "Wait."

Nina Thatcher's face was white. "I'm getting out of here," she said. She left me standing in the kitchen.

For about ten seconds. Then Nina Thatcher screamed. She screamed, "Mark." Then she screamed, "Robert." I ran outside to see what had happened.

Nina Thatcher was standing over Mark, who had rolled off the couch and was lying on the floor, wedged under the coffee table. Nina Thatcher was pulling Mark's arms, trying to move him. I pushed her away and got my own arms in back of his shoulders and yanked. He came clear, and I pulled him across the rug. His eyes were open. He was moaning. I bent over him and shook him by the chin.

"Mark," I said. "Mark."

He wasn't focusing too well. "Mark," I said. I shook him again.

"Hey," he said. He slipped out of my grasp and rolled onto his stomach. He started to do a breaststroke on the rug. I rolled him over again. I pulled at the zipper of his windbreaker. I got it open and slipped it off him. Threw it to Nina Thatcher. I held Mark by the shoulders.

"What is it?"

"Hey," Mark said.

"What did he do?" said Nina Thatcher.

"Took something," I said. I bent over Mark. "What did you do?" I said. "What did you do?"

Mark half smiled. "Downers," he moaned, he slurred. He rolled into a ball.

I unrolled him. "Help me," I said to Nina Thatcher. I got behind Mark, got him into a full nelson, and tried to stand up. It was impossible. Dead weight. "Help me," I said to Nina Thatcher. She pushed from the front, I pulled from the back, and we got Mark to his feet. We struggled to keep him erect. We got arms under his arms and dragged him to the bedroom. Nina Thatcher headed toward the master bedroom. "The other," I said. "Tape machine," I said.

We dumped him on the bed, face down. Pulled his legs onto the bedspread. Flipped him onto his back. It was like moving a corpse.

237

Nina Thatcher grabbed the bedspread and pulled it down, away. We worked the blanket and sheet down to the foot of the bed. I pulled Mark's sneakers off, and his socks. I unzipped his jeans and held his hips up while Nina Thatcher pulled them off from the legs. Mark wasn't wearing any underwear. I got his shirt off, and his T-shirt. Then we covered him up. Mark rolled onto his side. He took the pillow and hugged it. I pushed him back, took the pillow away.

"What did you take?" I asked. "Why did you do downers?"

"Bummed me out," he moaned.

"What?" I said. "What bummed you out?"

"The pictures," Mark said. He was talking very indistinctly. He rolled back onto his side.

Nina Thatcher pulled at my sleeve. "What do we do?"

"Wait," I said. I went back to the bed.

"How many downers did you do?" I said. I shook Mark. "How many did you do?"

"A few," said Mark. "Did a few."

"What did you do?" I said. "Mark, what downers did you do?"

"A few," he said.

"I know," I said. "I know, Mark. But which ones?"

"Ludes," he said. "A lude. Doriden. I did two tabs." He rolled onto his stomach and started dry-humping the mattress. I pressed him down and got him onto his back again. "Bummed me out," he said. "The pictures," he said. "Bummer," he said. "You sold me," he said. "Sold me out," he said. I stood up by the side of the bed. Looking.

Nina Thatcher and I stood over him like a couple of anxious parents. She held onto my arm.

Nina Thatcher looked at me. "You could have killed him," she said. "What was in the Coke, I mean."

I nodded. "I know."

"Would it have been worth it?" Nina Thatcher said. "Killing him?"

I looked at the kid on the bed. No kid, no story. "No," I said. "I was wrong.

"There are other ways," I said.

*chapter 21*_____

Maybe it was the euphoria of the Doriden. I never quite knew. People develop a tolerance for Doriden, just as they do for Quaalude. There were three 150-milligram Rorer Quaalude tabs wrapped in a Kleenex still in the pocket of Mark's jeans. There were also two blue-and-white caps of Doriden and three yellow quarter-inch-wide 5-milligram tabs of Ritalin. The kid was a walking drugstore. In his shirt pocket were three joints. Our lab later told me they were laced with both hash oil and PCP. I should have kept them.

I have an ethical problem with drugs. I smoke dope, and I have done cocaine. I always keep reefer in the house (although I do not ever have more than a few grams on hand at any one time). Yet I write about what dope does to people. I tell myself that I write only about the hard stuff: heroin, skag. Jones. Champagne for the veins, as Cocteau said. And yet . . . and yet I give heroin to my snitches just the way most narcs do, a cap, two caps at a time. I skim half a gram from what I buy with the paper's money. The dope goes to the lab. It gets tested. If it's bad, if there is chalk in the mix, or

kitchen cleanser, ground Alka-Seltzer or rat poison I flush my half gram down the toilet. If the dope is good, however, I bag it, or cap it, and deal information with it. Quid pro quo, as people are so fond of saying these days. Something for something. It's not nice, but it is necessary. My editors wouldn't understand this sort of thing. They don't cover narcotics. They don't comprehend the economics, the savagery of the trade. I don't like cops, but I understand them. They don't like themselves much, either, after a while. It's like a stew, perhaps. Cops, junkies, reporters—each with their own flavor at the start. Then as the pot starts to boil, things merge. "Everything is everything," a dealer said to me recently. "Can you dig it, man?" he said. "Everything is everything." I can dig it.

But I still have an ethical problem with drugs. If you write, you shouldn't use. But if you don't use, how the hell can you pass yourself off as a person who with a sniff and a taste can differentiate Maui Wowee from plain old Maui; Oaxacan Sinsemilla from seedless blue Hawaiian; Colombian Red Gold from plain old Colombian Gold? It takes tasting, takes a palate, just like wines. So I taste and sniff and snort and inhale. I tell myself it's part of the job. I lie to myself. I like it. Just like the cops.

Maybe it was the euphoria of the Doriden, which gives some people a rush. Or the combination of Doriden and Quaalude. Maybe Mark had dropped something before he came over, before Nina Thatcher retrieved him from his house. When he started to talk, lying there, I just stood, Nina Thatcher clutching my arm. I didn't realize what he was saying. When I did realize, I went for the tape recorder control. I sat on one side of the bed, holding Mark's hand. Nina Thatcher sat on the other side, holding his other hand. We didn't talk much, either of us. But we looked at each other a lot. Mark didn't mind. Mark had his eyes shut. Occasionally he would pull an arm away and cover his eyes. But always the hand would come back, searching for Nina Thatcher's hand or mine.

I love transcribing tapes, I do. I have always prided myself on my speed and accuracy. But afterward, it took me three,

four tries to get Mark's tape onto paper. I did the job alone. But I did not want to be alone. I needed to be held, sitting at the machine, the transcriber responsive to my foot on the pedal, the sound of Mark's voice in my ears. I wanted someone to share it with me. As Jack once said, a Nancy. Everyone needs someone: a Nancy; the idea of a Nancy. If I believe that there is a Nancy, then I'm not really alone. Alone now, but maybe not alone forever. God, I'm maudlin.

Maybe it was the euphoria of the Doriden. I don't know. I'm not strong in pharmacological chemistry. But something happened.

Mark's voice said, "It started out so smooth. It started out so beautifully, you know."

Nina Thatcher's voice said, "Uh-huh." Just "Uh-huh."

"Quiet evening, you know, at Larry's. Doing a little dope, lying around. Sip some wine, you know. No value judgments, you know. I mean Larry didn't hassle me. It was a place to go to, a home, see?"

"I see," Nina Thatcher's voice said. She said it as if she did see. She has that ability. It's something I admire.

"My mother is a drag," said Mark's voice. "She's a bitch. I hate my mother, you know, I think.

"We did some good dope," Mark's voice said. "Great dope, outstanding dope, you know. PCP dusted through it, but Larry said it was just hash oil, you know. Larry always said if he got me high enough, I'd let him fist-fuck me, but I don't think I could stand it, you know. Jack was never like that. Jack was the kindest, gentlest, wonderfulest lover in the world." A pause.

"Larry told me none of it happened," Mark's voice said. I could hear the bedclothes move, and I ran the tape again. "Larry told me none of it happened," Mark's voice said, "but after he was killed, you know, I started thinking it could have happened, but that would have been impossible because I was at Larry's all the time, you know.

"See, Larry wanted to fist-fuck me, which he had always told me. He said it would be okay, that I'd dig it. He said he'd fist-fucked Jack and Jack dug it, but I knew it was a lie because Jack wasn't into that kind of thing ever. Jack told me."

"I know," I said. "I know, Mark. You told me you loved
Jack the first time you called. The night you called."

"From Larry's house," Mark's voice said. "I called because
it said you loved Jack, too, and you did, didn't you?"

"I loved Jack," I said. "Yes."

"And he loved you," Mark's voice said. It was a plea.

"Larry said it never happened," Mark's voice said. "It was
the wine, he said, you know, the wine and the PCP, because
the hash oil wouldn't have done it, I think. But late, late, I
wanted to go to Jack's. Go to Jack's because I was afraid Larry
was going to fist-fuck me. Two friends of his, I think, came
over, maybe, I don't know. But I wanted Jack because Jack
wouldn't let them fist-fuck me. Jack would make it all right.
Larry was smoking a lot of dope, I remember. His friends
brought pills, I think. They gave me some Ritalin, you know,
or something. See, I was bummed out. I didn't want Larry to
fist-fuck me. I told Larry I wanted to go to Jack's. I loved Jack,
and he loved me. I didn't love Larry." Another pause. The
tape hissed.

Then: "Larry says it didn't happen. Maybe he's right. I
don't know, but I think it did happen, you know."

"What happened?" my voice said.

"Larry said it was a bad dream, you know," Mark said. "But
then I read in the paper what happened, and I didn't know if
the paper came first or the dream. Larry gave me some tranks
and said it was a dream, that I'd heard the TV news when I
was tripping, and I believed him, you know, but I don't
know what to think now, you know."

"Talk about the dream, Mark." Nina Thatcher said it. "Tell
me about the dream."

"It's a lousy dream," Mark's voice said.

"I know," said Nina Thatcher. "It's a lousy dream."

"Larry said a nightmare," Mark said. "Larry said it was
a nightmare later, but I didn't know what to think, you
know."

I rolled the tape back; I remember rolling the tape back.
Not to get Mark's voice but Nina Thatcher's. She was getting
hungry. She wanted Mark's dream. She was pushing for
Mark's dream. God, I thought, she was getting hungry for the

story. I pulled the plugs out of my ears and paced through my living room, lay down on the rug and stretched my back muscles. I didn't want to transcribe. Didn't want to work the keys of the IBM. Too many keys. Too many words. Maybe transcribe every fifth, sixth word. I get that way sometimes when I type. I want to skip words; hear them, but not have to put them onto the page. Too many pages, I think. Too many pages. I have to force myself to go back and work slowly. Word by word. Sentence by sentence. I want to be finished with it when it hasn't even started. The ultimate frustration. I love doing this, is what I tell myself. I love doing this, I say, sometimes aloud. And I go back. I always go back. The way I went back to Jack's tapes. The way I went back to Mark's.

"Larry said a nightmare later, but I didn't know what to think, you know." Mark's voice on the tape. Slurry voice on the tape. Which was working? The Doriden? The Quaalude? What else had he taken?

"God, it was a bad dream," Mark's voice said.

Nina Thatcher was impatient. "The dream," she said. "The dream, Mark. What was the dream?"

"Bad," said Mark's voice, "a bummer."

Nina Thatcher softened. "Tell me," she said. "Tell me."

My voice, my lie: "Tell me, Mark. If you tell, it'll go away. It'll go away, I promise."

"Dream bummed me out, you know," said Mark's voice. "Like every night. Like a smell that doesn't go away," he said. "I did it with a girl once," he said. "I did it with a girl in the basement of her house with her parents upstairs asleep. I was fifteen. Last year. And she made me use a safe, you know, because she didn't want to get knocked up. She gave me a safe, you know. It came wrapped in a piece of foil, man. I'll never forget the smell when I opened the foil, you know. It just stayed with me for days, you know. The smell when I unrolled it over my cock, you know. It smelled. It wasn't much fun fucking her, except we were in her basement and her folks were upstairs. She wanted me to eat her, you know. She said nobody ever ate her before, and she'd eat me if I ate her, you know, but I didn't want to do it. It was the smell, you know. The safe smelled. On my hands. I

couldn't get the smell off. I remember thinking it wouldn't come off.

"I told Jack about it, you know. He laughed. He told me it was more fun without a safe, you know. He said he'd never get me pregnant, you know."

"The dream," I said.

"Yeah," Mark's voice said. "Like the smell, I can't get rid of it, you know. My cock looked funny inside the safe. She had a green one. A green safe. My cock looked all greenish. She told me she had green ones because they made spades' cocks blacker, but I don't think she ever fucked a spade, you know, because she said nobody ever ate her before and spades like to eat you."

Nina Thatcher said, "What about the dream, Mark?"

"She was blond," Mark's voice said. "She didn't have much hair on her pussy, you know. I could see everything." His voice stopped. He shifted in the bed. "It wasn't as good as I thought it would be," he said. "It was the smell, you know. Then later she wanted to give me a hand job. She said she'd never seen anybody come, you know. So she pulled me off, you know. But it wasn't very much fun. I mean, like she didn't have any finesse, you know. Jack had finesse. He loved to watch me come. I loved that. He was so gentle, you know.

"I told Jack about the smell. He laughed, you know. He said he never wore a safe. He said he'd never get me pregnant. That was funny, you know.

"Larry said it was a dream," Mark's voice said. "But I'm not sure anymore. It's such a bummer, you know."

"Why is it a bummer?" My voice.

"Because," Mark said.

Nina Thatcher said something. Softly. I couldn't make it out. I ran the tape back. Nina Thatcher said, "He sounds like you. 'Because.' He sounds like you." She said it to herself, I guess. But it was on the tape.

"Because why?" I asked.

"I wasn't there," Mark said. "Larry told me it was a nightmare. But it's so real. I was so bummed out. Larry wanted to

fist-fuck me. I wanted to go to Jack's. I don't remember
going to Jack's, but in the dream I'm suddenly at Jack's, and
Larry throws me on Jack's couch, and he and Jack get into an
argument, and Larry's brought two friends, except I don't
know how they got there because I don't remember going in
the car or ringing Jack's bell.

"But in the dream I'm watching Jack, and Jack's drunk,
and he can't handle himself and Larry's friends say maybe
we should party and Jack says no and then they hit Jack and
he falls down and Larry says Jack should get up and he can't
and Larry's friends take Jack's watch or something and Larry
says don't do that and then it all becomes a mess, you know,
with things flying through the air and Jack lying there. And
then we're in the bedroom, Jack and Larry and me, and we're
in the bed together and then Larry says something and Jack
says something, it's all such a jumble. It has to be a dream,
and Jack says something about a tape, and Larry gets mad
and starts ripping up the room and finds a tape recorder and
it's been on, and he takes the tape out and starts pulling the
tape apart and then he hits Jack and I want to do something,
but I can't because I'm asleep, you know, and it's a dream
anyway, and then Larry gets a knife and hits Jack with it and
Jack goes down on the floor and Larry's hitting him with the
knife and I'm on the bed asleep and it's such a bad dream,
but I can't reach Jack because I can't wake up, you know.
And Larry's hitting Jack with the knife and screaming about
the tape and calling Jack names and I'm trying to crawl
where Jack's lying on the floor, but I can't reach him because
I'm asleep and you can never reach anybody when you're
crawling toward them when you're asleep, you know. Larry
told me that. He said it was true. He says nightmares are a
bummer, but you see maybe it wasn't a nightmare because
the next day I read about Jack in the paper, even though
Larry says I was tripping and I heard it on the news and it
gave me a nightmare. He says he couldn't sleep either, see,
and he was up all night.

"I thought maybe I dreamed it all before it happened, you
know, and then I felt bad because I didn't call Jack and tell

him what I had dreamed, but then it was too late, see, because I read in the paper that Jack was dead and that he was a reporter. I never knew that before.

"He never told me that, you know. Never said what he did, you know. It was like a secret and I thought maybe he worked for the CIA or something and I don't think Larry knew either, except in the dream Larry kept screaming at Jack for having a tape recorder and he was yelling, 'Liar, liar, liar,' at Jack and hitting him with the knife, you know, and pulling at the tape in the tape recorder and screaming, 'Where is it, where is it?' every time he hit Jack with the knife and Jack couldn't say anything, I don't think, but I can't remember, really, because it was all such a bummer dream, you know."

Nina Thatcher's voice: "Yes, you can remember, Mark. Come on."

My voice said: "The tape, Mark." Then there was a pause on the recording. I was thinking, rephrasing. "Mark," I said. "If there were a tape that Larry took, if there were an argument in your dream about a tape and a tape recorder, how would it have gone?"

"I'm not sure," said Mark's voice. "It's all crazy, you know. But I swear that Jack said something about a tape and some story and a recording, and Larry went crazy. That's what I dreamed, but Larry said it was just that—it was a dream."

"How did you get to Jack's house?" I asked. "Did Larry know where it was?"

"No," Mark said. "Larry was never at Jack's before. Larry used to ask me what it was like at Jack's house. I don't know how he got there. How I got there."

"What else do you remember?" I asked. "Do you remember leaving?"

"I told you," said Mark. "I told you it was all a dream anyway. I was at Larry's place, and I heard the news when I was tripping out. I heard the TV set. I must have heard the TV set, is what Larry said, and I freaked, you know."

"Then why is Larry dead?" I asked. My voice turned harder. "Why is Larry dead?"

"I don't know," said Mark's voice. "I don't know."

"Yes, you do," I said on the tape.

"I don't. I don't," Mark said. The words spewed quickly then, and transcribing became difficult. "It was all a dream. I was bummed out. It was all bogue, and it doesn't matter anyway, you know, because I was bummed out. Really bummed out. Besides, Larry told me that it was a dream, and I believed Larry, I believed Larry. Then Larry got killed, and I wasn't sure anymore, but, you know, it still doesn't matter because they're both dead."

"It matters," my voice was saying.

Contrapuntally Nina Thatcher was saying, "Mark, Mark, come on."

I slipped out of the earphones and paced some more. In front of the typing stand and transcriber. Back and forth on my Oriental carpet. Looked at the pattern. Stared out the living-room window. Looked across the wide street to the high rise where Jack had lived, had died, had lied. I live my life by rules. I lived my life by rules. I had broken them; not a wise thing to do. I had not wanted to write this story. I did not want to finish making this transcription.

Another rule to live by: Always finish a transcription. There is usually some small bit of information just before the tape runs out.

I did not finish the transcription. Instead, I called the corporate apartment. Nina Thatcher answered the phone.

"How's Mark?" I asked.

"Okay," said Nina Thatcher.

I looked at the decibel meter on the recorder attached to the phone by my bed. It was registering a normal level. The cassette was moving. "When can we take him home?" I asked.

"Soon," Nina Thatcher said. "What are you going to write?"

"I don't know," I said. "I have to finish transcribing the tape." I was lying. I was not going to finish. I would never finish transcribing that cassette.

"You've got to write something," Nina Thatcher said. "When's the latest you can get something in?"

"About four-thirty."

"Robert—"

"Oh, shit," I said. "You know what we have here." I waited. There was no answer, so I went on. "We've got hearsay, and stammering, and maybe a lot of fantasy. But there's nothing hard. Nothing the kid can prove. Like he says, maybe it was a dream."

"It wasn't a dream," said Nina Thatcher. "We know that, Robert. I know it, don't you?"

"I don't know what I know," I said. "I don't know any more. 'Write about Jack,' Mike said. 'Jack was your friend,' Mike said. All that bullshit about doing his memory a favor, Mike said. Shit." I paused. I took a big breath.

"What's left?" I said. "Jack lied. So I don't write about the Jack I thought I knew. I wrote about the Jack no one knew. Some obituary. Some goddamn encomium, huh?"

"That's the way the story turned out," Nina Thatcher said. "It's not your fault," she said. "It's not your fault."

"You're beginning to sound like me," I said.

"You're not always wrong," Nina Thatcher said. "You know, Robert, there are some things they never taught in J-school. Like how to handle a story like this. Like the feeling you get when you see an exclusive in the competition. Maybe the other guys don't have the whole story. But they have enough of it to put it into the paper. It doesn't matter afterward whether your story is better than theirs or not. They had it first. That's what hurts."

"I know," I said, "I know all that."

"So," Nina Thatcher said, "what happens when the competition does the story of Jack Fowler? And he's your friend, Robert? And they get to it first?"

I said nothing. The cassette spun.

"You feel like shit, Robert. On two levels. First, Jack was your friend. You can't renounce him no matter how you feel. So your friend's been flayed in print. And second, the other guys got it out first. No matter what you do after that, they broke the story; anything you write is purely a sidebar. It's all follow-up. It doesn't matter anymore.

"Look," said Nina Thatcher. "I have a hard time dealing

with you, Robert. You are not an easy person. Not to mention that you and Jack and I—well, I'm not going to go into that again. Suffice it to say that these past few days have not been easy for me, okay.

"I don't like the way that you work. I don't like your rules, or your taping, or your ethics. But underneath all that, somewhere, is a person, Robert. And it's the person in you—the human being in you—that's making this story so rough."

I was silent.

"Finish the story, Robert," Nina Thatcher said. "Finish it. Get it out of your system," she said. "Finish it, and then think about yourself. Think about your rules, and the way you live, and who you are. Call your friend in Los Angeles—"

"Nancy," I said.

"Nancy," Nina Thatcher said. "Call Nancy when it's all over. When you've had a chance to think."

Another pause. "But right now, get the story out. On paper. Out of your system. Put Jack to rest, okay? Just do it."

I sat there holding the receiver. A tear seeped from the outside corner of my left eye. I could feel it roll down my cheek, my chin. It plopped onto my shirt, a big, fat plop. A big, fat tear. "I will," I said. "I will. I'll finish."

"Good," said Nina Thatcher. "Good," she said. "Look, Robert," she said, "I'll get Mark home. Don't worry about Mark. You write. You finish." She took a pause here. I could hear her breath suck in. "Then call me," she said. "Call me, and we'll talk." Another pause. "When you're ready to be a person, call me. I'll talk to you. I promise." She hung up.

———

I told myself that I would go back to the transcription, that it was necessary. I'm not sure that I would have done it. But I was spared the work. Mike called. Mike called to tell me that Jerry Daley had just announced a press conference concerning Jack's murder. Our regular police reporter would be covering, of course. But Mike wanted me to know about it so that if I wanted to show up I could. I took a manila folder

from my files and slipped the unfinished transcript inside, changed the tape in my Nagra, grabbed a fresh reporter's notebook and a handful of pens, and drove downtown. Jerry had called the press conference in the press room at police headquarters. Strange for him to do, I thought, driving downtown. Usually he did such things from his office, which, unlike most ADAs' offices, he had decorated with his own money.

I swung the Bug into the potholed police parking lot across the street from 1300 Beaubien. It was an ancient building. I did not like going there. Few cops recognized me, but those who did were never friendly. Why should they be? It was my job to cream them in print. Yet we were so much alike, the cops and I. Those of them who worked on the streets had their problems, too. How does it feel to make $16,000 a year and know that someday you'll run into a dealer who'll take you aside and offer you $16,000 for one night's work? What do you tell the lieutenant who works behind a desk back at the station? Would he understand if you told him? Probably not. People behind desks don't understand those sorts of things. Mike certainly doesn't. Mike has his office, his desk, his secretary. He has a house account at the Chop House. He is an officer of the corporation. He tells me what we can and cannot do. But he doesn't understand the pressures. "Write about Jack," he told me; he asked me. He had no idea what he was asking me to do; none at all.

I swung the Bug into the potholed police parking lot across the street from 1300 Beaubien. I carried the transcription under my arm, legal-sized pages flopping out from the manila folder. Walked inside, past the reception area, press card on a chain around my neck guaranteeing my access to the press room. I was a late arrival. Already the TV crews had taken the best positions, their cameras and lights blocking the print reporters' access. One of the old desks had been selected for Jerry Daley to speak from. Two dozen microphones in clusters of three, four, five, sat in the middle of it. Yards of black cable ran to two dozen cassette recorders,

sound cameras, minicams. I worked my way along the wall to the front of the room. I saw Howard Mahler, our police-beat guy, and waved to him. "What's going on?" I said. I elbowed my way through the crowd to where he crouched in front of a camera tripod.

"Not much yet," Mahler said. "How's it going?"

"Slow," I said.

"At least you've been writing," he said. "I've been here waiting for something to happen for three days. How the hell did you find that guy Larry's place anyhow?"

"Luck," I said.

"It had to be," said Howard Mahler. "God, my knees hurt. Those sons of bitches took all the good seats."

I looked at him. He was close to retirement. He had covered the police beat for more than fifteen years. Pals with the cops. Never a bad story. If you'd read Howard's pieces, you'd never know the word "corruption" existed. We had talked about that once. He had told me, "What good would it do? All it would do is blow my sources here. I gotta live with these guys, Robert. You don't know what it's like to be frozen out." He had said that to me. Later, when my series about cops taking dope dealers' money for protection came out, he had complained again. He had said, "Now nobody's talking to me because of your stories. Couldn't you have checked with me first, Robert?"

I edged closer to where he knelt. "Luck," I said. "It was luck."

"Uh-huh," he said.

"What's this all about?"

"I don't know, nobody's said anything," he said.

"Did you call Daley's office?"

"It would have been a waste of time," Mahler said. "They would have said no comment."

I nodded.

"Matty—he's the PIO—said he didn't know anything either. So I just came over and settled down here. We'll know what's up soon enough."

"Okay," I said. "I'm going to move back closer to the

door." I was nervous around Howard. The same nervousness I get when I'm around press agents. He waved me off.

"Are you going to file?" he said. "If you're gonna file, then I won't bother. No sense both of us doing it."

"I'll file. It dovetails into something I've got working."

"It does?" Mahler asked. "What's that?"

I looked at him. Sure, I'd actually tell him what I was doing in a room full of reporters. I shook my head. "Just something."

I pushed my way against the tide, back down the wall, to a spot next to the glass-paneled door. I found a wastebasket and turned it upside down. I stepped on top of it. The view was much improved. I stepped down and edged outside the door, just in time to see Jerry Daley making his way down the hall. I waved to him.

"Jerry?"

He saw me. "Robert," he said. "Robert."

"What's up?"

"No scoops," Jerry Daley said. "Everybody finds out at the same time." He was holding a cigarette above his head. He brought it to his lips and inhaled, then waved it aloft.

"Come on," I said.

"Well, what the hell do you think?" he said. "I'm going to announce some arrests in a case you've been covering." He moved forward. He was abreast of me.

"I thought you were going to call," I stage-whispered as he pushed by.

Jerry Daley looked at me. He smiled. His long, horsey teeth showed when he smiled, just like John Tunney's teeth. "Did I?" He flicked the ash of his cigarette into the crowd. "Either I lied or I forgot, Robert," he said. "You figure out which." He pushed his way into the press room, smiling and shaking hands as he moved down the center aisle like a politician out campaigning. That, I thought, was exactly what he was.

Such a simple story, really, Neat, precise, full of detail. Jerry Daley stood behind the desk. The cameras rolled. The recorders were switched on. The notebooks were flipped open.

"I'd like to announce two arrests in the Fowler murder," is what he said. I stood there and took notes with the rest of them. I stood on my upturned wastebasket, the unfinished transcription between my knees, leaning against the wall for support, and took notes. Just like everybody else.

*chapter 22*_____

It was so simple, the way Jerry
Daley explained it. It was anticlimactic. Two suspects—Phil
Malatesta, also known as Petey Mustache, and William Eckhart, aka Billy Boy—were in custody. Eckhart, he said, had
contacted the police through an attorney, and had turned
himself in at nine-thirty that morning. Information he gave
the police led to the capture of the second suspect, Malatesta. The arrest had been made, said Jerry Daley, without a
struggle, at Malatesta's house in St. Clair Shores.

Daley added that the motive for the Fowler murder was
robbery. He said both suspects alleged that the actual killing
had been done by Larry Perkins. Each accused the other of
Perkins's murder, he said.

"As best we know," Daley said, "what happened was this:
The three men assembled at Larry Perkins's house. Perkins
had a lover, a minor, who was also involved with Jack
Fowler. The youngster, whose name is Mark, was at that time
under the influence of PCP, supplied by Perkins. Mark, in a
stupor, supplied the trio with Fowler's address. The three
then took the boy in Perkins's car. They went to Jack Fowler's
apartment. There, utilizing Mark's condition, they gained ac-

cess. It was to be a simple robbery. Fowler couldn't complain because his double life would then be open to scrutiny, or so they thought. But according to Eckhart, a fight broke out between Perkins and Fowler when Fowler boasted that he was a reporter, and he—Fowler—had been accumulating research on the homosexual underworld. It was after that, according to both suspects, that Perkins stabbed Fowler to death.

"Afterward, the three suspects vandalized the apartment to make it look as if a forcible-entry robbery had taken place. Larry Perkins removed a cassette tape from Fowler's apartment, a cassette that the suspects say he later burned in his fireplace. The ransacking, they say, was also done to search for other tapes that Fowler might have made. These, however, they never found.

"After the killing the three suspects removed Mark, who had passed out, from the apartment. They took the elevator downstairs, carrying with them a few small items: a wristwatch, a signet ring, a color TV set, and two cameras. The TV set was dumped in a garbage bin. It has not been recovered. The other items we found hidden in Malatesta's garage." Jerry Daley paused.

"That's the story," he said. "Questions?"

There were dozens of them. But I didn't stick around to find out what they were. Daley had known, had known at breakfast, that he'd be taking Eckhart into custody. He had played me for a fool. No, he hadn't. He had given me the story. I had recorded it. "Jack Fowler was killed by three guys," he had told me. "Larry was one of them. The other two are rip-off artists. It was a simple case of robbery that got out of hand." That's what he had said over breakfast. I hadn't listened. "The other two *are* rip-off artists," he had said. Are, are, are. He had known who they were. The obvious question never got asked. How do you know the other two *are* rip-off artists, Jerry? "Because one of them has had his lawyer call me and tell me, Robert, because he doesn't want to take the fall for killing Larry and Jack, Robert, because we lifted fingerprints from Larry's house, Robert, or discovered some other incriminating evidence, Robert, and

because you are not asking me the right questions, Robert, I will not answer, Robert, you shmuck." I played that scene in my head ten times in the five-minute drive between 1300 Beaubien and the paper.

I sat in the city room, at the desk I hardly ever use, and wrote the story. Straight news. Followed all the rules of construction. All I had to do was read my notes from the press conference. I never even looked at the transcription.

"Police authorities announced the arrests of two suspects in the murder of Jack Fowler," I wrote. "Philip Malatesta, 29, and William Eckhart, 32, have been charged in the killing. Eckhart turned himself in to the police through an attorney early yesterday. At a news conference Assistant District Attorney Jerome Daley said that Malatesta had been captured at his St. Clair Shores house without a struggle. It was announced that items from Fowler's East Side apartment had been seized in Malatesta's home." It went on, of course.

Actually it was a solid piece. Five and a half books in length, filled with facts. Larry Chesler, the city editor, loved it. I stood over him as he read it.

"Not bad," he said. "Even you stars know how to write a straight news story sometimes," he said. He spec'd the copy, put in the breaks and boldface, and stared at the green front-page dummy layout on his desk. "Okay, Robert," he said. "Go home."

I shook my head. "I want to write a backup," I said. "I've got Mark's eyewitness stuff on tape. I want to use it."

"No need," said Larry Chesler. "This is the story." His bony finger poked my copy. "You've got all that stuff about the kid right here." He pushed his chair from the desk and laid his feet on top of my story. "Go on," he said. "Go home. Get some rest. We'll take it from here."

I went back to my desk. I sat. I unlocked the top drawer and read through Mark's transcript. I called the corporate apartment. There was no answer. I dialed Nina Thatcher's house. There was no answer.

I felt empty. Alone. Betrayed. Vulnerable. I wanted to talk to someone. Nancy. Nina Thatcher. Jack.

I did something I hadn't done in three years. I dialed Nancy's number in Los Angeles. I let the phone ring for a long time. There was no answer. I locked the transcript back in the top drawer of my desk. I took a fresh roll of tape and walked into the men's room, where I changed the spool on my Nagra body recorder and shoved the machine back into the jockstrap.

I walked into the city room. I sat with my feet up on my desk and stared at the ceiling. I called Nina Thatcher again. Still no answer. I said, "Shit," aloud.

Juliet Walker, who worked at the desk facing mine, said, "What?"

"I said 'shit.' "

"Oh," Juliet Walker said. She had a copy book rolled in her typewriter.

I pointed at it. "Anything good?" I said.

She shook her head. "The usual," she said. "Corruption in high places; Cosa Nostra payoffs; organized crime controlling the steel-hauling business. Nothing special." She looked at me. "How're you doing?"

"I don't know," I said. "Not very well."

"Nice stuff on the Fowler story," she said.

"I got beat," I said, "on the arrests."

"We had the other stories first," she said. "You can't win all the time."

"I know," I said. "I know." I dialed Nina Thatcher's apartment. There was no answer. I hung the phone up. I felt terribly alone. I thought about Jack, about Nancy. There was no one to talk to. I unlocked the desk and took out the Mark transcript again. I looked at it because it was all I had to look at. I didn't want to, but it was all I had. I needed a new conversation, not an old transcript. I needed. I put it back and watched Juliet Walker attack her machine.

I really wanted to talk. I couldn't. After a while I said, "Which one?"

"Which what?" She stopped typing and looked at me.

"Corruption in high places, Cosa Nostra payoffs, or the steel-hauling business?"

"All three," said Juliet Walker, "plus heroin."

It's funny how fast moods change. "Talk to me," I said. "What about heroin?"

"I think the steel haulers are carrying it," she said.

"Sounds lovely," I said. "Good story."

"If it works out," she said. "But they're buying everybody off. From the mayor's office on down. Judges, cops, DAs—it's incredible."

"Sounds like history repeating itself," I said. "Corruption in high places. It's always been like that."

"Since when?"

"Since anytime. Rome, maybe. Selling papal bulls in the Middle Ages. Eighteenth-century England. The first musical play was about corruption in high places, did you know that?"

"What was the first musical?" Juliet Walker asked.

"*The Beggar's Opera*," I said. "John Gay wrote it in 1728. It was supposed to be George Washington's favorite show."

"No shit," said Juliet Walker. "I saw one of those eighteenth-century things on TV last night. *Tom Jones*."

"That came later," I said. "That was after most of the English playhouses had been shut down in 1737. The government forced them out of business because they spent a lot of time criticizing Walpole, and Walpole thought they were libeling him. So all those guys—Gay, Fielding—had to find other things to do. Fielding began writing in a new form called the English novel. *Tom Jones* was one of the first."

"No shit," said Juliet Walker. "How come you know all that?"

"I majored in trivia," I said. "No, seriously, I was an English major. I spent two years on Gay, Fielding, Swift, Pope, Richardson, Defoe—all those guys."

"Really?" said Juliet Walker. "Hogarth and all that stuff?"

"Right on."

"Incredible," said Juliet Walker. "Did you see *Tom Jones* last night?"

"No," I said, "I was working."

"I did."

"So you said. What did you think?"

"It was okay," she said. "It was a little beyond me, though. I mean all that stuff about rightful heirs and landed gentry— I didn't understand a lot of it. I'm a lot more comfortable with e e cummings or Eliot."

I nodded. "I'll explain it to you sometime."

"Okay," she said. She looked at the clock above the city editor's desk. "Christ," she said, "I gotta finish this."

"Sorry to interrupt," I said.

"It's okay," she said. "They want this today. Half an hour ago."

"I understand." I watched as she rolled a new copy book into her machine. She typed the way a romantic pianist plays, with lots of forearm and shoulder action. She swayed with the words; her whole body leaned into the carriage return. I tried Nina Thatcher's phone again. I hung up after twenty rings.

"This is one of the few times I've seen you work down here," Juliet Walker said.

"Huh?"

"You're never in the office," she said.

"I work at home," I said. "My files are home," I said. "It's easier."

Juliet Walker nodded. She pulled the copy set from the machine and laid the story on her desk. She penciled corrections, pulled herself a file copy, and then took the remaining pages to where Larry Chesler sat. I watched as she stood over him while he read the story. Just the way I had stood. Just the way everyone stood. Children waiting for the teacher to tell them, tell us, that it was all right, that we would not receive a failing grade today. He looked up. He smiled. He nodded. She nodded.

She wheeled away and returned to her desk. She sat down, facing me.

"Done," she said. "For today."

"It never stops, does it?"

"Never." She looked at me. "Are you all right?"

"Sure," I said. "Why?"

"You look pale," she said. "You don't look so good."

"It's the hours I've been keeping," I said. "I just need a drink or something." Or something.

"The Fowler story?"

"Yes."

"Incredible, wasn't it?"

"Yes."

"He was a friend of yours, wasn't he?"

"Yes."

"It must have been rough on you."

I said nothing.

"Good pieces, though," she said. "Good stories." She locked her copy of the story in her desk drawer. I toyed with the phone. I thought about Jack, about Nancy, about my rules.

"I need a drink," I said. I needed more than a drink. I needed a life. I needed to be held.

"It's like that," Juliet Walker said.

"Huh? What is?"

"You've got them. The depressions, right?"

"I don't understand."

"The story's finished; the next one hasn't started, and you're depressed because you don't have anything to do, right?"

I thought about it. "I guess so," I said. There was no guessing. I had those old postpartum, best-friend's-been-murdered-and-I've-just-dumped-all-over-him-blues.

"Yeah, I guess so," I said. I picked up the phone and tried Nina Thatcher again.

"Listen," I said, "can I buy you a drink or something?"

"I'd love to," Juliet Walker said. "But I have to go home and feed my dogs."

"Oh."

"Look," she said, "why don't you come over and have a glass of wine while I open half a case of Alpo? We can go out afterward."

"Half a case of Alpo?"

"Figuratively speaking," Juliet Walker said. "They're big dogs."

"I see," I said. "Sure."

She stood up. She pulled her coat off the stand next to her desk and shrugged into it.

"Where do you live?"

"Oh," she said. She wrote her address on a copy set. "Second floor, door on the left."

"I just have to make a couple of calls," I said. "I'll be over in a few minutes."

"Fine." She wrapped a seven-foot scarf around her neck. "See you."

"Okay," I said. I watched as she walked toward the elevator. Then I turned my attention to the phone. I dialed Nina Thatcher. There was no answer. I got up and walked to Mike's office. I rapped on the glass door. He looked up from his desk and waved me inside.

"Have you heard from Thatcher?" I asked.

Mike shook his head affirmatively.

"Where is she?"

"Detroit General," Mike said.

"What's wrong, what happened?"

"Nothing much," Mike said. "She took little Mark home from your question-and-answer session. Half an hour later I got a call. It seems he swallowed everything in his mother's medicine cabinet. They took him to Detroit General to pump his stomach and put him under observation. I put Thatcher on the story."

" 'Nothing much,' " I said, "Jesus, Mike—"

"Nothing much," Mike said. "It's not front-page stuff. We got what we needed from the kid, right? You took care of that. So I let Thatcher run with it."

He looked at me over his half-frame glasses. "It's sidebar stuff, Robert," he said. "Forget about it." He glanced at whatever he was working at. "What's next for you?"

"I don't know," I said.

"Make it something good, okay?" He toyed with his gold-plated pencil. "You got beat on the Fowler story," he said. "Don't make a habit of it."

"What?"

"You heard me. You got beat. First you held back on the

faggot stuff. Then you let Daley get away from you; he got Mustache Phil or whatever his name is, and that Billy Boy character, and you never heard a whisper about it. You were out playing with Jack's little kid."

"And everything else in between?"

"In between doesn't count, Robert. First counts. First is all that counts." Mike fiddled with his pencil. He took his half glasses off and laid them on the desk.

"Hey," I said, "you're the one who asked me to write about Jack in the first place. I told you then I don't write about my friends. It's a rule."

"Frankly," said Mike, "I don't give a rat's ass about your rules." He put his feet on the desk. "The only rules I care about are mine. I only have one. And my rule is that we're first. You broke my rule." He stared at me. "You screwed up."

"You prick," I said. "First you ask me to write about Jack; you literally beg me to do the story. Now you tell me I screwed up. You can't have it both ways."

"Oh," said Mike, "but I can. That's why I sit here." He clasped his hands behind his neck. "I make the rules, Robert," he said. "You forget that sometimes. You don't get in here very often. That's fine by me. You write good stuff. So I let you have your little peculiarities, like working at home. Just so long as you turn in your stories. Just so long as we're first. But don't screw up, Robert. Because if you do, you'll be back here working from your desk just like the rest of the peons." He looked up at me. "It's my shop," he said. "You play by my rules."

"And if I don't?"

"There are other papers," Mike said.

"You prick," I said.

"You're being redundant." His feet came off the desk. The glasses went back on. The pencil was picked up. I was dismissed.

"Fuck you," I said.

Mike smiled. There was a bump on his nose. He looked like a lizard in the half glasses. "You told me you weren't

into that kind of stuff," he said. "Or did the story make you want to change your mind?"

His attention went back to the papers on his desk. He didn't look up as I walked out of his glass-enclosed office. He never noticed me go to my desk and pick up my Olympia standard office typewriter. But I caught his attention when I tossed the fifty-pound machine through the middle of his eight by twelve-foot plate-glass wall.

I never said a word. I wheeled toward the elevators.

"You're fired," Mike shouted after me.

The city room had gotten very quiet. I pressed the down button.

"Hear me? Your ass is fired, Mandel."

The elevator doors opened.

"You're on my shit list, Mandel. You'll never work at a paper again."

The elevator doors closed.

*chapter 23*_____

Mike fired me, but I didn't stay fired very long. About thirty-six hours in all. I had to pay for his glass wall, of course, but I didn't care. And even though Mike and I haven't spoken in eight months, I'm back in his good graces. No shit-list stories for me. No pothole assignments or supermarket openings. The stuff Juliet and I wrote was just too good. We were a sensational team, and Mike knew it. Pragmaticism is one of his better qualities. If the stories are good, you can do no wrong in his eyes. And Mike's eyes liked our stories.

The best of them was a three-part series about a civic organization called Drugs Out of the People's Environment, DOPE for short. DOPE received money from the City of Detroit, the Law Enforcement Assistance Administration, the Drug Enforcement Agency, the U.S. Department of Health, Education and Welfare, and the State of Michigan. It had been created as a neighborhood self-help group under the leadership of a civic activist with the unlikely name of Melvin Nairobi to help the police chase dope dealers out of the West Side ghetto. But Juliet and I discovered that Nairobi and DOPE were tied to Leroy "Nicky" Barnes's New York-

based heroin smuggling and distribution operations.

It was a lovely exposé. The city rented DOPE its headquarters for a dollar a year. The mayor had even put in an appearance at its dedication. We ran a picture of him shaking hands with Nairobi in our first installment. Next to it we ran a police mug shot of Nairobi, whose real name was Dorrance "The Spook" Jones. The Spook had been arrested in New York, Newark and Baltimore no fewer than eighteen times, for everything from extortion and attempted murder to cocaine dealing, arson, and sodomy. It turned out that he was a suspected member of the so-called Black Mafia. Two of the other four members of DOPE's board of directors also had long, out-of-state police records. The others, a pair of Baptist ministers, had no idea what had been going on.

DOPE, Juliet and I found out, had "raised" more than $80,000 from neighborhood merchants in its first nine months of existence. The money, we were told, was extorted. The three "safe houses" that DOPE had purchased on the city's West Side, ostensibly to use as crash pads for runaway teenagers, were in reality warehouses for shipments of heroin, cocaine, and marijuana shipped in from Nicky Barnes's New York drug empire. Juliet's sources showed us how crime-connected steel haulers shipped the contraband through a network of business fronts. It was, all told, a multimillion-dollar operation, a beautiful scam. And all the while Detroit's television stations did regular public-service features on DOPE, singling it out as a neighborhood organization truly deserving of public support.

So I did not stay on Mike's shit list very long. On the other hand, I made neither of the two phone calls I had tried to dial in the city room the day Juliet and I first talked about Henry Fielding. I thought about calling from time to time, but I never did anything about it. There was no need to call anyone. Not while the stories were going so well. Not while there was a warm body in my double bed. No, in the eight months that I shared a byline with Juliet there was no past for me. Only the present. Only the stories.

Besides, I rationalized, there was no need to call Nina Thatcher. I didn't need those kinds of hassles. Call when you

are a person, she had said. Well, I was a person. I always had been a person. I was whole—or as whole as I am ever capable of being. Except for an occasional nightmare I never even thought of Jack. Juliet never knew about the dreams. In all the time we worked together she never spent an entire night at my apartment. We would work. We would make love. She would go home. When I had the nightmares, I had them alone. Juliet never heard me scream.

And calling Nancy? The thought honestly never occurred to me. Fantasies of Nancy I have all the time. But real contact, not at all. Besides, I was working so well. I was working with someone.

Then, yesterday, the gray envelope arrived from the Los Angeles Police Department, and my past caught up with me. Nancy is dead, and I am completely alone. Juliet slept with Johnny Psycho, and I am completely alone. Jack Fowler lied to me, and I am completely alone.

As of yesterday the rules have changed. As of last night there are no more rules—at least as I once knew them.

Nancy dead means no more fantasies. Jack was right about that. Everyone, he said, needs a Nancy. It makes the aloneness bearable; it allows for possibilities.

When I first came to Detroit, I would send Nancy copies of my stories. An envelope of clippings every week. I never received an answer, but that was all right. It was still communication—of a sort. She could follow my life by reading my articles. She would know about me. In the past three years the envelopes have dwindled to one every six weeks or so. But I never stopped sending them.

I have a file on Nancy. There are no tapes in it. Only cards, letters, and other relics. One is a receipt. A ten-year-old scrap of paper, from the Ace Motel, just outside Indianapolis. I called Nancy from there and told her that I loved her, and she told me that she loved me, too. I didn't tape the call. I didn't have to in those days. I was able to have conversations then. I was adored once. I had real conversations; I didn't need transcripts.

I haven't spoken to Nina Thatcher in eight months. Nor have I seen her at the paper. She works on the fifth floor; my

desk is on the third. We do not meet in the corridors or in the elevator. We do not see one another in the coffee shop. Yet there is communication—of a sort. I read her stories. I follow her life through what she writes. And I listen to her voice. Sometimes, on those nights after Juliet left and I had a nightmare about Jack, I played tapes of Nina. The one I play most often is the one in which she says she will be my friend.

Nina Thatcher once asked me why I tape. I told her, but she didn't believe me. Tapes, transcriptions, files—they are all real. They prove who I am and who I was. Memory, by itself, is so selective, so fragmented. It leaves only shards. Yet we must be able to substantiate who we are, who we were, at all times.

I can prove I loved Nancy because I have the receipt from the Ace Motel. I may know I loved Nancy, but with the receipt I can prove it. That is very important to me.

Similarly, I can verify that Nina Thatcher promised to be my friend because I have it on tape.

I know Jack Fowler lied to me because I have nightmares.

The files, the tapes, the transcripts. With them I can escape into the reality of my past. I can double-check my own existence. I can see where we all went wrong. And we all go wrong, believe me. I said that to Nancy once. I told her that every human being goes wrong. Nancy said in response that I acted as if I had been put on this earth to prove it. Maybe she was right.

The files, the tapes, the transcripts. Standing here, the water cascading down on my head, the LAPD comprehensive homicide report visible through my transparent shower curtain, I am unsure of things. In the pit of my stomach I may know that new conversations are just as valuable as old tapes. It's just that I'm not sure I know how to start conversations anymore. I know, too, that I want my rules to change. I need new rules. The thing is, I don't have any idea what they should be.

Nancy said I would be a lonely young man, me and my stories. She was right. But that is one of the liabilities of the profession. Compiling evidence is a lonely job. Assembling it coherently and presenting it in an orderly form is a solitary

assignment. Being a professional observer—riding those white paragraphs, as Nancy said—is a desolate craft. But it's all the craft I know.

For example, in my Will Be Back file I have a folder about a man who is going to run next year in the Democratic primary for governor. He has a good chance to win the nomination. But he is not entirely clean. Through a chain of blind corporations he owns fourteen West Side buildings that are used as shooting galleries.

He's a nice man. He has a pretty wife and three perfect children. He's active in his church. He gives handsomely to the United Way. His law firm argues cases for the ACLU. I'm going to hate myself for bursting his comfortable little bubble.

But sooner or later I'm going to do it.

I've got to. Before somebody else does.